Globalisation, Development and Culture

Globalisation, Development and Culture

Essays in Honour of Professor S.P. Nagendra

Edited by

C. Lakshmanna

Jugendra Sahai

Rawat Publications

Jaipur • New Delhi • Bangalore • Hyderabad • Guwahati

ISBN 978-81-316-0532-5

Published by
Prem Rawat for **Rawat Publications**
Satyam Apts, Sector 3, Jawahar Nagar, Jaipur 302 004 (India)
Phone: 0141 265 1748 / 7006 Fax: 0141 265 1748
E-mail: info@rawatbooks.com
Website: www.rawatbooks.com

New Delhi Office
4858/24, Ansari Road, Daryaganj, New Delhi 110 002
Phone: 011 2326 3290

Also at *Bangalore, Hyderabad* and *Guwahati*

Typeset by Rawat Computers, Jaipur
Printed at Chaman Enterprises, New Delhi

Contents

In Memoriam

Professor S.P. Nagendra

Professor S.P. Nagendra

A Tribute

It is a joy, pure and simple, for me and my wife to express our reverence and gratitude towards an eminent scholar, educationist, administrator, a teacher of teachers and, above all, a thinker with deep human sympathies with whom we had a long association. Our relationship graduated from his being my Guru, guardian, PhD guide to familial bond. He was always an elder brother to us known as "Bhayaji". My wife, Professor Shailly Sahai, too was his student in her under-graduate and post-graduate classes in Lucknow University.

Fortunately, for us, Professor Nagendra, belonged to that illustrious school of synthetic, multidisciplinary scholarship which was initiated by his own teachers and benefactors, Professor D.P. Mukerji and Professor A.K. Saran. While Professor Mukerji's academic training tutored Professor Nagendra's mind, Professor A.K. Saran's teaching and analytical power attracted him to his substantive and methodological repertoire. Professor Nagendra's close association with a practical, socio-political thinker like Acharya Narendra Dev enlarged his sensibilities. The result was that Professor Nagendra turned out to be not merely an academic thinker but also a person with deep human sympathies. His profound knowledge and insight in the field of sociological theories by imbibing the best philosophical traditions – both Indian and Western – had made him a voice of authority in his discipline. His thesis about religion in the sixties created some stir. That was the period when the mainstream of sociology in India was constituted by a vigorous fieldwork tradition.

Professor Nagendra had brought forth the traditional text to the core of understanding of religion and provided a sort of marriage between ideology and sociology.

Professor Nagendra was emphatic and clear in stating his position, expressing disagreement or disapproval with zest. One could feel the authority of a Guru in his pronouncement. He had set certain standards for himself, but allowed some concessions to his students. The requisite package of skills needed for attempting such a task would consist of a fair degree of competence not only in the study of original writings of a classical and modern theorists, but also in the history of ideas, the structure of logical reasoning and philosophy of social sciences. If one has to combine ideological material along with it, he or she would require a comprehension of the classical text, as well as Sanskrit. In the present context, such skills could be brought together probably one in a thousand students and would call for an investment of decade or two to catch a level of confidence. Few of his students at least enjoyed themselves attempting some steps in that direction, but it seems the effect of the Guru was carried forward more in oral tradition than the written one.

Professor Nagendra had worked as specialist on the various UGC panels and has ably represented India at various international fora. The fact that he remained Pro-Vice Chancellor for six years in Gorakhpur University and completed his full term as Vice Chancellor, University of Lucknow quite successfully is a positive evidence of his excellent administrative efficiency. It was in recognition of this rare blend of scholarship and administrative competence in Professor Nagendra's versatile personality that he was appointed as Director, Govind Ballabh Pant Social Science Institute, Allahabad, a prestigious centre for advanced studies in social sciences.

Professor Nagendra writings, as readers will find, were the result of rejecting modernity, the cult of the moment, and taking to traditional thinking based mainly on Anand Kentish Commaraswamy, Rene Guenon, Frithj of Schuon and the whole group of thinkers concerned with timeless truth.

Our association with Professor Nagendra as his disciple and recipient of his benediction makes us to assert with certitude that Professor Nagendra would be a light for generations to come.

Jugendra Sahai

Acknowledgements

First of all, let us applaud the decision of few of Professor Nagendra's old students who had assembled in New Delhi to bring out a volume in honour of Professor Nagendra. The occasion was to participate in a national seminar and luckily all of them were staying with Professor Lakshmanna. It was decided that Professor Lakshmanna and Professor Sahai will edit the volume.

We appreciate the effort of Professor R.C. Sarikwal in initiating the correspondence with the assistance of Professor C. Lakshmanna who was posted at New Delhi as state representative to the centre with cabinet rank. Professor Sarikwal used to visit him whenever required to handle the correspondence. It can be well imagined that in those summer days how difficult it would have been to travel from Ghaziabad to Andhra Bhawan, New Delhi. He never felt disappointed or disgusted even when replies were not coming. Reminders after reminders were sent, gradually affirmations started reaching. Taking into consideration the views of the contributors a common theme for the book could not be evolved.

We are grateful to the contributors who sent their articles, most of them were Professor Nagendra's students and rest of them were his colleagues who knew him closely. We are sorry for the delay in publication of the book due to the bad health of both the editors due to which the work had to be stalled.

Ever since, the work was restarted we have lost four of our esteemed contributors, Professor A.K. Saran, Professor B.R. Chauhan, Professor Raghuveer Singh and Professor S.P. Srivastava. We deeply pay our homage to the departed souls and convey our heart-felt condolences to their families.

We are grateful to the family of Professor Nagendra for their effort to collect the articles and got loaded in CD available for publication. Mrs Nagendra always kept reminding us of the timely publication of the book as she too is not well. Professor Nagendra's youngest son Professor Srivardhan Pathak deserves special mention as he always remained in touch with us and attended the queries promptly.

We also feel obliged to Professor Shailly Sahai for the hard work done by her. She did the proof reading of both the books and suggested improvements.

We have no adequate words to express our gratitude to Mr Ramesh Chand Tiwari who helped us in so may ways, whether it was a personal reminder to contributors or planning the publication of the book.

We delightfully acknowledge and feel obliged to Mr Kailash Rawat and Mr Pranit Rawat, Rawat Publications, Jaipur for accepting our proposal to publish the book in a shortest possible time. We are thankful for their suggestion to publish the book in two parts – one containing Professor Nagendra's own contributions and second having contributions of his admirers.

C. Lakshmanna
Jugendra Sahai

Contributors

A.K. Saran, Former Professor and Head, Department of Sociology, Jodhpur University, Jodhpur.

Raghuveer Singh, Former Professor and Head, Department of Political Science, Gorakhpur University, Gorakhpur.

Ramesh Chandra Tiwari, Former Reader, Department of Sociology, M.G. Kashi Vidyapith, Varanasi.

Yogendra Singh, Former Professor, Centre for the Study of Social System, Jawaharlal Nehru University, New Delhi.

Brij Raj Chauhan, Former Professor and Head, Department of Sociology, Institute for Advance Studies in Sociology, Choudhary Charan Singh University, Meerut.

Yogesh Atal, retired as UNESCO Regional Adviser for Social and Human Sciences in Asia and the Pacific. Earlier, he was Director at the Indian Council of Social Science Research, New Delhi.

C. Lakshmanna, Former Professor and Head, Department of Sociology, Osmania University, Hyderabad. Also, ex-Rajya Sabha member and ex-High Commissioner, Trinidad & Tobago.

Gyorgy Szell, Professor, Department of Social Sciences, Osnabruck University, Germany.

Jugendra Sahai, Professor, Department of Sociology, M.G. Kashi Vidyapith, Varanasi.

Rajeshwar Prasad, Professor, Institute of Social Sciences, Agra.

B.D. Tripathi, Former Professor, Department of Sociology, M.G. Kashi Vidyapith, Varanasi.

S.P. Srivastava, Former Professor Emeritus, Department of Social Work, University of Lucknow, Lucknow.

Bindeshwar Pathak, Founder, Sulabh International, New Delhi.

R.C. Sarikwal, Professor Emeritus, Department of Sociology, Institute for Advanced Studies in Sociology, Choudhary Charan Singh University, Meerut.

P.N. Pandey, Former Professor and Head, Department of Sociology, Banaras Hindu University, Varanasi.

D. Sundaram, Former Professor and Head, Department of Sociology, Madras University, Chennai.

Jagdish Kumar Pundir, Professor, Department of Sociology, Institute for Advanced Studies in Sociology, Choudhary Charan Singh University, Meerut.

Ashok Kaul, Professor, Department of Sociology, Banaras Hindu University, Varanasi.

Anita Mattoo, Lecturer, Government Girls Degree College, Varanasi.

Introduction

The book is a collection of essays giving a panoramic view of current sociological understanding of the emergent social reality. It could not be possible to have a common theme for a kind of discourse leading to logical conclusions. Majority of the contributors have voiced their concern about the social development and change. When we look at the enormous amount of literature on development, one thing becomes amply evident that development seems to define the world's agenda, divergent ideologies and viewpoints. Development appears to be the key concept, an eminently attractive idiom of the fast modernising economies and social systems the world over. Professor Nagendra once said emphatically that social and cultural development in India could only be achieved through a cultural renaissance. Few contributors have expressed their concern for sociological theory; it would not be out of place if I again quote Professor Nagendra's views that he expressed in a seminar in G.B. Pant Social Sciences Institute, Allahabad. Expressing his stand regarding theories and facts, Nagendra said, "Theory is theory", "facts are facts". The implied meaning was that theory could back mind along its internal logical structures; and that it could be discussed only in the abstract. In all probability he mentioned that a collection of facts that provided evidence to the contrary could not negate a theoretical formulation. At any rate, description of facts did not attract Nagendra's thought process with facts being crucial or relevant.

Rest of the essays are of different nature questioning the existential basis of human action, examining Nasr's philosophy on the religion and nature and caste has also to be taken into consideration. The essays are not only exhaustive but shed enormous light on the Hindu social theory. Two esteemed contributors have raised the issue of worker's participation and provided a detailed model to redeem the crisis. Taken together, all the eighteen essays provide a spectrum of concern about the emergent social reality. We hope, readers will find it refreshing.

A.K. Saran critically examines Nasr's views on religion and the order of nature. According to Saran, modernist idea of the order of nature is idiotic because it is concerned about the logos of the eco (and industry), so it does not fit in the order of nature. The order of nature as resource, if not altogether stupid, is the order that man chooses to impose upon it. Saran's commentary on Nasr is about "the world created by the demiurge is not only an order or cosmos but a living order directed to the good and teleological in nature". In response to it, Saran suggests that the traditional theory of religion and nature takes us to the doctrine: "all is sacred: each in its own way and at the appropriate level". Saran does not believe in the omniscience and omnipotence (modernists) to substantiate his views he has taken clues from Commaraswamy and Kaviraj.

Raghuveer Singh mirrors the salient features of the modern administrative state, its power structure and the relationship with citizens. His observation is that with the increasing rationalisation in the politico-administrative set-up humanity is fragmented and fractured within and between individuals. This further leads to blurring of private and public realms. The eighteenth century Enlightenment Project of universal progress and rational reconstruction of society is deeply in crisis. The concept of humanism is quite misleading unless integrated with trans-human and trans-temporal dimensions of reality.

Ramesh Chandra Tiwari's essay is about the existential basis of human action. According to him, man's actions and their objective are rooted in his mind. While performing actions and achieving their objectives there always remains a sense of incompleteness and imperfection. Though the explanations have been provided to overcome them by many religions, yet the Indian tradition provides a sound explanation to bridge the gap between the sense of completeness and incompleteness. To substantiate his views, Tiwari quotes from various Upanishads and Gita in which the theory of 'Nishkam Karma' and various other paths have been provided and shown how one could strive to achieve the highest reality, i.e., Brahma. Though, all the paths are mutually exclusive, yet they culminate into the action of individual according to his/her potential.

Yogendra Singh proceeds with the assumption that Indian society is temperamentally against the new courses of social change. Yet, after independence, revolution in some form or the other crept into the Indian social system. According to him, Indian sociology played a vital role in preparing the ground for such revolution. In course of time, the revolution overtook Indian society in three phases, namely, democratic social revolution, green revolution and finally, globalisation. The author, however, feels that with the onset of the third phase a wave of crises has set in in the Indian sociology and social sciences.

Brij Raj Chauhan states that theories do not arise from the void blue: they grow from the personal experience of the theorists. To substantiate this assumption, the author takes the example of Max Weber who talks of three types of legitimate power. To work out this concept, he gathered inputs during the course of his visit to USA. The major theme of Weber's book *Protestant Ethic and Spirit of Capitalism* is based on his first-hand experience that he gained from his close association with the Protestant workers in the capitalistic economy.

Yogesh Atal, while examining the socio-cultural dimension of development, finds that after the end of Second World War, war-torn European nations engaged themselves in the reconstruction of their socio-cultural life. Along side, countries independent from the colonial yoke opted for economic development. In the colonial phase of history, people of colonised countries looked upon their colonial masters as positive reference group and copied them blindly. In contrast, colonist nations looked down upon the natives as negative reference group. In spite of this, they studied native subjects language and customs only to govern them efficiently. After the colonial phase, the socio-economic priorities of the freed nations changed radically. Their focus of administration shifted from law and order maintenance to rapid socio-economic development. The author talks of different paradigms of development adopted by the decolonised countries. The major dimensions of development are endogenous, sustainable and human resource. In the latter part of the paper the author takes up the issues of reconstruction of culture, separation of culture from ideology, sub-culture and cultural identity.

C. Lakshmanna's paper on Indian diaspora is an analysis, which is based on the cultural history of India, as well as secondary data and personal observations. He asserts that settlement of Indian population in foreign countries does not belong to colonial rule. The population in ancient times also moved due to commercial and religious reasons. However, modern migration has its origins in the British colonial rule. In this period Britishers experimented with indentural system recruiting people for a specified period to work on plantations. It was for the cultivation of cane that the specialised workers from India were brought mostly from Bihar, eastern UP, Orissa and other North Indian states. Large number of migrants stayed back due to unwelcome and hostile home conditions. Further, the author observed that migration of Indian population also occurred for business and professions. Settlement of Indians in foreign countries has gained momentum in the recent decades. The major reason behind this is oneness of identity. They have distinguished themselves in politics, economy, science, literature, art and sports. Lakshmanna opines that Indian diaspora is not uniform. There is much diversity in numbers, economic levels, relations with other co-existing ethnic groups but common among all this is their adherence for Indian culture. Lastly, he finds that the key factors in the sustenance of Indian identities are religion, family system, love for land, attachment of soil, faith in the destiny and pride in cultural forms. Religion also played a positive role in survival and growth of Indian identity.

Gyorgy Szell asserts that corporate social responsibility (CSR) has been in the focus of EU's industrial policy, its employment relations and its environmental concerns since the beginning of the 21st century. In the background of the triad competition, i.e., between the EU, the NAFTA and East Asia – perhaps an East Asian Union – the EU tries to accomplish the highest quality of life and working life for its citizen. CSR is a concept whereby companies integrate social and environmental concerns in their business operations and also in their interaction with their stakeholders on a voluntary basis. 'Shareholder value' became some 15 years ago the dominant slogan for corporate governance. Social justice, worker's rights were put into the waste basket of history. CSR is not a new phenomenon. Early bourgeoisie and capitalists created charitable foundations for people's welfare by opening schools, hospitals, etc. Philanthropy can be even characterised as an essential element of modern bourgeois society to overcome part of its contradictions, but also promote the own class and recruit from the lower classes promising talents. Two excellent indicators for CSR on the macro level are tax payment and employment. This brings us to the issue of ownership: Some corporations like the German Bertelsmann, Rockefeller, Ford and George Soros have transferred their main assets to foundations, which are socially responsible. Research on CSR is still in an embryonic phase.

Jugendra Sahai's is an analytical paper, the major concerns being modernity and culture. Discussion advances with the comparison of two pioneering sociologists in this field, one from America and other from Germany. Daniel Bell's and Jurgen Habermas's views have been discussed in details to show how the former rejects modernity and the latter defends it. Bell and other post-modernists see the causes of social crisis and moral breakdown in the cultural system, whereas Habermas and other critical theorists in the capitalist economic system. Sahai is equally suspicious about the viability of their views.

Rajeshwar Prasad's major concern in his paper is the deteriorating standards of teaching, research and training in Indian universities. To posit his view, he starts from pre-industrial to industrial age. He observes, in pre-industrial age, the knowledge was integrated, i.e., leading towards the perfection of man. Hence, there was no division of humanities and social sciences. With the onset of industrial revolution, this knowledge got separated and become polar. With the result, internal theoretical contradictions and methodological biases surfaced. In sociology, empiricist and ideological orientations came into conflict leading to theoretical crisis. In Prasad's opinion, what is required is the interdisciplinary approach in dealing with social reality.

B.D. Tripathi discusses evolution of caste system under three sub-heads, namely, the origins, the growth and constraint phase and the current phase. He traces the origin of caste system in the varna order of Hindu social hierarchy. In the growth and constraint phase caste gathered new attributes of closure and exclusiveness. In this very phase caste multiplies by leaps and bounds. Originally, there were only four segments of the Hindu varna hierarchy. In the growth and constraint phase the number of castes touched the figure of 4,000. In the third phase, caste gathered many new traits. The author identifies twelve dimensions of such new traits. One dimension is the admixture of caste and class attributes that gives a new identity and name to caste. The author calls it 'clast'.

S.P. Srivastava's paper is a vivid description of changing notion of development. Earlier, development was linked with economic growth which has now been replaced by human development; the essential components being equity, sustainability, productivity and empowerment. The scope and coverage of issues under the broad umbrella of human development is pretty large to include all such issues, policies and programmers which contribute to strengthening of human capabilities and widening of people's choices. Srivastava further examines UNDP's various reports and finds that the concept of human development is much wider than what it can be caught in any set of indicators. With regard to policy perspectives he opines the top priority has to be accorded not only to sustained economic growth but also to equity, good governance and an effective human rights regime to remove discrimination and secure social justice. Though India has made tremendous progress in economic development, infrastructural resources and technological advancement, yet all these have, however, not resulted in the materialisation of universal human well-being, according to the author.

Bindeshwar Pathak's paper is divided into three sections. The first section deals with the understanding of the dynamics of globalisation, whereas the second section discusses the relationship between globalisation and Gandhian economic thought. The third section concludes with the relevance of Gandhian thought in the present scenario of globalisation. He asserts that whilst Gandhiji's opinion and views are the best ways to handle the problem of economic growth, yet they have to be recast, reformulated and restructured in coping with the factors and forces that make globalisation a reality and not to be easily wished away and confronted with. Globalisation is inevitable in view of the efforts of all nations to accelerate their economic growth and modernise their society.

R.C. Sarikwal discusses the concept of worker's participation its meaning, fullness and viability. Different countries have defined the concept according to their socio-political and cultural structures.

Hence, no single model can be followed. To substantiate his view, he examines the worker's participation models prevalent in different countries and finds that there is no disagreement about the merit and quality of the models implemented in these countries. In the last, he asserts that the situation in India is much more adverse due to various factors such as the half-hearted nature of state intervention, employees' reluctance to accept innovative changes, absence of strong trade unions, workers' participational incompetence, and the like.

P.N. Pandey, while discussing globalisation and cultural change, finds that in common parlance, globalisation refers to the transformation of society at the universal plane as initiated by highly industrialised countries of the western world. According to him, the impact of globalisation is both positive as well as negative. On the one hand, globalisation breeds uniformity in the cultural, social and economic fields and on the other, it proves detrimental to the survival and maintenance of cultural, social and economic diversity. In other words, globalisation sacrifices diversity for the sake of uniformity. On the one side, it integrates society at the universal plane, and on the other, it eats up local cultures, traditions and economies in the process of integration. However, the strident steps of globalisation sadden the author. He ends up his essay by the following words in deep despair, "the whole world is going to emerge as a computerised network rather than a natural entity".

The understanding of the issue of inequality through the culture of hierarchy is of how the hierarchy as a component of inequality is a locally variant one with the potentials of continuity and change. D. Sundaram, in his paper, observes that the traditional methodological approaches appear to be an excessively reductionist. While analysing the classical social structure, the power of the state and not the sacred prescription had great significance. The social order during the classical age was of continuity and change in the cultural features of hierarchy. The framework of individuality without individualism represented how the hierarchical concept could undergo change or transformation in a given context. The author's endeavour is to capture the cultural forces of hierarchy in the Indian social order.

Jagdish Kumar Pundir in his paper seeks to examine the relevance and applicability of social theories formulated by American sociologists in the context of Indian social reality. He bases his analysis on the reference group theory. Towards the end of the paper he tentatively concludes that reference group theory may be treated as an interpretative rule for the understanding of Indian social process.

The last paper by Ashok Kaul and Anita Mattoo begins with the quote from Indian Constitution to understand the meaning of secularism. The Indian Constitution declares that "the State shall not discriminate against any citizen on the ground of religion, race, caste, sex, place of birth or any of them". In other words, a secular state is pledged to equal proximity or distance in respect of all the castes and communities living within the premises of its national geography. The author feels that history of India and neighbouring nations polity after independence lends credibility to the policy of secularism and its growing acceptance as a policy of administration for multicultural countries.

C. Lakshmanna
Jugendra Sahai

1

A Nasr Sentence

Some Comments

A.K. Saran

> "The world created by the Demiurge is not only an order or cosmos but a living order directed to the good and teleological in nature."[1]

In *Religion and the Order of Nature* which forms the title of Professor Nasr's *magnum opus*, the conjunction 'and' is clearly one of internal transformation.

Logically, there are two kinds of connections (or connectors). Taking 'and' as a basic coupler or connector, we may distinguish between two kinds of connections or conjunctions: the additive and the internal modifier. The distinction does not go very far, nor does it delve deep. The distinction is yet important and can help us reach important insights.

My point here is to suggest that the traditional theory of Nature and Religion takes us to the doctrine: all is sacred; each in its own way and at the appropriate level. In any consistent and persistent analysis of phenomena and human experience, ultimately all truth is tautologus. This was the view of Wittgenstein in the *Tractatus Logico-Philosophicus*. A lie accordingly is a self-contradiction (or a pretension); needless to point out that the one is a logical, the other is a behavioural concept.

This paper was prepared for *The Philosophy of Seyyed Nasr* to be brought by The Library of Living Philosophers, Chicago La Salle, Illinois, Open Count, USA.

The effect, the impact of Religion upon Nature is not a circumstantial, nor casual; more important, it is not ideological, even more importantly, it has nothing to do with pre-modern, non-scientific theories. The 'and' in the title of the treatise *(Religion and the Order of Nature)*, is, as we said, internal, symbolic, suggesting a sacred, divinely given unitive relation. The Order of Nature is ordained by the Creator, the Supreme creation from the huge to the negligible from nature and man to Angels and Satan is sacred; it has to be accepted by man not as something out there, to be exploited in his own interests, as he may see them from time to time. Nature is sacred to be approached in awe and wonder – independently of the level and scope of his knowledge and power. The Order of Nature is sacred and is to be approached in fear and trembling; never and in no way is nature to be exploited for man's fancies nor for auto telic knowledge. (There is, of course, no auto telic knowledge or, in truth, nothing is auto telic for the word 'auto telic' (or concept) does not survive any careful analysis of its meaning.)

Today, however, the very idea of the Order of Nature is, for modern man, idiotic indeed blasphemous: the ultimate profanity in the eyes of the White world (and for the White man there is only one human world, namely, the whiteman's). And, for him, ecology, environmental concern, the planned endangering of (Only One) Earth – all this is a kind of new game: something of the kind of the vogue of J.L. Austin in Harvard and Cambridge (some twenty years ago). Man, the Master, simply need be concerned about the logos of the eco (and industry). (So, where does one fit in the Order of Nature? Is there an Order of a Resource? None. Except to be ordered about by the white man and him alone.)

The Order of Nature as resource, if not altogether stupid is the order that man chooses to impose upon it But "man" does not mean you and I (Asians, Africans, etc.). Man is synonymous with White Man. And he (=He) decided to impose upon nature and non-white man, the order that is becoming suicidal: especially when "new science" takes charge of the *ecological crisis*.

The crisis of the modern world is only a footnote to the nature as resource theory. Appearances to the contrary, ecology will be conquered by advances in modern science and technology. The key to this hoped-for wonder is simple: Abolish the eco and invent a man-created Logos. No home, no *economy;* only industry and commerce.

And yet: the higher the scale of affluence, the deeper and even more unmanageable and revengeful effluence. This is a hackneyed warning. And so ineffective. As we said, all major threats to human survivals are entrusted to science and technology: which is expected to reach omnipotence. Strangely, though, modern man does not care much for omniscience. Perhaps there is nothing so strange here. If one could always deal with all contingencies, all menace, omniscience is not indispensable: the only snag is that omnipotence cannot cover time except by abolishing it. An obvious limit of omnipotence is its inability to change the past if this is included (or reduced to a short history), Time itself will be abolished. That would be the end of the matter for the modern man who cannot and does not talk about timelessness. For modern man is or chooses to be historical and entertains talk of prehistory. Man makes history. Can he unmake the history he made? I raise this question but only tentatively to suggest a point I cannot formulate. However, so long as the irreversibility of time remains, omniscience and omnipotence are out of man's reach.

Consider: man can and does unmake it (if not wholly, certainly on a large scale). Did he make it? Can he do this to-day?

Professor Nasr's *magnum opus* is full of ideas and insights *absolutely* vital for our survival. Primarily for lack of competence but also for limitations of space, we will offer an elucidatory commentary on only one selected passage: "The world created by the Demiurge is not only an order or cosmos but a living order directed to the good and teleological in nature."

The Demiurge is a strange God. He is the primordial transgressor: he breaks the Primal Silence and disrupts the originary unity of phenomena. Demiurge is the archetypal Benefactor of Man and the Protector of all creation.

In the Hindu-creation myth, the Demiurge – Brahma – is guilty of the Primal Violation: of creation of another Time and another Space and Man. Siva the God of Time (and death) gives Brahma capital punishment: He cuts off Brahma's Fifth Head. The Guardian of the Non-manifest could not act otherwise. In consequence, Siva is declared guilty of Murder. The Assembly of Gods punishes Siva. He is to live for a time by collecting alms with the skull of dead Brahma as his begging bowl.

We have here a strange, even absurd, account of creation of Man.

Primordial creation is both Benediction and Benefaction. And also the Original Sin which, in the Hindu tradition, is committed by the Creator himself, in contrast to the Christian tradition where the Original Sin is of Adam and Eve, the Primordial Pair. The idea of Redemption belongs to the Sin and not necessarily to the Sinner. And so Siva had to live for a time on alms which the God had to beg Himself. It has always to be remembered that there is a sense (in traditional thinking) in which all thought and all action is ultimately absolute: its ordained consequence must follow.

All sin, that is, the very idea of sin, arises from the non-acceptance of the Absolute. And so modern man rationalizes every thing: making the Relative (pseudo-) Absolute. For contemporary "thinking" modernity and modernization are absolute, all time values for contemporary colonial people. Without this pseudo-absolutization of the fancies and phantasies of the brute power (sans authority) of the white man human authority (in its own name, or in the name of a "superior race") cannot be absolutized. Except Man be omniscient and omnipotent: a cherished and impossible dream. A dream modern man cannot give up.

For man – and modern man especially – omniscience and omnipotence may not suffice even if the possibility were granted of taking care of the internal tension between the two concepts. Firstly, omniscience logically and even more so praxiologically, implies, if not presupposes, omnipotence. The reason is this: whatever one comes to know by omniscience entails: (a) it is all that is to be known and (b) that he has the knowledge *and* certainty that it is all that is there to know. There is of course, the problem of the certainty of both past and future (it may look like cutting it too fine to include the present). Omniscience, therefore, clearly generates insoluble problems and impossible tasks. At least as far as past and (even) present are concerned. It may be objected that all this concerns the non-initiate. Yes, but if the omniscient is his own authority, then he can be certain about his omniscience. Only one has to remember: omniscience is a strictly closed, one may say, an impenetrably dark space and a temporal time.

If this be broadly accepted, the problem of omniscience and the problem of omnipotence remain a dark area. (There is, I think, no need to offer a separate analysis of omnipotence.)

What about the Coomaraswamy text which has been quoted[2] with acceptance. Does it not conflict with our strictures on the idea of the human attainability of omniscience and, apart from that. the impossibility of understanding the idea for man? The Coomaraswamy passage steers clear of the problematic here presented. He says: "It is, of course, "only as it were with a part of himself" (BG xv. 7) … ."

What is involved here is the necessary infinitude of both: the manifest and the non-manifest. There need be nothing strange or recondite about this statement. The idea of finitude or limit presupposes that of the limitless, the infinite. Finitude cannot be understood otherwise than as a modality of limit, which (limit) by itself cannot be given a "definite" meaning without presupposing the infinite. What Coomaraswamy points out is that omniscience and omnipotence are both limited and confined to the manifest. What *remains,* the non-manifest, the Uncreate, is beyond all possibilities: measurable and immeasurable.

Pure creation is residue less. This is impossible: the infinite is Uncreate: the create alone is finite. Yet it is always burdened with residues (which are unending by virtue of their necessary birth from the infinite). In the myth of Siva, Brahma, the Demiurges cannot but sin. Brahma (the Creator) is punished by 'Siva' who does what was to be done. This was Siva's duty; it was Siva's *dharma.* And it entailed the primordial, cardinal Sin of Brahmacide. And Siva was punished. He had to atone for his cardinal Sin. The Sin had to be redeemed. And Siva was redeemed by virtue of his travails.

As "fruits" and "creatures" of the primordial sin of the arch-creator, namely, violating the Uncreate, we have our originary, primal *dharma* of remembering the Uncreate and moving towards the Origin.

All askesis is a backward movement towards the Uncreate, the inviolate. Human askesis, at its deepest is repentance, (= Being in One's Right Mind). Our self-redemption-movement, askesis, *sadhana* is in terms of possibility. It is a silent, backward movement – to the Origin. This does not – cannot – make sense. Naturally, For Origin is what one leaves "behind". It is impossible to unite with one's own Origin or even to see what such a personal unity with one's origin could mean. It is no use pointing out that it is not a matter of Time and Space. Is not human askesis transcending temporality and spatiality? I am not sure, the Grand Originator is charged with sin: the

Original Sin in Hindu tradition is not of man but of the Creator who has, for this purpose, to disturb the Supernal Majesty of the Uncreate. Siva avenges and beheads the creator. And in turn He has to atone for this by serving time under condition not so much hard as demeaning for anyone: as for Lord Siva – he alone – and the myth makes it clear that the Greatest of the Hindu God, Siva is the Lord of Death and simultaneously of the Great Emancipation for the believer, the *mumuksu*. Clearly dharma of Siva is to avenge the primordial sin of Brahma: it does not follow that Man is born in Sin: the relation of man to the Creator is not filial.

Brahma is immediately avenged by Siva who is the Lord of Death. Siva cuts off Brahma' s head.

This is Brahmacide: the highest sin. And Siva has to repent and suffer the penitence. He has to beg alms for a year using the dead skull of Brahma as his begging bowl. But not at all as a repentance for the "sin", he committed. It was in response to his duty flowing from his being the Lord of Death.

Creation is thus a fractured Reality and is bound to remain so under all circumstances: for it follows from the logic of creation *ex nihilo*.

An order, we said, is necessarily asymmetrical. A teleological order repeals this asymmetry. Without using the means-end vocabulary (which in this and many other contexts is vulgar) one may certainly say that the *telos*, is the specific asymmetry that defines a given order. Without a given and freely accepted *telos* this asymmetry is a threat to the life and working of an order.

The key words in the succinct formulation are cosmos (order) and *living*. The Cosmos is not only a significant whole (at whatever level and with whatever be its dimensions, the most significant thing here is that it is (strictly) a whole and so it is holy.) and no less significant than other aspects of the cosmic reality: it is an ordered whole and *living* and teleological. Each of the three cardinal aspects of the cosmos is important and definitive: for it is not only that an aggregate. a totality can be just that: a number of things which one wishes to refer to as funning *some kind* of unity. In fact, some may distinguish between totality and a whole, an aggregate in terms or chance (as distinguished from purpose) however, I for one would not see the general point (for in the context of the Nasr Sentence to the whole either as an aggregate or a totality, would be to miss altogether the level of Nasr's book).

An ordered whole (eventually the concept of order) must presuppose if not imply a whole of one kind or another; the argument that follows endeavours to avoid a blanket presupposition of wholeness in the logic of the idea of order. (It should be mentioned that ultimately in any non-antitrans existential context, the holiness or order is necessarily entailed – except in a context divorced from man's humanity which entails transcendental realms.)

With reference to asymmetry as necessarily implicated in any concept (and theory) of order, I am now unsure about it. Indeed it is old problem of the labyrinth: it seems to me that if the symmetry of the labyrinth were perfect, airtight, the possibility of an actual way could not be admitted – even so I feel that the ultimate logico-dialectical asymmetry originates. with, is inherent in the relationship of the creator and creation and creatures. From time immemorial man or superman has denied his creature hood: the well known Indian mythological story of king *Trishanku* and sage *Vishwamitra* illustrates this. This story uncovers the inherent weakness of the twin concepts: omniscience and omnipotence which as pointed out early are confined to the manifest and do not extend to the non-manifest.

It seems to me that a symmetrical order entails reversibility and this possibility is cancelled by the reign of Time.

In any case, the full phrase refers to an order which is living and teleological: this already implies that because of the irreversibility of time for man. a living order has to be teleological if man is important to reverse time in the full sense of reversibility. In this context the teleological dimension of human life is one of the necessities of a *living* order *sans telos*, there will be no humanity in man's life.

In many ways, the keyword here is the adverbial adjective "living" (order). If I could be allowed to distinguish between an active and a passive adjective, "living" qualifies "order" in two ways: the order, here in question, is a highly responsive (where "response" is vitally distinguished from "reaction": a reaction [the word "action" notwithstanding] is passive. indeed even mechanical [if not automatic]). A response is an active. well considered dealing with a given situation: a response is ever free; a mere reaction is unfree (being an unthinking), mechanical, and hence a dead "response" to an inter-human situation (this includes interaction between man and animal, especially the tamed ones).

At this point too one has to race the problem of the nature and necessity of the *telos* of the creation. It can of course, be said that the asymmetry of human time entails a *telos*: the problem is: does not the mortality of the man create a chaos rather than a cosmos? In other words, the irreversibility of (human) time negates all (human) teleology: so that you and I can respond and act freely and positively. I must have faith in the ultimate goodness of the creation: in other words, faith in the ultimate truth (which is a monadic: of man and the cosmos).

"True and false" is unlike all other pairs; unlike good and evil: where the evil too is a matching power even more powerful. Truth is truth, is truth. (Truth is cosmo-existential: false is not an antonym of truth. only a limitation of ordinary language.)

To posit false as the opposite of truth would not hold: for the false, the untrue or untruth has no positive *locus standi*; unlike good and evil where the latter too could have a powerful positively: falsehood does not, cannot have any kind of positive status: indeed paradoxically a false statement must itself be believed to be true in order to serve its purpose as false (whereas evil does not have to be non-evil in order to be evil). Thus the grammar and syntax, of falsehood do not support any theory of its positively: for this very positively necessarily automatically makes it true. As far as I can see and argue truth is *ipso facto* true: absolute in the sense that its negation itself has to be true. (If it leads to a paradoxical situation, so be it.)

This hierarchical Firstness of Truth in the traditional triad of Truth Goodness and Beauty is designed to encapsulate the whole life-endeavour of man *qua* man.

"The hierarchical Firstness of Truth": this rather quaint-looking use of the Firstness of Truth is however, derived from Peirce.[3] In Pierce, broadly speaking, Firstness is a non-mediated experience: whether or not there be any such experience is not the point: even when one holds that all our experience is mediated the possibility of non-mediated experience is thereby already posited whether or not there be, in fact, any such. Indeed, spiritual askesis in some traditions (say Hindu and Buddhist) often see it as the goal of human askesis *(Sadhana)*.

In the triad of Truth Goodness and Beauty a hierarchical relation between the three is necessarily posited. As Coomaraswamy told Eric Gill: Take care of seeking, finding and seeing the Truth in any given context. And Goodness and Beauty will take care of themselves.[4]

How so; Coomaraswamy's primary truth and Peircean Firstness (Secondness, Thirdness) are appearances to the contrary, wholly compatible – on the basis of the transcendental theory of symbolism as the only theory.

I do hope that this formulation is not, in any significant way, incompatible with the traditional hierarchy of the four *Purusarthas* (cardinal Ends of human life), namely, *Dharma, Artha, Kama, Moksha*. The life of desire and its fulfilment, the life of pursuit or establishing oneself in a reasonably comfortable living; the life of askesis: working towards the attainment of absolute freedom, *Moksha*.

There are grounds (or reasons) for this: One: sensation and intuition belong semantically to the same family: what may be called sensory or sensate knowledge (or better, information) is the same as Kierkegaard's aesthetic level of human life [the other two being (a) ethical, and (b) religious]. For our purposes here, do not think that the further distinction between Religiousness One and Religiousness Two need to be examined here. The essential thing here is to remember that (a) the lower is always pregnant with the higher, and (b) the higher is all the time threatened with a fall (via pride or the persistence of the lower) in the higher (as a residue or as pride).

And so the asymmetry inherent in a living order (even when it is cast as a hierarchy) is redeemed by the *hieros*.

In the living order, teleology again is redeemed by the Unknown and Unknowable *Hieros*: unless and until man's *telos* be transformed, transmuted by the (Divine) Logos, no hierarchy can be definitively saved. The ultimate Release is a Leap. The essence of any genuine teleology is the *Logos* itself or else the *telos* could be a breeding ground for human pride.

Notes

1. Seyyed Hossein Nasr, *Religion and the Order of Nature* (Oxford: Oxford University Press, 1996), p. 85.
2. Here are two texts on omniscience and omnipotence. Each is from a cardinal authority of traditional thinking and scholarship:

   "It is, of course, only as it were with a part of himself" (BG xv. 7) that the Supreme Identity of Being and Non-being can be thought of as omnipresent, omniform, omniscient. For omniscience can be only of the possibilities and actuality of manifestation: of what remains (*ucchistam,* AV xi. 7, etc.) there can be neither science nor omniscience, and it is from this point of view that, as Erigena justly remarks, "God does not know *what* he is, because he is not any what" (cf. Buddhist *akimcanna*). It is only his possibilities of manifestation that become "whats" of which there can be science or omniscience."

   [Anand Kentish Coomaraswamy, *Coomaraswamy 2, Selected Papers – Metaphysics*, edited by Roger Lipsey (Princeton, NJ: Princeton University Press, 1977), p. 60]

   "All these views are centered on the fundamental thesis of Sankaracharya, viz., that omniscience, omnipotence, etc., are not *really* predicable of the Supreme Being. It is after and through the operation of Cosmic Nescience that these are attributed to Him. Since His essence is knowledge itself, it is only by a metaphor that He may be called all-knowing. Omniscience and omnipotence are, therefore, pseudo-real concepts and not real."

   [Gopinath Kaviraj, *Aspects of Indian Thought* (Burdwan: The University of Burdwan, 1966), p. 27]

   With this foreword let me return to omniscience and omnipotence. Kaviraj sees it with concentrated insight and astounding universal scope. Quoting Sankaracharya, he denies omniscience and omnipotence, even to *Supreme Being.*

   But today science – natural, social, anthropological; mathematical is constructed and ordained to serve the omniscience and omnipotence: God (if there be One) may or may not attempt to accomplish. Modern science and technology are hell-bent to pursue and achieve.

   The formulations of Coomaraswamy and Kaviraj may seem to differ on one point. Coomaraswamy seems to concede that with reference to the Manifest, omniscience and omnipotence may be possible; emphatically impossible if one thinks of the Non-manifest. No knowledge and no power are at all conceivable and so ruled out.

The seeming difference between the two formulations vanishes when one remembers that the Manifest is born out of the Womb of the Non-manifest. And except one has power over the Non-manifest one can have no worthwhile power over the Manifest. Then again, one can have knowledge of the Manifest: past, present and future {assuming the last has an antic-existence). This knowledge must be related in a certain manner; when there is a given relationship the future follows, and if it is not as predicted by the omniscient, there has to be an intervening variable which ought to have been known to the omniscient. If the omnipotent intervenes and disturbs the knowledge of the omniscient the two are working at cross purposes.

The modern age defines itself by its Faustian will to know – at all costs. I shall know all or shall not live. And by its Promethean will to possess all – or life is not worth living.

If Modern Science and its latest advances are a promise of the fulfilment of a Faustian will – never mind if Faustian Spirit is hellish. The Universal White Imperialism is Modernization of the ignorant people: Asian and African. Modernization being seen following Husserl as the "humanization" of non-white peoples toward self-chosen slavery of the white West.

All modern science – physical, chemical, zoological, anthropological – hides in its inner spirit: this grand intent.

The message of the East is: Be the willing slaves of the White.

There is one other aspect of the twin concepts – Omniscience and Omnipotence: the omniscient person can know the past and the present and the future of a given world, small or vast. He can by virtue of his omniscience envision the past, the present and the future of a given and presumably unchanging present but the present is, by definition, just a moment and thus a continually vanishing present. By omnipotence he can affect the present and the future. Even here there is a huge problem: how to deal with the sheer moment that the present is? The exercise of power over the moment runs into trouble because the purpose of this kind of exercise of power would be based on the totality of the concatenation of each passing moment. And once the moments are changed then this can change the future but this would be an unknown future which *eo ipso* falls outside both omniscience and omnipotence.

As to omnipotence, it is totally powerless over the past. Does the omniscient has memory? By the logic of omniscience memory is abolished: for the omniscient the distinction between past and present and future is lost.

The ideas of omniscience and omnipotence have persisted in human history and mythology; they seem to be a kind of superstition. If every thing is like a cinema reel, there is no purpose in knowing them. Maybe in order to avoid this logical result, the idea of omnipotence has been invented to give "meaning" to the idea of omniscience. That is perhaps why the Hindu Avataras never act: they playact (*Lila*). This is a view maintained by some scholars of Buddhism: *The Buddha Acts in a Nirman Kaya*.

3. "The idea of First is predominant in the ideas of freshness, life, freedom. The free is that which has not another behind it, determining its actions; but so far as the idea of the negation of another enters, the idea of another enters; and such negative idea must be put in the background, or else we cannot say that the Firstness is predominant. Freedom can only manifest itself in unlimited and uncontrolled variety and multiplicity and thus the first becomes predominant in the ideas of measureless variety and multiplicity. It is the leading idea of Kant's "manifold of sense." But in Kant's synthetic unity the idea of Thirdness is predominant. It is an attained unity; and would better have been called totality; for that is the one of his categories in which it finds a home. In the idea of being, Firstness is predominant, not necessarily on account of the abstractness of that idea, but on account of its self-containedness. It is not in being separated from qualities that Firstness is most predominant, but in being something peculiar and idiosyncratic. The first is predominant in feeling, as distinct from objective perception, will and thought.

[Charles Sanders Peirce, *Collected Papers*, Vol. I, edited by Charles Hartshome and Paul Weiss (Cambridge: The Belknap Press of Harvard University Press, 1960), pp. 148–49]

4. Anand Kentish Coomaraswamy and Eric Gill: In a letter to Coomaraswamy, Eric Gill suggested that in the triad of Truth, Goodness and Beauty the most important is Goodness given which Beauty and Truth will follow. Coomaraswamy wrote back to disagree: No, it is Truth that is primary and essential: Seek Truth and Goodness and Beauty will be added unto it.

[This letter is not included in Lipsey edition of Coomaraswamy Correspondence. It is in earlier collection of AKC's Correspondence by Durai Raja Singam]

Kumar Ajai Srivastava, Research Assistant to the *Collected Works* of Saran Project of the Central Institute of Higher Tibetan Studies, Sarnath, Varanasi (India) has spared no trouble and worked overtime in making of this short essay something my draft respectable and reasonably free of inconsistencies, repetitions and other blemishes. For more significant is his positive contribution to my thinking and the draft of this essay. Thanks would be incommensurate with the importance or what he has done for me and for this brief contribution to the Philosophy of Professor Nasr – the latest work in the Library of Living Philosophers.

I pray for God's Grace for his continued advance in this direction. May God's Grace let him overcome difficulties and disturbances so that they do not prove too much for his intellectual work.

2

The Administrative State and the Home Politics

Raghuveer Singh

The transformation of the modern democratic state from the 'police state' to the 'social service' or 'welfare state' system is a widely acknowledged fact, but the exact nature and implications of this phenomenon are only recently being realised with any appreciable degree of precision and perspicacity. The nineteenth century democratic state was based on the assumption that the people have a well-articulated and clearly recognizable will of their own which is expressed through an elected body of representatives. The business of government is carried on by this representative body, but ultimately the people are sovereign and their representatives are the deputies who work under their direct control and according to the mandate given to them. This postulates an intelligent understanding and active role on the part of citizenry, a subordinate and subservient position of the government and its administrative organs, a determinate source of authority and well-structured system of ruler-ruled relationship with precisely definable locus of authoritative command and obligations and assignable centres of power. All this has radically changed with modern mass democracy. We no longer have a system of command and obedience, a determinate sovereign and an obligated subject, a

---

Professor V. Raman Endowment Lecture, delivered at Lucknow, 1999.

definite ruler and a definable set of individuals who are ruled, but an impersonal, ubiquitous network of power relations without a subject and working without any meaning and purpose, with inexorable necessity and perfect objectivity. In it there is hardly any place for human will and purpose, rights and obligations which are only disguised of relations of power. Long before Foucault, Max Weber had clearly discerned this view of modern state system though with different analytical perspective. He said: "In the final analysis, in spite of all 'social welfare policies', the whole course of the state's inner political functions, of justice and administration, is repeatedly and unavoidably regulated by the objective pragmatism of reasons of state. The state's absolute end is to safeguard (or to change) the external and internal distribution of power."

From the Foucauldian point to view, it would be more appropriate to say that the end of the state is itself a function of the external and internal distribution of power or power knowledge. The gigantic growth of administrative machinery of the state following upon and necessitated by the demands of technological-industrial apparatus of contemporary civilisation and the acquisitive ideology of modern man has transformed the old Reichstag* into the modern so-called administrative state, which is rather the administered state, in which there is hardly a place for the free play of individual will and discretion and every thing is done by way of objective necessity, governed by instrumental relationality which joins given end and relationally discovered means in the casual nexus. Here, ends are important, but are beyond reason and are simply presupposed whereas the means are discovered by rational cogitation, logical deduction or empirical generalization. Science of politics or administration becomes value-natural or purely objective and rational. The idea of an objective and rational science of public administration to which the theory of politics seems to have been reduced by the protagonists of the autonomous discipline of public administration was well expressed some forty years back by the authors of a well-known textbook which has survived, even today: "Knowledge of administration, like all knowledge, is amoral. It becomes 'good' or 'bad' only in, terms of value assumptions, added to it by the person who uses it in terms of his attitudes towards goals and methods. Knowledge gives man power – but power to do either good or evil … ."

* A historical edifice in Berlin, Germany, constructed to house the parliament of the German empire.

The book also states: "Knowledge of administration is amoral in even deeper sense, for it is knowledge of how to manipulate other human beings, how to get them to do the things you want done. The study of administration discloses techniques of influencing human action."

In other words, just as knowledge involves manipulation of symbols, administration implies manipulation of men. Leonard White's famous definition of public administration as "the management of men and materials in the accomplishment of the purposes of the state" is of a piece with this approach. Here, the distinction between men and materials tends to vanish, for men themselves are treated as materials to be manipulated and used for the sake of the purposes of the state which are defined by those who happen to be in power. The nomenclature currently given to what used to be called the Ministry of Education in India, namely, the Ministry of Human Resource Development is only symptomatic; it signals the dawn of the age in which men are nothing but resources to be used or misused in accordance with the aims of public policy set by the powers that be. The end may be called the public good, but the good cannot be objectively ascertained. Hence, it must be a matter of subjective preferences, idiosyncratic propensities, individual or collective or personal whims and caprices of those who happen to capture power by hook or by crook.

Thus, the science of administration is, in the ultimate analysis, the rational science of irrational goals, the collective pursuit of non-justifiable socialised values authoritatively allocated and inculcated by propaganda and mass indoctrination.

"The time has come", says Lasswell, "to abandon the assumption that the problem of politics is the problem of promoting discussion among all the interests concerned in a given problem. Discussion frequently complicates social difficulties, for the discussion by far-flung interests arouses a psychology of conflict which produces obstructive, fictitious and irrelevant values. The problem is less to solve conflict than to prevent them, less to serve as a safety valve for social protest than to apply social energy to the abolition of recurrent sources of strains in society."[1] "It is by exposing and perhaps destroying the interpersonal relationship", he adds, "which have held true in the past that the scientific effort produces the most far-reaching results."[2] This means virtually the abolition of man as homo politicos and the end of politics as a mode of human activity consisting of speech and action. The preoccupation of current sociological and administrative theories with the concepts of 'mass society' and 'organisation man' reflects this tendency. According to Simon, the well-known theorist of organisation, "Organisations are the least 'natural', most rationally contrived units of human association."[3] The subject of science of administration is a "drastically simplified model of buzzing, blooming confusion that constitutes the real world."[4] This drastically simplified mode is fashioned on the "criterion of efficiency" and involves a well-conceived plan initiated by a controlling group. "The rational individual is and must be an organised and institutionalised individual." Through "his subjection to the organisationally determined goal's and through the gradual absorption of these goals into his own attitudes, the participant in an organisation acquires an organisation personality rather distinct from his personality as an individual."[5]

The above profile of public administration may appear to be one-sided and oversimplified in view of the emergence of comparative, ecological and developmental perspectives in the writings of theorists like Fred W. Riggs, Dwight Waldo and Spitz and Weidner. Yet, and the fact remains that in much of the public administration literature there is hardly any idea of the public. In fact, the very science of public administration owes its origin to a blurring of distinction between the public and the private realm or rather the assimilation of the public to the private; in other words, modelling of the state activity on the lines of private business management geared to the need of efficiency and economy. Hannah Arendt, with her characteristic insight into the nature of the modern world, shows how the growth of the social, by an inescapable logic, necessitates the growth of bureaucracy, which is "the last stage of government in the nation state just as one-man rule in benevolent despotism and absolutism was its first." She also observes that bureaucracy is the rule by no-body," but it is not necessarily no-rule, it may indeed, under certain circumstances, even turn out to be of its cruelest and most tyrannical versions."[6] Karl Marx oft quoted observation that in a prefect communist society the government of men will be replaced by administration of things does not require any great imagination or intellectual exercise to understand it because of the simple fact that in a perfectly socialised community there will hardly be any men to govern.

The enormous growth in the administrative powers of the modern state and the consequent loss of individual initiative and liberty follows as a natural corollary of the concept of rationalisation that has characterised the modern European consciousness since the time of Descartes and Bacon and which Weber made the very foundation of his theory of social and economic organisation epitomised in the notion of bureaucracy. Bureaucratic rationality has a tendency towards totalisation. It is "not confined to governmental arrangements; it has deeply penetrated all modes of social life so that distinctions have lost their salience."[7] The greater and greater use of technical power and more and more systematisation and rationalisation, co-ordination of means and ends, balancing of inputs and outputs, have reduced the play of contingency and variability and have made everything calculable, determinable and predictable. Everything has been systematised. "System, a term which is widely used and revealingly combines a technical bioengineering meaning with a technocratic, bureaucratic one, signifies the transmutation of the state into the economic polity ... . Unlike the monocratic structure, in which dominance was the basic political and social fact, the basic fact about power under the regime of the technologically advanced economic polity is its pervasiveness."[8]

This brief note was aimed to bring out the salient features of the modern administrative state, its power structure and its relationship with citizens. It shows how radically the twentieth century administrative structure differs from what it used to be earlier. The difference is due not only to the growing complexities of modern life arising out of the vast network of national and international agencies and corporations impinging on or fast changing and modernising lifestyle and ever increasing demands and expectations of the people, but also to the homogenising and totalising tendencies inherent in the very nature of modern rationality seeking to transform the condition of man beyond recognition. Are we not here faced with the death of man as many philosophers have recently suggested? Is Foucault's prophecy that soon man would be erased like a face drawn in sand at the edge of the sea coming to be true?

The ideological crisis of the western world is presently reflected in the modernity-postmodernity problematic. The eighteenth century Enlightenment project of universal progress and rational reconstruction of society for the attainment of freedom, equality, prosperity and the conquest of nature culminated in the rise and growth of industrial capitalism with all its homogenising and totalising tendencies. The postmodern thought has strongly reacted to it and has emphasised plurality, specificity, contingency and difference (differance). In the Anglo-Saxon world the communitarian critics of liberalism have sought to resuscitate the values of social ethos, traditional norms and different 'spheres of justice'. The reigning doctrine, however, continues to comprise rationalistic individualism, scientific advancement, industrial growth and material development of which globalisation and privatisation are the latest expression in concrete terms, and of which India seems to have been the most helpless victim in spite of all its rhetoric of cultural nationalism, Hindutva and Swadeshi. The result is that the ruling elite and bureaucracy have to choose between serving the people and serving the market, and under the pressure of international forces and agencies like the World Bank and the IMF it has opted for the latter. Global economy and world trade lead to cut-throat competition and ceaseless strife and the ideals of cumulative growth of material resources and ever increasing physical control of nature as universal desiderate accentuates the disparity and widens the gulf between the 'developed' and 'developing' nations. "World trade and world wars", says Coomaraswamy, "are congeneric evils". People who are conscious of the dehumanising and disintegrating tendencies of unlimited economic growth have started talking of human development and the older mechanistic theory of scientific management is giving place to what is called humanist framework of administrative theory. But, the concept of humanism is quite misleading. Unless integrated with a transhuman, transtemporal dimension of Reality intends to reduce himself into a psychophysical phenomenon, as the rational cut off from its source in Divine Intellect succumbs to the infra rational.

"The word 'humanism'", says Schuon, "constitutes a curious abuse of language in view of the fact that it expresses a notion that is contrary to the integrally human, hence to the human properly so called: indeed, nothing is more fundamentally in human than the 'purely human', the illusion of constituting a perfect man starting from the individual and terrestrial, whereas the human in the ideal sense draws its reason for existence and its entire content from that which transcends the individual and the earthly."[9]

"In any case, man by attributing to himself his own self-sufficient reason, cannot remain what he is; if he no longer believes in that which transcends him and if he does not place his ideas above himself he condemns himself to the sub-human."[10]

The concept of human development as envisaged in the United Nations Development Programme (UNDP) devoid as it is of a metaphysical perspective hardly conducive to a proper solution of our present-day problems. In fact, the entire paradigm of development is meaningless because it posits no end, *telos* or *summum bonum* and substitutes the means for the end. Continuous and indefinite development means that there is in fact nothing to achieve and therefore the pursuit is fruitless. In the classical theory all meaningful evolution or growth is one from matter to form or from potency to act. The *telos* puts an end to all development. The whole process is governed by a fixed 'measure' or ratio. The idea is never development but harmony, balance, repose, equilibrium or order. In traditional civilizations this idea is expressed in such terms as Tao, Rta, Dharma, Dyke, justice or righteousness. This implies a proper balance, a hierarchy (sacred order) of the metaphysical and the physical orders of being, a superordination of contemplative to active life of man. The crisis of the modern world arises out of this inversion of order. It cannot be resolved by material development and technological advancement. What is needed is St. Augustine's "Wisdom uncreate, the same now as it ever was, and the same to be for ever more."

Notes

1. Harold Lasswell, *Psychopathology and Politics*, Chicago: The University of Chicago Press, 1930, pp. 196–97.
2. Harold Lasswell, *The Political Writings of Harold D. Lasswell*, Glencoe III: The Free Press, 1951, pp. 524–25.
3. Herbert Simon, *Models of Man*, New York: Wiley, 1957, p. 199.
4. Herbert Simon, *Administrative Behavior*, New York: Wiley, 1957.
5. I have adopted this formulation from my discussion of scientific rationality in the essay "Causality, Meaning and Purpose in Politics", *The Review of Politics*, Vol. 47, No. 3, July 1985.
6. Hannah Arendt, *The Human Condition*, Garden City, New York: Doubleday Anchor Books, 1959, p. 37.
7. Sheldon S. Wolin, "Democracy and the Welfare State", *Political Theory*, November 1989, p. 489.
8. Ibid., p. 491.
9. Frithjof Schuon, *From the Divine to the Human*, Bloomington, Indiana: World Wisdom Books, 1982, p. 9.
10. Frithjof Schuon, *The Transfiguration of Man*, Bloomington, Indiana: World Wisdom Books, 1995, p. 13.

3

Man's Yearning for Fulfilment in Life

The Hindu Traditional View

Ramesh Chandra Tiwari

Among the various attributes of a man two can be said to be outstanding, viz., praxis, the capacity of action and lexis, the capacity of speech. These two provide the bases that give rise to the realm of human affairs. Although these two can be distinguished from each other, yet, if one analyses their interrelationship in depth, it can be seen that the two are very closely interwoven. The interlinkage between the two is grounded in human mind. This explains why, in common parlance, mind, speech and action, *Mana, Vachana* and *Karma,* are often taken into consideration together. The mind of the individual sets the goal and direction of his action and speech. Without a goal there can be no action. In his day-to-day existence man always seeks to pursue one end or the other, no matter how high or low these may be. It is extremely rare to find someone acting without reference to an end. Truly, man is a goal-seeking being.

All action, guided and directed by mind, has its roots in human needs and desires. If man has to exist – physically, socially and psychologically – his basic needs and desires must be fulfilled. Fulfilment of needs is the basic condition for an individual's existence. The range of

---

This paper is based on a lecture delivered by the author during a month-long conclave on the 'Existential Study of Hinduism' organised by the Christian Retreat and Study Centre, Rajpur in 1984.

human needs is extremely wide and diversified. There are certain needs which man shares with animals, e.g., the need for food, sleep and sex. But there are certain needs that are specific to man, such as socio-cultural, aesthetic and spiritual needs. Although each of these needs is distinct from others and each activates man to satisfy it, yet, they are not to be seen as independent of each other. The interdependence of the various needs of man is a major factor in shaping human life. The interdependence of man's existential needs brings about a co-ordination, directly or indirectly, between his diverse actions. Man's effort to fulfil one need impinges upon other needs and in the process his different activities react upon and modify each other. That being so, the interdependence of needs and that of actions go together and this gives unity to human life. After all, man's life is not to be seen as a conglomeration of various needs and related actions. Seen in proper perspective, it is a unity, a whole.

Though man is a goal-seeking being and his actions are directed towards the satisfaction of needs, yet it is a fact that in his normal life he is not generally satisfied with the outcome of his efforts. Very often he finds a gap between his conception of the satisfaction of a particular need and the actual outcome of his action to meet it. Moreover, there always exists a possibility of failure of one's action. This generates a sense of incompleteness giving rise to anguish and, consequently, he thinks more in terms of "I ought to have acted in such and such a manner" rather in terms of "I have performed well under the circumstances". He hankers to achieve perfection in his actions. He desires to achieve a level of perfection where there is no gap between idea and performance, between thought and action. But, as the things stand, for an individual there is hardly any escape from the feeling of imperfection and incompleteness generated by that gap. The hiatus between thought and action is one of the basic conditions of human existence.

The almost inescapable sense of incompleteness and imperfection experienced by man is rooted in the very nature of human action. Analysing the nature of human action, Hannah Arendt says that the each action can be seen as having two parts, the beginning *(archain)* and the achievement *(prattain)*.[1] The beginning initiated by an individual is very much different from the actual achievement. While performing an action under the given circumstances, one can only be sure about making a beginning. He can never be sure about the end product of his action. It may click or may not. Chances of complete failure or partial failure are always there. Imperfection and incompleteness are the in-built characteristics of human action. Unpredictability of outcome is its inherent feature.

As matters stand, one can see that man constantly finds himself placed in a predicament. While, on the one hand, he longs for the achievement of the perceived goal, on the other hand, neither is he sure of the success of his effort nor is he likely to achieve complete satisfaction out of it. It is rare that an individual in the course of his normal social life gets complete satisfaction with regard to the yearning for fulfilment. It is even rarer that he stops to yearn for fulfilment. He longs for perfection and fulfilment but at the same time he is also gripped by the feeling of imperfection and incompleteness. Nevertheless, if one takes the realities of human condition into consideration, it is undeniable that against all odds man does not forsake the quest for perfection, for fulfilment. It is his eternal quest and this eternal quest is a part of his existence.

It is in the context of man's existential quest for perfection or fulfilment that religious traditions assume significance in one way or the other, and each religious tradition offers help and guidance to man in finding his way out of his existential predicaments, including that relating to the yearning for fulfilment in life. There are varieties of such traditions – Taoist, Judaic, Hindu, Buddhist, Christian, Islamic and the like and each of them offers guidance to its adherents through its own unique approach. Here, we have chosen to delineate some major aspects of the Hindu approach in order to find out how does Hinduism deal with the existential problems and predicaments of man. So, now, let us see in what manner the Hindu tradition treats the problem of man's yearning for attaining fulfilment in life. What is the Hindu idea of perfection or fulfilment? How to attain it? What are the problems related to its attainment? How they are dealt with?

II

Human desire to achieve perfection in life greatly hinges on one's conception relating to the meaning and purpose of life. Therefore, to begin with, it will not be out of place to have a brief idea about the meaning and purpose of life in the Hindu tradition.

It is a firm belief in the Hindu tradition that behind and beyond everything there is one or the infinite. This infinite, generally referred to as *Brahman,* manifests itself everywhere and in all possible forms. *Brahman* has been described as the creative, cosmic principle. It is the very being, the very truth of all things and, at the same time, it is the creator who wills the cosmos into existence, as *Brahadaranyak Upanishad* says: "It wears all forms, it does all acts, all movements, everywhere in all times."[2] However, as far as human beings are concerned, its nearest manifestation is the human consciousness. Man experiences it as self-consciousness. It is the self-conscious man who takes up the questions concerning the meaning and purpose of his life.

The purpose of human life is the achievement of happiness as *Mahabharata* declares: "All human acts have for their end the attainment of happiness."[3] The Hindu seers have talked of two kinds of happiness, viz., the worldly happiness and the supreme happiness or bliss. Man can attain both kinds of happiness by following the four *Purusharthas,* the four goals of life. Of these four *Purusharthas,* the pursuit of the three, i.e., *Dharma, Artha* and *Kama*, brings worldly happiness. *Artha*, the pursuit of wealth and prosperity and *Kama*, the pursuit of the pleasure of the senses both have to be guided and directed by *Dharma,* the supreme moral principle, which gives meaning to human endeavour and regulates all forms of human activity. It is true that the Hindu tradition gives due recognition to the importance of worldly happiness and thus takes man's biological, psychological and social needs and potentialities into consideration, but it also makes one realise that the pursuit of such happiness has its limits as it does not fully meet man's basic longing to attain perfect happiness. He can achieve perfect or supreme happiness when he pursues the highest goal of his life, i.e., *Moksha*. In fact, *Moksha* or the final liberation is the release from the bonds of the previous three goals of life. It is the release from the bondage created by the yearning for worldly happiness. At the same time, it has to be appreciated that there exists a profound integral combination of bondage and necessarily ever present opportunity of freedom.[4] Without delving further into the metaphysical intricacies involved in the dialectical relationship between bondage and freedom here, it will suffice to say that *Moksha* is the final release as it frees the individual from the endless cycle of births and rebirths. Thus, the quest for perfection achieves its culmination in *Moksha*.

This very brief review of the Hindu ideas relating to the purpose and goals of human life makes it clear that in the Hindu tradition the course of action to be followed by man has been charted out in unambiguous terms. The extremely comprehensive concept of *Dharma* in its various forms unmistakably lays down norms to be followed by man in carrying out various social and individual responsibilities and in the course of the pursuit of wealth and pleasure. In this way, performing actions is not a matter of one's sweet will, but of the conscience grounded formally in *Dharma*. But howsoever meticulously one follows the norms of *Dharma*, it is held that the pursuit of *Artha* and *Kama* has its limits. The pursuit of worldly happiness may be necessary for man and it may also generate some sense of achievement and satisfaction in him, but it cannot give him ultimate satisfaction and happiness. A lifestyle, which puts premium on this world with its pleasures and possessions, can never be satisfying in the true sense. One who clings all the time to the world is bound to be overtaken sooner or later, by a sense of emptiness and meaninglessness. Hence, the Hindu tradition accords highest place to the happiness, which fills one with the experience of the eternal. This happiness transcends the manifest world. It is the final and last freedom.

It becomes obvious that the Hindu tradition takes into account all the basic existential needs of man. The various needs are not seen as independent of each other. Societal, individual, physical and spiritual needs are seen as interdependent. Dealing with the existential traits of the human beings, the noted existentialist philosopher Martin Heideggar holds that 'being-in-the world' is also 'being-with-others'.[5] Leaving apart the vexing question of the 'automatic existence' dealt by Heideggar, if we see that the societal existence of man is an important dimension of his total existence, then even from the purely existential point of view it becomes necessary to establish balance and harmony between the social and individual life of man. This may be one way to understand why the Hindu seers with all their emphasis on the transcendental yearning of man have not ignored the worldly pursuits and relationships. They did not shut their eyes to the realities of human existence. The Hindu doctrine gives due recognition to both the finite and infinite, the temporal and eternal and the worldly happiness and the supreme happiness.

Since the temporal and eternal are not to be viewed in their exclusiveness and their interdependent nature has to be recognised, it implies that the two-fold purpose of life, i.e., *Abhudaya*, the pursuit of worldly happiness and *Nihsreyas*, the pursuit of supreme happiness, is not to be seen as unrelated. In a way, the two appear as polar opposites. One affirms the world, the other negates it; one leads to attachment, the other to renunciation. But, if one looks at the situation from a wider or holistic perspective, there does not exist such a dichotomy between the two evidently; they are contradictory, but they are mutually dependent also. One cannot exist without the other. Both contradiction and unity exist side by side. These seemingly opposite poles are interrelated and bound to each other. The *Upanishad* declares: "In darkness are they who worship only the world, but in greater darkness are they who worship the infinite alone. He who accepts both saves himself from death by the knowledge of the former and attains immortality by the knowledge of the latter."[6] To those who are used to analyse things in terms of neat logical categories this may sound as illogical and confusing. But as the things stand, the interdependent and contingent nature of opposites is a reality, a stark reality. Here it would not be considered out of place to point out that though this line of thinking in India was initiated by the *Upanishads,* it was at a later stage of Indian cultural history that it witnessed its real fruition. It was left to the *Madhyamika* school (of Buddhism) to take this line of thinking to its culmination. The concept of *Sunyata* or emptiness, as enunciated by Nagarjuna, does not distinguish between *Samsara* and *Nirvana,* between existence and non-existence. This may all sound as paradoxical, but if realities are actually paradoxical then they have to be seen as such. The distinction between bondage, *Samsara,* and liberation, *Nirvana* lies in the state of one's consciousness. The enlightened consciousness is unaffected by the rising and setting of likes and dislikes, mental action and supra-mental consciousness. When one is firmly established in the infinite and unconditioned consciousness, i.e., *Prajna,* even these distinctions vanish.

III

The way the individual's existential needs have been taken care of and the way the purpose and aims of human life have been spelled out, it is clear that in the Hindu scheme of life every individual is expected to make full use of all his potentialities. The entire fabric of social and individual life is integrated in such a manner that everyone can realise his or her own perfection. Ananda Coomaraswamy writes:

> Where there is agreement as to the nature of man's last end, and that the way by which the present and the paramount ends of life can be realised is that of sacrificial operation, it is evident that the

form of society will be determined by the requirements of the sacrifice; and that order *(Yatharthta)* and impartiality *(Samadrishti)* will mean that *every man shall be enabled to become, and by no misdirection prevented from becoming, what he has it in him to become* (emphasis ours).[7]

Undoubtedly, actualising the potentialities of man has been accorded utmost significance in the Hindu tradition.

The emphasis on the fulfilment of the potentialities of the individual indicates that the Hindu tradition has taken up one of the fundamental problems of man: the problem of being human. In the eyes of the Hindu seers, to be human is to actualise the potentialities of man. If the underlying aim of all human activity is such an actualisation, a new dimension is added to the meaning of life. The entire life is then seen as a *Sadhana*. The term *Sadhana* comes from the root *Sadh* which means to accomplish an aim, to fulfil, to gain control over or to subdue. Broadly speaking, *Sadhana* can be said to mean the process of perfecting of man or the process of fulfilling the potentialities of man. Seen as *Sadhana* human life becomes an endeavour, a pursuit to attain the aim of perfection. Commenting on the aim of perfection in Indian culture, the renowned Indian sociologist Radhakamal Mukherjee says: "The individual's aim of perfection is the same as the group's aim of culture, complete, balanced and practical the realisation of the Universal Self and the Universal Community."[8]

This brings us back to one of our leading questions that we raised in the beginning. If to attain perfection is the goal of life, how one is going to attain it? What way or ways are suggested by the Hindu tradition? Let us take it up as briefly as we can.

Since the times of the *Upanishads,* it has been maintained that one can attain the goal of perfection by following any of the three different *Margas* or paths. These are: the *Jnann Marga,* the path of knowledge; the *Bhakti Marga,* the path of devotion; and the *Karma Marga,* the path of action. The assumption behind the formulation of the three paths is that all men are not alike and they differ from each other on account of their intellectual, emotional and practical qualities and capabilities. If we find that some individuals are primarily emotional in their disposition, some others appear to be primarily reflective and yet some others may be found to be more disposed towards work and activity. However, such a classification of human beings is not to be treated as exclusive. It simply takes this fact into consideration that certain qualities are found more dominant in the personality make up of certain individuals than others than one says that someone is endowed richly with reflective qualities it does not mean that he is totally devoid of emotional or other qualities. Thus, the three paths to perfection are distinguished on the grounds of *Adhikari Bheda* – the difference based on the kind of worthiness of an individual.

Jnana Marga is the pathway to wisdom or the supreme knowledge. Wisdom is not to be confused with the knowledge based on theoretical, philosophical or scientific learning. It is the knowledge of the reality behind all things, it is the knowledge of *Brahman*. It lies beyond the discursive realm. It is not to be achieved by analysis or argumentation. It is experienced directly. *Jnana* is the polar opposite of *Avaidya*, which is desire as well as ignorance about the reality behind the phenomenal world. Once wisdom dawns *Avaidya* disappears. As *Avaidya* or ignorance is the cause of action that binds man to the world and to the incessant process of births and rebirths, therefore, with the dawning of wisdom actions do not bind the individual any more. He is liberated. This state is achieved by means of *Dhyanayoga,* the way of meditation and development of the personality in such a manner that passions like envy, anger and malice fade away. The mind becomes tranquil. The tranquillity of mind and the absence of desires make one experience the ultimate reality. A verse in *Kathopnishada* reads: "When all the desires hidden in the heart are loosed, then the mortal becomes immortal, then here he enjoys Brahman."[9] Describing the qualities of a *Jnanayogin* or one who has attained the highest knowledge, *Bhagavadgita* states, "He whose undertakings are all free from the will of desire, whose works are burned up in the fire of wisdom, the wise call him a *Jnani.*"[10] The actions performed by such a wise man melt away and they are not bound by their actions. "The work of a man whose attachments are sundered, who is liberated, whose mind is firmly founded in wisdom, who does work as a sacrifice, is dissolved entirely."[11] The *Jnana Marga,* or the path of knowledge, is steep and austere. It is often said that "treading the path of knowledge is like walking on the sharp edge of a sword". Only few individuals can follow this path. Usually it is pursued by the *Sanyasins,* the world renouncing monks. But it is not necessary that only the world renouncers can tread this path or only they can gain success. The path is open to all those who are its real *Adhikaris,* those who are worthy of it.

The second path leading to fulfilment is known as *Bhakti Marga* or the path of devotion. As the path of knowledge, this seeks to realise the supreme reality, which is *Aryakta* or unmanifested and is extremely difficult. The path of devotion is open for all those who are ready to devote themselves completely to a deity or the *Ista-Devta,* the chosen deity. This path can be pursued by the weakest of the weak and the lowliest among the low. Hindu *Puranas* and the epics are full of innumerable stories illustrating how even the most ignorant and seemingly unworthy individuals got liberated by the grace of the deity. The word *Bhakti* is derived from the root *Bhaj* which among many other things also means to attend upon or serve. Thus, *Bhakti Marga* is the path of service of the chosen deity. Choosing a deity depends upon one's personal choice or his or her local and family tradition. *Bhakti* demands total surrender and total dedication. The *Bhagwatpurana* declares: "Whatever we do and achieve through our body, speech, mind, sense, organs, intellect or our own self-nature, should be surrendered and dedicated to *Narayana*."[12] The edifice of *Bhakti* is raised on the foundation of *Sraddha* or faith. Devotion demands unflinching faith. Such a faith generates supreme love. According to the Hindu tradition, it is the supreme love for the *Ista-Devta* that makes one qualified to receive his benign grace. By his grace the devotee is assured the fulfilment in life. He reaches the goal of perfection. Dwelling upon the significance of unswerving devotion, Lord Krishna says: "Those, who, laying all their actions on me, intent on me, worship, meditating on me, with unswerving devotion. These whose thoughts are set on Me, I straightway deliver from the ocean of death-bound existence, O Partha (Arjuna)."[13] It is through unflinching devotion that the devotee is ultimately freed from bondage and attains supreme knowledge or *Jnana* by the grace of the Lord. The destiny of a true *Bhakta,* the devotee, is assured if he forsakes everything for the love of his chosen deity. "Abandoning all duties, come to Me alone for shelter. Be not grieved, for I shall release thee from all evils."[14] Among all the paths for attaining perfection and fulfilment, the *Bhakti Marga,* or the path of devotion, is the most straight and direct. It is open to all without any man-made distinctions and hierarchies.

Karma Marga, the path of action, is the third path to be followed in one's attempt to approach the goal of life. As the name suggests, this path is based on action or *Karma*. The concept of *Karma* is one of the important concepts of Indian thought. It is this concept which overarches all the major religions of India, viz., Hinduism, Buddhism and Jainism. This concept has been enunciated and analysed by all the Hindu scriptures. One of the fullest expositions of this is to be found in the *Bhagwadgita*. *Karma* is considered to be ubiquitous in human society because every individual performs one action or the other at almost every moment of his life. It is the condition of being human. The Hindu tradition holds that the concept of *Karma* explains why an individual is leading a particular kind of life and what he can make of his life. Only through *Karma* can man actualise his potentialities and also make his destiny. It makes man to realise that it is never late to set things right. Gokhale writes: "*Karma* looks both ways; glances back into the past and it looks forward to a bright future."[15] Therefore, it is no wonder that the path of action, *Karma Marga*, is counted among the major paths leading towards fulfilment in life. In many respects it is the best path.

One who pursues the path of action never allows himself to be caught in the mire of inaction. But, at the same time, it is necessary for him to know the subtleties of action and he should very well understand which line of action he has to pursue. His mind must be very clear about it. The Indian tradition generally holds that the performance of *Karma* or action is invariably followed by its consequences, which have to be faced sooner or later by the performer of the action. The oft-repeated proverb puts it in most simple words, "as you will sow, so you will reap". None is above the law of *Karma*. All created beings are under the sway of *Karma*. *Devi Bhagwat* puts it briefly in these words: "All, *Brahma* (The creator) and the rest, are under its sovereign rule."[16] Men are caught in the unending cycle of births and rebirths because of their *Karmas*. Unless one is not liberated from this cycle, he cannot achieve perfection. But, notwithstanding the inexorability of the law of *Karma*, there is a strong belief in the Hindu tradition that it is given only to man, not to others, not even to gods, that he can cross the ocean of death and free himself from the bondage of *Karma* or action itself, not by inaction. Man must not desist from the path of action. A verse from the *Isopnishad* tells us, "A man should try to spend his life-span of hundred years only in constant performance of actions."[17] But it does not mean that one should go on performing actions with a hedonistic set of mind. *Isopnishad* has advanced the view that all actions must be performed in view of the ultimate purpose of human life, i.e., the final liberation or *Moksha*. This approach seeks to synthesise and integrate the life of action with the life of knowledge. We are told, "To pitchy darkness do they go who pursue the path of ignorance, namely, the path of action. To greater darkness still they go who devote to the life of knowledge for its own sake. Sages have told us from very ancient times that knowledge leads to one result, while action leads to the other. But he alone who can synthesise the claims of knowledge and action is able by means of action to cross the ocean of death and by means of knowledge to attain immortality."[18] Thus, *Isopnishad* tells us that the life of bare knowledge or contemplation and the life of bare activity are to be abhorred alike. Only that person can attain the ultimate goal of life who knows how to harmonise the two different paths.[19]

This strand of thought found its highly sophisticated and most advanced enunciation in the *Bhagwadgita* – the most celebrated *Hindu* scripture – which erected a complete philosophy of *Karmayoga*. The central principle which the *Gita* enunciated is its well-known concept of *Nishkama Karma,* or desireless action. *Gita* reinterpreted the concepts of *Jnana, Bhakti* and *Karma* resulting in a new synthesis which does not see any contradiction between *theoria* and praxis – *Jnana and Karma.*[20] This synthesis saw its culmination in the metaphysical concept of *Nishkama Karma* which is grounded on spiritual knowledge – *Prajna/Buddhi.* This concept is the guiding principle of moral and religious life. *Gita* does not subscribe to the idea of pure *Jnana* which looks down upon all action and advocates *Naiskarmaya,* or non-action. The wise persons advocating this idea argued that all action springs from desire and ignorance. *Gita* declares that both individual and social survival depend on action and actionless life is an impossibility. But, at the same time, it holds that a genuine wise person can act as an uninvolved disinterested spectator. Such a person does not pretend to engage himself in immobilising his mind and body both. As a matter of fact, he realises his inner aloofness even when engaged in action. He never acts to achieve his selfish ends. He acts out of duty, out of love and out of empathy, with equanimity and inner serenity.[21] Thus, the idea of *Nishkama Karma,* propounded in *Gita,* is the most important concept which stands for performing action that leads to liberation – *Moksha* – the supreme goal of a human being. This concept synthesises the apparent duality between *Jnana* and *Karma*. Lord Krishna says: "Works do not define me; nor do I have yearning for their fruit. He who knows Me thus is not bound by works."[22] In this way, action performed without attachment does not lead to bondage. *Gita* differentiates between three kinds of *Karmas,* viz., *Karma* that binds, *Vikrama* which not only binds but is also a wrong action and *Akarma* that is not binding in its nature. As the man must perform some action, therefore, the best thing is to perform actions, which are non-binding. One of the most famous couplets from *Gita* reads: "To action alone has thou a right and never at all to its fruits; let not the fruits of action be thy motive; neither let there be in thee any attachment to inaction."[23] One has to perform all his duties as laid down by *Dharma,* but, without concern for the result. This is *Nishkam Karma,* or action without attachment. By enunciating the concept of *Nishkama Karma, Gita* has shown the path which helps man to steer away clear from the two extremes, i.e., inaction and the attachment to the fruits of action.[24]

IV

In our present enquiry relating to the nature of the Hindu response to man's yearning for fulfilment in life, we have so far dwelt upon the Hindu idea of perfection or fulfilment in life along with the prescribed ways to achieve it. However, there is yet another dimension of the problem under consideration. All said and done, one may rightly ask, "Well, I have understood the theory alright. It is complete in itself and takes into account all the major aspects of human existence and human nature. But, the question arises how does all this help man in overcoming that sense of incompleteness and imperfection which is related to one of the basic problems of our existence, viz., the hiatus between thought and action, between conceptualisation and actualisation." No one can say that a person pursuing the goals of *Artha* and *Kama* by faithfully following the rules of *Dharma* will always get success and will never experience the feeling of imperfection. Even a devout *Sadhaka,* a seeker of truth or a *Sanyasin,* cannot be sure that all the penances he undertakes, the righteous life he leads and the meditation he practices will definitely enable him to make it. He may or may not achieve the goal. As was indicated in the first part of this paper, given the conditions of human existence, there is no guarantee that once an action is initiated it will lead to the desired goal. Therefore, the question is how does the Hindu tradition deal with the problem of imperfection in achievement?

At this juncture, it is necessary to point out that, by and large, in the Hindu scheme of things there is no static end or goal to be attained by the individual. It is correct that the *telos* of man's striving, the goal towards which he moves, is *Moksha,* the final liberation. But what is significant is man's act of striving towards the goal and not the actual achievement. In this context, Troy Wilson Organ presents a nice distinction between the perfected man and the perfecting man. He writes: "The goal of Hindu Sadhana turns out to be not perfected Man but perfecting Man. Hinduism is not Donatism, demanding that man become perfect, rather it is concerned with the melioristic direction of man's life, individually and getlerically."[25] The perfecting man is one who by making use of his potentialities is moving in the right direction. Man perfected is the ideal to be approximated whereas the perfecting man is the reality to be attained. The process of perfecting is the process of becoming.

In the Indian tradition the emphasis on striving in the right direction is underscored by the frequent use of the term *Marga* or path. The striving for attainment of wealth and possessions is called the *Pravartti Marga*. Similarly, the path of renunciation or of liberation is known as the *Nivritti Marga*. The terms *Pravartti* and *Nivritti* are often used as synonyms for *Abhudaya,* the worldly happiness and *Nihsreyasa,* the supreme happiness, respectively. The term *Marga* is also used widely in other contexts, e.g., the *Jnana Marga, Bhakti Marga, Karma Marga, Yoga Marga* and so on. This wide use of the term *Marga* underscores the fact that emphasis is laid on the path one treads and not on the goal which is standing somewhere over there. Man's effort to actualise his potentialities and his striving for perfecting, as different from perfection, is supremely important. Nothing more is expected of him. If he continues his journey onwards along the *Marga,* it is laudable. It is enough that he is marching along, no matter he ever reaches the end of the path, if there be any. Thus, man's striving is his *Sadhana*. It is the process of eternal becoming. Only that justifies his being as man. On many occasions the Hindu scriptures refer to *Moksha* as a pursuit for immortality. *Mahabharata* describes it as "the pursuit of the Brahman or self-knowledge".[26]

For ages the ideal of constantly and whole-heartedly devoting oneself to perform his duties and to fulfil the social and individual obligations with an attitude of resignation towards the fruits of his actions has been the general trait of the Hindu way of thinking and acting. We have already referred to this ideal, known as the ideal of *Nishkama Kama*. Of course, it would be ridiculous to suggest that all Hindus follow this doctrine faithfully. That is beyond the line of argument being followed here. What is significant is the fact that down the millennia the doctrine has inspired millions and millions of people. Speaking about the unity of the doctrine and their realisation in the Hindu tradition, Rene Guenon observes: "Theory is always accompanied or followed by an effective realisation for which it merely provides the necessary basis; no realisation can be embarked upon without a sufficient theoretical preparation, but the history is ordained entirely with a view to this realisation as the means towards the end, and this point of view is presupposed, or at least tacitly implied; even in the exterior expression of the doctrine."[27]

Like any living cultural ideal or doctrine anywhere in the world, the concept of *Nishkama Karma* is a widely accepted ideal in India. Generally speaking, whenever an average Hindu strives to achieve some end, this ideal remains, in one way or the other, in his mind. It has percolated deep down the recesses of Hindu psyche. One can easily find out that in India in most of the cases whenever an Indian faces disappointment in the context of an action undertaken by him he finds ready succour in this doctrine which holds that to engage himself in action is in the hands of man but he has no control over its results. He may or may not achieve the desired end. If anyone controls the results, it is God alone. Let us taken an instance which may give some idea of the working of the mind of an average Indian living in the present-day world, and, to be more specific, living in the last decade of the 20th century. This speaker is known to a father who is faced with the serious problem – in India it is definitely major social, familial and individual problem of finding a suitable match for his daughter who has reached her marriageable age. As is prescribed by the custom, it is the duty of the girl's parents to find a match for her. Consequently, when a girl's parents approach the parents or guardians of the prospective bridegrooms, the latter adopt a hard stance and there is a lot of tough bargaining regarding the dowry to be given by the former. The Indian marriage market is out and out a buyer's market where the bridegrooms dictate all the terms. Thus, to get one's daughter's marriage settled is a terrible ordeal. So, as the matters stand, the father of the girl has been literally running from pillar to post for the last two years or so and has, till now, drawn a blank. In the process he has travelled hundreds of kilometres and has lost much of his valuable time and money. But, even in the face of his failure in finding a suitable boy for his daughter he has not raised his hands in despair. He faces the situation with equanimity. Talking about the problem, he often says, "I am doing my duty. I will continue to do so. If I succeed it is fine. Even if I do not I will accept His verdict. Only engaging myself in action is in my hands. I have no control, whatsoever, over the results of my action. It is only He who decides what is good for me." Thus, his search for the bridegroom continues. In Indian society such instances are galore. Go to far-flung tiny hamlets and villages, go to the towns or even go to the giant industrial-commercial metropolises, you will find that the attitude of a common Indian relating to his action is more or less similar. In general terms, it can be said that an average person faced with the problem of attaining perfection in his endeavour is more or less guided by the dictum of the *Gita:* "Action alone is your concern, never at all its fruits." This ideal could not have been better put in words by anybody else than Sant Jnaneshwara, the famous saint-poet, who says, "If one meets with success while engaged in action, it is God. But if for some reason the success eludes, that is also God If one does not meet with success one should not think that his action has remained unfulfilled; because if the action in its totality is offered to God then take It as fulfilled."[28] To avoid any misunderstanding, it must be emphasised that an ideal is meant to be kept before oneself. Like the Pole Star, it guides those who cherish it. It can never be achieved. The ideal is not the actual.

The emphasis laid on striving by the Hindu tradition implies that if one fails to attain perfection it need not cause despair. Despair and disappointment have no place in this scheme of things. Under all circumstances one who is pursuing a path has to keep on going. One can keep on going only when he does not loose enthusiasm and steadfastness, which sustain him in his onward journey. Man's existential condition ordains that the goal of attaining perfection or attaining fulfilment in life is an ever receding goal. The *Aitareya Aranyaka* says, "Whatever the man reaches, he wishes to go beyond. If he reaches the sky, he wishes to go beyond. If he reaches the heavenly world, he would wish to go beyond."[29] The existential problem of the yearning for fulfilment in life is resolved, when one sees that the movement or progression towards the goal of perfection is a fact and not the hankering for the actual achievement of the imagined picture of the goal. *Charaiwati, Charaiwati,* i.e., move on, move on, is the credo of the perfecting man.

Notes

1. Hannah Arendt, *The Human Condition*, Doubleday Anchor Books, Garden City, New York, 1958, p. 168.
2. *Brahdaranya Upnishad*, I, vi, pp. 1–3.
3. *Mahabharata Shanti Parva*, 190, pp. 6–7.
4. A.K. Saran, *Traditional Thought*, Central Institute of Higher Tibetan Studies, Sarnath, Varanasi, 1996, p. 20.
5. See, Edward A. Tiryakian, *Sociologism and Existentialism*, Prentice Hall, Englewood Cliffs, NJ, 1962, p. 112.

6. Quoted by S. Radhakrishnan, *The Hindu View of Life*, George Allen and Unwin, London, 1927, pp. 79–80.
7. Ananda Coomaraswamy, *Hinduism and Buddhism*, Philosophical Library, New York, 1943, p. 26.
8. Radhakamal Mukerjee, *The Culture and Art of India*, George Allen and Unwin, London, 1959, p. 18.
9. *Kathopnishad*, II, vi, p. 14.
10. *Bhagwadgita*, IV, p. 19; English translation by S. Radhakrishnan, *The Bhagwadgita*, George Allen and Unwin, London, 1948, pp. 163–64.
11. Ibid., IV, 23, p. 165.
12. Quoted by Bal Gangadhar Tilak, *Srimadbhagwadgita Rahasya*, Hindi translation by Madhav Rao Sapre, Tilak Bandhu, Bombay, 1928, p. 431.
13. *Bhagwadgita*, XII, 6, p. 7. English translation by S. Radhakrishnan, op. cit., p. 294.
14. Ibid., XVIII, 66, p. 378.
15. B.G. Gokhale, *Indian Thought through Ages*, Asia Publishing House, New York, 1961, p. 100.
16. *Devi Bhagwati*, IV, ii, p. 8. English translation adopted from, *Sanatan Dharma*, Theosophical Publishing House, Adyar, 1940, p. 132.
17. *Isoupnashada*, S. 9.a.
18. Ibid., S. 9.b.
19. R.D. Ranade, *A Constructive Survey of Upanishadic Philosophy*, Bhartiya Vidya Bhawan, Bombay, 3rd ed., 1986, pp. 218–19.
20. G.C. Pande, *Foundations of Indian Culture*, Vol. I, Motilal Banarasidas, New Delhi, Reprint, 1996, pp. 191–92.
21. Ibid., pp. 193–94.
22. *Bhagwadgita*, IV, 14, op. cit., p. 163.
23. Ibid., p. 119.
24. See, Mahamahopadhyaya Gopinath Kaviraj, *Bhartiya Sanskriti aur Sadhna*, Vol. I, Bihar Rashtrabhasa Parishad, Patna, 2nd ed., 1977, p. 213.
25. Troy Wilson Organ, *Western Approaches to Eastern Philosophy*, University Press, Ohio, 1975, p. 82.
26. *Mahabharata*, Udyoga Parva 42.
27. Rene Guenon, *Introduction to the Study of the Hindu Doctrines*, Luzac and Company, London, 1945, pp. 171–72.
28. Quoted in *Siddhayoga* (Hindi Monthly), Vol. XVII, No. 2, 1984, pp. 3–4.
29. *Aitareya Aranyaka*, 2, 3, pp. 1–2.

4

Sociology and Social Revolution in India

Challenges and Responses

Yogendra Singh

In the Indian situation, sociology had its growth first, through colonial encounter with the West and then normatively and intellectually imbibed the cultural, social and the political discourses of the Indian national movement. And, when India gained independence it performed both its pedagogic and instrumental functions for the society. As the Indian society is up against new forces of social change brought about by globalisation and revolution in the information technology, sociology once again is called upon to take up the challenge. It has now to move ahead with a new pedagogic and pragmatic strategy to achieve the goals both of the promotion of the discipline and the development of the society in the 21st century.

The Democratic Revolution

India, since independence, has gone through at least three phases of social revolution. The period between 1947 and 1967 could be broadly described as the first phase of this revolution – we may call it the democratic social revolution. It was marked by the adoption of a Constitution, which enfranchised the Indian people and politically empowered them as the citizens of India, irrespective of the differences of birth, gender, religion, race and class, etc. Radical land reforms were introduced that gave the right of ownership to the peasantry. The federal structure of the past was abolished. A national policy of positive discrimination in favour of the Scheduled Castes (SCs), the Scheduled Tribes (STs) and the Other Backward Classes (OBCs) was included in the Constitution. Institution-building for the development of the country was undertaken on a massive scale. A beginning was made for the establishment of the heavy industries, particularly steel and petro-chemicals, and the construction of dams and irrigation systems. The Community Development Programmes (CDPs) were started throughout the country. Side by side, heavy investment was made in the establishment of a chain of institutions to conduct and promote advanced research and training in the fields of natural sciences, technology, medicine, agro-sciences, management, etc. Also, during this period, an unprecedented expansion took place in the number of institutions of art, culture and higher education, particularly the universities and colleges in India. These policies paved the way for radical social transformation. Some changes that these measures brought about could be witnessed immediately, but most others had a revolutionary potential for growth and change, only to bear fruits later.

Consensual Sociology

The Indian sociology played a significant role in planning and implementation of these revolutionary social changes. Despite the debate on the indigenisation of their categories, social sciences reflected their universalistic character in theoretical constructions, research methods and generation of data. We find in this period a growing partnership between the researches in social sciences and the developmental needs and goals of the state. India adopted a model of import substitution and welfare planning for economic growth. Within a quasi-federal structure the state occupied a centrality of position in this process. This historicity has significantly influenced the institutional structure of social sciences and sociology in India, its pedagogy, scope and method. Moreover, state remained a major source of funding of research, and most researches were sponsored by its research establishments or through various autonomous institutions which were also its own creation. Sociology, social sciences and its community of scholars reflect, during this period, a spirit of consensus about the state's policies of development and planning.

Probably, it was a legacy of the Indian national movement and its ideology of social, economic and political development. The state was not perceived as an adversary but as an enabler to achieve the national objectives of development, nation-building and reconstruction of the Indian society.

Despite this grounding in the national ideology of development and social transformation, sociology and other social sciences did not remain impervious to the normative, theoretical and methodological influences derived largely from the United Kingdom and the United States of America. In sociology and social anthropology, large-scale studies of villages, towns and cities were undertaken; the social and economic impact of the community development, its group dynamics and the contribution of leadership in the adoption of technology and its diffusion of innovation, etc., were systematically explored for their role in the economic, social and political development. In this context, the comparative roles of social categories, communities, tribe and caste, etc., were observed and analysed in order to measure the impact of social policies on the processes of development and also to identify the shortcomings in the execution and formulation of these policies. In most of these studies, one may witness a significant level of influence of the Euro-American social sciences, particularly in the choices of methodology and operationalisation of conceptual categories.

In political science, the shift from the focus on political theory and the study of its macro-institutions to the study of voting behaviour, the social and institutional structures and processes of the political parties, political mobilisation and leadership, etc., introduced a new discourse. The goal of family welfare and balanced population growth being central to the process of planning, the demographers played a key role in the study of family structure, its gender profiles, the occupational mobility and social change. Several studies on the quality of life, health and education, etc., were undertaken. The psychologists contributed richly by their systematic studies of the pattern of the Indian 'achievement orientation', and its structure and function. A few studies, using interdisciplinary method, offered insights into the nature of the personality structure in India and its implication to social change and modernisation. Among the social sciences, however, economics made the most focused contribution to the process of planning and development, not only by generating benchmark data on significant economic variables but also by systematic studies of the macro- and micro-economic structures and processes of strategic significance for the economic growth.

However, the paradigms of almost all Indian social sciences, including sociology, of this period demonstrate reliance on the 'motivational approach' in planning, rooted implicitly, in the ideology of rational individualism. The primacy was accorded to the unit actor in making choices about goals of development, whether the objective was innovation in agriculture, entrepreneurship, family welfare or voting behaviour. The principle of universal rationality in choice-making was assumed. This assumption was, no doubt, valid for many spheres, such as the enforcement of the legal and citizenship rights, economic choices in matters of trade and investment, etc. But, in the spheres of culture, social structure, politics and political mobilisation, etc., this assumption was not valid because it neglected the historicity of social forces and their unique initial conditions, needs and experiences. This ideology of rational individualism, which guided the strategies for the implementation during the first two decades of planning in India, was not only Euro-centric; it was also flawed in its understanding of rationality. It relied heavily upon the social scientist's or the planner's definition of rationality, and neglected the people's or subject's own notion of rationality.

I may illustrate it by one example from the 'family welfare' programme. The studies revealed that the high rate of fertility was most frequent among the poorer sections of society. So, in order to reduce their birth rate, the strategy adopted, during the first two decades of planning, relied heavily upon 'motivating' the people with financial incentives, technical helps and other instrumental measures to adopt small family norm, which was considered to be entirely rational. This approach, however, did not take into account that rationality was operationally altered by social structural conditions of the subjects which may not harmonise with the planner's definition of rationality. In this case, the defining structural condition was the high rate of infant mortality among the poor. It was caused by poor nutrition, health care and illiteracy, etc. So, it was rational for the poor to have larger number of children if only one out of eight or nine infants survived by the age of five! Mere reliance on 'motivation' for adoption of small family norm could not work under these circumstances.

Its realisation did come in the following decades when the focus in family welfare programmes began to emphasise improvement in health and nutritional standards of the child and literacy of the mother to reduce the infant mortality rate. We find in Kerala a successful example of this strategy, which is now being adopted in the rest of India.

From Democratic Revolution to Green Revolution

The democratic revolution, however, has provided an enduring structure and impetus for social change and transformation of the Indian society. The decades of 1947–1967 released social forces of change which could be defined as "a domain of potentials and high expectations". In concrete terms, economy was not yet powerful enough to support the scale of welfare and employment needs as required or as expected. The country was pathetically dependent on food imports for existential survival. The fissiparous and separatist movements were emerging in several states on the basis of linguistic, ethnic, ideological and other forms of identities. Country had to face conflicts with China and Pakistan. All in all, these were the 'dangerous decades' for India. So, the question arises: what was the nature of the forces and their source which could provide strength and resilience to the country to face up with these challenges? The answer without hesitation is: the constitutional framework of the governance of India and its democratic revolution. The measures undertaken for social, economic and political growth reinforced the social resilience. Although, still in an incipient stage, democracy released hopes and consolidated the aspirations of the Indian people to withstand these challenges. Integrative energies were released which added strength to the nation-building process. The investment in the sectors of industry, agriculture, higher education, research in advanced areas of science and technology, administration and management, etc., resulted into growth of productive energies of the people and consolidation of their national self-awareness.

The political revolution slowly began to expand its potential in the fields of economy and human resources. The decades of 1968–1988 ushered India into a new phase of economic and social transformation. It is epitomised by the green revolution of the 1970s. Apart from making India self-sufficient in food production, the green revolution had major sociological and economic consequences. It activated a modern entrepreneurial and technological ethos which blended with the tradition of joint family mode of production. Apart from production, it involved rational management of resources, credit and market. It necessitated networking with several institutions: the cooperatives, political leadership and development administration. The green revolution, therefore, had deeper economic, social and cultural consequences. It reflected a process of the modernisation which was rooted in tradition since the contribution to it was made by the traditional peasant castes. These have also been defined as the backward classes. In most regions of India, they comprise middle-sized cultivators, and following green revolution they emerged as a new middle class in the rural society. They increasingly challenged the political and cultural hegemony of the upper castes and classes. It resulted into the countrywide growth of the backward class movement.

The green revolution and the policy of positive discrimination in favour of the SCs, STs and the OBCs enlarged the scope and the momentum of social mobility and the size of the middle classes in India, which today comprises nearly one-third of the total population. The 'new agriculture' intensified the scope of the market for the consumer industries and made them increasingly dependent upon the rural market. Today, about 80 per cent of the market for such goods exists in the rural sector and an adverse agricultural productivity puts consumer industries into crisis. In some regions of India, particularly in Andhra Pradesh and Karnataka, the green revolution has not only enlarged the scale of agricultural entrepreneurship, but also led to its linkages with the mercantile and industrial entrepreneurship. Interestingly, linkage has not taken place at the same scale in the north Indian states of Punjab and Haryana, where the green revolution started much earlier. In the other north Indian states, the impact of the green revolution was uneven and localised.

The green revolution mainly benefited the middle-sized peasantry. They also took maximum advantage of the reservation policy. The marginal-sized peasantry and the lower castes or the working classes did not benefit from it in equal measure. It was soon recognised that the process of social and economic mobility that the green revolution and the reservation policies set into motion favoured the better-to-do castes and classes. The poor and the marginal farmers and working classes did not benefit as much as others. Indeed, in many parts of India, green revolution led to agrarian violence. It set into motion structural contradictions at various levels of society.

The Critical Phase of Sociology

The sociologists and social scientists in India soon realised and their studies increasingly confirmed the fact that state policies of development have so far been advantageous only to the relatively better-to-do sections of society. The overemphasis on the 'motivational approach' to development neglected the need for structural reforms which could empower the economically and socially weaker and marginalised classes in society and could render the benefits of development accessible to them. Their voices and their needs had no centrality in the state policy and strategy of development. Even in the sectors where the state was empathic to their needs, the administration and implementation of policies was flawed. This realisation contributed to a break in the consensus within social sciences in India on the approval of the state's development policies. It led to a major shift in the theoretical orientation of social sciences and the choice of methodology. Social sciences increasingly became 'critical' in their orientation. The uses of the functional theory, or the behavioural approach or the liberal uses of the motivational theory of social action based on the principle of rationality came under severe criticism. The Marxist model of historical or dialectical materialism was increasingly made use of in the studies of agrarian structure, social and political movements and the structure of the rural, urban and industrial economies. The studies now focused upon the role of conflict and alienation in the systems of family, community, industry, polity, caste and class, etc. The Dalit and subaltern paradigms for study and research in the social sciences came increasingly into vogue. The institution of state and its organs themselves became a matter of critical enquiry.

From a broader comparative perspective, the shift in the orientation of the Indian sociology from 'consensus' during the 1947–1967 periods to 'criticism' during 1968–1988 coincides with global shifts in the centre of gravity of the social sciences. It is admitted that after the Second World War, the global supremacy of the United States reached a peak not only in political and economic sectors but also in the domain of knowledge, e.g., social science theorising and methodology. Europe lost its leadership and almost receded into the background. But this enchantment with the American model of social sciences was short-lived and began to crumble with its involvement in the Vietnam war; a deeper schism in the psyche and value system of the youth in America, Latin America and Europe took place on a large scale. The youth movements of the 1968, which spread all over the world, were prompted by an ideology which rejected the profit-oriented capitalist model of economic growth and its culture of technocracy and consumerism. This movement gave added legitimacy to the critical models of social science theorising and once again, though slowly, European traditions of theorising became acceptable. These gained momentum not only in Europe but also in the United States of America. The narrow positivism was rejected and the preference for reflexive and phenomenological theoretical paradigms increased. As the legitimacy of state was questioned increasingly, the role of the non-governmental organisations (NGOs) increased not only in the activities related to development but also in social science researches.

These changes left their impact upon the Indian sociology and social sciences. During the early years of 1970s India had to get involved into a conflict with Pakistan, leading to the emergence of Bangladesh. It came as a strategic victory but the country had to pay heavy economic costs, which resulted into political protests and movements later with far-reaching consequence. A national emergency was declared, Congress lost its political supremacy, a political ideology of the coalition politics surfaced, the role of the backward classes in politics emerged powerful as never before, and the government got more and more sensitive to the needs for radical economic reforms. These social and political changes, compounded as they were with a crisis in economy, did set a process of re-thinking in the Indian social sciences, including sociology. It also oriented the social sciences towards multi-directional theoretical choices. A process of restructuration in the theory and ideology of the social sciences set into motion, but its consequences revealed their potential fully only in the third phase of the social revolution in India.

The Information Revolution and Globalisation

The third phase of the social and economic revolution was broadly set into motion with the economic reforms initiated since 1991. Its consequences and processes continue to unfold as an ongoing process.

Even though, the need for economic reforms was realised from 1978 onwards both by Indira Gandhi and Rajiv Gandhi, its more focused implementation began from the time of Narsimha Rao. Coincidently, it was the time when the USSR disintegrated and the disenchantment with the state-sponsored model of the planned economy and the import-substitution paradigm of economic growth became universal. Consequently, India began to open its economy to foreign investment, capital and market and also establish linkages with multilateral institutions such as the World Trade Organisation (WTO), and entered into a new framework of relationship with the World Bank and International Monetary Fund (IMF). It also increased its active involvement with several regional institutions which aimed at multilateral economic cooperation. These reforms have exposed India to the forces of globalisation whose consequences are not only economic but also political, social and cultural.

The initial condition for the take off of globalisation process is provided by the revolution in the technology of information and communication. The space technology, satellite communication, computerisation, telephony, internet, etc., have revolutionalised people's mode of communication, the pattern of their social and cultural interactions and the processes of economy. India has, for historical reasons, been relatively more prepared to absorb and take advantage of this information revolution than many other developing societies. Its heavy investment in higher education, particularly technological, managerial and scientific education, has not only brought into existence a substantial middle class with rich human resources to take the maximum advantage of the information revolution, but its social and cultural plurality give it unique resilience to withstand its impact. It also has had the advantage of entering early into the space research programme led by Homi Bhabha and Vikram Sarabhai who had anticipated the significance of space research in leapfrogging over many infrastructural hurdles in India's path of development. A sizeable population of the English-speaking middle classes, containing a substantial pool of the scientific and managerial manpower, estimated as the world's largest, has helped augment and absorb the positive impacts of information revolution and globalisation.

No doubt, both information revolution and globalisation have augmented employment opportunities, rendered it possible for the

Indian entrepreneurs in the information and many other sectors of economy to go global. It had made the reach of telephony available to far-flung villages, to fishermen, farmers and the trading communities, and they tend to profit from its rather effectively. It enlarges the possibilities of making best educational resources and expertise available to people living in the remotest and most backward areas. It expands the scope of health care, management of natural resources, protection of environment, rationalisation of the cropping pattern, social forestry and fishery, etc., to an optimum scale. Its benefits have revolutionary potentials for the future. It is also an irreversible process.

Nevertheless, globalisation remains a cause for universal anxiety and discontentment. There are many substantial reasons for this. First, it is driven by market mechanism and quest for optimisation of profit. Privatisation of economy draws capital into sectors which yield maximum profit. Thus, the social and welfare sectors of investment, such as education, health, nutrition, ecology and infrastructures, etc., which primarily serve the needs of the poor, marginalised and less empowered sections of society, are neglected. Secondly, the main sponsors of globalisation, such as the IMF, World Bank, WTO, etc., often put pressure on states to withdraw from the administration and investment in the sectors of social welfare. This is disruptive in societies where a large population remains below the poverty line. Thirdly, globalisation also implies massive mobility of capital from the multinational corporations, located mainly in the developed economies, to the developing economies in search of profit and cheap labour, on a global scale. This brings money and jobs to the developing economies. To a certain extent the poor and the marginalised sections may also benefit from it as it creates employment. However, it favours only those who are educated and socially empowered. But even for these, the employment that globalisation offers is perpetually subject to structural displacement due to the flight of capital as it is in perpetual search of more lucrative markets for investment. It leads to massive unemployment and recurrent retrenchment. Devoid of welfare insurance, globalisation can compound the miseries of the poor and the marginalised people, more particularly in a developing society such as India. It may also create a crisis of cultural identities and constitute a threat to the local cultures and value system of the people. The social and cultural inequalities already existent in society are compounded by a 'digital inequality' by structural regimentation of access to information technology.

Crisis in Sociology and Social Sciences

This third phase of social revolution has brought a 'crisis' in sociology and the social sciences in India. The social science ideologies of 'consensus' and 'criticism' are now faced with a deeper crisis which is structural as well as ideological. The structural threat to sociology and the social sciences arises due to the random shifting of priorities in these disciplines. These priorities are no longer governed by the long-term visions of social and economic transformation of the Indian society or the creation of values, knowledge and skills to achieve those objectives. On the contrary, it is governed by the market forces which tend to fluctuate. Education, anchored on the market, promotes profit-driven areas of teaching and research. It is devoid of the long-term vision and is partial to fundamental researches which in the social sciences are essentially ideological. From a different perspective, the same ethos in sociology and social sciences is also the guiding principle in the researches by the NGOs who now have a sizeable presence in India. Moreover, globalisation and market economy prompt the state to withdraw more and more from its commitment to the promotion of higher education, and particularly in the social sciences. The market forces and private investment in education favour applied research. The liberal, humanistic and critical aspect of education is secondary to its goals. Market-governed education is oriented to gain skill and 'information', rather than 'knowledge'. This ethos in education, which is driven by market, has arrived in college and university premises on a large scale. The short-term job-oriented courses are launched and taught which are governed by the opportunity of the moment rather than an enduring perspective and value system.

There is a cleavage at present within the worldview of the Indian sociology, social sciences and humanities. The market worldview of these disciplines does not always integrate with the 'knowledge-discovery' worldview of the social sciences. In many parts of India the enrolment in the social sciences is declining and very few students opt for research degree in social sciences. Even in the management schools and the IITs, doctoral research no longer attracts students. The crisis in the normative principle of knowledge is compounded by a crisis of values in pursuit of higher education.

In India, we are at the crossroads of a revolutionary transition. Our history, civilisation, and social and ethnic plurality have given us resilience to face up with all challenges. It is urgently required that we evolve a systematic strategy to overcome the crisis that sociology and social science teaching and research encounters today. Some pointers in this regard are obvious. The state has to continue its involvement actively not only with primary and secondary education but also with higher education. Institutionalised mechanisms should be evolved to bring about a synergy between the contending two worldviews of the social sciences that I have mentioned above. The role of the corporate sectors and private agencies in the field of social science and sociological researches is limited by the market, but it cannot be ruled out altogether. The need is to formulate an enduring perspective and vision of teaching and research in sociology and the social sciences as a part of the national agenda of social, economic and cultural ideology of development which could provide an integrative principle to determine the future planning and investment in sociology and social sciences. The Indian business houses and corporate groups should, as in the USA, come forward for investment in higher education not only in the sectors such as business management, information technology, engineering and medicine, etc., where they are drawn by market forces, but also in the field of advanced researches in the social sciences and humanities. The need today is for investment at much higher scale. This cannot be achieved without the pooling of all resources and the Indian social scientists themselves rising up to the challenge of this historical and revolutionary moment. Along with higher investment, there is also an urgent need to revive the process of professional development of the faculty involved in teaching and research in sociology and social sciences. The existing listlessness and ambiguity in the policies of the state towards promotion of sociology, social sciences and humanities would retard our competitive ability in the international realm and would render us vulnerable as members of the future 'knowledge society' for which all of us aspire. A future knowledge society cannot attain stability based merely upon material or technological gains. It has to be anchored deeply in culture and values which optimise the emotional and spiritual well-being of the members of the society. For this, and also in order to resolve a string of institutional problems that the future knowledge society in India is likely to be confronted with, major and continued investment in sociology, social sciences and humanities is indispensable.

5

Sociological Theories and Their Empirical Bases

Brij Raj Chauhan

Studies in sociology through the writings of masters of sociological thoughts are enlightening as well as problematic. Enlightening because they reflect the working of a curious mind on determining the agenda for probing into questions considered as worth attempting for their own societies as well as bringing about methodological innovations and satisfaction. Problematic because the effort leads to certain conceptual formations that have specific meanings and application and certain possible conclusions that have questionable relevance beyond the time and place of their formulation. Special different societies begin to aid to these problems. Thus, we get more careful writers talking about a phenomenon like 'class and class conflict in industrial society,' 'developing societies,' or 'agrarian societies,' or try to combining more than one aspect for delimiting their inquiries as is the case with 'industrial democracy'. Such efforts could come under the development of what Robert Merton called the 'Middle Range Theories', the obvious reference being to the macro perspectives of theories of social system or social conflict. Several specific theories within each perspective or all interplay on them begin to appear. Is there one sociology or there are two sociologies or unreality or they are both manifestations of one, one being the more general and the other a special case of it. One is easily reminded to discourses in Indian philosophy on the relationship between the *'Jiv'* and the *'Atma'*, the *Sagun* and *Nigun* forms of the Almighty and the smart ones developing *advaita* or *vishishtadvaita*. Other parallel examples can be drawn, but such a treatment of ideology and sociology would require separate treatment. For the moment we might return to the present era in which the claim of sociology as a discipline involving cumulative growth is seriously advanced.

When one writer is associated with one perspective or a set of theories flowing there from the task is well set and further progress takes the form of commentaries or innovative refinements. That defines the nature of commutative efforts. What then happens to the contributions of the original masters? The originality may lie at one point or it may get diffused to several points of inquiry. Some of them could be woven in one perspective and some may cross those limits. The argument of the paper is that masters of the sociological thought combined more than one perspective, operated in multipolar situation and their classification into one extreme of thought would do injustice to the wide range of their thinking and writing. Such a situation has been tried to be overcome by commentators using phrases like "The young Marx" and "The old Marx" or the "Mature Marx". Likewise, one can think of Talcott Parsons beginning with a General Theory of Action. Then to social action to social system and parts of society like economy and polity. Examples can be multiplied, when a writer is classified as belonging to one school. It reduces the plurality of a writer to a singularity. When other writers are also listed under that approach it is quite easy to say that there are differences among the writers as is evident from the treatment of writers classified under different schools by Sorokin in his classic work *Contemporary Sociological Theories*. 'Contemporary' here means 1927 when the book was published. Later commentators have brought out specialised books on different approaches. Where does a beginner in sociology stand at the beginning of 21st century? What is the relevance of masters of the sociological thought for him. Merton tried to give answer quoting with approval philosopher A.N. Whitehead: "A science which refuses to forget it founders is dead". Merton agreed with the high status of the founders calling them Giants, but visualised his own role as that of riding, "On the Shoulders of the Giants". Merton's students in a similar vein responded with the work *On the Shoulders of the Merton*. Likewise, we have works of the work like *Marxism since Marx*. The dilemma of the students of sociology has been partly tried to solve through framing the model syllabus drawn by experts assigned for the purpose by the University Grants Commission of India. They have selected certain perspectives and mentioned under them a few selected authors by way of illustration. The purpose of getting the illustrations from the respective authors may be solved in the process, but it comes though a partial exposure to the author whose totality gets disjuncted, and whose creative encounters with varied situation get push to the back burner. The next section of the paper undertakes a critical examination of the way the scientific nature of the sociology has been advanced and questioned, and what has happened to Max Weber.

II

Scientific nature of sociology has been propounded by Auguste Comte and 'demonstrated' by Durkheim with Radcliffe-Brown going to the extent of asserting it as a natural science of society. The field work tradition replaced 'conjectural history' and comparative method strengthened the significance of such studies beyond the designated area of study. History, however, remained in constant dialogue with the nature of social science. Dilthey considered the human aspect of feelings and emotions central to the study of man and society which could not be subjected to objective enquiries. Two propositions were advanced: firstly, subjectivity was central to human concerns not objectivity; and secondly, uniqueness and search for specificity provided the core methodology, not generality. Max Weber tried to combine history and sociology for the study of significant trends using the construction of ideal type and comparative method. One of the key points was concerned with social action involving the role of subjectivity of the actor as distinguished from social fact which Durkheim had located outside the individual. Weber's combination of theory and method attracted universal attention both for the initiating a new approach and for raising controversies. The point under examination is not so much the internal structure of Weber's formulation as to what the proponents of different perspectives later did to Weber.

Writers developing the phenomenological approach anchored their efforts on the subjective nature of social action. The argument revolved around the meaning of action for the actors thereby seeking a departure from rationality. Thus, one part of Weber was accepted and the other given a goodbye that ideal types were mental constructs seemed also to encourage discussion on those constructs rather than on their derivation and relevance for the understanding of social situations. Empirical referents could also be there and had best a second class status. The nature of discussions centred on the concept per se. It is argued here that such a disjunction between perceived facts and conceptualisation is not found in Weber himself. His earliest work was on the economic history of the Europe at a very young age. He was sent on a holiday to Rome. Relaxing himself in surrounding of world class paintings and architecture, he also looked at the original sources for study the agrarian systems of Rome and Spain, enabling him to bring out his thesis. Thus, he widened his interest in economic history over time and space, analysing original sources.

Saying that the real meaning should have been authority implying the legitimacy was built into it. As one looks at Weber's discussion on three types of legitimacy of power, he/she can understand the academic and experiential inputs gene into it. Weber's visit to the USA enabled him to see first hand the working of the political machine' which controlled the affairs of the two major political parties and made him to conclude that bureaucratic control was an essential part of a large-scale organisation. Weber had also added to his live experiences the working of the protestant ethic in a capitalistic society. Back home in the early years of the 20th century, Weber got interested in what was happening on the eastern frontier—the unsuccessful Russian revolution. Here again, his information was based on the Russian newspapers as he acquired competence in that language. Cutting across political systems Weber realised the inevitability of bureaucracy as an essential feature in large-scale organisations and its dehumanising effects. Finally, one may locate the source of interest of religion in the study, particularly the Indo-Christian tendency. His grandfather was a Jew but had embraced Christianity or Protestantism to be able to continue living in Germany as a citizen on the practical side of the politics, be it recalled that Weber was present at the signing ceremony of the treaty of Versailles marking the end of the First World War as part of German delegation a defeated monarchy which later laid to the enactment of the theoretically best drafted constitution of a democratic order, the Wiener Republic, which only collapsed with Hitler. It would be now clear that the existential experiences of author have some relevance for his academic concerns and the themes on which he concentrated his attention. Such empirical inputs and their review would make it possible to situate Weber's formulations in their historical setting. Weber, as a social scientist and teacher of sociology, distinguishing between the two roles of political actor and a teacher, observed the distinction in what to lecture in the classroom and what to talk in public platform. Thus, Weber's choice of concepts and their treatment are not so abstract as to be devoid of empirical or existential base; hence, confining the discussion to abstract categories as treating the author in isolation of the existing realities could give to code Weber a picture that might come to what he used in a different context "one-sided accentuation of reality".

The empirical base door propounding the significance of the protestant ethic for capitalistic development is supplied by Weber through the relative distribution of students in the streams of sciences and humanities, where the protestant showing greater percentage for sciences. The position of Jews is also recorded. Of course, the derivation of the ethic is based on a textual exercise in which Weber's own thinking process in the development of ideal type finds full expression from the methodological point of view. It is whoever significant that Weber used comparative method for locating the emergence of capitalism or its absence or perhaps late development under different religious dispensations. This theoretical exercise led to the possibilities of generalising in sociology. It is here that chances for growth of sociology as a science of society get strengthened. This aspect of Weber's efforts gets underrepresented in phenomenological discourses. Thus phenomenology traces its rise in one part of Weber's writing, namely, the subjective aspect of action, keeping his other contribution on comparative methodology and generalisation on the back-burner. It has been also maintained in this presentation that Weber's peep into the existential base in the formation of some of the leading concepts propounded by him could be enlightening. The family background was characterised by the presence of political and legal experts. The drawing room was the meeting place for the galaxy of persons connected with public affairs. The political set-up was monarchy maintained by a disciplined military in Prussia. Military training for two years was compulsory for graduates and Weber had undergone the training in gymnasium quite efficiently. The first hand experience of such a training in the particular political set-up of Germany made Weber understood the strength of the concept of the bureaucracy. Secondly, his own uncle ran a factory which provided a model of a capitalistic spirit in action. This could explain Weber's intimate interest in capitalism. It further appears that concerns with the nature of power had got expressed actively as said earlier in the drawing room of the family. To this when we add the professional training in law, we realise the basis for his interest in discussion on legitimacy of power, that is, authority. At times the translation of German words into English created some problems. When Talcott Parsons used the word 'domination' to describe the phenomenon to which Ralph Bendix vigorously objected own concerns and orientations had empirical base and experiential ingredients generally overlooked. While discussing his conceptual categories. As Weber's writings became more widely available through translation in English and a few scholars conversant with German, efforts began to be made for reviewing specialised ethics of groups traditionally involved in trade and questioning the general attitudes of people towards religious factor with a new formulation appearing that the Indian case could be one where the religious ethics did not play a limiting role in economic development. Towards the beginning of the 21st century, it is being increasingly demonstrated that managerial skills of the modern era have brought forth even a competitive edge in the growth of information and space technology, heavy industry, listing on New York Stock Exchange and managing the richest cricket board in the world.

6

Socio-Cultural Dimensions of Development

Yogesh Atal

The end of the Second World War ushered in an era of reconstruction and development – reconstruction of Europe that was devastated by war, and development of the countries of the Third World getting freed from the yoke of European colonialism. In one word, it was a process of decolonisation affecting both the colonialists and the colonies. This was the period when the colonialists had to withdraw from their erstwhile colonies and develop new equations with the emerging new nations. The new nations had to rapidly respond to the rising revolution of expectations from the people by initiating a process of planned development to bring about changes in the economy, polity and society.

Having severely suffered from the devastating war, the countries of Europe took immediate measures to bring in normalcy in their social and cultural life. They also realise that it was no longer possible for them to contain the rising tide of nationalism in the colonies governed by them. That is why, they took steps to reconstruct their infrastructures and rejuvenate their cultures on the one hand, and decolonise the non-western world, on the other. Decolonisation

Presented at Indo-Russian Symposium held at G.B. Pant Social Science Institute, Allahabad, 5–6 November, 1998.

entailed not only a process of transfer of power to the natives, but also a process of building new nations. While the West had to reconstruct their cultural ruins, the non-West had to initiate a process of constructing a new the infrastructure that was needed to run a modern society.

The concept of *reconstruction,* which emerged in the aftermath of the Second World War, related more to the western world where the devastating war led to the destruction of cultural property and ruined a number of cultural institutions including educational institutions. Against this, the countries coming out of the colonial yoke had to engage in the project to come out of continuing underdevelopment. The other concept, namely, *development,* became a synonym for nation-building. While in the West, reconstruction exercise focused on the culture, the non-West embarked upon a programme of economic development. Reconstruction meant cultural reconstitution, and development came to signify nation-building that involved social and political development and economic growth. It is this twin concern that was reflected in the fuller name of the World Bank, that is, International Bank of Reconstruction and Development or IBRD.

After half a century's effort of the world community to attain the twin goals of reconstruction and development, several efforts are now being made to assess the gains and failures so that future strategies can be chalked out to make up for the deficits.

II

It is common knowledge that during the colonial period, the colonisers focused more on the *cultures* of their colonies, rather than on their economic development. This was guided by two considerations: theoretical and practical-administrative. The prevailing social theory of the times was evolutionary – drawing inspirations from the Darwinian contributions to biology. Scholars found in the primitive, non-western societies evidence of the earlier stages of evolution of societies and cultures. They tried to put them on the evolutionary ladder at a lower step than their own to justify their own superiority. Borrowing from Darwin the concepts of *struggle for existence* and *survival of the fittest* they advanced the view that the non-West has lagged behind in its struggle for existence and has surrendered itself to the 'fittest'. The colonialists regarded themselves as a 'superior' race and took upon themselves the task of helping the primitives to climb the evolutionary ladder treating the West as the 'positive reference group'. Cultural development, in the conception of the colonialists, was a process through which natives gave up, at the instance of the West, their own practices and customs and adopted elements of western civilisation. Of course, there were some scholars and administrators who wanted the native cultures to be 'preserved', that is, to be left untouched by the winds of change coming from the West. These people were criticised for having the ill-intention of treating the tribal cultures as 'anthropological zoos' – as exemplars of the queer and the exotic – so that curious tourists can come and visit them. More articulate amongst the protagonists for the preservation of tribal cultures put different and more convincing arguments to support their stand.

The practical-administrative interest in the native cultures was guided by the consideration of governance; to govern the colonies better, they needed to know their cultures – their language, behaviour, habits, traditions, and even the customary law – all in the domain of anthropology. To be sure, they were not so much concerned about changing the primitive cultures as about the understanding of them. The changes that they introduced were those that were regarded as instrumental in keeping a stronghold on the natives. To prove their superiority, they highlighted those aspects of the native culture, which they regarded as primitive and undesirable. There existed certain ambivalence towards native cultures – criticism of undesirable practices, and maintenance of the exotic forms of behaviour. All this was, now said with the wisdom of the hindsight, 'false philanthropy'.

This period witnessed a number of changes in the non-western world. And, they were described by the umbrella concept of 'westernisation' or 'modernisation'. Rising rates of literacy, urbanisation, industrialisation, and conversion to Christianity were regarded as useful indicators of the twin processes of westernisation and modernisation.

III

The attainment of independence led to the change of orientation towards social and cultural change. The focus of the new administration by the nationals moved from maintaining law and order and "keeping the natives subservient" to accelerating the process of economic and social development. Of course, this orientation gave further support to the processes of westernisation and modernisation, but created multiplicity of positive reference groups located abroad. It is striking that those very cultural changes that the colonial masters initiated to strengthen their foothold in the colonies helped the natives in developing a front against the colonialists. They not only used the exposure to the West to stage a revolt against the alien rule, but also took steps both to decry some of their own traditions that were retrogressive, and to revive many of the traditions that they regarded useful in fostering solidarity.

The national leadership adopted an economic agenda for development. To hasten the process so as to "keep up with the Jones" – that is, to follow the path of western development – they had to depend on external support. With the arrival of IBRD to provide financial support, and the setting up of agencies under the umbrella of the United Nations, such support was available from a variety of sources, and not only from the colonial masters. This support came in the form of men (as experts), machines (modern technology), money and modern system of management – both of business and of the government. Externally induced but nationally approved programme of change began to characterise what came to be known as the 'western paradigm of development'.

In this paradigm, there was marginal place for culture. At best, culture was regarded only as an instrumentality, not an aim of development that was defined in economistic terms. Foreign experts (all invariably western) enthusiastically tried to transplant their institutions, and their machinery in strange settings with a view to increasing productivity. Many of these narrow specialists were unfamiliar with local cultures, or with anthropological approaches that were developed during the colonial rule and focused on the holistic character of culture and hinted at the integrative nature of cultural traits and complexes. Social scientists entered the arena at a later date only to study the impact of change or to explain the failures of an innovation. All analyses of change thus attempted used culture as a variable to explain the failure of a project, or non-acceptance of an innovation. Culture was regarded either as an *obstacle* to development, or as a *victim* of development.

A good deal of claim was made by the social scientists for the inclusion of culture in the planning process. But nobody offered just how this can be done. What was available was not the methodology of how to do it, but post-mortem of failed events – all invariably indicating that it was the neglect of the cultural factor that was responsible for the costly failure of a good intentioned change brought from without. Social sciences began clamouring for the inclusion of the socio-cultural factors in planning, but they were not ready with the recipe. Even today, the situation remains more or less the same.

IV

The decade of seventies ushered in an era of disenchantment resulting in the shift in emphases in the development paradigm. First came the need for the reintroduction of the concept of *endogenous development,* then the emphasis shifted to *sustainable development;* later, the international community introduced the concept of *human resource development.* In all of these proposals the importance of the human factor was emphasised. Understood broadly, the human factor is a part of the concept of culture – after all, it is culture that transforms the biological brute of *Homo sapiens* into a social animal.

The stocktaking exercises initiated under the aegis of the United Nations in the present decade have highlighted the concerns related to population growth, environmental crises, gender issues and default on the social development front. More important is the point that for the first time a consensus emerged that piecemeal and sectoral approach to development is hazardous, and that there is a need for a *united thrust.* As a result, all agencies of the United Nations system joined hands to commonly evolve a programme of action to implement the various commitments made at the recently held world conferences on different aspects of development. It is for the first time that the world community recognised that there cannot be a single cure for a social ailment that may be commonly shared by many societies. Common problems need not necessarily have common solutions. While we have to think globally, we must act locally, we are told. There is a clear recognition of the cultural specificities and a recommendation that solutions to problems of social development should be sought in the light of those specificities. What may work in a given situation, may not work in another.

Towards the end of this century, we have learnt one great lesson: neither the western capitalism nor the eastern communism holds the key to success. While people in the non-communist world rejoiced the collapse of the Soviet Union, and thus almost a demise of communism, they did not fail to notice that even the non-communist world did not succeed on the social development front. It is important that the World Summit for Social Development, held in Copenhagen in March 1995, identified three main issues for discussion, namely, *poverty, unemployment* and *growing tendencies towards social disintegration of societies*. The main reason behind the selection of these three issues for discussion in the Summit was the point that these problems confronted all societies – be they of North or South, rich or poor, capitalist or communist. Since economic development could not arrest these tendencies – in fact, it even gave rise to them – it could not be considered as the cure for these ailments. In this regard, one is reminded of the views of Professor Amartya Sen, Nobel laureate. His study of the famines clearly indicated that they were caused not by the paucity of economic resources, but by other, and more potent non-economic factors. While all for globalisation – a trend that is now almost irreversible – Sen has been advocating the need to focus on education, health, and other social sectors.

Chilean Ambassador Somavia – the pioneering force behind the holding of the World Summit for Social Development – acknowledged the fact that such a Summit was unthinkable during the period of Cold War. Neither party to that war accepted any deficits on the social front. But, the end of the Cold War, with the disintegration of the Soviet Union, changed the scenario. The West felt the need to review its welfarist approach, and the former communist countries also began cutting public expenditure on the social sector. It now appears that the welfarist approach of the West was an answer to the socialistic stance of the communist states. That is why, they now feel that the state is unable to bear the rising cost on welfare and will like the market forces to operate. The decline in the social sector expenditure in the former communist states, likewise, has caused unprecedented unemployment, and increased the ranks of the poor, not sparing even the intelligentsia. The former communist states that denied the existence of poverty now openly acknowledge the growing phenomenon of poverty. The poverty phenomenon in these countries cannot be understood in the prevailing paradigms emanating from the West. The cultural context and the historical experience of these economies in transition are very different from those of India, or other countries of the Third World. In these cultures, ethnicity-based identification is resurfacing to cut across class-based identities that were forged during the communist era. Clearly, these communities feel that the communist ideology had eroded their cultural identities and superimposed the economic calculus of development. Strangely enough, even the capitalist mode of development also gave primacy to the economic factor and regarded traditions as functionless vestiges. Both these strategies contributed to the museumisation of culture. Neglect of the cultural factor led not only to the failure of these strategies but also politicised culture in the process. It will indeed be instructive to explore this phenomenon in a cross-cultural framework (see Atal, 1999).

This emerging context gives a special meaning to the phrase 'socio-cultural dimensions of development'. The World Commission on Culture and Development set up by UNESCO and the United Nations under the chairmanship of Javier Perez de Cuellar focused on this aspect and, as the title of the report of the Commission suggests, it underlines *Our Creative Diversity*. The report argues that culture is to be seen not only "as a servant of ends, but as the social basis for the ends themselves. We cannot begin to understand the so-called 'cultural dimension of development' without taking note of each of these two roles of culture" (p. 24).

The key question is: how do we bring culture in the development process? There are three different views on the issue of culture-development interface:

1. Use of native ideologies/religious faiths in promoting development. This approach suggests that a justification for change may be sought in the native categories of thought. The analysis of the indigenous ideologies may indicate that native cultures are not opposed to change, but that they are not prepared for all kinds of change. That change, which is in tune with the native ideology, is always acceptable.
2. Developed societies are using this paradigm of culture-development interface in the context of newly emerging issues of national integration caused by massive international migration. The colonial phase created many pluricultural societies by amalgamating different regional regimes, and also introducing populations from other cultures, e.g., through indentured labour. Now, the West is experiencing a form of 'reverse colonisation'. The homogeneity of the European states is giving way to heterogeneity caused by a plurality of cultures arriving through migration. In these contexts, the new phenomenon of what I have christened *sandwich cultures* (Atal, 1989) has become significant. In these societies, the word 'culture' is used almost as a synonym of 'ethnic groups' and

efforts are being made to ensure that the dominant culture of the host society maintains its position.

3. Another perspective is to examine the relationship between exogenous development and indigenous culture. Such an approach hints at the discrepancy between traditional norms and values and the values of industrial life, and it highlights the adverse impact of new technologies in accentuating inequalities.

While there is so much talk of the role of culture, there are several methodological questions that need to be properly addressed. Let these be briefly discussed:

- How to construct culture? And how to deduce it?
  While culture has been the subject matter of anthropology, there is still considerable grey area relative to its definition. Describing culture as a way of life of the people makes it very difficult for an analyst to draw the contours of culture, particularly of plural societies. The various claimants to the core of a given culture require careful scrutiny, and acceptance by the members of the society. The insider-outsider perspectives on culture do not always tally; each of these carries its own biases. Moreover, it is not only the outsiders who may have differing views and perspectives – as the outsiders have different origins – differences abound even among the insiders. In the context of India, Srinivas referred to the 'book view' and the 'upper caste view' which are again related only to the Hindu segment of Indian society when he underlined the need for field work at the grass roots to get the empirical view of the existing reality. Present criticism of the Hindu view of society as being 'Manuvadi' by the Dalit leadership is an instance of the disagreement that prevails. Also, there are the problems of distinguishing between the prescribed and the prevailing, and the prevailing and the desirable. Who defines the desirable? What are the good values to be imparted and what values to be rejected? Dube's criticism of characterisation of Indian traditions is pertinent in this regard: "In describing the Hindu ethos there has been an unjustifiable emphasis on religion, ritual and spiritualism. After all, Hinduism did not produce only *Dharmasastras;* it also produced *Arthasastras* (works dealing with the science of economics and statecraft), and *Kamasastras* (works dealing with the science of love and bodily pleasures). Similarly,

Buddhism did regard *nirvana* as the ultimate objective but without neglecting intermediate concerns governing the everyday life of the people The egalitarian emphasis in Islam constitutes one of its significant characteristics. It encouraged economic pursuits, with one important provision that a part of the earnings were to be earmarked in the forms of *zakat* and sadaqa for collective good" (Dube, 1990: 10–11).

- How to separate culture from ideology?
  While there is an agreement that ideology and culture are two separate entities, they are also so much intertwined that it poses problems for the analyst to extricate them from each other. People of the same culture may subscribe to different ideologies – homegrown or imported from abroad. Their followers may establish cultural parallels to justify their attachment to them and to attract new followers. In yet another sense, the totality of ideologies in vogue in a given society may be considered as components of a heterogeneous culture. Can culture be regarded as an ideology of conservatism, and ideology as a culture of forward-looking? A good deal of conceptual analysis and methodological sophistication is needed to clarify this relationship and to see their respective roles in the process of development.
- Whose culture is being referred to, particularly in a multicultural context?
  This point has been clarified in the previous queries. Suffice it to say that modern societies are facing the crises of managing the multiplicity. The conflicts between various sub-cultural identities are becoming more prominent, and the whole paradigm of core and periphery is under severe scrutiny. When talking about the cultural factor, this question assumes special significance.
- Who wants to save culture, and what culture?
  This question is related about the desirability of change. There are situations where the people themselves wish to bring about change but outside agencies intervene to save the cultures. Environmentalists speaking on behalf of the poor have led several movements to halt the process of modernisation – be it promotion of tourism, building of dams, construction of hydroelectricity projects, or introduction of alternatives to swidden cultivation.

- Is culture an alternative to exogenous development?
  It will be wrong to assume that those who plead for the place of culture are opposed to any change inspired from the outside. What is implied is the point that no culture accepts any change without its proper screening and its acceptance depends upon its compatibility with the prevailing infrastructure. A culture is an organic unity and it responds to changes brought from the outside as a functioning whole. A careful preparation is needed to receive foreign elements so that the host culture does not lose its identity and assigns a proper place to the immigrant cultural trait to ensure its integration in the new milieu.

How, then, to view culture in the context of development? Generally, scholars have tried to analyse the influence of development on culture and the role of culture in influencing development. But treating culture as a living entity, developmental process is to be viewed as part of the cultural process. Viewed thus, it is not a question of either/or. The old approach to preserve/save culture also needs to be reviewed. One needs to ask the question: does disappearance of certain cultural traits amounts to the erosion of culture, or its total destruction? The phenomenon of cultural growth will be inexplicable if this process did not involve both attrition and accretion processes. Changes occurring in the ambit of culture do not erase its identity. Fifty years of development experience has clearly indicated that cultures possess different degrees of resilience – like a bamboo they might bend when hit by a gush of wind, but are able to rise again – bending is not equivalent of breaking.

Cultures around the world have experienced significant changes, mostly caused by the so-called development exercises, carefully planned and meticulously implemented. But, despite these changes, cultures have not lost their individual identities; in fact, what has occurred in the past decades is a rising revolution of identities. Cultures have remained distinctly identifiable, even though their demographic composition and ethnic constitution have significantly altered, and their material cultural profiles are drastically different from what they have been a few decades ago. All this goes to suggest that westernisation, modernisation, and now globalisation, do not ensure homogenisation of cultures. What happens is a growth of complexity of individual cultures with multiple layers consisting of elements of international culture, emergent national culture – deriving from its civilisational base and giving the country its cultural identity, and regional-parochial cultures. A quote from Claude Levi-Strauss is very apt for what I am trying to say:

> "The notion of world civilization can only be accepted ... as a sort of limiting concept or as an epitome of a highly complex process. There is not, and can never be, a world civilization in the absolute sense in which the term is often used, since civilization implies, and indeed consists in, the co-existence of cultures exhibiting the maximum possible diversities. A world civilization could, in fact, represent no more than a world-wide coalition of cultures, each of which would preserve its own originality" (quoted from the report of the World Commission on Culture and Development, p. 29).

It is wrong to assume that traditions are static and unchanging. The vast reservoir of tradition possessed by ancient cultures provides support not only for the maintenance of status quo, but also for radical reconstruction and imaginative innovation. The false dichotomy of tradition and modernity posited by the western scholarship has to be discarded in favour of treating cultures as dynamic entities acting to preserve the good in human heritage and constantly innovating to enrich human life.

References

Atal, Yogesh (ed.), 1991, *Culture Development Interface*, New Delhi: Vikas Publishing House.

——, 1999, *Poverty in Transition and Transition in Poverty: Recent Developments in Hungary, Bulgaria, Romania, Georgia, Russia, and Mongolia*, New York and London: Berghahn Books.

Atal, Yogesh, 1989, "Outsiders as Insiders: The Phenomenon of Sandwich Cultures: Prefatorial to a Possible Theory", *Sociological Bulletin*, Vol. 38, No. 1, pp. 23–41.

Dube, S.C., 1990, *Tradition and Development*, New Delhi: Vikas Publishing House.

Masini, Eleonora Barbieri and Yogesh Atal (eds.), 1993, *The Future of Asian Cultures*, Bangkok: UNESCO, RUSHSAP Series #38.

UNESCO, 1995, *Our Creative Diversity and Development*, Report of the World Commission on Culture and Development.

7

Indian Diaspora

Some Reflections

C. Lakshmanna

> "These Indian hands – whether in British Guiana or Trinidad – have fed all of us. They are, perhaps, one and only jewels of a true native thrift and industry. They have taught us by example the value of money, for they respect money as only people with a high sense of communal responsibility can."[1]

Indian diaspora, as a concept, is of recent origin but as a phenomenon, it is very old indeed. The concept of diaspora itself gained recognition with Scottish and Israeli diasporas. It is generally believed that more number of Scottish people live beyond the frontiers than within. Israelis, likewise, were spread throughout the world and looked forward to uniting in the "promised land" which, in actual fact, came into existence as Israel in post-Second World War period. Obsession with "promised land" prevented the Jews from integrating into the lands of their settlement and migration. Integration, however, has to be differentiated from assimilation. Integration stands for the harmonious co-existence of different identities present in the society. Dreams of "chosen land" acted, however, as mental blocks for the Jews and they showed reservations in identifying with the country where they were living. It resulted in

This paper is a revised version of my inaugural address at a Conference on Indian Diaspora, organised by the Indian Diaspora Centre of the University of Hyderabad, Gachibowli, Hyderabad.

serious problems for them in many a country. Indian diaspora, today, is second only to China, in members and spread across the world.

Migration and Diaspora

It is evident that diaspora is the manifestation of people's aspirations and attitudes and of the forced or voluntary migration. People in groups or as individuals get scattered in a different place from the home country and society. It is amazing that distances and hardships did not deter them from undertaking these long, adrous and hazardful journeys. Here, we do not intend to enter into discussion concerning migration. Suffice to say that migration takes place due to aspirations for social climbing, employment and educational opportunities, or due to natural calamities, and even marriages. Migration always paved way for mobility of people – spatial, social and economic. Motivation for socio-economic mobility spurred people to move from one place to another. Migration has been both temporary and permanent. Both stable and unstable societies provided opportunities for migration and mobility. Diaspora illustrates these processes. Diaspora refers to the dispersed people or communities living outside their mother or home countries, having direct or vague connections with the lands of their origin.

Classical Migration

Indian diaspora, as is being researched and studied, reflects modern-day migration, mostly of the colonial and postcolonial periods. But Indian society had experienced migration of the people, even much earlier, to different parts of the world, in particular to South and South East Asia. These migration patterns occurred in ancient and medieval periods. The ancient and medieval migrations are characterised by the absorption of Indian communities in the countries where they had migrated, not without leaving deep impact on those societies. Distinct Indian cultural traces are evident in Tibet, Thailand, Indonesia, Vietnam, Cambodia, Korea, Philippines and even China. Malaysia, Singapore and Hong Kong stand distinguished in their own way. These three last named countries received migrant Indian population both in ancient and medieval and modern periods. Cultural evidences, if not historical data, indicate Indians' contacts with outside world before the origin and development of Buddhism, During the period of growth of Buddhism, instances are abound when

Buddhist monks and emissaries visited several countries and settled down to preach and propagate their religion. Buddhism spread Indian culture to all these countries. Buddhist and post-Buddhist "classical age" influences on different parts of Asia are historical facts. Caves, temples, pagodas and monasteries, existing in these countries, are standing testimony to the cultural interaction between India and these far off societies, and the indelible imprint the Indian society and culture have made on them. The enactment of the marriage ceremony of Arjun and Subhadra and other Hindu mythological episodes are part of the Indonesian heritage. Angkora and Boribudoor temples are shining examples of this fascinating phenomenon. Bali, of Indonesia, is abound with evidences of living Hindu (Indian) traditions and the practice of Hindu religion. The prevalence of the Indian alphabet even in distant Korean language illustrates the cultural contacts with them. The Thai kings, even today, are Hindu in their religious and cultural bearings. Many more Illustrations can be brought forth in evidence. Due to various reasons, these cultural relations were snapped over a period of time, but their impact and influence did not diminish in passing it can be mentioned that the cases of Srilanka, Nepal, Afghanistan and Myanmar are unique and their history is more intimately interlinked with India.

Modern Migration

The Indian society was at crossroads at the beginning of the 19th century. The Moghul dynasty's influence had waned. Several local and regional kingdoms had surfaced all over the country. The Indian caste society was decadent with pernicious hold of superstitions and Brahmanic hegemony. European trading companies, specially the East India Company, were making inroads into the Indian economy. The industrial revolution in Europe was helping with mass production of consumer goods. They were in search of durable markets. From the time of Spanish and Portugese expansions, they had an eye on Bijantan India. These traders faced stiff competition from the indigenous cottage and traditional industries. They further realised that they would not have strong foothold unless they destroyed these competing skills and production process. The feudal order had ugly implications for the people. Many middle order and lower groups were reduced to the position of serfs. Constant famines, pestilence and contagious diseases were ravaging the social fabric.

These were the ominous 'push' for out-migration in the country. What they needed was the emergence of 'pull' factors. The British, the French, the Dutch and other Westerners had colonised several parts of the globe, particularly Caribbean, Oceana and Indian Ocean areas. Sugarcane cultivation and sugar industry was thriving in those colonies. The colonial masters had largely depended for sugarcane cultivation on African slaves who were imported from different parts of Africa. The uprooting of African population and their import into colonies was followed by the complete destruction of African culture. The African slaves were forced to lose their religion, language, lifestyles, family system and, in essence, their culture. Slavery denied all rights to the salves. They became the property of colonial masters just as the land and moveable property. Masters became the mentors and the role models for the salves. Human misery was heaped on them. Sixty years of slavery in the Caribbean robbed the African slave population of their very human existence. The result was the rebellion. Briton by then had acquired colonial power in most of the islands from Jamaica to Trinidad. A few islands were under the French and Dutch colonial powers. Similar drama was enacted with some variation in Oceana and Indian Ocean areas. The African slaves, however, yearned for freedom and struggled for their emancipation. Haiti was the first to succeed in forcing the abolition of slavery. There was a bloody revolt which left a death blow to the savage institution of slavery. The British Parliament had to follow suit with the abolition of slavery in 1830. The former African slaves, who were in sugarcane cultivation in British Caribbean islands, gave up cane cultivation in the wake of the abolition of slavery. Attending to work on land in general, and cane cultivation in particular, became symbolic of slavery for them. They moved away from rural areas and concentrated in urban pockets. They gave up cultivation and took to other occupations such as defence and police services, bureaucracy and administration. They opened a new chapter in their own lives and in the history of British Caribbean, nay, in the entire West Indies. Consequent to these developments, the British colonial masters experimented with indenture system, recruiting people for specified periods to work on the cane plantations. In this direction, they, in the first instance, brought indentured labour from China. The Chinese did not stick to the islands. Among them many moved on to US, mainly to the Western Coast. They were later on replaced by the Lebanese and the Syrians. The Middle East workers were not familiar with cane cultivation. The experiment thus ended in a failure. At this stage, the attention of British masters turned to India. They lured the cane farmers and others by design, deceit, bait, temptation, motivation and force. The prevailing political, economic and social conditions also facilitated their task. Most of the indentured Indians were recruited from western Bihar and eastern Uttar Pradesh (which is known as Bhojpuri area), Bengal with indentured labour, Orissa and other North Indian states. Eighty-five per cent of the ships sailed from Calcutta port between 1838 and 1917. The rest of the ships sailed from Madras Andhra Pradesh, Kerala and other southern states. Similarly ships travelled to Mauritius, South Africa, Malaysia and several other islands in Indian Ocean and Oceana. These indentured labourers were contracted to stay in service for five years on a fixed sum of money as wage. Indenture was thus a contract service. The work was, however, as hard, harsh and demanding as was experienced by the slaves. Colonial masters, and their henchmen, extracted work from the indentured labour by heaping filthy abuses and physical torture The indentured tolerated the hardships, perhaps, for two reasons:

(i) They were looking forward for the end of indenture period with some savings which could be helpful to them on their repatriation to the homeland.

(ii) Working on the sugarcane plantations satisfied their underlying urge to cling to land, a characteristic feature of rural people in India, and if possible gain ownerships of the land with the savings on the termination of the indenture. A large number of people, however, returned to India on the completion of the period of contract and an equally large number of them retracted due to unwelcome and hostile home conditions. Yet, they were in two minds. On one hand, they realised that their lot had been cast with the lands of migration and that they had to make their way up the ladder in those countries. On the other hand, they nourished a belief at the back of their mind that they would be in a position to return to the motherland later after India gains freedom with better economic position and social status. These attitudes and aspirations sowed the seeds of achievement orientation among them.

Migration of Business and Professional Indians

Decades after the termination of indentureship, there were fresh waves of migration. In the beginning, it was the business people and tradesmen, who migrated to both the colonies and the developed countries to seek their livelihood and fortune with their efforts and skills. Hindu ethic of thrift and tradition of family helped them greatly in establishing themselves in the sphere of business, trade and small-scale industries. After India's independence, with the expansion of educational and technical opportunities, a new wave of migration started. It is distinct with earlier phases in the sense that these professionals, when migrated, landed in the middle and high levels of the societies in countries of migration. Hard work and basic intelligence were there assets and thus they made a mark in the competitive and complex situations. Basically, there had been two essential differences between colonial indenture migration and postcolonial professional migration. First, the contact between the indentured immigrants and the mother country was minimal. This was so because of the distance between them and also because of the lower level of status – economic and social – of the immigrants when they left India, compared to the section which they had left behind. In addition, communication networking was selective and prohibitive. Second, the religion and culture played a significant part in the relations between the indentured and the social forces operating in the societies into which they had migrated. Distances and lack of communication, thus, allowed minimal contacts for the indentured populations with the homeland. The position was different with the professional migrants. In addition to religion and culture, language and the region of their origin in India also played an important role in the networks. The rapid development of communication networks and the better economic and social positions which professional and technical migrants enjoyed in their new settings further augmented the new trends. During this period, there was also 'second step migration'. The second half of the 20th century witnessed emancipation of several African nations from colonial imperialist rule. This new development had resulted in unanticipated, and perhaps unintended, victimisation of the Indian settlers in these countries, specially in Uganda and a few other African states. These Indian settlers in the wake of atrocities and attacks immigrated to UK, US, Canada and some of the island countries with their enormous skills, capacities and business acumen and settled down in the fiercely competitive market conditions in these western countries. The migration of professionals and those of the second step migration changed the entire complexion of the diaspora.

Indian Diaspora, People of Indian Origin and NRIs

Indian diaspora has gained currency in the recent decades. During the last few decades, the migrant Indian population in several parts of the globe came to be known as 'People of Indian Origin' or PIO. Conceptually, they connote a different term though all of them embody the same phenomenon. In connotation and context, suitable differences exist between them. While Indian diaspora emphasises the inter-connection and interface between the migrants and the homeland from where they had emigrated. PIO looks at the structure and functions of Indians in the lands of their settlement. It does not, completely, rule out the underlying ties between the two peoples. A third concept, which has gained currency in recent years, more particularly in India, is NRI (Non-Resident Indian). NRI as a phenomenon refers to the process of migration of Indians, skilled and unskilled. in pursuit of better or even simple and ordinary employment opportunities either with a temporary but prolonged stay abroad with no intention of settling down or even if they intend to naturalise as citizens where there are no such legal provisions and possibilities. Strictly speaking, NRI stood for change of residence at least for one year or more. But, the legal definition of NRI has been broadened. Under this position, all PIOs can be termed as NRIs. But, an NRI is not automatically PIO but Indian. But emergence of Indian diaspora has diminished this distinction. The concept dearly, however, makes it easier to comprehend the phenomenon in clearer terms. The economic reforms, the opening up of economies and the emergence of free market conditions should, ordinarily speaking, facilitate labour mobility. But borders between the countries divide the nations and peoples. Free access is being advocated but it is being observed more in breach than in actual practice. Passport regulations and visa restrictions exist more today than any time in the past. Connected with this is the dual citizenship issue and the holding of more than one passport. While lateral integration is attempted in culturally homogeneous blocks such as European Union, ASEAN, etc., yet movement across blocks is becoming more and more difficult. Indian diaspora can become a more viable proposition if the knotty issue of dual citizenship is solved. But, the realisation of solution to this problem appears to be still a distant dream.

Oneness of Identity in Indian Diaspora

PIOs living outside India, including NRIs, are estimated to be about 15 million or a little more. They are spread in all the continents. They belong to all strata in those societies. Most of these people, however, are achievers. They have distinguished themselves in almost all fields – politics, economy, science, literature, art, sports etc. But it is necessary to recognise the psychological distance which separates PIOs from NRIs. The fault lies with both. Suspicion and distrust exist between these two groups. It is built on the imaginary sense of superiority and inferiority. Tendencies to structure the relations into hierarchy are in a way responsible for the unhappy and undesirable developments. But, the recent years have witnessed reduction in such tendencies. Greater mutual appreciation seems to govern these relationships now. I would like to illustrate this with a few personal anecdotes. Some years back, I was on a visit to Miami of Florida in USA (while I was serving as Indian High Commissioner in Trinidad and Tobago and other West Indies). The International University at Miami was celebrating Annual Day function of its International Students Union at the time of my visit. The immediate past President of the Students Union was an Indian Trinidadian whose parents had migrated to Trinidad a few decades back and settled down there. We have friendly relations with the family learning of my visit, the past President of the Students Union raised about it, perhaps, with the President of the University who suggested that I might be invited as a guest for the function. Accordingly I attended the function. At the end of the function, some Indian students wanted a get-together with me. They numbered about hundred. Among them, it so happened that one haired forms my neighbourhood in Hyderabad and, hence, he appeared to claim special attention from me. At the gathering, yet another student attempted to introduce himself where upon the boy from Hyderabad tried to brush him aside saying that he was a Jamaican. At this the former got visibly disturbed and shouted down the latter by addressing me, "Your Excellency, this gentleman is showing too much of his importance. His father migrated to US a little more than a decade back and my great grandparents came to Jamaica a century back. That is the only difference. As he is an Indian American, I am an Indian Jamaican, Sir, there are also in this group Indian Trinidadians, Indian Guyanese and so forth." This incident explains my observations knowingly or unknowingly if there is a tendency to display superior attitudes; it also illustrates the efforts to identify with each other often among the migrants belonging to different periods of migration and different parts of the globe. I would like to add a few other personal experiences to further support my observations. Sometime in 1992, Mr V.S. Naipaul and I were together in Port of Spain at a dinner reception along with our families. A few weeks before the meeting, he was denied the Noble Prize for Literature, though he was nominated for the same in that year and few years more before. Obviously I was disappointed at the event.[2] In my conversation, I mentioned the same to him. But his reply was more pertinent. He said, "R.K. Narayan does not figure among the Prize Winners over the years. (He mentioned one or two other names as well). So I don't bother about it. Did I miss much by not getting the Noble Prize?" In an direct sense, it points to the solidarity and the feeling of belonging to the Indian diaspora. Here, another instance comes to my mind. Sometime in late seventies, I met an Indian looking gentleman in London. Innocently, I asked him, "Are you from India?" He looked at me with visible contempt and answered with airs, "No, I am from East Africa." He was not prepared to associate with India altogether. After about two decades, I observe now among people from all parts of the world including the ones from East Africa a strong desire to identify with India and a pride to be part of Indian diaspora. Several similar incidents can be narrated to show the change in the perception about India and Indian connecting. Volumes can be written to show how Indian culture is flowering in different countries without, at the same time, conflicting with the other cultural shades of fellow citizens in those countries.[3]

Classification of Indian Diaspora

Indian diaspora is not uniform. There is much diversity in numbers, economic levels, relations with the other co-existing ethnic and social groups, cosmopolitanisms, religious perceptions and above all political participation. But, common among all these Indian communities abroad is their adherence, with enthusiasm, for Indian culture. In many countries, both overtly and covertly, they have joined hands with other ethnic communities and groups to shape their cultural mosaics in their countries without, at the same time, losing their own cultural identity. Not that there are no differences, contradictions and conflicts altogether. These again vary from country to country. We can classify these Indian diaspora countries into five categories as described below:

1. Countries with Indian Majority or Indians as the Largest Majority Group

In this group of countries, Indians constitute either an absolute majority group or the single largest group. (The numbers given below in table are approximate figures). The Indians' presence in these countries had considerable bearing on the polity, economy and society. In almost all these countries, Indians had either enjoyed full power or shared power with others. They are a force to reckon with in the political processes. In Mauritius, Guyana and Trinidad, for example, Indians are the rulers or part of the ruling hierarchies. In Surinam, after the recent elections, Indians again occupy key positions and one of the Indian readers has been the king maker. In Fiji, Indian leaders are locked in fierce struggle for political supremacy. In the last three countries, the Indians represent the Islands as the representatives (Deputies) in French Parliament, since these countries are still part of the French Union.

		Country	*Percentage of Indian Population*
(A)	(i)	Mauritius	68%
	(ii)	Surinam	54%
	(iii)	Fiji	62%[4]
	(iv)	Guyana	48%
	(v)	Trinidad	44%
(B)	(vi)	Guadeloupe	38%
	(vii)	Martinique	30%
	(viii)	Reunion	52%

2. Countries with Dominant Indian Presence (Indians as an Influential Minority Group)

In this category of countries, a fairly large population of Indians lives, which is visible for its role in the larger society. These countries include:

(i) South Africa, (ii) Malaysia, (iii) Singapore, (iv) USA, (v) UK, (vi) Canada, (vii) Grenada, and (viii) Hong Kong (of China).

In these countries, Indians represent the creative minority. They are hardworking, productive and achieving in orientation. Their presence in the society and economy is felt by the larger community. They are effective participants in the production and development process. In countries like South Africa, Malaysia, Singapore and Grenada, they have representatives in the political governance. In US, UK, Hong Kong and Canada they have been occupying prominent positions in the recent past. Economically, they have climbed the status ladder and are among the prosperous groups.

3. Countries with Recognisable Indian Population

Indians in these countries are recognised by the mainstream society as a competitive and productive. They are mostly professionals, business people and workers. These countries include: (i) Jamaica, (ii) Netherlands, (iii) Kenya, (iv) Uganda, (v) St. Lucia, (vi) St. Martin, (vii) Aruba, (viii) St. Vincent, (ix) Australia, and (x) Indonesia.

In the rapid development of these countries Indians have played an important role. Sometimes, their prosperity aroused suspicion and envy among the local people. But, on the whole, they are a recognisable group in these countries.

4. Middle East

These countries, with their new found wealth and prosperity due to resources like oil and gas, were in need of labour force and professionals. They turned to India among others for the supply of abundant human resources. India responded to this call generously and sent, large number of professionals and labour force – skilled and unskilled – to these countries. Residence and immigration laws in these countries are such that they do not ordinarily allow to gain citizenship. The Indians living in theses countries are mostly NRIs in the strictest sense of term. Those countries include: (i) United Arab Emirates, (ii) Oman, (iii) Kuwait, (iv) Iraq, (v) Yeman and PDR Yeman, (vi) Qatar, (vii) Saudi Arabia, (viii) Bahrain, (ix) Iran, (x) Lebanon, (xi) Libya, and (xii) Algeria etc.

In these countries, Indians occupy different types of technical, administrative and service positions for a specified period under definite contracts. Their contracts are renewed periodically and allowed them to continue their stay.

It is certain that these economies largely depended upon such labour force. The laws of these countries are so harsh that the immigrant population always lacks the special identity which they enjoy elsewhere. As and when these countries find alternate manpower sources, the Indian migrants are repatriated to their homeland as has been witnessed in recent months.

5. Other Countries with Small Indian Population

There are many other countries where a small size of Indians live as professionals and business people. These include France, Germany, St. Kits, Virgin Islands, Seychelles, Nigeria, Zimbabwe, Malawi, Tanzania, Thailand, New Zealand and others. Here, they are in small numbers and, however, are keeping their identity.

I have, purposefully not included neighbouring countries like Srilanka, Nepal, Bhutan, Burma, Bangladesh, Pakistan and Afghanistan in my discussion. In Indian diaspora, they, no doubt, occupy a very special and significant position. They stand distinguished by themselves.

The nature and pattern of emergence of the immigrant Indian communities in different parts of the globe depended on factors such as (i) distance, (ii) communication, (iii) culture and society of the host country, (iv) religion and language of the place of their original home, and (v) opportunity structures. Distance played a significant role in the preservation of the particular type and nature of Indian community patterns in the lands of their settlement. In Malaysia, Singapore and Srilanka, for example, Indians maintained, being nearer to their homeland, close contacts even at the level of the families in the native villages. In Mauritius, they could not keep contact with the village, but have preserved their languages and castes (to a less extent and only in few aspects). Some of the strengths and weaknesses inherent in the Indian society are reflected in Mauritian society. But, on the other had, distant Caribbean countries have preserved the religion and culture but have, by and large, lost the language. Caste has almost vanished. Inter-marriages have made this possible. Today, a strong Hindu society in these countries lives without caste. Recent contacts with Indians and the migration of Indian professionals in the past few decades have, however, done some damage by arousing caste consciousness among a select few individuals and groups. Communication networks likewise shape the patterns of emerging Indian community structures. US, Canada and UK are also distant countries. But, the strong communication links with India enabled Indian migrants in these countries to mirror all aspects Indian society in their living patterns. Caste animosities, regional disputes, language controversies, communal cleavage and other features reflect in the living of the Indian communities in these countries. It becomes more conspicuous when the higher literate professional and social status of these communities are taken into consideration. It needs deeper attention and study. In the case of Gulf workers and professionals the extent to which Indian communities evolved and developed there depended on the host country. Where liberal atmosphere prevailed, it allowed growth of strong Indian communities. It also depended on the extent to which Indian communities struggled to preserve their identity. While in Jamaica, Indian identity was lost due to the assimilation of Indians in the larger society, the case is different in Trinidad. In Guyana and Surinam Indians showed greater keenness to preserve their identity while co-existing with the rest of the ethnic groups in the larger society. All this, however, depended on the availability of opportunities for such struggle and survival. French colonies, such as Guadeloupe, Martinique and Reunion Island, preserved the frozen forms of the Indian culture of the period of their emigration from India. I had on occasion to witness the performance of a form of Bharata Natyam dance which I have not seen anywhere else when the Martinique Bharata Natyam dance group participated in Indian Caribbean dance festival in Trinidad. The point in question refers to the lack of opportunities for greater exposure and contact with Indian connections due to the isolation of French colonies caused by distance and barriers in language communication. Centres for the study of Indian diaspora need to investigate these issues.

Key Factors in the Sustenance of Indian Identities

It is necessary to examine the key factors responsible for the sustenance and survival of Indian identity among the diaspora population. The fact that they belonged to rich and hoary culture gave them strength to stand against odd situations which confronted them in the new circumstances. Religion, family system, love for land and attachment to soil, faith in the destiny and pride in cultural forms could be identified as the key factors in this connection. Religion played a positive role in the survival and growth of Indian identity in different countries where the Indian had migrated. People had pride in their religions and their social background. The indentured Indian immigrants in Trinidad had to contend with other ethnic groups such as colonial white masters, former African slaves and indentured Chinese and Syrian or Lebanese. African, Chinese (to some extent), Syrian and Lebanese immigrants lost their religion, culture and lifestyles. Was it due to lack of pride in them for their own religion and culture or to some other pressing reasons? Investigation alone can answer this question. The Indian indentured immigrant hoisted a flag when he lacked the facility of temple for worship and created a place of worship. Hindu Indian homes today display cloisters of flags in their front yards to proclaim their identity. Religion became a symbol of cohesion and unity when interacting with other ethnic groups. Sarah E. Mortan, wifc of John Mortan, the pioneer Canadian Presbyterian priest in early 20th century, narrated an interesting incident about Indian pride in an indentured labourer.

She quotes her husband: "I never had all adequate notice of what pride was until I saw it in a priest. One day after service on an estate, one stepped forward and shook hands. He was lithe and straight as a palm tree, though his white head and beard proclaimed him in the winter of his years. He drew himself up before me with the dignity of a prince, and addressed me as a fellow Brahman. He was poor, he said, his savings have been stolen. He had to work now, though old, but he had been a gentleman in India and was so in spirit still. And his eyes flashed with haughty dignity as he claimed me for a brother though a carriage stood at hand for me and his hoe awaited him."[5] This incident indicates the pride in his own being even though he might have been forced by circumstances to work on the cane farm. His religion taught him the dignity of labour. The immigrants preserved the religious forms, devotional songs and the faith in the correctness of their religion. The construction of the shore temple by Seva Das, single handedly, against all odds of estate laws and the non-recognition of Hindu practices by colonial Trinidad, sufficiently demonstrates the will to preserve the Indian identity.

The institution of Indian family largely helped Indians to remain knitted together. The joint family system and the Indian ethos taught them thrift and the virtue of living together. The institution taught them the nobility of raising and giving, and also helped in preserving strong kinship bonds. The Indian family advocated concern not only for the present but also for the progeny. The strong kinship bonds helped them in the networking in space and time. This stood in contrast to the family ties seen in the rest of the groups. The permanent nature of marriage and relative absence of divorce laid secure kinship relations among the Indian migrants. Indians' love for land is proverbial. Land is Mother Goddess to them, they worshipped land with reverence. The Indian community, therefore, showed tenacity in preserving their strong links with land. The Blacks displayed exactly the opposite attitudes towards land. Land had become a symbol for slavery and they prided in their assimilating and interacting into white man's culture and religion. The Indians remained in the rural areas which is turn facilitated them for living in strong family groups. Depending on rural area they developed the values of self-reliance and self-dependence. The vast developed culture which was their heritage helped the Indian immigrant communities to maintain their identity. The strong tradition of song, dance, music and drama supported their urge for creative contingence of their social values and institutional framework.

Conclusion

From the preceding discussion, two paradigms emerge:

(i) persistence and co existence, and

(ii) pluralism and unity in diversity.

  (i) Indian immigrants when they spread to different parts of the globe were presented with certain dilemmas. Not merely the 'pull' factor existing in the countries of their destination, such as employment opportunities, scope for social mobility and opening up of new vistas but also 'push' factors, motivated them to undertake weary journeys to distant lands. They had the urge to both preserve and persist with their cultural forms of living patterns. They could not have succeeded in the new locations if they lacked flexibility and inclination and intention to adjust and co-exist with the new environment. They needed to live and let the others live. While they had pride in their being, they were not reluctant to let others practise their own beliefs and lifestyles. The paradigm of persistence and co-existence which again formed part of their cultural heritage helped the Indian communities abroad largely.

(ii) Indian society for centuries had been a plural society. Plurality is the core value of Indian existence. Instinct of preservation and presentation also added to the possibility of plurality. The migrating Indian community, with its determination to preserve its identity, was adding to the already existing plural streams in the country of their destination or by their addition to the homogeneous host country were leading to new plural solution. But it is not centrifugal in orientation under all circumstances. One other, it stands for centripetal syndrome. These paradigms, however, need closer observation and sharper examination to identify the variable, which plays the significant part in Indian diaspora.

Let me conclude the discussion with the following observations: It is said that you can take a man out of India but you cannot take India out of him. Would it be more appropriable to say that you cannot take Indianness out of him.

Notes

1. George Lamming, "The West Indian People", *New World Quarterly,* Vol. 2, No. 1, 1966, p. 60.
2. He was, however, awarded with the Nobel Prize for Literature after ten years in 2001.
3. See my forthcoming essays in a book on Trinidad, Tobago and other diaspora countries.
4. After the coup and the establishment of Rebuka government, the population of people of Indian origin has come down to 48 per cent with waves of migration to New Zealand, Australia, etc.
5. Cited in "Pundit of Chaguanas" by Anthony de Verteuil, C.S.S.P. in his work *Eight East Indian Immigrants*, Paria Publishing Company, Newtown, Port of Spain Trinidad and Tobago, 1989.

References

Birbalsingh, Frank (ed.), 1989, *Indenture and Exile: The Indo-Caribbean Experience*, TSAR, Toronto, published in association with the Ontario Association for Studies in Indo-Caribbean Culture.

Dabydeen, David and Brinsley Samaroo (eds.), 1987, *India in the Caribbean: Special Commemorative Edition 1838–1938*, Centre for Caribbean Studies Publication in cooperation with the London Strategic Policy Unit, Hansib Publishing Limited, London.

Deen, Shamshu, 1994, *Solving East Indian Roots in Trinidad*, H.E.M. Enterprises, (Freeport) Trinidad and Tobago.

de Verteuil, Anthony, 1989, C.S.S.P. *Eight East Indian Immigrants*, Paria Publishing Company, Newtown, Port of Spain, Trinidad.

Gosine, Mahin, 1992, *The Coolie Connection: From the Orient to the Occident*, Windsor Press, New York.

Jain, R.K., 1994, "Reality and Representation: Aspects of the Electronic Media in Contemporary Indian Society and Diaspora", *Sociological Bulletin*, Vol. 47, No. 2, September.

Naipaul, V.S., 1969, *A House for Mr. Biswas*, Penguin Books, New Delhi.

Ryan, Selwyn (ed.), 1991, *Social and Occupational Stratification in Contemporary Trinidad and Tobago*, Institute of Social and Economic Research, University of the West Indies and St. Augustine, Trinidad and Tobago.

Singh, Kelvin, 1994, *Race and Class Struggles in a Colonial State: Trinidad 1917–1945*, University of Calgary Press, Canada and University of West Indies, Trinidad and Tobago.

Varma, Pavan K., 2004, *Being Indian*, Penguin Books, New Delhi.

8

Corporate Social Responsibility in the European Union and East Asia

Gyorgy Szell

Corporate Social Responsibility (CSR) has been in the focus of European Union's industrial policy, employment relations and environmental concerns since the beginning of the 21st century. When at the EU Lisbon summit in 2000 and the Gothenburg summit in 2001 the heads of governments and states decided to make the European Union (EU) the leading knowledge-based economy in the world, including fair work and ecological sustainability, this signalled a new approach. In the background of the triad competition, namely, between the EU, the NAFTA and East Asia – perhaps an East Asian Union – the EU tries to accomplish the highest quality of life and working life for its citizens. This should not be understood as a negative or even destructive competition. Setting a good example, or a best practice, the EU hopes that the other nations and blocs will follow this path of sustainability. CSR is a concept whereby company's social and environmental concerns in their business operations and interaction with their stakeholders on a voluntary basis. It is about enterprises deciding to go beyond minimum legal requirements and obligations stemming from collective agreements in

---

Public lecture delivered at Hyderabad on 24 November, 2008.

order to address societal needs. Through CSR, enterprises of all sizes, in cooperation with their stakeholders, can help to reconcile economic, social and environmental ambitions. As such, CSR has become an increasingly important concept both globally and within the EU, and is part of the debate about globalisation, competitiveness and sustainability. In Europe, the promotion of CSR reflects the need to defend common values and increase the sense of solidarity and cohesion" (EC, 2006: 2). My basic thesis in this context is that the ongoing outsourcing and privatisation of public goods, based on neo-liberal ideologies and practices, is the reason for the necessity to introduce the concept and hopefully also the praxis of CSR. I think it is worthwhile to come back here to the writings by Karl Marx, although for many he seemed to be completely outdated with the breakdown of really existing socialism in the Soviet Union and its satellites. I will try to demonstrate the validity of Marx's main approach in this context. There is no doubt that we are living in really existing capitalism. Marx phrased accurately as main principle of the capitalist system: "Enrichissez vous, enrichissez vous!" ("Enrich yourself, enrich yourself!").[1] Not as a person, but for the corporation. Because the corporation will go down within the competition under capitalist conditions, if it does not accumulate the highest possible surplus value, i.e., profits to reinvest. CSR has no place in this logic of primitive accumulation and primitive capitalism.

'Shareholder value' became some 15 years ago the dominant slogan for corporate governance. Social justice and workers' rights were put into the waste basket of history. But, the end of the 'Bubble Economy' in Japan and elsewhere together with the ecological crises were indicators to the "Limits to Growth", as the first Club of Rome Report in 1973 was titled (Meadows et al., 1972). So, the newspapers are full of scandals, in summer 2004 in Italy Parmalat set a new landmark with a bankruptcy of more than 14 billion Euro, although by far not reaching the ones by ENRON, Worldcom, etc. However, after ten years, fortunately the euphoria around the shareholder value has largely disappeared, because it could not fulfil its high promises. So, we are back at the fundamental crossroads.

History

Companies and organisations are embedded in their geographical, cultural, political, societal and economic environment. From thereon a social responsibility is a condition for their long-term survival and sustainability. To understand the relevance of the issue and its further prospects, I propose to first have a look backward, i.e., into history, because in my view without history we do not understand anything, and therefore also cannot explain the reasons for problems and conflicts. And so we also cannot then find solutions.

Although, as Fernand Braudel, in his magnificent three-volume on the material civilisation, the economy and capitalism (1979), has demonstrated, the market has been a universal phenomenon since the beginning of human civilisation; it has always been regulated differently, according to the divergent needs and stages of human development. And apparently the market itself regulates behaviour and produces its norms in a dialectical relationship. Karl Polanyi has very well described this process in his book, *The Great Transformation*.

So, economic activities were always regulated for political, social and cultural purposes. And it is not at all the so-called "Invisible Hand", as Adam Smith formulated so nicely. On the contrary, it was through law and legal action that public authorities looked for the proper functioning of the economy, because the economy is not an end in itself – or at least should not be. We may differentiate between two main actors in the field of regulation: the state and the social partners. I try to square the circle with the following figure, which may illustrate the four main forms of regulation:

Figure 1
Forms of Regulation

		Social Partners	
		+	–
The	+	Tripartism	Law
State	–	Collective Bargaining, Codetermination	Market, Finance, Capital

Legal Regulation

This is the first form of regulation, historically speaking, and the regulation of employment relations by the state through law, without letting formally participate the social partners in this process. Apparently, this form of regulation is here ideal-type-sized (as the other three forms as well), as in modern times there is always a hearing in a legislature before passing of each new legislation. Even before these hearings, it is the social partners, who through lobbying try to influence the legislation through the political parties – who are close to them – or the administration itself, which prepares the law.

Regulation by the Social Partners

In this form of regulation there is in principle no state intervention, besides that it has to legalise the existence of social partners at all. Normally, this right is regulated in the national constitutions. In authoritarian regimes trade unions, and even sometimes employers' associations, are not allowed at all. The normal form of regulation by the social partners is collective bargaining. This collective bargaining can be done at the micro, meso, macro or even transnational level. There we find profound differences, due to the diverse historical background of each nation.

A specific form of regulation done at the micro level, i.e., the company level, is co-determination. This means the representation of workers' representatives in various decision-making bodies of the company. This may go even to a partial representation – as in the case of the German co-determination law (1976). But this form of regulation by the social partners needs a legal base too, because it interferes into the property rights of the capital owners of the company.

Tripartite Regulation

The modern welfare state has brought the state and the social partners closer together. Mostly it is under social-democratic governments that this form of regulation is practised. In extension of the collective bargaining principle, the state intervenes into collective bargaining in establishing fora, where principles and guidelines for its macro policy and the wage policy of the social partners are agreed on. One of the most famous of these agreements is the Wassenaar agreement (1982) in the Netherlands.

But, the interconnection goes also the other way round: the social partners become constitutive bodies within the institutions of social security, as the old age retirement schemes, the health and safety systems, the employment agencies, etc. This type of regulation refers also to the concept of 'corporatism', which means that the social partners become constituent bodies of the state itself. The effect of this model of regulation is generally great social peace and very few social conflicts, i.e., strikes, etc. Again, this model is regionally centred, i.e., mainly to be found in Northern Europe. It may have come out, that these first three forms of regulation are closely intertwined and complementary. There is no sharp line of differentiation. According to different national traditions, the balance between them may change, but it is something, which may be termed as specific European in contrast to the United States of America and Japan, the latter had been largely forced to copy the American model after the Second World War.

But we have also the role of the state as employer itself, which steps in directly in this property into employment relations too. The state in the OECD countries is also the biggest employer – including its own administrations at the different levels – the military, the educational and health systems, science and research, para-statal agencies, energy, transport, etc. This state ownership is naturally one of the main targets of deregulators, asking therefore for the full privatisation of state property.

Market Regulation

Partly as a reaction against this kind of social regulation, we find the renaissance in the so-called "free market economy", promoted by the neo-liberals on the (never realised) ideal of the laissez-faire state of the 19th century. This ideology came mainly from the Chicago Boys around Milton Friedman in the 1970s, and largely applied by Margaret Thatcher in the UK from 1979 on, to be known as "Thatcherism", and in the form of "Reaganomics" in the US. This strategy of deregulation intends to liberate the market from constraints of the state and of oligopolistic associations (i.e., the trade unions).

Though it is true that sometimes in Europe we have in the economy and in the state still vested interests, which by the way stem often even from feudal, pre-modern times, this strategy has largely failed in not bringing economic growth or reducing unemployment. On the contrary, however, it was successful in changing massively the distribution of wealth and income, as well as the tax burden in favour of capital in the last twenty years. Perhaps, Thatcher has best resumed the ideological base of this strategy, when she said, "There is no such thing as society. I know only individuals and the market!" But that's where the problems of CSR start all about.

The principles of the honest merchant are such traditional rules. Notwithstanding that there always have been breaches of the rules, and certainly always will be – if we will not be transformed into angels. But this is the exception; otherwise the economic system will break down. Interestingly, even criminal organisations like the Mafia or Yakuza have their clear rules to follow within their own economic system – although it may relate to another kind of social responsibility than in the main economic sectors.

In the pre-industrial period, in Europe, the guilds regulated economy, safeguarding quality, employment and sustainability. This role was more and more taken over afterwards, i.e., since the development of modern nation-states, by the modern state itself, which introduced welfare systems, to which the companies had to contribute. These welfare systems are often autonomous, independent structures co-managed by employers and workers, or by tripartite structures, including the state.

The role of the state is to guarantee the infrastructure, law and order to promote society and the economy. However, since the beginning of industrialisation, public companies (health, education, water, energy, transport) were created to supply public goods. This has been done on the local, regional and national levels. So, public corporations producing public goods are, by their very conception, practising social responsibility.

Apparently, in a socialist system, all corporations are by their very definition already socially responsible. I cannot extend this argument here due to the restrictions of my topic. In really existing socialism at least some sort of transnational cooperation on social regulation existed, as the principles of Soviet corporate social responsibility have been exported to the other COMECON members.

The question arises, why has then the issue of CSR come so much to the fore since a couple of years? About 70 per cent of all leading managers in these companies of the recent scandal-ridden corporations like Enron, WorldCom, Vivendi, Mannesmann, nearly all Japanese banks, Nokamura investment, etc., had an MBA. So, is this just a problem of false training – then the responsibility of academia would come in? But, business ethics and CSR are taught in a number of business schools since last several years – already apparently an indicator for the need.[2] However, this does not seem to have had any great effect on business practices so far. So, the problem with corporate governance and CSR seems to me more deep and fundamental.

CSR is not a new phenomenon. Earlier, bourgeoisie and capitalists created foundations which were sponsoring charity and welfare, hospitals and kindergarten, schools, universities, housing for their workers, culture, theatres, operas, music, arts, sports, etc. Philanthropy can be even characterised as an essential element of modern bourgeois society – not only to overcome part of its contradictions, but also to promote the own class and recruit from the lower classes promising talents. By the way, the old philanthropy has certainly not died out, as George Soros demonstrates. But today's CSR is not only a new term, but has definitely new characteristics. So, the question stands: Why has it come up over the last ten years ago or so? After the defeat of the Soviet Union, and as Francis Fukuyama proclaimed the end of history there seemed to be no alternative to really existing market capitalism.

"Socially responsible initiatives by entrepreneurs have a long tradition in Europe. What distinguishes today's understanding of CSR from the initiatives of the past is the attempt to manage it strategically and to develop instruments for this. It means a business approach, which puts stakeholder expectations and the principle of continuous improvement and innovation at the heart of business strategies. What constitutes CSR depends on the particular situation of individual enterprises and on the specific context in which they operate, be it in Europe or elsewhere. In view of the EU enlargement it is however important to enhance common understanding both in Member States and candidate countries" (EC, 2002: 5).

Excursion: Germany

I would like to make here some remarks on the German system of co-determination, because it is in my opinion closely related to the issue of CSR. And, because it is of high relevance for the understanding of historical processes. Besides, Germany is still the third biggest economy in the world, although China is quickly catching up and might overtake it in the coming years. But Germany is without any doubt the most important EU member-state and has played an important role together with the Nordic countries in the shaping of the EU, especially in regard to CSR.

This model has been developed over the past hundred years. One remembers Marx's criticism of the Gotha programme of the SPD in 1875, and the debate on reformism at the beginning of this century with Rosa Luxemburg, Karl Liebknecht, Eduard Bernstein and Karl Kautsky. In a way, after the failed revolution of 1918–19, the work committee act (*Betriebsrategesetz*) of 1920 was an historical compromise, which was questioned again by the fascist regime.

This model was further developed by Fritz Naphtali in the 1920s under the concept of 'economic democracy', which included the level of companies, and economic and social councils at the sectoral, regional and national levels. One can still find this model today in the fundamental programmes of the DGB (Deutscher Gewerkschaftsbund, the German Trade Unions' Federation). This perspective includes the nationalisation *(Verstaatlichung)* of key industries and banks. The so-called *Gemeinwirtschaft,* mutual economics, which includes production and consumption co-operatives, insurance companies, banks, etc., complements this model. The most renowned example of that sector is the building society "Neue Heimat", Europe's largest trust in this field – before its bankruptcy in 1986 – and the Bank fur Gemeinwirtschaft, formerly Germany's fourth largest bank, now owned by the Swedish SEB.

This model does not only cover the economic dimension, but also education, culture, sports, etc. In the pre-fascist years, there were people's universities *(Volkshochschulen)* in the workers' quarters, as well as theatre groups, choirs, etc. Islands of socialist municipalities still existed in the capitalistic society, for example, "Red Vienna" of the 1920s, which would become a fortress against fascism.

There was a division of labour between the social-democratic party and trade unions. The party led the political struggle to get to power through elections at all levels: city, province and country. The economic fight was led by trade unions, in order to earn higher incomes and better living and working conditions.

After World War II, work committees were set up spontaneously all over the western zones of Germany which began the reconstruction work and brought about the German "economic wonder". After the fascist rule, the Socialist Democratic Party expected victory during the general elections, but it did not come. Although, the events taking place in the Russian zone and the Cold War were greatly responsible for this failure, but there were also other factors. The allies, especially the Americans, had already intervened to prevent the socialisation of industries and banks, etc., to weaken the left and the trade unions. After a general strike, co-management at company level was introduced in the coal and steel industry (mines, and steelworks) in 1951, and in all firms with more than five salaried workers in 1952 (*Betriebsverfassungsgesetz* – Company Constitution Act). The Co-management Act in the metal works industry was probably passed with the approval of the allies, for they might have thus hoped to weaken German firms, which were showing up again in international competition.

After these initial laws, some others also followed to regulate the co-management in public sector, the social security institutions (retirement and sickness insurance), the national employment board, the chambers of commerce and industry, that of craftsmen *(Handwerkskarnrner)* etc.

Under the social-liberal government from 1969 to 1982, the Company Constitution Act was reformed in 1972 – without satisfying trade unions,[3] and the Company Co-management Act was voted in 1976. This law applies in principle to all firms with over 2,000 employees. It did not achieve complete parity, because of the Liberal Party's intervention. The liberals have firstly created a separate group for executives/white-collar officers *(Leitende Angestellte)*, generally not organised in trade unions/members; and secondly, they gave a double vote to the chairman of the board in case of "patt" situations.[4]

The co-management's reality in Germany is too complicated to be described here exhaustively. But, the following table might give a modest insight into the system (Briefs, 1989):

Table 1

Co-management in the FRG

Degree of Participation	*Form of Participation*						
100%							G
50%						F	
49.9%					E		
33%				D			
25%			C				
10%		B					
0%	A						

A Firms with less than five salaried workers or without company boards (almost half of SMEs).

B Firms with 5 to 19 salaried workers, who can elect a company delegate.

C The public sector, generally having only a right to information and consultation (i.e., personnel council).

D Firms with 20 to 2,000 salaried workers (from 300 workers on, with the right to have one permanent representative on the company board for every 300 salaried workers and one-third of the seats of the administration board).

E The chambers of commerce and industry, of craftsmen, the national employment agency (one-third of the seats respectively for salaried workers, employers, state).

F Co-management Act; a few communal public enterprises.

G Employers/salaried workers parity (metal industry law, retirement schemes, health insurances), mutual economics *(Gemeinwirtschaft)*.

The above table would have been even more complex if the part played by trade unions was taken into account. In the wake of the Second World War, trade unions of various political streams tried to settle their differences and set up a single union. But, this did not serve the purpose. Unions saw differences in opinion amongst workers' organisations in the pre-1933 period as causes of the weakening of democratic forces. However, the only ones to come together within the DGB in 1949 were the communists, the social democrats and many trade unions close to the former Catholic "Zentrum". Alongside the DGB were the CGB, a Christian trade union (200,000 members), the DAG, an executives' union (500,000 members), which is now integrated into the new services union ver.di, and the Deutscher Beamtenbund, the civil servants' organisation (800,000 members). The DGB federations have a 7.5 million strong membership, representing a 45 per cent overall unionisation rate and a 35 per cent rate for the DGB alone. The DGB has only eight members, for it is in fact a federation of trade unions. The size of the federations varies from 30,000 members, for the leather federation, to the 2.5 million, for the "Metall" organisation or to 2.7 million for the newly merged union ver.di – the biggest single union in the world. Various political trends are represented within the federation, with a majority of social democrats everywhere.

Corporate democratisation in the FRG has taken place within a codified *(Verrechtlichung)* and representative framework, contrary to the Anglo-Saxon model, where industrial relations, with their shop stewards and closed shops system, are governed by customs and habits, and provide a greater degree of direct democracy on the work place. Co-management has become a highly skilled business. Unions have become increasingly bureaucratic and difficult to monitor.

If we look back into past CSR, the picture in general is not very convincing. It took about 50 years after the end of the Second World War until German companies were ready to write their company history including the Nazi period from 1933 to 1945.[5] And it took another ten years until at least a large part of them under pressure was ready to take responsibility for the use of forced labour and pay compensation. Together with the Federal Government US $ 10 billion were collected to compensate the surviving victims.[6]

Actually, in this sense of codification, it is very important to look into the Fundamental Law (*Grundgesetz,* equivalent of a Constitution) of the Federal Republic of Germany from 1949. This was at the height of Cold War. And, even the Conservative Party CDU has voted in its Ahlen Programme from 1947 for a socialisation of key industries, as well as the DGB in its Fundamental Programme from 1949. In the background that the workers had largely self-managed and reconstructed large parts of the German industry after 1945 and with a strong presence of socialists and communists in transition governments, the Article 15 was formulated in such way that property is socially responsible. In case of failure it can be socialised.

The Basic Principles

I will try to answer the question what is CSR all about, with the following figure, which only roughly and in two dimensions gives a sketch of the complexity of the interrelations and their dialectics:

Two excellent indicators for CSR on the macro level are:

1. tax payment, and
2. employment.

Definitely every society needs some public authority, and this has to be paid by the community – corporations and citizens. So, tax evasion is the absolute contrary of CSR, however, all kinds of tax evasions are regarded by most companies as normal practice. So, the

Figure 2
CSR Relationships

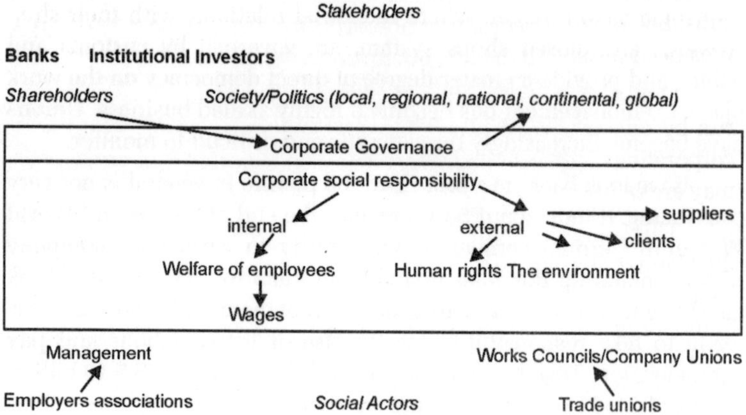

part of taxes paid by companies had radically decreased over the last couple of decades in all OECD countries, e.g., 60 per cent of US companies did not pay any corporate tax between 1996 and 2000 (Pearlstein, 2004). In Third World countries companies practically never paid taxes, and the former socialist countries have enormous problems to establish a tax system – that is something, which the neo-liberal consultants did not teach them.

In regard to employment it is for sure that a company does not exist to create employment, but goods and services. So, it can definitely not be the main objective of corporations to create jobs. It is one of the biggest lies that they defend jobs when they are fighting against ecological and other restrictions. Again and again workers and their representatives go into this trap, not realising that this argument disappears in the wind under other circumstances. Fortunately, the time seems to be over when share prices rose when a company made a larger number of workers redundant, because investors realise that then the situation must be very serious. However, again, it is a different issue to practice a "hire-and-fire" policy by management, where all risk is born by the employees, and management after their mistakes even leave with a golden handshake.

In really existing capitalism it is true that the corporation has to make at least no losses, because otherwise the costs have to be borne by somebody else. So, social policies have to be mainly formulated by public authorities, which may be complemented by subsidiary and social networks. And for structural change public compensation and subsidies may be necessary. However, for that purpose, the authorities need public funds, i.e., tax revenues.

One other important point: CSR cannot be practised in the long run by one or several corporations alone; it has to be shared by all corporations, otherwise as with ecological standards, social dumping may arrive.

This brings me to the issue of ownership. Some corporations like the German Bertelsmann[7] and also Rockefeller, Ford or George Soros have transferred their main assets to foundations. Apparently, these foundations are by their very definition already socially responsible. This holds also true for another form of ownership: the co-operatives. The biggest co-operatives in the world – Desjardins in Quebec and Mondragon in the Spanish Basque country – are economically and financially very well functioning corporations. They do not need a Code of Conduct, because it is built in into their ownership structure. More radically in this regard are even the Kibbutzim, although they are in some crisis now – not unrelated to the difficult political and with it the economic situation in Israel.

Coming back to the core issue. If CSR should be voluntary or obligatory, the historic experience shows as with the length of working day, health and safety, starting in the 19th century, all need legal, binding regulation, otherwise most companies will just not follow. The case of the optical producer Zeiss in Germany (which turned later into a foundation) is interesting so far. The philanthropic owner introduced voluntarily the eight-hour working day, and this set the example for the workers' movements to ask for a generalisation of this rule. But this historic experience also exemplifies that all these regulations could only be won through organised, collective efforts by social movements and their political organisations, which by the way is also true for all other fundamental, human, social rights.

And, a similar argument holds true for environmental protection. "In most cases, factors other than the given voluntary approach seem to explain the major part of any environmental improvement that has taken place" (OECD, 2003: 62).[8]

After all, for social regulation as well as for the field of labour relations the nation-state is still the main framework. Employers' associations and trade unions are therefore mostly limited in their action within this area. But in the present age of globalisation financial speculation is one of its main driving forces. About US $ 1.3 trillion are being circulated every day around the globe in the search of profitable investment. Of this, 95 per cent is for speculative purpose, the rest to settle commodity and service moves.[9] Twenty years ago it was the other way around. The main actors in this computerised world are the banks, hedge and pension funds, and collective investors. And, all this happens without any political or social regulation. Actually, one of those who profited most of these deregulated financial markets, the Hungarian-American George Soros, wrote in 1998 a book with the title *The Crisis of Global Capitalism*.[10] In this book he claims that these unregulated markets are more dangerous for freedom than Stalinism has been.

Research on CSR is still in an embryonic phase. It is only recently that some research centres have taken it up. The CEC has funded a number of research activities since a number of years. And also, the EUU Tokyo Consortium – as mentioned above – has selected it as one of its main research areas. Corporate Sustainability Research (CSR) organisations from across Europe, including EIRIS, PIRC and SERM of the UK, have come together to form the Association of Independent Corporate Sustainability and Responsibility Research (AI CSRR). The corporate sustainable and responsible research sector continues to expand throughout Europe due to increasing popular interest. At the same time pressure on CSR research groups to raise quality and be transparent and professional has grown. AI CSRR, therefore, has been created to develop and promote high professional standards for organisations in the field. In a joint statement the three UK groups announced: "Transparency is no longer an optional extra; we consider this initiative crucial for SRI research organisations to demonstrate the same level of accountability they rate most highly in listed companies" (Via3net, 3 November 2005).

Using another theoretical perspective, sociologists were active. In the London-based Tavistock Institute, they focused their studies on the so-called Socio-Technical System (STS) in the fifties and sixties. In these projects, researchers from different countries took part. Some of them were of British or German origin, but there were also the Norwegian Einar Thorsrud and the Australian Fred Emery (Emery and Thorsrud, 1969, 1976). Their studies had a great impact not only on Britain, or perhaps even less there, but on Scandinavia and Australia, where Thorsrud lived. Thorsrud founded the Work

Research Institute in Oslo (Qvale, 1992). Its main contribution to industrial democracy was the (semi-) autonomous working group, which reached in the Volvo car factories in Kalmar and later in Uddevalla in the eighties (Sandberg, 1992, 1995).

Following the same model of tripartite partnership between the state, the employers and the trade unions – which is actually the structure of the ILO – the Arbetslivscentrum was founded in Stockholm in the seventies. The Norwegian Bjorn Gustavsen was and is some kind of a link between Oslo and Stockholm. He contributed immensely to the critical reflection and implementation of industrial democracy in Scandinavia and beyond (Gustavsen, 1979, 1986). Due to conflicts with the employer's side, which is common all over, the world within the neo-conservative and neo-liberal 'revolution' led by Ronald Reagan and Margaret Thatcher, the Arbetslivscentrum was partly dissolved and integrated into the National Institute of Working Life in the nineties. Still, we can speak of a Scandinavian model of industrial democracy. During the Swedish EU-Presidency in 2000 it was the first time that a great number of conferences on working life were organised within presidency (Ennals, 2000).

The experiments conducted in the small island of Malta after its independence make out a special case. They were carried out mainly in the dockyards. The sociologists of the Workers Participation Centre of the University of Malta intervened effectively into this self-managed institution (Kester and Zammit, 1992; Zammit, 1996).

The Industrial Democracy in Europe studies, published in 1981, gave a big push in the field. The studies covered 12 countries. It was possible to discern three forms of industrial democracy at that period: the Nordic, the Anglo-Saxon[11], and the socialist, i.e., the Yugoslav form. The latter gave more *de jure* than *de facto* rights. Since these studies more than 25 years ago both the world and Europe have changed. Yugoslavia does not exist anymore and from the former six republics only Slovenia has entered so far the EU and even the Euro zone. The former COMECON countries have partly changed radically to a neo-liberal market model as in the Anglo-Saxon world. Others have adopted a tripartite strategy. However, the problem in these countries for a functioning social partnership is the weakness of trade unions as well as of employers' associations.

The main problem in regard to CSR as a common EU strategy is this diversity of labour relations and ownership structures. We are still far away to the historical and cultural differences from a real Social European Union (Busch et al., 2000).

With regard to research promotion, Ricardo Petrella within Directorate General Research of the European Union introduced the FAST (Forecasting and Assessment of Science and Technology) programme in the eighties. This programme was not only promoting science and technology, but also industrial democracy by the way of "human-centred technology". The follow-up programme Targeted Socio-Economic Research (TSER) of the European Commission also had as one of its foci industrial democracy. Finally, the Sixth Framework for Research of the European Union had explicitly as one of the main research areas citizenship and governance.

The EU's CSR Policy

The European Union has first of all just been an economic community, creating a single market for free trade and free movement of capital and labour. However, the European Social and Regional Funds to promote social justice and solidarity to help less favoured regions have soon complemented it.

The European Commission is sub-divided into Directorates General, they have the function of three ministries concerning CSR:

- The DG Industrial Policy (III)
- The DG Employment. Social Affairs and Equal Opportunities (V)
- The DG Environment (XIII)

Without any doubt, the DG Employment, Social Affairs and Equal Opportunities is the most active in the field of CSR, as also the Dublin Foundation for the Improvement of Living and Working Conditions is its realm.

The European Commission hosts a number of homepages concerning CSR. The most active is DG V – Employment and Social Affairs, followed by DG III – Enterprise and Industry, whereas the DGs Trade as well as Environment, to which links were laid from DG V, were outdated (2002) or non-specific. DG V published most interesting documents including references and funded research projects permanently at: http://europa.eu.int/ comm/employment_social/socdi al/csr/. To promote further CSR the Directorate General of Employment and Social Affairs of the CEC has published the following support materials since 2002:

- ABC of CSR instruments
- Mapping instruments for CSR

Another initiative is to discern the 100 best EU workplaces within the following three categories:

- Organising life-long learning
- Creating diversity at workplace
- Implementing gender equality

In 2004 the DO V also published an overview of "National CSR Public Policies" for the then EU 15.

"An increasing number of European companies are promoting their corporate social responsibility strategies as a response to a variety of social, environmental and economic pressures. They aim to send a signal to the various stakeholders with whom they interact: employees, shareholders, investors, consumers, public authorities and non-governmental organisations (NGOs). In doing so, companies are investing in their future and they expect that the voluntary commitment they adopt will help to increase their profitability" (EC, 2001, Green Paper: 6).

Europe needs business to do what it does best: to provide products and services that add value for society and to deploy entrepreneurial spirit and creativity towards value and employment creation. However, Europe does not need just business but socially responsible business that takes its share of responsibility for the state of European affairs. In its contribution to the March 2005 Spring Council, the Commission recognised that CSR can play a key role in contributing to sustainable development while enhancing Europe's innovative potential and competitiveness. In the Social Agenda, the Commission announced that it would, in cooperation with member states and stakeholders, present initiatives to further enhance the development and transparency of CSR. In the revised Sustainable Development Strategy, the Commission called "on the business leaders and other key stakeholders of Europe to engage in urgent reflection with political leaders on the medium and long-term policies needed for sustainability and propose ambitious business responses which go beyond existing minimum legal requirements" (EC, 2006: 3).

Different activities have been developed under the Finnish presidency, during the second half of 2006. On the EU level a Social Charter has been voted in 1992 together with the Maastricht Treaties. And in 1994 the Directive for European Works Council was finally introduced after many years of preparations. Similar initiatives are starting within Mercosur. In the meantime some companies like VW, Siemens and Daimler Chrysler have even established World Works Councils. In this regard, European companies, and foremost German ones, are in the lead. Now, the European company (SE) is also a new legal form, which includes workers' participation in decision-making. It allows co-determination on the supervisory board level. Here again, the German co-determination was the model to follow, although it was not possible to have a common structure for the supervisory board.

The EU tries to be on the lead since its Green Paper on CSR in 2001, and follow documents in 2002 and 2003. However, a Green Paper is not a White Paper, i.e., it is a discussion paper. It defines the subject as follows:

CSR covers social and environmental issues, in spite of the English term corporate social responsibility; CSR is not or should not be separate from business strategy and operations; it is about integrating social and environmental concerns into business strategy and operations; CSR is a voluntary concept; an important aspect of CSR is how enterprises interact with their internal and external stakeholders (employees, customers, neighbours, non-governmental organisations, public authorities, etc.) The Green Paper rightly differentiates between:

1. The internal dimensions:
   - Human resources management
   - Health and safety at work
   - Adaptation to change
   - Management of environmental impacts and natural resources
2. The external dimensions:
   - Local communities
   - Business partners, suppliers, consumers
   - Human rights
   - Global environmental concerns

However, there is no explicit mentioning of the kind of decision-making, i.e., involving unions and employees. The Green Paper goes on in developing a holistic approach, which includes:

- Social responsible integrated management
- Social responsible reporting and auditing
- Quality in work
- Social and eco-labels
- Social responsible investment

Here, we are at a very important point for realising CSR. The pension funds have become the biggest worldwide investors. And, they invest globally the money of employees, not of corporations. They can and do invest already more and more into companies with CSR strategies.

The European Foundation for the Improvement of Living and Working Conditions

One of the tools of EU policy is the European Foundation for the Improvement of Living and Working Conditions in Ireland. The Foundation is a tripartite structure, consisting of representatives of employers' associations, the trade unions, and the member-states as well as of the European Commission. It is a scientific and consulting agency. Its Director always comes from the employers' side, whereas its Vice-Director is always a trade unionist. The Foundation has published an excellent report on CSR in 2003. The following table gives according to that study a good summary of the different approaches, used in CSR research:

Table 2

CSR: Variety of Approaches

fragmented	vs.	systematic
voluntary	vs.	regulatory
centre	vs.	periphery
pro-active	vs.	reactive

When we differentiate the first approach, we arrive at four different forms of action as shown in the following table:

Table 3

CSR: Fragmented versus Systematic Approaches

— low level of interaction

— relatively peripheral activities

— all stakeholders on certain issues

— all stakeholders connected to all aspects of activities

The main forms of CSR, depending of the direction on the initiation and the internal or external focus, are shown below:

Figure 3

CSR: Types

Direction	Internal	External
Top-down	Management	Government
Bottom-up	Trade unions	NGOs

When we relate countries or regions to this scheme, we arrive at the following classification:

Table 4

CSR: Types according to Countries and Regions

— management-driven: USA, Japan

— government-driven: Denmark

— trade union-driven: Ernilia Romagna, Greater London, Germany, Norway

— NGO-driven: Austria, Belgium, Germany, Hungary, The Netherlands, UK

Trade Unions and Consumers

Trade unions are the biggest democratic organisations in our societies, and they play a crucial role in the production process for goods and services. This process is and will always remain the centre for the power question, i.e., who decides what, where, when, for whom and when will be produced.

To be honest, the trade unions did not always escape the temptations of capitalism and corruption, just to mention the *Teamsters* in the USA, but also the scandal around the German *Neue*

Heimat, than the biggest construction company in Europe, which accumulated more than 10 billion Euro debt, for which trade union members had to pay in.

With participation in decision-making and co-determination at the heart of corporate governance trade unions in Europe have a special responsibility in this respect. However, they woke up rather late to participate in the ongoing debate on CSR. Fortunately, *Transfer* – the quarterly journal of the European Trade Union Institute – has focused on CSR in its fall issue 2004.

Trade unions developed since the end of the 19th century with their international units first forms of transnational cooperation. Since a couple of decades this dimension of transnational cooperation has been flourished more substantially. In the 1960s first initiatives of international sectoral unions, including the International Federation of Chemical Workers, started to initiate global works councils. But, the time seemed not yet ripe then, and – the two so-called oil crises helping – these institutions did not sustain. So far, the international trade unions have been very slow to catch up with the debate on CSR. An exception is the recent publication by UNI, the Union Network International, and the worldwide confederation of the national service unions. They start their analysis with the crisis of corporate governance, referring to the recent scandals. They ask for "fair shares" and "worker-friendly regulations", develop an action plan and designate themselves as "global stakeholders". But, as the World Bank reported, all this is still at the initial stage.

Actually, the unions have already been somewhat active in regard to CSR since the 1970s and 1980s, however, more on the local and regional level, in small nations like Belgium and Denmark also at the national level. One outstanding example has been the movement on socially useful goods in the UK and beyond, which is linked with the name of Mike Cooley (1986), an engineer and trade union leader with the then big arms producer Lucas Aerospace. The debate around arms conversion – which unfortunately died out with the end of the Cold War instead of really starting – had CSR in its centre (Szell, 1987, 1990).

Cooley was able to implement his ideas into the Greater London Council (GLC) in the 1980s, until Margaret Thatcher dissolved the GLC out of political reasons. The UK is the only country so far, which has since 2001 within the New Labour government a Ministry for CSR, as the pressure by NGOs has been very strong. This may be a late effect of the earlier movement for arms conversion. Other similar experiences continued elsewhere in Europe. The Emilia Romagna Region in Italy has become well known for its successful regional policies. Belgium introduced a Social Label (cf. Anne Peeters in Transfer 2004/3: 393–400). And, Denmark is another interesting case, although the focus of government policies was directed more and more only on employment issues. But I will come back to the regional and local levels, as they have become – especially with the weakening of the nation-states within the EU – more and more important for sustainable social development in the last couple of years. The European Trade Union Institute in Brussels was very active in helping to pass the directive for the constitution of European Works Councils in 1994. There are some 1,600 companies now, which fall under this regulation. But only about half of them have so far implemented the ruling. This form of industrial democracy is coined on the German experience and model of co-determination (Szell and Schlatermund, 1993). This is probably today the biggest experiment in industrial democracy on a continental level. Quite a few studies accompany it.

It seems in the meantime sometimes more successful to force companies to respect their own principles via the consumer law than via employees rights, as Andre Sobczak demonstrated in his article in Transfer 3/2004: 401–415.

Social Responsible Investment

Within a capitalist system the banks have a core function. It is not only that their representatives in two-tier governance sit in all supervisory boards, but they also exert an enormous influence on the main decisions of corporations, as these have only between 20–40 per cent, in average around 30 per cent of own capital. The rest has to be borrowed from banks. So, the banks could exert the decisive influence for the introduction of CSR. And, there are in their eyes many good reasons for doing it, as they can then better control their investment and have a long-term perspective.

In this line, since a number of years, different indexes have been developed, which reflect social responsible investment, e.g., the FTSE4Good does not include companies, which produce tobacco, nuclear energy and arms. The Dow Jones Sustainability Index has no exclusions, but functions on a 'best in class rationale' with benchmarks sector by sector. These indexes have in average a 25 per cent higher yielding than the average index. So, it seems it pays off to invest into CSR companies.

Social responsible investment has become also an issue for trade unions, as the pension funds have become the biggest investors. The Norwegian government decided to invest its oil riches only into 'ethical companies' (*Japan Times*, 21 November 2004, p. 16).

The European CSR Stakeholder Forum and Alliance

In 2003, the European Commission has established a Multi-Stakeholder Forum on CSR, which is co-ordinated by the European Foundation for the Improvement of the Living and Working Conditions – an organisation, which has been promoting since more than a quarter of a century transnational co-operation on social regulation by social dialogue, consulting and research (Krieger, 2002). The Forum worked in four round tables as under:

- Round table on improving knowledge about CSR and facilitating the exchange of experience and good practice
- Round table on fostering CSR among SMEs
- Round table on development aspects of CSR
- Round table on diversity, convergence and transparency of CSR practices and tools

The round tables worked with interesting case studies, which may be downloaded through its website. The Forum concluded its 18 months' activities with a meeting and final report in Brussels on 29 June 2004. This is an outstanding performance, as for the first time all relevant stakeholders agreed on the basic principles.

"Acknowledging that enterprises are the primary actors in CSR, the Commission has decided that it can best achieve its objectives by working more closely with European business, and therefore announces backing for the launch of a European Alliance on CSR, a concept drawn up on the basis of contributions from business active in the promotion of CSR. The Alliance is an open alliance of European enterprises, for which enterprises of all sizes are invited to express their support. It is a political umbrella for new or existing CSR initiatives by large companies, SMEs and their stakeholders. It is not a legal instrument and is not to be signed by enterprises, the

Commission or any public authority. It is a political process to increase the uptake of CSR amongst European enterprises. Backing for the new Alliance should be understood as a key component of a wider partnership that the Commission wishes to pursue with all stakeholders involved in CSR. In presenting this communication, the Commission draws on several years of public debate and consultation with all stakeholders, most particularly in the context of the European Multistakeholder Forum on CSR, which presented its final report in 2004. The Commission continues to attach utmost importance to dialogue with and between all stakeholders, and proposes to re-convene meetings of the Multistakeholder Forum at regular intervals with a view to continually reviewing progress on CSR in the EU" (EC, 2006: 1–2).

Finland

During the second half of 2006 the Finnish government took the initiative to massively promote CSR policies, and it staged a conference with the topic, 'Corporate Social Responsibility Policies-Promoting Innovation and Competitiveness' in Brussels on 22 November 2006. The successful Nokia company served as a case for best practice to be presented.

"Following the annual EU CSR conference tradition of recent years, the Finnish EU Presidency even brought together experts from government, business and civil society across Europe. This year, over 230 people participated ... Building on previous conferences, the Brussels conference focused on the links between corporate social responsibility (CSR), innovation and competitiveness. The issue of innovation was an over-arching theme of the Finnish Presidency, and reflected Finland's own commitment to the development of a knowledge-based economy. As one participant expressed it, 'knowledge and innovation were the 'beating heart' of EU growth and competitiveness'. Speakers and participants were specifically encouraged to several things. These included to identify broad CSR and related trends, both in the EU and abroad, assess their implications for EU and organisational CSR policy, use the forum to share examples of best practice, and explore dilemmas, and identify possible responses. Although the meeting was not a decision-making one, participants were encouraged to make recommendations for ways in which superior CSR performance could drive innovation and improved economic performance, and vice versa" (Finnish Presidency, 2006b: 1). In the same report the following figures are given: "European companies are leading the way: 90 out of the top 100 European companies report on social and environmental performance, while the figure is 59 per cent in the USA and 61 per cent of the rest of the world's top 100" (ibid.: 5).

Asia

In this part I will mostly treat the evolutions in regard to CSR in the three major economies within North-East Asia, i.e., China, Japan and the Republic of Korea. For evident reasons I have to neglect in this context of the Peoples Republic of Korea. And also, it would be worthwhile to treat the situation in Hongkong and Macao as well, however, it is not enough space and time to do it here.

South-East Asia comprises Singapore, the Philippines, Indonesia, Myanmar, Thailand, Brunei, Malaysia, Vietnam, Laos and Cambodia. All these countries are under strong American influence within the Association of South-East Asian Nations (ASEAN). ASEAN counts today 10 members besides China, Japan, South Korea, as well as Australia, New Zealand and India. Apparently, all these countries are too diverse to treat them here too. I will treat first the three North-East countries separately, and will compare them later in regard to convergences and differences.

Japan

Japan was the first non-European country to have started modernisation of its industries in the second half of the 19th century, by restoring its monarchy under the Meiji emperor. It was until recently the only non-western country to have succeeded to catch up and even overtake the western nations in regard to its economic, technological and industrial performances. Japan has, since several decades, remained the second strongest economy in the world. In spite of its long economic crisis since the early 1990s, it is still among the top countries in regard to its per capita income and its quality of life (cf. Human Development Index of the World Bank). Japan has for sure long time copied the most advanced countries – as did and do many more – notably Germany. This modernisation process was full of contradictions: in copying the western model, they also copied its imperialism, the exploitation of its own workforce and that of other countries. Having annexed first Taiwan in 1895 and Korea in 1910, Japan tried since 1931 to realise under its hegemony the grand area of well-being in Asia. As we know, this dream has completely failed with the total defeat on August 15, 1945.

But, similar to Germany, what Japan could not win by arms, got it through its economy: the domination of Asia and even of large parts of the world economy. However, in spite of its soft appearance – and Koreans know especially well – Japan has not become a world leader in many areas by this quality, but also by a strategy sometimes quite hard, and even arrogant. The Swiss author Friedemann Bartu described this expansionist attitude on the Asian markets in his book with the pertinent title *The Ugly Japanese*.[12]

Definitely attitudes cannot explain by themselves the success of Japanese companies on the global markets, where at the beginning they even were disdained, especially in the USA. Their success is first of all based on the quality of their products. And there we arrive very closely at the CSR versus their clients. That means to start with the use value instead of the exchange value (reversing capitalist logic in the sense of Karl Marx) – as the French author Benjamin Coriat explained so well in his "Penser a I envers: travail et organisation dans I entreprise japonaise" (1992) [Thinking the other way round]. In this regard, Toyota, the most successful company in the world, and now number one in the world, is the best example (Reingold, 1999; Toyoda, 1987). Its chief engineer, Taiichi Ohno, has also reversed another capitalist production logic: Not to put the technology in the first place, but the human being. One more time in the sense of Marx: Man is the only productive force (Ohno, 1989). Most probably, Ohno has never read Marx, however, it is striking to find out that his logic quite well with the one the German philosopher.

This phenomenon may be explained by the weak role of the shareholders. The American Michael Gerlach has analysed and very well designated this structure in his book *Alliance Capitalism* in 1992. This capitalism is based on the great economic trusts, the keiretsu, sometimes already founded in the 16th century, around a bank, and with cross-shareholdings.[13] This structure allows to plan on very long term, i.e., 20 or 30 years, and not in a short term as in the USA, i.e., for periods of 3 to 5 years maximum.

To satisfy the needs of clients in a very large sense is the primary objective of Japanese management – even before profit or market share. This quality approach is not at all recent, but goes back to centuries. The craftsmen, already in the period of the Shoguns, i.e., between the 16th and 19th centuries, have tried to realise the highest possible quality in their products. Long training was a precondition to reach this goal. This is by the way also still the case today. The big Japanese companies have still some of the best vocational training systems in the world. Total quality, zero default are therefore no miracles, but logical consequences. Japanese modernisation was built on the structures of the traditional rice producing society. It demanded a strong solidarity by the community, the le (Szell, 2001). This model has been transferred into the industrial sphere from 1920s onwards. It seems therefore to be evident that it is not possible just to copy the Japanese success recipe, neglecting the historical and cultural context. However, this success has also its weaknesses.

First, the trade unions are weak, and like in the USA are company unions. In effect, this situation is, as quite often, a historical compromise. After Second World War, to break the resistance of the unions, in majority communist or socialist, the principle of seniority (with salaries rising regularly with age), the principle of bonus (going up to six monthly salaries per year) and life-long employment (Ishikawa, 1992; Silvestre, 1992). As these principles were only valid for the regular employees, i.e., only for about 30 per cent of the workforce, this system contributed largely to relative stability of labour relations in Japan, to some of the highest incomes in the world, nearly to full employment, and absence of labour conflicts. The great losers of this system are the employees with limited des contracts and those who work with suppliers, which go down to seven levels,[14] women, immigrants (mostly illegal or Koreans), even the Brazilians of Japanese origin (Szell, 1983) and, since the crisis of the 1990s, the young ones (Pons, 2007).

Since a number of years Japan has lost the first place in record to the length of working hours of the industrialised nations to South Korea, not to forget China, and even in the USA working time is now longer than in Japan. Nevertheless, the notion of *karoshi,* meaning "death through overwork", has entered international language (Tieste, 2000). Every year more than 45,000 Japanese die due to this phenomenon. Another illness, which has had large repercussions in the whole world, is the Minamata disease, poisoning through industrial waste. Until the 1960s, Japan has been one of the most polluted countries – like China today. Tokyo Metropolitan Area remains the biggest agglomeration world wide, with more than 35 million inhabitants.

Social security was at the beginning only guaranteed by the big companies, but has become in the meantime a state affair. The problems of its financing have not yet reached the European level, however, as Japan has the most ageing population it is quickly approaching a collapse.

Another weakness concerning CSR is the gender inequality. There is definitely a strong discrimination in regard to women in the world of labour. Here, apparently, CSR is limited by the glass-ceiling (Vianello, 2000). And social rights are not very well protected either, e.g., the labour courts have just recently been introduced, following the German model. Japan has so far ratified six of the eight fundamental ILO conventions.

One more negative point concerning CSR is the widespread corruption, known under the notion of 'iron triangle'. It means the close cooperation between the LDP, the party in power since more than 50 years, nearly as a single party, and big industry as well as the bureaucracy. This system has also been named 'Japan Inc.'.

However, there is another very positive side in the picture: the social economy, which by definition has CSR as its core strategy. Japan is one of the countries with the highest number of cooperatives in the world, with still an increasing tendency. To summarise this short tour d'horizon on Japan, we have to accept that the Japanese reality is full of contradictions in regard to CSR. The American author D.M. Kenrick (1988) is going even as far in designating Japan, as the country where Communism really functions.

South Korea

The country shares its past and recent history largely with Japan and China – being situated between its greater neighbours and solicited by them. For sure, sharing the ancient culture, especially Confucianism,[15] is still relevant today, however, it seems that period of Japanese colonial rule, *de facto* from 1895 on, and *de jure* since 1910 until 1945, had more serious effects in regard to CSR.

Its modernisation followed initially the Japanese model under its control. The most striking results are the large industrial units, the *chaebols,* similar to the Japanese *keiretsu* (Shin, 2002). Some of them are now known all over the world: Samsung, Hyundai, LG etc.

The political, economic and social structure is largely influenced by the Korean war from 1950 to 1953, which resulted into the division of the country into the North and South, even today without a peace treaty, but only an armistice. Both countries have some of the biggest armies in today's world, having each of them more than 600,000 soldiers. This division served also as legitimisation (Shin, 2003) for the military dictatorship in the South between 1950 and 1987, *de facto* until 1992 – supported by the USA (which has a large military presence until today).

During this period, the forced industrialisation started and brought in 2007 the country to the eleventh rank within the world economy – with a population less than the French one. During the dictatorship, the trade unions were not allowed, the salaries were amongst the lowest and human rights non-existent (Shin, 2002). The entry of OECD in 1996 was accompanied by conditions to safeguard workers' rights and those of the unions. Social security develops slowly now, especially within the big companies, but it is far away from a decent coverage. The Ginicoefficient (measure of the degree of social inequality by revenue) remains one of the lowest within industrialised nations – largely away from the critical threshold of 0.40. South Korea counts amongst the OECD members the lowest number of foreigners – less than 1.3 per cent – the illegal apparently not included. The latter are – as everywhere else – terribly exploited and maltreated.

Production is mainly oriented towards mass production, although a move towards high-tech has been realised over the last couple of years – a similar development like Japan, but with a delay of some 20 years. The suppliers and their employees are exploited like the ones in Japan. The Asian financial crisis of 1997 has squeezed out non-performing companies and strengthened the strong ones. In this chase for international acclaim not only social rights are neglected, but also the environment. Korea has so far ratified four of the eight fundamental ILO conventions as many or as few as China.

There is, however, one very strong point: gender equality. In Korea the emancipation of women is more developed than in Japan, although Korea is certainly the most Confucianist country in the world, and in many regards still very traditional, but until recently the Prime minister has been a woman. And, women have a strong influence in a large number of companies.

To conclude, one has to state that CSR in Korea is nearly non-existent. Only 12 companies, of which the majority are foreign and the other public, take part in the Global Reporting Initiative.

China

To give an assessment of China in a few lines – a country with more than 1.3 billion inhabitants – on the topic of CSR is nearly an impossible mission. Since 2007 it has been ranked third in the world economy, having overtaken Germany. Since the reforms of Deng Xiao Ping in 1978, China has radically transformed itself and developed its potentials. With an economic growth of more than 10 per cent over the last couple of years, the end of this catching up has certainly not yet been reached. But, the statistics, by their average, hide a reality: China is a country socially and economically divided. In effect, the coastal areas as well as some new economic centres in the interior like Qngqong or Wuhan, inhabiting 40 per cent of the population, concentrate the large chunk of all activity. In those regions, the growth rates are sometimes around 30 per cent; in some sectors, as real estate or the automobile, it is even more than 40 per cent.

The provinces, which have up to 100 million habitants, are given considerable autonomy, but we should not forget that the country is still dominated by an authoritarian, with *de facto* one-party rule, and strong industrial and economic policies on the national level. The state owned enterprises (SOEs) play even today, thirty years after the beginning of the reforms, quite an important role in the national economy with some 30 per cent of the GDP and notably in the key sectors. They should by definition be socially responsible, although in reality it is quite different, as has been the case in the really existing socialist countries. The basic structure of these SOEs is the *danwei*, the production unit, which guarantees the well-being of all employees from birth to the grave (Li, 1993). But CSR did not extend neither to the customers – nearly at the contrary, if you look for the quality of the products or the services – nor the suppliers, not to speak of the environment.[16] Through privatisation of a large number of the public enterprises, dozens of millions of workers have been made redundant or remained formally members of their *danwei*, however, without being paid, at least keeping their lodging. Through the absence of unemployment benefits and social security[17] etc., the state has not taken over the CSR companies, which had closed down or had been privatised (He, 2003; Wang, 2004; Szell, 2004). In this process of internationalisation and modernisation, all started with the joint ventures (JV) – often together with SOE (Szell, 2002). These enterprises – like also the private companies – are subject of direct political control. They all have their party secretary, which have the position of a co-director – sometimes even the director is the party secretary. These secretaries should, in principle, safeguard a certain CSR. However, incompetence and corruption[18] do not allow an efficient control. Besides, there are no real free trade unions with bargaining power and right to strike. The All China Confederation of Trade Unions has some 60 million members, which makes it the biggest in the world, however, the remainder in the Leninist jargon 'transmission belts' of the CCP. It is the weakness of the Chinese unions it that a growing number of wildcat strikes develop: more than 90.000 have been counted in 2006.

In this context, the migrant workers are the greatest losers in regard to the non-CSR. Estimates go as far as 250 million of them within a working population of about 800 million. They are workers from the countryside, who abandon their home, looking for some employment in the city centres. However, there is no social security for them or any other rights or protection, because they are illegal. The freedom of movement does not yet exist in China. The citizen is still fixed to his *hukou*, the place, where s/he is registered.[19]

Human rights are neither respected by the state nor by most enterprises. However, China has in the meantime signed four of the eight fundamental ILO conventions. Therefore, it is not surprising to learn that the debate about CSR is just beginning. Practically, no Chinese company takes part at the GR1. Nevertheless, there is hope: a part of the political and economic establishment has understood that the ongoing development is not sustainable, and that the quality of life, or even the life of their own children is at risk. Enlightened managers and bureaucrats have formed, together with intellectuals and scientists, associations to promote CSR (cf., e.g., http://www.syntao.com/E_index.asp). And, more and more courses are taught on CSR in universities, which expresses not only a growing sensibilisation of academics but of the public at large.[20]

Convergences and the Future of CSR in East Asia

CSR has become a weapon in economic warfare, as has been underlined by the then American under secretary for democracy, human rights and labour, Lane Croner, during a conference on 18 June 2002. The irony is that it is just the USA, which has so far signed just only two of the eight fundamental ILO conventions, whereas the EU has signed all of them.

What is in common? The three countries, viz., Japan, South Korea and Japan, have been winners of globalisation so far. Together they possess nearly one quarter of the world population and produce about the same part of the world GDP. They have accumulated the biggest currency reserves in the world, and realise growth rates largely above the average – although they are in different phases of their development.

All three have already organised Olympic Games. Japan was the first Asian country to do so in Tokyo in 1964, followed by South Korea with Seoul in 1988; and in 2008, by China, in Beijing. Today, the organisation of Olympics is a demonstration to show the world that a country has successfully moved itself to the top level. But it is also the occasion to take responsibility – not only towards the hosts, but also in regard to its own population.[21] In 1964, Tokyo was probably one of the most polluted big cities in the world – as it is Beijing today, and Seoul was in 1988. Beijing has promised to celebrate the greenest Olympic Games in their history, and started to clean the environment at its best. So, the three Olympic Games in Asia were all the starting point for more ecological consideration and even in some respect of human rights. At least for South Korea it was a turning point for more democracy in the country.

Even if Confucianism may be considered as the basic Weltanschauung, there exist considerable differences (Lee, 2002). Besides, Confucianism is not without contradictions in its relationship to CSR. For sure it propagates the responsibility of the superiors towards their subordinates, of the elder towards the younger, of men towards women, however, there is a strict hierarchy, which does not give the same rights to everyone. Korea remains the country with the most Confucianist society in the world, followed by China and Japan. To summarise, the following table is proposed to make an assessment of the performances of the three countries in different domains of CSR:

Table 5

Different Dimensions of CSR in North-East Asia

Dimensions	*Japan*	*South Korea*	*China*
Shareholder	+	–	–/+
The state/community	–	–	+/–
Political parties	–	0	–
Employers	0	–	–
Trade unions	–	–	–
Employment	+	+	–
Salaries	+	–	–
Gender	–	0	+
Suppliers	–	–	–
Customers	+	–	–
ILO fundamental conventions	+	0	0
Non-discrimination of foreigners	–	–	–
Environment	0	–	–
Social security	0	-	–
Gini-coefficient	+	+	–
Non-corruption	–	–	–
Total	–2	–9	–11

Japan comes out as the winner in this comparison, although with a negative total. This may be explained by different factors. First of all, business ethics are still often based on the one of the samurai – the *bushido*. And, then, a business structure in the form of alliance capitalism, where a disloyal competition is prevented. The role of shareholders is therefore reduced, limiting the power of shareholder value. This weakness and a certain political regulation make it that the other stakeholders have some influence on decision-making. The result is a certain quality of life (Human Development Index) and of working life – amongst others the highest life – expectancy in the world.

South Korean capitalism cannot be understood without its historical context – as any other social phenomenon. The destruction of its traditional society by Japanese colonialism, which wanted to assimilate the Koreans, and its recent history of division and military dictatorship, allowed the appearance of a rather crude capitalism without much CSR. That may explain the relatively poor performance in regard to CSR in Korea.

China is the last in this comparison. In China, as well, traditional society, which transported certain values of responsibility, was as well destroyed by colonial interventions of the western forces in the 19th and 20th centuries, and later by the Kuomintang dictatorship, Japanese intervention and finally by Maoism. The brutal Manchester-type capitalism today is, however, partially regulated by political forces, which co-manage the SOB and also private companies and joint ventures. All this reminds of the theory of regulation, which insists on the embeddedness of economic structures, including CSR into their historical, cultural and social context (Hollingsworth et al. 1997).

Conclusions

There are many activities in regard to CSR going on. Besides unions and NGOs thousands of leading companies are involved together with the main global organisations like the UN with their sub-organisations such as ILO, UNCTAD, UNIDO, UNEP, UNRISD, the World Bank, and the OECD, the EU and many others – however, not the International Monetary Fund (IMF). So, it seems that CSR is more than just a fad, a public relations activity for many companies, governments and social actors worldwide and especially in Europe. Although it is for sure that there is still a long way to go to fully implement it. As CSR has now a history of more than 15 years, the conservative, market-radical critiques seem to be more and more marginalised. However, some of the critique I am sharing: CSR demands both transnational co-operation and social regulation. Voluntarily followed guidelines are not sufficient in the long run. They are a good beginning; however, they have to be made sustainable – not to be an object of the ups and downs of the economy and the markets, and changing leaderships as well as political majorities. They have to be transformed into corporate accountability. CSR is best exercised by co-management and co-determination; otherwise it remains a paternalistic, but not a democratic, responsibility. This leads directly to the issue of participation and economic democracy (Kester and Pinaud, 1996; Lammers and Szell, 1989; Szell, 1988, 1992, 2002).

CSR in the words of some protagonists is a question of survival of capitalism. Marc Benioff and Karen Southwick plead for a "compassionate capitalism".[22] Much clearer are the words of Sir Geoffrey Chandler, the Shell CEO, who was responsible for its much lauded first General Business Principles in 1976: "Doing right because it is right, not because it pays, needs to be the foundation of business, with principle, not profit the point of departure. There does have to be a choice about priorities … . If we are to preserve the most effective mechanism the world has known for the provision of goods and services – that is the market economy with the public limited company its main instrument – then it has to be underpinned by principle. Financial failures can destroy individual companies. Moral failure will destroy capitalism" (cited in Nelson, 2004: 10). Is this then neo-capitalism? However, for the more critical CSR proponents, CSR is at best a step forward into the direction of a post-capitalist society.

But it is clear that the dominant shareholder-value principle, which actually means shareholder dictatorship, is in sharp contrast to stakeholder democracy. Democracy is always more difficult to practise than an authoritarian rule. It takes long negotiations and at the end the outcome should be a win-win situation. But for a functioning economic and social democracy we need two fundamental elements as under:

1. consciousness, and
2. competence (Szell, Blyton and Cornforth, 1989).

Until the German co-determination started to really function, it needed about 30 years, i.e., a whole generation (KiBler, 1989). During this period thousands of elected works council members and members of the Aufsichtsrat (supervisory board in a listed company) were trained during extra-legal educational leave.[23]

It is interesting to note that the British – who in general refuse all kind of regulation – tend to regulate by law the duties of directors of companies. But it depends on the management perspective and strategy to decide what is in the best interest of a company. In a shareholder perspective, three months' economic results are the time frame. Hedge funds calculate on a time horizon for their investment of three, maximum five years. However, most investments, including those in human capital, are only profitable on a time horizon of 20–30 years. Taking into account the environment and the community, this latter is the only responsible way to act for a corporation.

Notes

1. This reminds us strangely of the slogans for the economic reforms by the late Deng Xia-ping in 1978.
2. One-third of MBA programmes in Europe already offer CSR modules, and 12 per cent have dedicated CSR programmes (Survey Teaching and Research in Europe on CSR, International Centre for Corporate Social Responsibility/European Academy of Business in Society, cited in Christian Aid, 2004: 8).
3. It was again reformed in 2005 under the so-called red-green government of Chancellor, Gerhard Schorder. Under the pressure of globalisation, the codetermination law shall be reformed anew. A commission under the chairperson, Biedenkopf, who already chaired the first codetermination law commission 35 years ago.
4. The chairman of the administrative board is elected by shareholders only.
5. The same, by the way, holds true also for German universities.
6. Unfortunately, Japanese companies in general – except for Mitsubishi – refuse until now to take their responsibility for the period from 1931 to 1945, or even including the colonial period in Taiwan and Korea.
7. The second biggest media-conglomerate in the world and Europe's biggest.
8. Cited after Christian Aid (2004: 8).
9. The American Economic Nobel Prize winner, James Tobin, proposed some 25 years ago a tax on all capital transfers to be invested in the Third World. So, at least it would have some social benefits. The introduction would definitely be a form of trans-national co-operation on social regulation (Cf. for on overview on the ongoing debate *http://www.ceedweb.orp/iiro/*).
10. But for sure also the trade unions are in a crisis. The one may be linked to the other.
11. In the Anglo-Saxon countries, the promotion of industrial democracy was substantially supported by the European Foundation for the Improvement for Living and Working Conditions in Dublin over the last quarter of the century. One of the outstanding projects was the EPOC project on Employees' Participation (Krieger, 2002).
12. Following after a similar book a couple of years earlier, *The Ugly American* by William Lederer and Eugene Burdick.

13. After the Second World War the US-Americans tried to bring down these structures – like in Germany structures – however, in vain.
14. Only about 30 per cent of the whole production is realised within the mother companies that means that the remaining 70 per cent are done by the suppliers. The Japanese were the first to accomplish on a large scale what is known now as outsourcing, even into developing of virtual enterprises. This is their strength within the international competition, combining quality at reasonable prices, i.e., the best quality/price relationship. It is this system which allowed them together with Germany, even during the crises years, to be world champions in regard to trade surplus.
15. These ways of philosophical, moral, political and to a lesser degree religious thinking have influenced China, Japan, Korea and Vietnam.
16. Five of the most polluted cities in the world are Chinese.
17. China is at the 189th place among 191 countries in this respect according to the statistics of the World Health Organisation.
18. China has started to fight this millenary disease in progressing in 2008 to 70th rank from last year's 82nd place among 164 countries, according to Transparency International, *http://www.transparency.de/tabellarisches-Ranking. 954.0.html*
19. The most dynamic centres are in the South of the country, like Shenzen or Guangdong, where growth rates of 1.5 per cent create already a problem of shortage of labour because many internal migrants are not ready any more to accept the conditions of exploitation, which are still widespread. So the local communities, which consisted of 80 of largely illegal migrant workers from the countryside, started to offer them the right of residence, which includes also bringing in their families, health coverage, schooling for their children, etc.
20. The author of this article is invited regularly since more than six years to lecture on this subject at the most prestigious Chinese universities like Tsinghua, Renmin, Beijing, Tongji, Wuhan, Yunda, etc.
21. These lines are written in July 2008, so just a couple of weeks before the beginning of the Peking-Games. The unrest in Tibet and the riots around the tour of the Olympic flame have shown that the authoritarian regime in China is not fully up to its own expectations and the expectations of the world.

22. This sounds very near to George W. Bush's 2000 election campaign slogan "compassionate conservatism".
23. They had legal rights of three weeks per year, in the first year after election even four weeks.

References

Bartu, Friedemann (1993) *The Ugly Japanese: Nippon's Economic Empire in Asia*, Tokyo, Yenbooks.

Bé, Dominique (2004) *Corporate Social Responsibility*, Commission of the European Communities, Brussels, *http://www.eujapan.com/japan/presentation_BE.pdf*

—— (2006) *EU CSR Strategy Origins*, Asia Invest Project, Brussels, 29 May.

Braudel, Fernand (1979) *Civilisation matérielle, économie at capitalisme, XVe-XVIIe siécle*, Paris: Armand Colin.

Briefs, Ulrich (1989) "Co-determination in the Federal Republic of Germany: An Appraisal of a Secular Experience", in György Széll et al. (eds.), *The State, Trade Unions and Self-Management: Issues of Competence and Control*, Berlin/New York: Walter de Gruyter, pp. 63–74.

Busch, Klaus et al. (eds.) (2000) *Ways to Social Peace in Europe*, Osnabrück: Secolo.

Christian Aid (21 January 2004) *Behind the Mask: The Real Face of Corporate Social Responsibility*, *www.christianaid.org.uk/indepth/0401csr/index.htm*

Commission of the European Communities, DG Employment and Social Affairs (2002) *Corporate Social Responsibility: A Business Contribution to Sustainable Development*, Brussels, COM (2002) 347 final. *http://www.Europa.eu.int/comm/employment_social/soc-dial/csr_index.htm*

Commission of the European Communities [COM (2005) 12] *Strategic Objectives 2005–2009. Europe 2010: A Partnership for European Renewal. Prosperity, Solidarity and Security*, Brussels.

Commission of the European Communities [COM (2005) 24] *Communication to the Spring European Council – Working Together for Growth and Jobs. A New Start for the Lisbon Strategy. Communication from President Barroso in Agreement with Vice-President Verheugen*. Brussels [02.02.2005]. DG Employment, Social

Affairs and Equal Opportunities: CSR IN ENGLARGED EUROPE. 20 February 2006, Brussels (press release).

Commission of the European Communities, DG Employment and Social Affairs (2001) *Promoting a European Framework for Corporate Social Responsibility*. Green Paper. Brussels. *http://www.Europa.eu.int/comm/employment_social/soc-dial/csr/csr_index.htm*

Commission of the European Communities, DG Employment and Social Affairs (2003) *Mapping Instruments for CSR*, Brussels.

Commission of the European Communities, DG Employment and Social Affairs (2004): *ABC of CSR Instruments*, Brussels.

Commission of the European Communities, DG Employment, Social Affairs and Equal Opportunities, Unit D2: European Employment Strategy; Corporate Social Responsibility; Local Development (2006): CSR – *National Public Policies in the European Union*, Brussels.

Commission of the European Communities: Communication from the Commission to the European Parliament, the Council and the European Economic and Social Committee: Implementing the Partnership for Growth and Jobs: Making Europe a Pole of Excellence on Corporate Social Responsibility, Brussels, 22.3.2006, COM (2006) 136 final.

Commission urges greater Corporate Social Responsibility in Europe'. Press release 2001.

Cooley, Mike (1980) *Architect or Bee?: The Human Technology Relationship*, Slough: Langley Technical Services.

Coriat, Benjamin (1992) *Penser à l'envers: travail et organisation dans l'entreprise japonaise*, Paris: Bourgois.

Corporate Social Responsibility and Environmental Management. Review edited by Wiley since 1994 (4 volumes/year).

Croner, Lane, *Promoting Corporate Social Responsibility Abroad: The Human Rights and Democracy Perspective*, Remarks at the 2002 Surrey Memorial Lecture, National Policy Association, Washington, DC, June 18. *http://www.state.gov.g/drl/rls/rm/11405.htm*

Dongfang, Han (ed.) (1996) *Menschenrechte, Arbeitsverhältnisse und Gewerkschaften in China – internationale Perspektive*, Universitat Bremen.

Eli, Max (1990) *Japan Inc.*, New York: McGraw-Hill.

Emery, Fred E. and Einar Thorsrud (1976) *Democracy at Work*, Leiden: Martinus Nijhoff.

—— (in co-operation with Eric Trist) (1969) *Form and Content in Industrial Democracy: Some Experiences from Norway and Other European Countries*, London: Tavistock and Assen: Van Gorcum.

Ennals, Richard (ed.) (2000) *Work Life 2000 – Yearbook 2000*, London: Springer.

Finnish EU Presidency Conference: *Corporate Social Responsibility Policies: Promoting Innovation and Competitiveness*, Brussels, 22 November 2006a http://www.csr2006.fi

Finnish EU Presidency Conference: *Corporate Social Responsibility Policies: Promoting Innovation and Competitiveness*, Brussels, 22 November 2006b, Informal Synthesis Report.

Fritz Naphtali (ed.) (1928) *Wirtschaftsdemokratie. Ihr Wesen, Weg und Ziel*, Berlin, Köln: Bund-Vlg., 1984.

Geffken, Rolf (2006) *Labour and Trade Unions in China*, Brussels: ETUI-REHS.

Gerlach, Michael L. (1992) *Alliance Capitalism: The Social Organization of Japanese Business*, Berkeley: University of California Press.

Global Reporting Initiative, *http://www.globalreporting.org*

Gustavsen, Bjørn (1979) "Liberation of Work and the Role of Social Research", in T. Burns et al. (eds.), *Work and Power*, London: SAGE, pp. 341–356.

—— (1986) "Social Research as Participative Dialogue", in F. Heller (ed.), *The Use and Abuse of Social Science*, London: SAGE, pp. 143–156.

Hask, René (2004) *Theory and Management of Collective Strategies in International Business: The Impact of Globalization on Japanese-German Business Collaboration in Asia*, Basingstoke: Palgrave.

Hayashi, Shuji (1988) *Culture and Management in Japan*, Tokyo: University of Tokyo Press.

He, Faping (2003) *Strucktur und Funktionsweise des chinesischen Arbeitsmarkets – Der Gestaltungsprozess des Arbeitsmarktes unter dem wirtschaftlich-sozialen Strukturwandel in der VR China seit 1978*, Frankfurt: Peter Lang.

Hollingsworth, Joel Rogers and Robert Boyer (1997) *Contemporary Capitalism: The Embeddedness of Institutions*, New York: Cambridge University Press.

Hwang, B.D. (1989) *Nachholende Industrialisierung und autoritärer Staat. Das Beispiel Südkorea: Politik, Ideologie und weltmarktorientierter Kapitalismus*, Berlin.

Industrial Democracy in Europe (IDE) International Research Group (1981a) *Industrial Democracy in Europe*, London: Oxford University Press.

Industrial Democracy in Europe (IDE) International Research Group (1981b) *European Industrial Relations*, London: Oxford University Press.

Institute of Social Sciences (1994) *Market Economy and Social Justice*, Tokyo: Chuo University Press.

International Institute for Sustainable Development/IISD (n.d.): *ISO CSR Standards, http://www.iisd.ord/standards/csr.asp*

Ishikawa, Akihiro (1992) "Japan", in György Széll, *Concise Encyclopaedia of Participation and Co-Management*, Berlin/New York: Walter de Gruyter, pp. 454–460.

Ishikawa, Akihiro, Roderick Martin, Witold Morawski and Veljko Rus (eds.) (2000) *Workers, Firms and Unions, Part 2: The Development of Dual Commitment*, Frankfurt: Peter Lang.

Junji, Banno (ed.) (1997) *The Political Economy of Japanese Societies, Vol. I, The State or the Market?* Oxford: Oxford University Press.

Kawasaki, Yoshimoto and Shigeto Sonoda (eds.) (2000) *Globalization in East Asia: Past and Present*, Tokyo: Chuo University.

Kenrick, D.M. (1988) *Where Communism Works: The Success of Competitive Communism in Japan*, Rutland and Tokyo: C.E. Tuttle.

Kester, Gerard and Edward Zammit (1992) "Malta", in György Széll (ed.), *Concise Encyclopaedia of Participation and Co-Management*, Berlin/New York: Walter de Gruyter, pp. 506–512.

Kester, Gérard and H. Pinaud (eds.) (1996), *Trade Unions and Democratic Participation in Europe: A Scenario for the 21st Century*, Aldershot: Avebury.

KiBler, Leo (1989) "Codetermination Research in the Federal Republic of Germany: A Review", in Cornelis Lammers and György Széll (eds.), *International Handbook of Participation in Organizations, Vol. I, Organizational Democracy: Taking Stock*, Oxford: Oxford University Press, pp. 74–90.

Krieger, Hubert (2002) "The European Foundation for the Improvement of Living and Working Conditions", in György Széll and Gian Primo Cella (eds.), *The Injustice at Work: An International View on the World of Labour and Society*, Frankfurt/Bern/New York: Peter Lang, pp. 172–194.

Laaksonen, Oiva (1988) *Management in China during and after Mao in Enterprises, Government and Party*, Berlin/New York: Walter de Gruyter.

LAI, Qi (2006) *Corporate Social Responsibility of SMEs in China: Challenges and Outlooks*, Bremen: Universität and Hochschule [Berichte des Arbeitsbereichs Chinaforschung Nr. 18; http://www/iwim.uni-bremen.de/publikationen/pdf/c018.pdf].

Lammers, Cornelis J. and György Széll (eds.) (1989) *International Handbook of Participation in Organizations, Vol. I, Organisational Democracy: Taking Stock*, Oxford: Oxford University Press.

Lang, Nikolus S. (1998) *Intercultural Management in China: Strategies of Sino-European and Sino-Japanese Joint Ventures*, Wiesbaden: Deutscher Universitätsverlag.

Lederer, William J. and Eugene Burdick (1958) *The Ugly American*, New York: W.W. Norton.

Lee, Eun-Jeung (2002) *Konfuzianismus und Kapitalismus. Markt und Herrschaft in Ostasien*, Mänster: Westfälisches Dampfboot.

Legewie, Jochen and Hendrik Meyer-Ohle (2001) *Corporate Strategies for Southeast Asia after the Crisis: A Comparison of Multinational Firms from Japan and Europe*, London: Palgrave Macmillan.

Li, H.L. (1993) "Das Danwei-Phänomen und die chinesische Modernisierung", in Peter Atteslander (ed.), *Kulturelle Eigenentwicklung*, Frankfurt, New York: Campus.

Martin, Roderick, Akihiro Ishikawa, Csaba Makó and Francesco Consoli (1998) *Workers, Firms and Unions: Industrial Relations in Transition*, Frankfurt: Peter Lang.

Marx, Karl (1969) *Das Kapital*, Berlin: Dietz Verlag, 3 vols. (MEW 23–25).

Meadows, Donella et al. (1972) *The Limits of Growth: Club of Rome*, Harvard: MIT Press.

Moon, Woosik (2004) Globalization and Social Challenges: The Case of Korea, paper prepared for the international conference 'In Search of a Humanized Globalization', held on 28–30 April in Nagoya, Japan.

Morita, Akita (1987) *Made in Japan*, Hammersmith, London: Fontana Press.

Nippon Keidanren Committee on Management and Labor Policy (2003) "Summary of Position Paper 2004 on Management and Human Resources. Creating Higher Added Value, Utilizing Diverse Human Resources: Employers Sense of Duty and Aspirations are the Key", Tokyo.

OECD (2003) *Voluntary Approaches for Environmental Policy: Effectiveness, Efficiency and Usage in Policy Mixes*, Paris: OECD Publications.

Ohno, Taiichi (1989) *L'esprit Toyota*, Paris: Masson.

Pearlstein, Steven (2004) "Easy Laws + Tax Dodges = Zero Corporate Tax", in *Japan Times*, 13 April [originally Washington Post].

Pons, Philippe (2007) "Le Japon, l'île des enfants perdus", *Le Monde*, 10 août 3.

Quintin, Odile (2004) Activities of the European Commission on Corporate Social Responsibility: Address to the Japanese Business Federation, Tokyo, 9 February *http://europa.eu.int/comm/employhment_social/speeches/2004/oq090204_en.pdf*

Qvale, Thoralf U. (1992) "Scandinavia: Direct Participation", in G. Széll (ed.), *Concise Encyclopaedia of Participation and Co-Management*, Berlin/New York: Walter de Gruyter, pp. 708–14.

Reingold, E. (1999) *Toyota: People, Ideas and the Challenge of the New*, London: Penguin Books.

Ryder, Guy (2003) "The Social Responsibilities of Business and Workers' Rights", in *Labour Education # 130*, special topic 'Corporate Social Responsibility: Myth or Reality?', pp. 21–24.

Sakiya, T. (1987) *Honda Motor: The Men, the Management, the Machines*, Tokyo and New York: Kodansha International.

Sandberg, Åke (1992) "Sweden", in György Széll (ed.), *Concise Encyclopaedia of Participation and Co-Management*, Berlin/New York: Walter de Gruyter, pp. 842–48.

Sandberg, Åke (ed.) (1995) *Enriching Production: Perspectives on Volvo's Uddevalla Plant as an Alternative to Lean Production*, Aldershot: Avebury.

Schienstock, Gerd, Paul Thompson and Franz Traxler (eds.) (1997) *Industrial Relations between Command and Market: A Comparative Analysis of Eastern Europe and China*, New York: Nova Science Publishers.

Shin, Jin-Wook (2003) *Modernisierung und Zivilgesellschaft in Südkorea. Zur Dynamik von Gewalt und Heiligkeit in der modernen Politik*, Wiesbaden: Deutscher Universitätsverlag.

Shin, Kwan-Yeong (1996) *Characteristics of the East Asian Economic System: Authoritarian Capitalism and the Developmental State*, Aalborg University, Denmark: The Research Center for Development and International Relations, Working Paper # 52.

—— (2002) *Droits humains et valeurs asiatiques: un dialogue possible?* Adhérent: Bruylant-Academia, pp. 187–200.

—— (2007) The Economic Crisis and the Neo-liberal Globalization: Democratization, Globalization and Casualization in Korea, paper presented at the Korean Sociological Association Conference 'Diversity and Dynamics of Globalisation: Socio-economic Models in the Global Capitalism', Seoul, 14 September.

Silvestre, Jean-Jacques (1992) *Le systéme d'emploi dans les grandes entreprises japonaises. Mise en perspective avec la France et la RFA*, Aix-en-Provence: CNRS/LEST.

Soros, George (1998) *The Crisis of Global Capitalism: The Open Society Endangered*, New York: Public Affairs.

Széll, György (2005b) "Corporate Social Responsibility in the Age of Globalisation", *The Review of Business Administration Soka Keiei Ronshu*, Vol. 29, No. 3, Tokyo, March, pp. 17–32.

—— (2000) "Developing Competitiveness and Social Justice: The Interplay between Institutions and Social Partners", in Debi S. Saini and Sami A. Khan (eds.), *Human Resource Management: Challenges in the New Era*, London: Sage, pp. 270–79.

—— (2002b) "Fifteen Challenges for a European Social Model", in G. Széll and Gian Primo Cella (eds.), *The Injustice at Work: An International View on the World of Labour and Society*, Frankfurt/Bern/New York: Peter Lang, pp. 588–606.

—— (2002) "Japanese Joint Ventures in China: Some Preliminary Findings of a Research Project", in Ulrich Teichler and Gisela Trommsdorff (eds.), *Challenges of the 21st Century in Japan and Germany*, Lengerich: Pabst Science Publishers, pp. 215–28.

—— (2005a) "Labour and Social Issues in the Enlarged European Union", in *1st EU Institute in Japan Conference at the ICU on 10 January 2005*, Vol. 29, No. 3, Tokyo: ICU, pp. 143–52.

—— (2007) "Labour Market Policies and Currencies in an Integrating Europe", in Eiji Ogawa (ed.), *The EU Economy*, Tôkyô: Keizô [in Japanese].

—— (1995) "Le siécle de l'entreprise?", in M. Legrand, J.F. Guillaume and D. Vrancken (eds.), *La sociologie et ses métiers*, Paris: L'Harmattan, pp. 121–28.

—— (1990) "Möglichkeiten partizipatorischer Konversion auf der Basis der Mitbestimmung", in L. Köllner and B.J. Huck (eds.), *Abrüstung und Konversion: Politische Voraussetzungen und wirtschaftliche Folgen in der Bundesrepublik*, Frankfurt/New York: Campus, pp. 491–510.

—— (1998) *Participation, Workers' Control and Self-Management: Trend Report and Bibliography*, London: Sage, Current Sociology 36 # 3.

—— (2002a/2004) "Sociology and Industrial Democracy", in Nikolai Genov (ed.), *Advances in Sociological Knowledge*, Paris: International Social Science Council and Opladen: Westdeutscher Verlag, pp. 396–418.

—— (2001) "To Learn from Japan?", in György Széll (ed.), *European Labour Relations*, Vol. 2, Aldershot: Gower, pp. 191–205.

—— (2004) *Transnational Co-operation on Social Regulation in 10th Euro-Asia Research Conference on Corporate Social Responsibility*, Yokohoma: National University of Yokohama, 28–29 May [CD ROM].

—— (2003) "Workplace, Democracy and Alienation: A Modern Drama until now in Three Acts with a Prologue", in Heinz Sünker, Russell Farnen and György Széll (eds.), *Political Socialisation, Participation and Education: Change of the Epoch*, Frankfurt: Peter Lang, pp. 35–42.

Széll, György (ed.) (2004) *China and the WTO: Effects on Employment, Labour Relations, Intercultural Management and Economic Welfare*, Osnabrück: University of Osnabrück, aepi.

—— (1992) *Concise Encyclopaedia of Participation and Co-Management*, Berlin/New York: Walter de Gruyter (Studies in Organization 38).

—— (2006) *Corporate Social Responsibility in the EU and Japan*, Frankfurt: Peter Lang (Vol. 1 of the series *Labour, Education and Society*).

—— (2001) *European Labour Relations*, Aldershot: Gower, 2 vols.

—— (1987) *Rüstungskonversion und Alternativproducktion*, Hamburg and Berlin (West): Argument-Verlag.

Széll, György and Heiko Schlatermund (eds.) (1993) *Arbeitsorientierte Wissenschaft und Forschung in den Neunziger Jahren in Europa: Labour Oriented Science and Research in Europe in the Nineties*, Osnabrück: Secolo.

Széll, György and Ken'ichi Tominaga (eds.) (2004) *Environmental Challenges for Japan and Germany: Interdisciplinary and Intercultural Perspectives*, Frankfurt: Peter Lang.

Széll, György, Blyton, Paul and Chris Cornforth (eds.) (1989) *The State, Trade Unions and Self-Management: Issues of Competence and Control*, Berlin/New York: Walter de Gruyter.

Széll, György, Carl-Heinrich Bösling and Johannes Hartkemeyer (eds.) (2005) *Labour, Globalisation and the New Economy*, Frankfurt: Peter Lang.

Széll, György, Compte rendu de 'J.H. Galjaard: A Technology Based Nation; Kamata Satoshi: Japon: l'envers du miracle; Reveue Française de Gestion (# 27/28, 1980): Le Japon, mode ou modèle?', *Autogestions*, # 14/1983: 120–122.

Széll, György, CSR in the EU + East Asia 33 Tairako, Tomonaga, Die Modernisierung Japans und 'Die Modifikation der Tradition. Kritik an Tominagas, Modernisierungstheorie', *Mesotes* # 3/1992: 295–311.

Takashi, Y. et al. (eds.) (1998), *Management Strategies of Multinational Corporations in Asian Markets*, Tokyo: Chuo University Press.

The Council of the European Union: Resolution of the Employment and Social Policy Council on CSR, Brussels, 2–3 December 2002.

The Economist (2004) "Corporate Social Responsibility: Two-faced Capitalism", 22 January.

Tieste, Oliver (2000) *Karôshi, ein japanisches Phänomen? Ursachen und rechtliche Hintergründe betreffend den Tod am Arbeitsplatz. Eine rechtsvergleichende Studie*, Frankfurt: Peter Lang Verlag/Europäischer Verlag der Wissenschaften.

Toyoda, E. (1987) *Fifty Years in Motion*, Tokyo: Kodansha International.

Toyota (1990) *Production at Toyota: Our Basic Philosophy*, Tokyo.

Transfer (2004) Corporate Social Responsibility: A Threat or an Opportunity for the Trade. Union Movement in Europe? Autumn, Vol. 10, No. 3.

Uemura, Hiroyasu, A. Ebizuka and A. Isogai (1997) 'L'hypothèse de la relation hiérarchisée marché-firme et l'économie japonaise de l'aprés guerre: une analyse en termes d' incitation et de flexibilité', *Année de la regulation*, pp. 297–315.

van Kemende, W. (1997) *China AG Maos Utopie and die Macht des Markets*, Munich.

Vianello, Mino (2000) *Gendering Elites: Economic and Political Leadership in 27 Industrialised Societies*, New York: Palgrave Macmillan.

Wang, Weihua (2004) *Das System der chinesischen Basiskrankenversicherung: Eine Betrachtung und Analyse des*

Systems und der Steuerungsmöglichkeiten aus der Sicht der Verfügungsrechte, Frankfurt: Peter Lang.

Womack, James P., Daniel T. Jones and Daniel Ross (1991) *The Machine that Changed the World: How Japan's Secret Weapon in the Global Auto Wars will Revolutionize Western Industry*, New York: Harper Collins.

Yuan, X.W. (1999) *Industrielle Beziehungen Chinas am Scheideweg: Der wirtschaftlich-soziale Strukturwandel und das Besispiel von VW Shanghai*, Frankfurt: Peter Lang.

9

Modernity and Culture

Some Reflections

Jugendra Sahai

Never before has the fate of mankind been so precariously balanced. Its destiny seems intimately bound up with the questions of whether and how it can cope with accelerating scientific advance and channel its potential away from human self-destruction towards socially useful ends. The problems posed by science and technology had, therefore, best be seen as a challenge to the socio-cultural framework of society in the form of requiring us to understand their cultural significance and to create the social conditions in which their misuse – which seems to be programmed into our political order – can be avoided.

Such a task would necessitate learning processes in the sphere of the inter-subjective determination of ends and purposes in line with the steady increase in instrumental knowledge. That the latter should have come to outstrip public control can be seen as symptomatic of the atrophy of modernity which is being hastened by the encroachment of scientific rationality upon the communicative determination of a meaningful social existence.

It appears that sociology has, on the whole, not only failed to counteract this development, but has also itself been instrumental in the demise of communicative rationality. It has largely failed to enlighten us about ourselves through widening our horizon to the point at which something qualitatively better, a more adequate way of organising society, could have come into view. Instead it remains content with mirroring conditions in which individuals are fragmented both within and between themselves. It can be argued that the tendency within sociology towards the gathering of instrumentally useful knowledge and away from the generation of practically relevant insight relates to the trained inability to take account of the dimensions operative in the study of social phenomena and the reluctance on the part of sociologists to engage in self-reflection.

The above scenario takes us to a new mode of understanding and explaining social reality, a new synthesis of conservatism and radicalism. Neo-conservatism as a philosophy has its roots in American academicians. Among these academicians, Daniel Bell and S.M. Lipset are the pioneers. Bell certainly ranks higher among these sociologists who have had a substantial interest in the analysis of culture in general and the connection between capitalism and culture in particular. Jurgen Habermas yet is another sociologist who also takes into account culture as a fact and goal to understand modernity. He explores the meaning and significance of modernity as a cultural variant. The objective of this small piece is to examine the views of Bell and Habermas with reference to modernity and culture.

Habermas' defense of modernity as a viable cultural goal starts from the point of view of Weber's 'Entzauberung', or the disenchantment of the world. From Weber's point of view culture has lost its ability to legitimate the statues quo while it has also lost its will to social change. This is due to the world historic process of rationalisation. Rationalisation has come to mean the use of means-end rationality – a purposive rationality – in all spheres of human conduct and inquiry. Indeed by a distortion of Weber's concerns about purposive rationality in relation to value rationality, rationality as such has come to be seen as purposive rationality. In a further distortion culture has been constructed to be the cause, or at least the scapegoat for the crisis of our time.

From the point of view of the present, the deepening worldwide economic and political crisis is said to have its origins in the decline of that culture that made capitalism as enviable economic system. This economic system is said to have been guided by sense of purpose – a sense of rationality that had its roots in the protestant ethic. The crisis of capitalism today can be found in the demise of the replacement of the protestant ethic with a culture of consumerism.

Bell's analysis of modern capitalism begins from these premises. In short, for him, the analysis of capitalism is neither an economic analysis, nor a class analysis. Instead, he places the failure of capitalism in the failure of the culture that used to and should guide capitalism. Bell's analysis of culture hinges on the distinction between modern culture and a more conservative older culture. Put differently, Bell equates all that is excessive in our culture with the notion of modernity. For Bell, anti-modernity is rampant. It manifests capitalism, post-industrialism, back to basics and the beliefs of the moral majority. In so far as we can identify diverse interests under the mainly political label of postmodernism, neo-conservatism, as an ideology of anti-modernity, has penetrated society, that is, political, economic, educational, religious, and even cultural institutions. By way of milder thesis, we can say that the culture and institutions that reflected and espoused liberal or conservative ideologies have been transformed into a neo-conservative ideology.

Collectively post-industrialism Bell professes allegiance to capitalist economics to conservatism in culture, to religion and the nuclear family as protector of culture and to culture as a source of contemporary discontent of individuals and the general malaise.

Habermas, following earlier propounders of the Critical Theory Tradition, who were always interested in the critique of culture, would agree with postmodernists that contemporary culture and society are in a mess. However, critical theorists and postmodernist differ sharply about the causes and cures and most importantly about the sociological theory and methodology most appropriate to cultural, social and economic analysis that would lead to culture, social and economic renewal.

While the postmodernists see the causes of social crisis and moral breakdown in the cultural systems, Habermas and critical theorists see the causes of breakdown in the capitalist economic system. Postmodernists prescribe a cure for the general social malaise in the form of the re-institutionalisation of religious fundamentalism and cultural asceticism via an intellectual neo-conservative elite to the revival of laissez-faire capitalist economics. Habermas speaks of social, political, cultural and economic emancipation and the achievement of what Aristotle has called the 'good life' based on social norms that reflect system of value meaning and knowing while we worked out collectively and aim at the transformation and elimination of capitalist, technists economics – be it in the form of the capitalism or bureaucratic socialism.

Habermas' sociological analysis starts from the point of view of philosophical anthropology that accounts for knowledge as an expression of interests, where both are coupled to culture understood as imaginative expression, creation and experience on the one hand and understood as interaction of social institutions, on the other. Knowledge and interests are tied to social evolutionary imperatives of work language and family, which in turn are connected, by way of knowledge projects that 'objective' work language and family and by way of critique and extension, to the culture in which they had origin.

Bell's critique of modern culture lies for example in *The Cultural Contradictions of Capitalism* (1976): "... what I find striking today is the radical dysfunction between the social structure (the techno-economic order) and the culture." For Bell, modernism in the form of counter-culture has infiltrated the everyday life of citizens, robbing them of motivation to moderation and restraint that was once attached to the protestant ethic and puritan temper upon which successful capitalism – as an aspect of social structure – had been built. According to Bell, the loss of the protestant ethic and the puritan temper is one of the roots of the crisis of capitalism as a social system because this loss unleashed a trend towards self-actualisation, guided by the ideology of entitlements. Religion in general, the protestant ethic as Weber had analysed it and puritan metaphysics are pushed aside to make room for hedonism of many sorts.

Bell does not distinguish sufficiently, between culture, which is the totality of symbolic and material institutions within which individuals and collectivities live while shaping the structure and content of that same culture, and the institutions through which culture manifests itself. By way of clarification it can be said that when culture moves into the past it becomes traditions and when it explores the future, it becomes the avant-garde. Bell argues on the priority of culture but not in the way he means it. Yet, culture and culture alone legitimates society and all the other institutions are sub-systems of culture; they never bequeath an essence to social existence. Elsewhere, however, Bell invokes religion, particularly the protestant ethic and puritan temper to provide a transcendental set of ultimate meaning. To distinguish legitimation of society is not to be confused with the legitimation of the economy where the latter is extracted from the culture. In psychological terms culture, and not society, is legitimated by way of mechanisms that assure happiness. Social structure ... the array of institutions in which Bell has used the term ... and the economy are legitimated by way of mechanisms that are meant to assure success. Bell seeks the salvation of capitalism in religion because culture has become one huge dark canvas of modernism. That this is counterfactual need to be addressed. But what needs to be addressed is the individual and collective meaning of modernism.

A Critical Theory of Modernity

Habermas sees modernity as the expression of an epoch that sets itself against antiquity while it sees itself as a result of the transition from the ancient to the modern. Modernity is a process and projects more than a product.

For Habermas it is only culture that can legitimate a social order. And central to the problem of legitimation is the spontaneousness of a culture. We may say that culture in this restricted sense must appear, particularly like nature. An explanation by analogy may help. Legitimation functions in culture somewhat like friendship among individuals. Friendship works themselves out, so to speak slowly, mostly without conscious direction, without will and certainly without design. For Bell, religion carries out this function of legitimation, but religion for him is not one of many institutions. It is primary and prior to culture. We always need to start our analysis from the point of view that religion is a contingent upon culture as is the economy and that they interact dialectically in any social formation. Habermas puts it that reason should be able to create its own normatively out of itself through self-reflection. He inaugurates a philosophical discourse on modernity or try to create a universal language into which all languages describing modernity the life of enlighten reason ... could be unified. A firm belief – in the infallibility of reason and efficacy of social services to improve the lot of humanity – has been the faith of Habermas. He poses a basic issue of a cultural heir to the enlightenment of modernism and the avant-garde of a progressive modernity and reactionary postmodernity. He affirms the modern refusal of the 'normative' but warns against 'false negation' and at the same time he denounces (neo-conservative) anti-modernism as reactionary. Opposed to both revolt and reaction, he calls for a critical reappropriation of the modern project.

Concluding Remarks

Bells' structural-functional analysis lies at the root of the dichotomy of culture and social structure. It is as if culture satisfies both the functional pole and social structure pole in this perspective. The social consequences of this sociological perspective are as follows: Bell sees need for rationalisation in the one; he is against it in the other. Modern economics and bureaucracies that are expressions of social structure are modern because they are rational. At the level of sociological theory, Bells' dichotomy of culture and social structure is untenable and confusing.

Habermas' assertion that 'Modernity is Dead but Dominant' (in one of his public lectures at Frankfurt) reflects his position. For him modernity is going to stay as it is an incomplete project. According to him, it is only culture that can legitimate a social order and central to the problem of the legitimation is the spontaneousness of a culture.

The weakness with western sociologists and thinkers has been to tailor their institutions according to the needs and demands of modernity. Now to overcome this crisis in social structure their approach lies in reorienting institutions.

References

Bell, Daniel, 1973, *The Coming of Post-Industrial Society*, New York: Basic Books.

Coser, Lewis A. and Irving Howe (eds.), 1976, *The New Conservatives (Revised edition)*, New York: Meridian Books.

——, 1976, *The Central Contradictions of Capitalism*, New York: Basic Books.

Habermas, J., 1990, *The Philosophical Discourse of Modernity*, Cambridge: Polity Press.

Nisbet, Robert A., 1966, *The Sociological Tradition*, New York: Basic Books.

Steinfels, Peter, 1979, *The Neoconservatives*, New York: Simon and Schuster.

10

Research, Education and Training in Social Sciences and Humanities

Some Issues and Policy Concerns

Rajeshwar Prasad

In may be well recognised that without proper education and training research has hardly any significance. And again, for excellent teaching and training, research is not only a necessary element but it may of course be auxiliary in these cases.

Secondly, I do not propose to either review the process of education, training and research or attempt any evaluation of standards of education (including training and research) in the areas of humanities and social sciences in the country in this paper instead. I only propose to raise certain issues that indicate the policy concerns. It is perhaps not possible due to the huge education enterprise obtaining in India and due also to the fact that it entails an investigation by another commission.

I may honesty submit that being educated and trained in social sciences in an educational milieu which is trichotomised into science, social sciences and humanities, in the country, I am only partly competent to speak about social sciences. Humanities is not my cup of tea but since it is an essential component of any educational enterprise, at all levels in any society, I would certainly like to make

---

This paper has been taken from *IASSI Quarterly*, Vol. 23, No. 3 with formal permission.

brief comments in this respect more particularly at the foundation or school level that may point to some policy concerns.

Crisis in the Humanities

J.H. Plumb edited a book *Crisis in the Humanities* (1964). In its introduction Plumb writes: "A hundred fifty even twenty years ago, a tradition of culture, based on the classics or scriptures on History and Literature, bound the governing classes together and projected the image of a gentleman. It was a curious mixture of humanistic principles and a national pride … . These subjects – History, Classic, Literature and Divinity – were with mathematics the core of the educational system and were believed to have peculiar virtues in producing politicians, civil servants, imperial administrators and legislators" (p. 7). According to Plumb, traditional culture was based on the classics, scriptures, divinity, etc., that projected the image of a gentleman and bred civil servants, legislators, politicians, etc., but the common man was out of its pale. The folk culture or the cultural element of the toiling masses was perhaps not the concern of humanities. And, it was not true of only the UK or the other western world; in other traditional societies too it was equally true. For example, in India, the classical language – Sanskrit and for that matter the classics, the divinity, the holy scriptures – were restricted to only the higher varnas, especially the Brahman and the Kshatriya, and thus the humanities did not touch the large chunk of our population. The traditional ancient education, as also the feudal/imperial education, encompassed only a smaller chunk of the privileged castes/classes of the Indian population. This amply clarifies the role of humanities in producing gentlemen.

Plumb's observations that the rising tide of scientific and industrial societies, combined with the battering of two world wars, has shattered the confidence of humanists in their capacity to lead or instruct, is indeed true. Uncertain of their social function, their practitioners have taken refuge in two desperate courses – both suicidal. Either they blindly cling to their traditional attitudes and pretend that their function is what it was and that all will be well so long as change is repelled, or they retreat into their own private professional world and deny any social function to their subject. And so the humanities are at the crossroads, at a crisis in their existence: they must either change the image that they present, adapt themselves to the need of a society dominated by science and technology, or retreat into social triviality. Thus arises the crucial problem facing the humanities – History, Classics, English, Fine Arts, Divinity, Philosophy … (ibid.: 7–8). The response to change by any society is too slow and feeble that corresponding changes in other established institutions, e.g., education, are hardly visible. It took a fairly long time for the educational system in the West to adapt to the changes brought about by the revolution in science and technology. Humanities in this march have lagged sufficiently behind. The story is not very different in other societies the world over including India.

Yet another setback to the positions and prestige of humanities has occurred due to the contemporary processes of liberalisation, privatisation and globalisation (LPG) which have boosted commercialisation and bolstered consumerist culture the world over. It has thus overtaken sophistication, social/moral valuation, humanism and refined citizenship, which were at one time the hallmarks of a gentleman. The rise of umpteen professions, due to science, technology, international trade, commerce, industry and business, gave an impetus to subjects/disciplines, other than humanities. These new disciplines have a dominance over old traditional subjects of study.

The metropolitan-urban, the imitational-capitalist, the multinational-industrial and the global-elite orientations have given birth to subjects like Management, International Trade, Information Technology, e-Commerce, etc., pushing aside Classics, Fine Arts, History, Literature, Divinity and Philosophy.

And, the knowledge which was at one time contained in Natural Philosophy and Moral/Social Philosophy, first got divided into Science and Liberal Arts, and then into sciences, humanities and social sciences. In fact, in the humanities are grouped such subjects of study which are literary, related to culture, devoted to human interest, and classics and scriptures. As argued earlier, with the change in human interest, people inclinations, community's culture and economic devaluation of scriptures, classic philosophy, etc., the humanities got relegated to obscurity. The key objective of any education, particularly higher education, in the contemporary context, is professional/occupational placement of the educated, economic security of the individual, higher earnings and ensured employment of the educated masses. The humanities in the changed context failed to fulfil these objectives. But, at the school level, the humanities are still functional in one way or the other. At the level of higher education, the humanities are in search of a new role, supplementing the new emerging areas of study at the universities, colleges and other technical and professional institutions. Let us first examine the place of humanities at the school level.

Ian Lister in 'The Teaching of the Humanities in the Schools' said: "So far the part to be played by the humanities in the schools has been seen from a point of view of looking outwards from their own position; it is even more important to access it in general perspective of the debate concerning the patterns of education in the schools and more particularly in its relationship to the problems of specialisation, and that polarization between the humanities and science which C.P. Snow has said is a sheer loss to us all as people, and to our society" (in Plumb, ed., 1964: 162). Lister has pointed to these important problems in relation to the humanities in the school: (i) pattern of education in schools (in UK the public and grammar school systems also indicate to differential patterns of education); (ii) problem of specialisation; and (iii) polarisation between the humanities, and sciences (and now between humanities, social sciences and science). These problems, it may be noted, are not merely restricted to the school-level education but extend to the higher level too, which we shall discuss latter.

Lister further comments about specialisation: "Many writers have alluded to our distinctive propensity of specialization and the peculiarly English problem of specialization in the schools, shortage of university places, and the resulting competition, as one of the great causes of premature specialization and university expansion and the easing of the fierce competition for places would greatly reduce the difficulties of the schools. This problem of specialization is faced not only by public schools and grammar schools but our whole system is permeated by the specialist idea. It has even challenged some of the secondary modern schools, which were set up to provide a good all round secondary education, not focused primarily on the traditional subjects of the school curriculum but developing out the interests of children" (ibid.). It is expected that the expansion of the university education and easing of competition in the system will act as correctives in the situation of premature specialisation but this is yet to be corroborated by new facts. However, the polarisation between humanities and science has now encompassed social sciences, as the third pole, in the school education system. This polarisation is responsible for truncated education of young pupils.

A world of caution in respect to specialisation: "Some schools have ignored the deeper contributions that religion, the Classics,

Literature, and History can make to education. Other schools, fearing that their scholarship results will decline in a highly selective educational system whose ultimate achievement is to reject almost everyone, have introduced programmes of non-specialist work, which are more decorative than effective" (Lister, ibid.: 165). It may indeed be quite difficult to compare the situation obtaining in the UK with the Indian school education system but one may notice that non-specialist subjects, viz., social service, project work, etc., introduced in 1986 by the new education policy in India, are only decorative. Vocationalisation at the school level, so vehemently recommended by the Education Commission, has been violently flagellated.

Apart from the colonial system of school education, the *Sanskrit Pathashalas* and *Arabic Madarsas* are still functioning in the country. From montessory, kindergarten to *tat-pattis* pre-primary schools, from suburb play group to so-called "public" schools – all cater to the educational needs of the tribal, rural and urban children in India. At the primary, post-primary, middle and secondary educational levels, there are different types and varieties of schools in the country. From big church-sponsored schools to secular state educational institutions to privately-run 'education shops', there are innumerable centres which impart 'education' to the children of the growing population. Innumerable commissions and committees, especially after the independence of India, have looked into the education enterprise – its quantity, quality and quagmire – in the country from time to time. But even today, on the one hand, we have building-less schools, single-teacher schools, pupil-less schools, and on the other hand there are coming up air-conditioned schools transporting their students in air-conditioned buses, and catering lunch, etc., that being done by five-star air-conditioned hotels. This has resulted in a flagrant violation of our National Policy on Education (1968) that aimed "to promote national progress, a sense of common citizenship and culture, and to strengthen national integration. This depressing development in education in the country also infringes from the egalitarianism as enshrined in the New Educational Policy of 1986 that laid down that the concept of a national system of education implies that, up to a given level, all students, irrespective of caste, creed, location or sex, have access to education of a comparable quality. To achieve this, the government will initiate appropriately funded programmes. Effective measures will be taken in the direction of the common school system recommended in the 1968 policy. Not only that the objectives of the National Education Policy are unfulfilled but the different education systems, as described above, have created dangerous hierarchies in Indian society.

In the existing differential educational scenario it is a shame to talk of any improvement in the existing educational efforts or to discuss about either the role or quality of school education, more particularly about the education of humanities or social sciences, and for that matter even that of science, in the majority of our schools. Yet, it may be relevant here to once again refer to the National Education Policy, 1968 that had envisaged a common educational structure – 10+2+3 – which has been accepted by all the states. However, the 1986 policy had stipulated a further break-up of the first 10 years, to move towards a quality elementary education, into five years of primary education, three years of upper primary, followed by two years of high school level of education. In spite of the fact that it has now been stabilised, no uniformity in the syllabi and/or standards of teaching and learning has been accomplished yet. This could not perhaps be achieved due to the fact that there are more than 18 major State Boards of School Education apart from the CBSE, ICSE, NIOS and a few universities that prescribe course and conduct examinations at the 10th and intermediate levels of education, and innumerable other agencies – governmental, quasi-governmental and others – that regulate pre-primary, primary and middle level education.

The existence of this plethora of curriculum setting and examining bodies belies the pious pronouncements made in the NEP, 1986: "The National System of Education will be based on a national curricular framework which contains a common core along with other components that are flexible. The common core will include the history of India's freedom movement, the constitutional obligations and other content essential to nurture national identity. These elements will cut across subject areas and will be designed to promote values such as India's common cultural heritage, egalitarianism, democracy and secularism, equality of sexes, protection of the environment, removal of social barriers, and observation of the small family norm and inculcation of the scientific temper. All educational programmes will be carried on in strict conformity with secular value." These objectives, largely normative, highly value-loaded, needed political will, mass awareness and above all a strong base of humanities and social sciences in educational curriculum at different levels. It is imperative to mention here that both the policy documents of 1968 and 1986 give emphasis to science and technology education and the reference to humanities is peripheral.

A brief comment on history teaching may be apt here. In the recent controversies in regard to the books on humanities and social sciences produced by the National Council of Educational Research and Training (NCERT) the books on the subject of history have evoked wider criticism. In the UK the scholars are trying to free history from Anglo-centric, Euro-centric and Christian-centric influence whereas in India an attempt was made to make history Hindu-centric. Not only history but other subjects in the humanities are also soft targets of politically enthusiastic scholars and need careful treatment at the hands of experts, especially at the school level.

I may end this discussion on the place of humanities at the school level by quoting Lister once again that points to future policy concerns: "Basically, we must appreciate that the nineteenth century classification of knowledge is not always appropriate to our own day, and we must see the dangers of projecting those divisions of learning – necessary at a higher level of scholarship and research – down to the lower levels in the schools, where they often become artificial, obsolete and harmful. We must realize the limitations of an educational system in which we tend to abstract out of life instead of contracting into it. We must acknowledge that the very liberty, flexibility and variety of the educational structure have ensured that experiments should be limited and isolated, and have often encouraged tribalism in educational organizations and staunch conservatism in educational practice. We must postulate that we live in an industrial, scientific society: and that the aim of teaching the humanities in schools should be not only to develop people as individual but also to help us to understand and improve the world in which we live" (in Plumb, ed., 1964: 165).

In India, it is important to recognise that humanities are an important aid and tool for higher learning. Languages, Philosophy and Logic are important to comprehend theories and conduct research. Hence, the need to strengthen education of humanities not only at the school level but also at the university/college level of education is an urgent one.

Education at the University Level: Humanities and Social Sciences

In India, the university/college education was patterned on the British model but with increased interaction with American universities, it has deep imprints of US higher education. But it may be recognised that both in the humanities and social sciences there are no effective links between the school educational system and higher educational enterprises in the colleges and universities. This link is further disjointed due to the liberalisation and unfettered privatisation in the educational sector. The problems however are similar both at the school and higher levels of education.

Seriously reflecting on the division of knowledge into separate compartments and the skewed development of social sciences, Immanuel Wallerstein et al., in the report of the Gulbenkian Commission of the Restructuring of the Social Sciences, observed: "The idea that we can reflect intelligently on the nature of humans, their relations with each other and with spiritual forces, and the social structures that they have created and within which they live is at least as old as recorded history. The received religious texts discuss these matters, as do the texts we call philosophical. And, there is the oral wisdom that has been passed on through the ages, and often put into written form at one point or another. No doubt, much of this wisdom was the result of culling inductively from the fullness of experienced human life in one or another part of the world over a long period of time, even if the results were presented in the from of a revelation of a national deduction from some inherent eternal truths ... what we today call social sciences is a heir to this wisdom. It is, however, a distant heir, and perhaps often an ungrateful and un-acknowledging heir, for social science consciously defined itself as the search for truths that went beyond such received or deduced wisdom, social science is an enterprise of the modern world" (1996: 1). The industrial revolution, the rise of science and technology, and the complexity of social and other social forces, had resulted in this division of knowledge. The emergence of new occupations, new professions and new social concerns has further accentuated this artificial division.

While discussing the artificial division and consequent specialisation (also polarisation) in different branches of knowledge at the school level of education, we have dilated on its effects on the pupils and society. The Gulbenkian Commission Report averred: "By the beginning of the nineteenth century, the division of knowledge into two domains had lost the sense of these being 'separate but equal' spheres and took on the favours of a hierarchy, at least in the eyes of natural scientists – knowledge that was certain (science) versus knowledge that was imagined, even imaginary (what was not science)" (ibid.: 5). This is important to understand the debate which is still quite fierce in the domain of social sciences in relation to 'empiricism' which, the natural scientists believe, leads to the objective understanding of reality. For a proper understanding of this new perspective of 'objectivity' one should first understand that the division of knowledge that was divided into two worlds, the worlds of science and social sciences, sciences claiming definitive, objective, verifiable and universal truths and the other part being dubbed as speculative, subjective and stoical, was in itself subjective and vulgar. In other words, the resultant knowledge based on physical facts constituted sciences and those based on social facts were called social sciences. The Gulbenkian Commission Report further stated that thus, between 1850 and 1945, a series of disciplines came to be defined as constituting an arena of knowledge to which the name 'social sciences' was accorded. This was done by establishing in the principal universities first chairs, then departments offering courses leading to degrees in the discipline. The institutionalisation of training was accompanied by the institutionalisation of research: the creation of journals specialised in each of the disciplines; the construction of associations of scholars along disciplinary lines (first national, then international); the creation of library collections catalogued by disciplines" (ibid.: 30). In spite of this entire establishment at the university level, 'sciences' commanded more prestige in the changed social context and in the hierarchy 'social sciences' occupied a lower status. And, the whole exercise of adopting the science model: of organising social science disciplines, insisting on 'objectivity' in studying social phenomena and persisting 'scientism' in the outlook of social scientists may be understood within this web of dichotomy and/or tracheotomy of knowledge. But there also exists another dominant trend of non-empiricism (and anti-empiricism), in social sciences, which rejects the very idea of objective and certainty; for most scholars of this stream science is a pseudo-knowledge. With fragmented knowledge through tracheotomy we cannot understand the 'whole reality'. Not only that we find the division of knowledge in two worlds but there also grew umpteen disciplines in science and social sciences: "The creation of the multiple disciplines of social sciences was part of the general nineteenth century attempt to secure and advance' objective knowledge about' reality' on the basis of empirical findings (as opposed to 'speculation'). The intent was to 'learn' the truth, not invent or intuit it" (ibid.: 13). The non-empiricists have forcefully reputed the claims of sciences to be able to comprehend 'reality' and that too 'objectively'. Even the staunch empiricists after realising the limitations of empirical methods to understand the most volatile social phenomena revert to non-empirical approaches. The observations of Paul Abrecht in this regard may further clarify the situation: "I was raised in the tradition of a strictly empirical approach to the social science, with an emphasis upon fact-finding and upon neutrality with respect to human values. But the more I have reflected upon that approach, the more I have come to feel that a fundamental self-deception is involved in it. And, I have not seen a very effective challenge to those traditional approaches" (1968: 81). Without going into the nuances of the controversy I would only indicate its futility. For, more important is to examine the very merit of the division of knowledge that has created innumerable problems in regard to the holistic comprehension of the phenomenon or total reality. The scenario has vastly changed from what it was in the nineteenth or early twentieth century. "Today, the discovery of common themes and approaches seems to be occurring on different bases than in the past. Natural scientists are talking of the arrow of time, which is what has always been central to the more humanistic wing of the social sciences. At the same time, literary scholars are talking of 'theory'. However, hermeneutic such theorising is and however hostile it proclaims itself to master narratives, theorising is not what literary scholars used to do. No doubt, this is not the kind of theory that has always been central to the work of the more scientific wing of the social sciences .... What is clear is that the tripartite division between the natural sciences, the social sciences, and the humanities is no longer as self-evident as it once seemed. It also seems that the social sciences are no longer a poor relative somehow torn between that two polarised clans of the natural sciences and the humanities; rather they have become the locus of their potential reconciliation" (ibid.: 68–69).

In the discussion on humanities we have dilated on the artificial specialties that need to be removed for the sake of a proper understanding of the social milieu. It equally holds true of social sciences. Not only is the polarisation but also the fragmentation of knowledge into specialisations that began, again in the nineteenth century, no more functional. About economics, which is considered more 'scientific' today, as compared to other sister social science disciplines, and to whom J.R. Sargent (1964) calls as "The Would-be May-be Science", was not a distinct discipline at one point of time. "However, only in the nineteenth century do we begin to find a discipline called economics, sometimes within the faculty of law, but often within the faculty (sometimes ex-faculty) of philosophy" (Wellerstein et al., op. cit.: 17), and today, economics itself has got divided into many 'super-specialties' – welfare economics, labour economics, micro-economics, macro-economics, business economics, managerial economics, etc., with volumes of research and professionalised activities having little concern for human betterment. Super-specialties sometimes lead to vulgar conclusions. Radhakamal Mukerjee (1960) concluded: "Equally significant for the philosophy of social sciences is the cognate conception of the multi-dimensional character of social environment, relations and values. It is this philosophical notion, which can bring about a unity of the social sciences on the one hand, and the widening of treatment of the social universe with its metaphysical laws, postulates, norms and values on the other … . Man is today divided in his mind, loyalties and ways of living because psychology, Economic, Sociology, Political Science, Law, Ethics and Religion, all interpret human motives and actions in different ways and refuse to see man, society and the way of human living as integrated wholes. In fact, the crisis in modern culture is largely the outcome of the segregation of different aspects of life, and disciplines concerned with them".

Ramakrishna Mukherjee (2004), in this context, only recently averred that by the expression, "social science … we mean that it is one organized body of knowledge for understanding society and, therefore, there is one discipline This emphasis on primary relevance of interrelationship among the social science subjects is dictated to by the fact that their union on the principal axis denoted by culture, economy and polity is such that one of the three axial ingredients cannot operate without an equal operative power of the other two, unless we conceive of society to be fissiparous and moving toward oblivion. Therefore, the social science subjects may not be regarded as just systematically related (or for interdisciplinary explorations): instead, they should be regarded as related symbiotically, in order to appraise and mould social reality in a wholesome and durable manner But without unity of all these specialties on a generic axis denoting the mechanics of society, i.e., of its static of in being at points of time in the past and at the present moment, and of he dynamics of the same society in becoming (i.e., moving forward) in the future social reality becomes obfuscated, diffused and, finally, distorted and destructive for the society in view." So, it is evident that instead of creating specialties and super-specialties, there is a need to integrate, and get the holistic view of man, culture and society. So, perhaps, the emergent issues to critically look into are the polarisation of knowledge and artificial specialisation of subjects/disciplines in our education system in the universities and colleges.

I have earlier referred to the hybrid nature of our education having the British traditional organisation of our universities and American imprints on the educational system. The lack of effective links between the school and university education, the permeation of 'specialisations' in the domain of studies at the high school and intermediate levels (10+2 levels) and the general neglect of humanities and social sciences at the foundation stage of education have not only created a general crisis of sound academic socialisation of pupils but also a kind of vacuum thus damaging the goal of personality development. This may be attributed to the hybrid nature of our educational system and our incapacity to evolve an indigenous system suitable to our own needs. The traditional Indian educational system was composite and holistic, with effective links between the different rungs. Even with the existing specialisations (in social sciences and humanities), we need to seriously examine as to whether their continuation from standard 10 to the Master's levels has any relevance both in terms of enforcing a knowledge base on the learners as well as on the understanding of social reality holistically. I plead for progressive enforcement of disciplinary knowledge from eighth standard to the twelfth, and at the Bachelor's level, one may specialise in specific subjects/disciplines (Economics, Sociology, Political Science, etc.) with related subjects as minor courses, or there may be introduced a five-year course in social science(s) after 10+2 level. However, at the Master's level, without an integrated social science course, with adequate grounding in theory, methodology, philosophy, logic and techniques of dissemination, objectives of higher research and goal of application of social sciences for social development may not be fully accomplished. I am conscious of the fact that it needs a major policy shift, and in the present context where the universities are autonomous and steeped in stagnation, the decision in this regard may be rather impossible. But a beginning may be made at the level of University Grants Commission and the Association of Indian Universities.

Yet another issue facing social sciences are the way it is taught in schools as well as at institutions of higher learning. The manner in which social sciences are taught is not only monotonous but also irrelevant and non-innovative. Yogesh Atal, as far back as 1976, observed: "It is rather sad that social science teaching in universities and colleges (schools included in India) is, by and large, still carried out on traditional lines. The disciplinary boundaries are jealously guarded and the syllabi offered to the students are characterised by an annoying degree of constancy rather than by needed innovativeness … . Very little of India is introduced, and fewer if any, Indian references are cited. It is this feature which has been described as 'academic colonialism', roots of which are much deeper" (1976: 42). There are innumerable causes for this morass but it may be apt to briefly refer to a few of these factors so as to clinch the future policy options.

Let us now take the issue of irrelevance of social sciences: the excellent centres of teaching and research in social sciences teach concepts, theories and other material which is hardly relevant to the Indian situations. I have been putting this question to fellow social scientists as to why very little knowledge based on the Indian context has been generated in social sciences. One cannot point to any theoretical construct by any Indian social scientist which may have been internationally established and accepted. C.T. Kurien has succinctly remarked: "Our knowledge about the problems of our own societies is largely bookish, and the books that we read are mainly from the West. We are rather like the beggar that Rabindranath Tagore wrote … We are beggars, all of us-we sneak under many an academic table to gather the crumbs under them. And we mix these bits and make a hash which we pretend to relish but one we can hardly digest" (1968: 17).

The new awakening in Asian societies has shaken the social scientist of hue. It is now realised that the values so trusted by the western social science model have not only been dysfunctional but detrimental to local societies. A.C. Espiritu forcefully argued: "It is now becoming increasingly evident that the validity of such (Western) social sciences, uncritically trained to think in western terms through the medium of western language, some are experiencing a reawakening to the reality of their situation … . Asian intellectuals are undergoing and agonising period of soul-searching. Their system of values, developed through years of training in, and broad exposure to, Western philosophies, is being shattered by a realization that these values may not be suitable to the Asian environment" (1968: 35). Espiritu points to a very delicate aspect of 'reawakening' of the social scientists in most countries of Asia that creates distaste for western concepts, theories, methods and philosophies and consequently motivates them to search for alternatives that may be locally relevant, suitable and widely acceptable. In this search, the uncritical mind may turn to obscure, fundamental and obsolete concepts. For, after all, all the western concepts, etc., have been accepted by the 'uncritical indigenous intellectuals', and the possibilities of a total about-turn on progress, modernity, development, democracy, secularisation and concomitant processes of equality, social justice and fraternity, is quite possible. When we say western, we refer to the 'imperial' and 'Christian' origin of social science so dominantly steeped in 'Asian psyche'. The observations of Von Leeuwen may further clarify the situation: "... social sciences, in their best manifestations, are products of the Western Christian Secularization Process, and therefore they must come into conflict with all traditional, 'sacral' structures of life ... I think this (Western bias) is one of our most – difficult problems, because in a sense a kind of western cultural imperialism inevitably creeps in through the ideological bias of social sciences, and we have not been very successful in discovering the exact nature of that bias. There is no doubt in my mind that the secularization, in the special way in which it is usually defined in reference to the social sciences, is a good thing, and can be defended as such from Christian perspective. But the real meaning of that fact in terms of Asian traditional and Asian social values seems to me to remain very much an open question" (1968: 78–79). I may only add that the Asian Christian is 'Asians' and the 'Christian perspective' of Asian Christians may not be homologous to Western Christians and thus 'Christian perspective' as such may not be homogeneous. This apart, Leeuwen's observations in regard to the creeping in of the western cultural imperialism through the 'ideological biases' of social sciences, need immediate attention of the Asian intellectuals.

Parochialism of social sciences poses another potential threat to its claims to universalism; this threat is equally there in the sciences, but in social sciences it is more real and vociferously raised by many affected groups. The Gulbenkian Commission has rightly observed that "the late 1960's was initially, and perhaps most fundamentally, a challenge to its claim to represent universalism. Tile critics argue that it was in fact parochial. This critique was made by feminists challenging a masculinist orientation, by the various groups challenging Euro-centrism, and later by multiple other groups raising questions about still other biases that they saw as built into the premises of the social sciences" (op. cit.: 53–54). Earlier, in the context of history (and for that matter some other disciplines of humanities also) we have talked about freeing these disciplines from Anglo-centrism, Euro-centrism and Christian-centrism; it is equally true for social sciences which need to be freed from the above shackles as also from gender biases predominantly male. In India, social sciences for long neglected the poor, weaker, deprived, marginalised and socially and culturally ostracised groups from its serious studies, analyses, discussions and policy actions. To be universal, social sciences may have to change its perspective and orientation, particularly in the Asian societies. The movement to free social sciences from biases in India has been heralded by Marxist, Dalit and feminist scholars and the hopes of relevant changes are rightly expressed by social analysts.

I am inclined to specifically mention the damage done to both humanities and social sciences by the modern process of privatisation in the field of education, both at the levels of schools and universities. The higher educational institutions in the wake of diminishing state financial support are opening courses in management, computer application, technology, bio-technology, emerging branches of engineering, multimedia and information sciences, e-commerce, business economies, etc., which offer job opportunities to the graduates. In the process there is decreased enrolment not only in the humanities and social sciences but the transitional science disciplines too have suffered greatly. This has largely affected the educational complex and the quality of learners. The schools too are now concentrating more on science, commerce and on other applied education which has meant an increased infrastructure, highly increased fee and other costs for the students. The poor-class learner is thus pushed out of the access circle of education. More and more youngsters are thrown out of the educational enterprises creating a host of other social problems in the country.

Training and Research in Social Sciences

I am not keen to touch upon the aspects of training in greater detail for the simple reason that I am not associated with it in any serious manner. However, I may briefly mention that both humanities and social sciences have a crucial role in training a variety of personnel needed by society. For research too, in any discipline, training constitutes an important component. Education, training and research are thus interconnected and complementary.

Training may be essential to not only prepare persons for certain occupations, professions, etc., but also upgrading skills for better performance of people. There are established training institutions to train and mould civil administrators, police personnel, judicial officers, army and defense personnel, etc. To name a few of these institutions, Lal Bahadur Shastri Academy of Administration, Mussoorie, Sardar Vallabh Bhai Patel Police Academy, Hyderabad, National Defence Academy, Pune, etc., are very important. There are other institutions which provide in-service training, viz., Indian Institute of Public Administration, Administrative Staff College, National Institute of Social Defence, National Institute of Criminology and Forensic Sciences, National Institute of Rural Development, National Institute of Banking, etc. For the academia there are Academic Staff Colleges established in some of the universities in the country to train university teachers. All these institutions impart training of some or the other sort, to train persons to do specific jobs skilfully and efficiently. But, all the training institutions necessarily depend on humanities, especially language, and inputs of social sciences, apart from the specialties related to their own job, occupation or profession. Economics, sociology, social work, criminology and anthropology are important components of most of the training modules. Similarly, history, political science, public administration, law, etc., find an important place in the curriculum of most important training curricula for administrators, police personnel and judicial officers.

The stakeholders in training of personal are the central/state government, employers in industry, trade and commerce, professional technical educational institutions, e.g., medical colleges, engineering and technology institutions, agricultural colleges, etc., and the universities. In the western professional/technical institutions both humanities and social sciences occupy a place of prominence in the training programmes. In India, the situation is not very encouraging. For this the humanists and social scientists, particularly those working in the universities, are to be blamed. First, they have not been able to recast their specialties not only to suit but also to become a necessity for any training basket. And, secondly, they have failed to spearhead a movement to get humanities and social sciences accepted as essential components of any training project and programme. For, we do not need socially ignorant, culturally deprivated and humanly deficient professionals; instead we need sufficiently aware, moderately humane, socially conscious citizens as administrators and professionals, hence, the importance of humanities and social sciences in training enterprises.

Researches again are highly technical and advanced professional persons not only in academics but in other areas of societal operations like law and order, defence, industrial production, trade, commerce, banking, etc. So far, in India, research is perceived as an activity confined only to the academia. The diversified research operations in umpteen fields of human activity in fact need rigorous training. We need to examine it seriously and reorient our research training and operations accordingly.

Currently, research may be broadly classified into two main categories. First, university/college research which is carried on by individual scholars largely aiming at the university degrees. There is also project-research carried out by an individual/group of scholars in college and universities, but this area is still not very strong like the US, Canadian and other western universities. Secondly, research being conducted in research institutes in the area of social sciences. Such researches are carried out in approximately 27 research institutions established/supported by the Indian Council of Social Science Research (ICSSR). Thirdly, research being conducted in other establishments both government and voluntary. The purpose, objectives, goals and functions of these different types of social science research vary. But one thing which may be noticed is that not only the interest orientations of researches working in these varied organisations widely differ but their mode of functioning too greatly vary. Besides, the research outcomes of most researches in these sectors are hardly used by policy makers. The usage of research findings thus is too low. Also, the dissemination of such researches, even in the extension sector, is negligible. And, it is certainly doubtful that most researches conducted due to the individual interest or interests of the funding agencies, or even whims of researchers, have hardly any relevance to the people at large. Policy-related and policy-oriented researches are few and this is the crisis that is quite evident in social science research in India.

It may not be out of place to briefly mention that the researchers involved in projects and other commissioned research, though quite large in number, are employed at a lower rung or stratum at despicably low wages, lower self-esteem and least security of employment. Above all, the training in research in our institutions is at the lowest ebb. One or two theoretical papers in research methodology at the Bachelor's and/or Master's level(s), with some dose of statistical methods, does not prepare persons to handle sophisticated research project in social sciences. Most university departments offer a course in 'Dissertation'/'Project Report Writing' having inputs on 'literature review', 'field work' and 'data collection'. In most universities it has become a source of amassing marks/grades instead of a real effort in gathering experience in nuances of research. The existing examination system does not afford an honest evaluation of these reports, and lack of time and interest among the faculty in the universities and colleges does not, in the real sense, impart research training to the learners honestly. Philosophy, logic, social science theory and the language of research reporting (which is different from literacy writings), are hardly taught with any seriousness to the students. These unprepared and ill-trained persons handle 'researches' in research organisations of hue. It is another serious crisis largely put under the carpet. The University Grants Commission (UGC) and the Indian Council of Social Science Research (ICSSR) had initiated a scheme to impart specialised training in research methodology in social sciences for university and college teachers which is still in vogue, but its results are not satisfactory at all.

Partha Chatterjee (2002) observed that there are two themes that occur repeatedly in most discussions about social sciences today in South Asia. One is an apparently pervasive sense of crisis, an idea that the institutions and practices of social science research are on the point of irretrievable collapse. The other – and associated – theme is the idea that the crisis is the result of the precipitous decline of major institutions of social science research built mainly in the decades following the end of colonial rule. Those who put forth these arguments have many observations to present as symptoms of the decline or crisis and many examples to illustrate their case. A closer study of the facts, however, shows that the decline-crisis story does not hold true for all regions of South Asia and for all social science disciplines. However, in the context of India, I would like to refer to certain facts given by Partha himself, which point to the crisis and decline of the apex body of social science research – ICSSR, Partha said that "one often-cited reason for the decline is the familiar bureaucratic phenomenon of the expansion and entrenchment of the administrative apparatus at the expense of the activities of the organization." Quoting from ICSSR's report of 1998, Partha said that "in

1996–97 the ICSSR received a total grant of Rs 96.9 million from the Government of India, of this Rs 46.6 million, i.e., 47.9 per cent, was distributed in the form of grant to the ICSSR research institutes. Only Rs 4 million, i.e., just over 4 per cent, was given as research grants to scholars, while a whopping Rs 22.5 million, i.e., 23 per cent was spent under various heads on the ICSSR's own administration" (ibid.: 43). The situation has worsened now with an increased number of ICSSR institutions and highly increased costs of administrative functions. This, indeed, is a crisis because ICSSR is one of the major institutions of research funding and its malfunctioning is reflected in other associated institutions and sectors related to social sciences.

Let us now examine the role of the UGC in this decline or crisis of social science research. UGC's allocation of funds for social sciences (also humanities) is awfully low as compared to sciences. Apart from this, the recent steps taken by the UGC and the policies pursued by it, in the realm of higher education and research, have been detrimental for social sciences and humanities – education and research. The progressive decrease in the Commission's grants and opening up education to the private sector has boasted technical, management, computer and other similar courses that are earning propositions, at the cost of humanities, social sciences and even traditional branches of sciences. It is very unfortunate in a society like ours. The worst victim of this policy is 'research' of social sciences and the humanities.

In all policies of recruitment and promotion of teachers, enunciated by the UGC, instead of aiming at excellent teaching the dictum I publish or perish has been zealously followed. It has resulted in lesser interest by the faculty in teaching and more interest in the publication of so-called research papers: it has proved problematic to both teaching and research. The norms of evaluation of excellence in teaching are difficult to determine as is true of evaluation of 'excellent research'. In my considered opinion norms for evaluation of quality of teaching need to be evolved to improve university teaching.

Again, the UGC's oscillating stand on M.Phil degree, Net and research degree for recruitment to college/university teaching positions has proved a watershed, particularly for the social sciences and humanities research standards.

A disturbing note on university research leading to doctoral degree is given here both as a caution and a warning. In one of the old and established universities in the state of Uttar Pradesh, the Vice-Chancellor tried to raise the standards of research by enforcing certain rules and academic norms. On 6th November, 2004, the affiliated college teachers not only protested but virtually attacked him. He had tried to break the caucus and demolish the racket of research. Beware: this racket is there in a large number of universities. It is very much there in all faculties and all subjects but it is more pronounced in humanities and social sciences and needs to be demolished by well-meaning scholars.[1]

A brief note on the social science research in the research institutes and organisations, other than the universities, may be relevant here. T.S. Papola (1983) averred that "a large part of social science research today is going on in organizations established either exclusively or mainly for conducting research. Most of these institutions of social science research have come up during the last two decades in the wake of the somewhat restrictive atmosphere of the university system for promotion of research on the one hand, and increasing realization on the part of social scientist and policy makers for the increasing need for research on various aspects of economic development and social change taking place in the country on the other … of late, they seem to have scored over universities in terms of the research output and variety of research themes". Most of these research institutes were ICSSR institutions. Leaving aside a very few of these research institutes, which are on a sound footing, most of these organisations today are not healthy both academically and functionally. They are in a real crisis. Partha says that "the single most important reason for the prevailing sense of crisis is the recent shortage in the assured government funding of established institutions of social science research … . The general climate of lack of expansion in higher education and greater opportunities in other professions as well as in higher education abroad has led to a critical shortage of qualified and motivated students wanting to take up a career in social sciences research … . The shortage of government funding has meant smaller faculties. In University departments, the result is increased teaching load for faculty and less time for research. In the institutes the way out has been to seek sponsored projects from outside agencies with an inadequate faculty size find hard to undertake from out-side agencies … Institute with an inadequate faculty size find hard to undertake team research or indeed to create a viable academic community to foster new ideas" (op. cit.: 45–48). The new climate in the country has forced the science-related institutes and organisations to generate to big chunk of funds for their existence and operation by the researches themselves. Here, the industries and other funding agencies come forward to sponsor research projects, and if this condition of generation of funds is applied to social science research institutions too, it may then perhaps be difficult for most of them to sustain themselves for long; and those who will still operate may do so with foreign and other dubious funding sources (including the funds from Brettonwood institutions), which will prove catastrophic for society.

ICSSR should not have either established or co-opted these institutions of research for, the UGC, another similar body, does not establish college and/or universities in the country. It is a norm-setter and funding organisation with specific roles of monitoring and evaluation. The ICSSR should have emulated it so as to release more funds for individuals and specific project research. How would this crisis be reconciled is a moot question.

The research institutes, which did excellently well at one point of time, are not only ailing from financial asphyxia but also suffering from proper academic leadership. It is very difficult to say with any certainty that the researches conducted in these institutes are either used by policy makers or get any respectable place in social science teaching in the universities. The dilemma today is that the faculty engaged in these institutions has either forgotten pedagogy or feel shy of associating themselves with university curriculum. And, on the other hand, the universities do not want to either recognise them as research centre (except a few which have succeeded after long lobbying) or affiliated them as teaching intuitions. This crisis has to be squarely faced sooner or later by these research institutes.[2]

In 'Social Science: Quest for Relevant Research', presented as a working/discussion paper for the Dialogue on Social Science Research held in G.B. Pant Social Science Institute, Allahabad, in September 1996, I had raised certain structural problems, basic issues and core questions related to social science research. These issues, problems and core questions are repeated time and again in research-related seminars and conferences including this 'Hyderabad Meet'. These relate to the infancy of social sciences; limits of quantification; problems of measurement and analysis of qualitative data;

issues related to value-free/neutral researches in social sciences; ethical questions associated with the social science researches; empiricism vs. non-empiricism, problems related to objectivity, verifiability, universality; theoretical fundamental vs. applied and action research interdisciplinary approach and issues related to ideology in social science research. These issues are still relevant and the issue of relevance of social science research carried out in the country, is still alive and throbbing. I had remarked then, and I repeat, "It is a Rondo – a piece of music with a leading theme to which return is continually made" (Prasad, 1996).

In the end, let me close with an asserting note that our efforts and crusade for formulation of a National Social Science Policy are directed also to take care of these problems facing social science education and research in the country.

Notes

1. Research in most institutions, particularly in the universities, is carried out as an academic ritual. In most colleges and many universities students are enrolled under such teachers who have not published even one research paper in any established journal. Some of these teachers 'guide' up to eight research scholars at a time on subjects which have hardly any research flavour or any relevance to society/regional concerns/social development. Students scoring as low as 48 per cent marks are permitted to pursue research whereas the entry to the profession of teaching and research may be had only when one scores at least 55 per cent marks at the Master's level. Some teachers have produced more Ph.D's in number than their age/teaching experience.

   The colleges are too poor in their library collection suitable for any viable research. What to talk of standard journals, even the standard texts are not available in these libraries. The State Universities too have deficient libraries. The UGC is the culprit again, by pruning funds of libraries and by putting restrictions on the purchase of research journals, especially foreign, the research operation has greatly suffered.

   Research is a repetitive, cut and paste and xeroxing operation. The libraries in some way or the other connive in this 'big business' and the beneficiaries are unscrupulous teachers. I have already mentioned as to how the UGC, by accepting M.Phil/Ph.D degree up to a certain cut-off date by obviating the compulsion of NET qualification, introduced corruption in the whole process of research. Let me frankly admit that there is now a racket, inter-university indeed, that 'awards' Ph.D degree to undeserving candidates. And, to my own assessment, the outburst of college teachers against the Vice-Chancellor on 6th November, 2004, Dr B.R. Ambedkar University, Agra, was due to the fact that the Vice-Chancellor of this university tried to introduce reforms so that research standards may be improved. On the forefront of this agitation are the teachers belonging to humanities and social sciences. And I have all apprehensions that institutions and persons who will make attempts to rectify the situation, will face similar protests and agitations.

2. I have taught social science for forty years in an institute where teaching was incidental to research and where both teaching and research were not prisoners of disciplinary boundaries. But slowly, however, due to vested interests, institutionalised in traditional academic bounds, the traditional rules and obsolete structure have been reinforced to damage the academic freedom and research standards.

   Apart from this, I have served as Noorul Hasan Senior Fellow in a research institute where the faculty was small as a mere five, and the clerical staff was four times the number of the research faculty and research funds were so meagre that even the field work and consultation with other institutions/libraries could not be supported.

   I have also been on the Governing Board of the Tata Institute of Social Sciences, Mumbai, Centre for Studies in Social Science, Kolkata, Omeo Kumar Das Institute of Development and Social Change, Guwahati and worked closely with the Kasturaba Rural Institute, Rajpura and thus have some knowledge of working and functioning of research institutes. I have visited a number of other research institutes and interacted with the faculty there at academic and other meetings. I am therefore sufficiently aware of the situation obtaining in research institutes.

References

Abrecht, Paul, 1968, "The Uses of Social Sciences in Asia", in *The Relevance of Social Sciences in Contemporary Asia*, World Student Christian Federation, Tokyo.

Atal, Yogesh, 1976, *Social Sciences: The Indian Scene*, Abhinav Publications, New Delhi.

Chatterjee, Partha, 2002, *Social Science Research Capacity in South Asia: A Report*, Vol. 6, Social Science Research Council, New York.

Espiritu, A.C., 1968, "The Limits of Applicability of Western Concepts: Values and Methods in the Social Sciences to the Concrete Realities of Asian Societies", in *The Relevance of the Social Science in Contemporary Asia*, op. cit.

Government of India, 1968, National Education Policy Document.

Kurien, C.T., 1968, "Planning in Asian Countries: A Critique", in *The Relevance of the Social Sciences in Contemporary Asia*, op. cit.

Leeuwen, Von, 1968, quoted by Paul Abrecht in "The Use of Social Science in Asia", in *The Relevance of the Social Science in Contemporary Asia*, op. cit.

Lister, Ian, 1964, "The Teaching of the Humanities in the Schools", in J.H. Plumb (ed.), *Crisis in the Humanities*, Penguin Books, Middlesex, England.

Mukerjee, Radhakamal, 1960, "The Unity of the Social Sciences", in *Philosophy of Social Sciences* (also see Integral Sociology, An Anthology of the writings of Professor Radhakamal Mukerjee, G.R. Madan and V.P. Gupta (eds.), 2000, Radha Publications, New Delhi, pp. 282–284).

Mukherjee, Ramakrishna, 2004, Unitary of United Social Science, Inaugural Keynote Address at the National Seminar on Futuristic Vision of Social Science-Social Science in India in the 21st Century. Organised by the Indian Social Science Association, Agra, October 9–12 (Unpublished).

Papola, T.S., 1984, "National Perspective on Social Science Development in India", *IASSI Quarterly Newsletter*, Vols. 3 and 4, December.

Plumb, J.H. (ed.), 1964, *Crisis in the Humanities*, Penguin Books, Middlesex, England.

Prasad, Rajeshwar, 1996, Social Science: Quest for Relevant Research, Discussion Paper Submitted for Dialogue/Agenda for Social Science Research, G.B. Pant Social Science Institute in September.

Sargent, J.R., 1964, "Economics: The Would-be, May-be Science", in J.H. Plumb (ed.), op. cit., pp. 139–54.

11

Evolution of Caste System

B.D. Tripathi

Caste system has passed through several phases. These can broadly be grouped into three distinct ones, namely, the origins, the growth and constraint phase and the current phase. This article takes a look at these three phases one by one.

The Origins

Caste (jati) came into being in the form of varna in the deep past on the Indian soil. Varna is theologically believed to have emerged from different parts of the Primeval Being's body. The four varnas – Brahmin, Rajanya (Kshatriya), Vaishya and Shudra – are respectively born from the mouth, arms, thigh and feet parts of the Virat Purusha's body. Such a description of the emergence of the four varnas is found in the most ancient and sacred book of the Aryans, known as Rigveda.[1] In Yajurveda also there is such a description.[2] Later, in Manusmriti[3] and Gita[4], almost the same thing is said though worded differently.

Varna literally means colour. Each of the four varnas is ideally-typically symbolised by a particular colour. Brahmin's colour is white, which is supposed to be free from all blemishes and impurities. White colour symbolises the pure guna of satva. Satva is the symbol of knowledge and wisdom. Brahmin being white in colour is supposed to be free from all the infirmities, imperfections and weaknesses. He is the mind and vision of the community. He is the forerunner and the whole caravan (masses) followed his foot steps.

The second varna is Rajanya (Kshatriya). Its colour is red. This colour symbolises Rajas Guna, an attribute of fortitude, self-sacrifice, self-initiation, invincibility, courage and movement, on his shoulders, rested the defence and security of the whole community. The third varna, i.e., Vaishya is the carrier of yellow colour, a symbol of both Rajas and Tamas. Tamas symbolises inactivity, lethargy, idleness, dependence and such other bad attributes. Vaishya is thus a combination of good and bad attributes. The fourth varna, i.e., Shudra is the carrier of the pure Tamas. Its colour is black. As such, a Shudra seen as full of all blemishes, evils, infinities and impurities. He is looked down as personified ignorance, lethargy and passivity.

Each varna is a semi-closed system integrated with the rest in varying degrees ranging from the most integrated to the loosely integrated. Bond between the two upper varnas is most integrated. The Vaishya varna is fairly attached to the dyad of Brahmin and Rajanya. The two (Brahmin and Rajanya) along with the Vaishya constitutes a trinity of varnas. The bond between the trinity and Shudras of course is very loose. In fact, the Shudra fold is virtually annexed or appended to the trinity. There is big social gap between the trinity on the one side and Shudras on the other. In spite of this social gap, the Shudra varna is treated as an integral part of the grand system. The upper three varnas observe big social distance from Shudras as is evident from the following facts:

(1) Shudras were barred from the study of Vedas. They observed their own native rituals from birth to death. They were not entitled either to recite or to listen to the Vedic hymns. Brahmin did not officiate in the ceremonies of Shudras.

(2) Shudras were not entitled for initiation ceremony. It was this practice which separated the Shudras from the trinity. This discrimination was probably based on the assumption that Shudras, full of Tamas, as they are, may not respond to the various initiations meant for intellectual training and spiritual upliftment.

(3) Discriminatory social codes were formulated by different law-givers for Shudras in respect of punishment for deviance, social intercourse and education.

(4) Shudras were accorded the lowest socio-ritual rank and status. They were subjected to several socio-religious disabilities such as rolelessness in the *yajna* performance, non-entry into temples, untouchability, of course, exceptions apart. They were discriminated against in almost all the walks of life.

Shudras were a discriminated lot, so were Vaishya, though to a lesser measure. Tamas probably was the cause of such discrimination. In Gita[5], Vaishyas, Shudras and women have been grouped together and branded as papyoni (sinful folk). Women of all the varnas were ordinarily treated at par with the Shudras because of their association with the Tamas. As person by herself, a woman's status was equivalent to Shudra but her position or rank elevated or relegated in correspondence with the varnas, she was linked to, in the course of her marriage. A Shudra bride's status was elevated if she was married to a Brahmin. Oppositely, a bride's position born in the Brahmin family, relegated if she was married to a Shudra groom. For example, Akshamala and Sarangi were born in Shudra families but they rose in status because of their marriage with Vasishta (Brahmin) and Mandpal (Kshatriya) respectively.[6]

Among the four varnas, Brahmin and Rajanya were very close to each other. This was due to their complementary attributes (gunas). What one needed the other possessed? Brahmin needed physical power for the expansion and consolidation of the Aryan culture and society which Rajanya possessed. Similarly, for the same goal, Rajanya needed wisdom and insight which Brahmin possessed. The dyad of Brahmin and Rajanya maintained maximum possible social distance with Shudras as they were possessed of Tamas. The dyad intact carried the Shudras with them for menial roles. Vashya's was mid-way position. The dyad retained distance with them as they were tainted with Tamas but deemed them indispensable because of their Rajas attributes. Vaishyas were granted entry into the inner fold of the dyad only because of their Rajas attribute. The trinity went by the common name dwija (twice-born) as against the Shudra who was called ek-jat (once-born).

As regards the number of varnas, Manu[7] is quite emphatic that they are four only while others talk of the fifth varna (pancham varna). Now, how is it that in the varna hierarchy, Brahmin is on the top and Shudra on the lowest rung, while Rajanya is next to Brahmin and Vaishya is just above the Shudra? There are several theories to solve the riddle of varna hierarchy but the one formulated by Louis

Dumont[8] is acknowledged as the best one by sociologists. According to Dumont, it is the principle of purity-pollution that is the ultimate determinant of the ranks of the varnas. Brahmin is on the top of hierarchy because this varna contains utmost purity element in it. On the opposite side, Shudra's rank is the lowest because this varna contains maximum amount of pollution. This very principle determines the relative higher rank of Rajanya and lower position of Vaishya. Rajanya has greater amount of purity and lesser amount of pollution as compared to Vaishya, so former's rank is higher than the latter's. The varna system may be likened to a ladder with four rungs at varying distance. The top and next-to-the-top rungs are quite close to the each other while the third is at a little more distance. The fourth rung lies at the farthest end of the ladder, almost touching the ground.

Now, two more questions, one related to varna membership and the other to the nature of marriage in the varna system. Membership to different varnas largely depended on the birth. If both the parents of the progeny belonged to the same varna, the latter was a natural member of the varna concerned. In case, varnas of the parents were different, the progeny had to be pushed off to a new caste along with the parents. Sometimes, there were provisions for inter-varna migration under restricted conditions, both upward and downward. Downward migration was a punishment awarded to those who transgressed varna rules. Upward migration was marriage-based. If the girl progenies of the Shudra are married to Brahmin grooms consecutively for seven generations, in the last generation, the progenies attain the status of Brahmin. But this does not amount to Brahmin as such. In the reverse process, the Brahmin girl may fall to Shudra status but not Shudra as such.

Now, about the nature of marriage in the varna system. There were three types of marriages. Intra-varna, hypergamous inter-varna and hypogamous inter-varna, Out of the three, most preferred marriage was intra-varna. The next best was hypergamous inter-varna though the union of the top and the bottom as groom and bride was heavily condemned. Hypogamous inter-varna union was deemed against the spirit of varna hierarchy and was viewed as a most serious offence.

The Growth and Constraint Phase

If caste is Ganga, varna is Gangotri, the source of caste. As Ganga becomes entirely different at Gangasagar from its original tiny structure at Gangotri, in volume and content, so became caste with respect to varna. In the second, i.e., growth and constraint phase, caste multiplied, spread to new areas, cultures and societies and evolved new traits and attributes as dissimilar from varna. Further, caste headed toward closure and constraints, from openness and freedom. Caste, the progeny though broadly resembling its mother, varna, gathered certain new features leading to an identity of its own. The new identity of caste emerged in response to several new social practices which may be enumerated as (a) differentiation, (b) insulation and segregation, (c) migration, and (4) induction.

(a) *Differentiation:* Caste multiplication through differentiation refers to the practice of siring progenies by the male members of the Aryan fold through inter-varna hypergamy and hypogamy. Under the practice of hypergamy the male members of the upper three varnas were entitled to take brides from their respective lower varnas. Progenies of such marriages along with their parents were disqualified to inherit their native varna: they were expelled from their respective varnas. Expelled people constellated to from their own endogamous groups winch amounted to new castes. Thus, at the first stage, there arose six castes, known as Murdhobhisikta, Ambasta, Ugra, Karan, Nisad and Parasava. Those born of hypogamous marriages were rated as inferior in rank to the ones born of hypergamous unions. The six castes from the hypogamous marriages were Suta, Magadh, Vaideh, Ayogava, Chhatta and Chandal. Chandal was rated as lowest as all, He was born from the marriage between Shudra groom and Brahmin bride, the most forbidden category of inter-varna hypogamy. He was looked down as most despised, dreaded, obnoxious, repugnant and unclean. So from the four original varnas sprouted 12 castes at the first stage of varna differentiation or varna fission.[9]

The practice of inter-varna and inter-caste marriage continued unabated leading to the geometrical progression of the number of castes within the varna fold. Such marital unions set forth the principle of caste and sub-caste formation which may be termed as expulsion-constellation. Progenies of inter-varna and inter-caste wed-locks were expelled from their native varnas or castes along with their parents. Thus segregated from the native fold, the affected people constellated into new endogenous groups called caste. Out of the four factors responsible for caste multiplication mentioned above, differentiation alone accounted for the majority of such branches and sub-branches of the varna and caste tree.

Along with the formation of new castes, the original varnas, particularly the upper three sustained as ever by following the practice of intra-varna marriage within their respective sub-folds. Due to country-wide migration, such people were divided into several regional groups, each of which had to practise regional endogamy. In the course of migration, Brahmins were divided into ten broad endogamous groups called Pancha Gauda and Pancha Dravida. Similar was the case with Kshatriya and Vaishya varnas as well. Can such endogamous groups be called caste sociologically? In my view, it is improper to call such groups as castes. They may instead be called endogamous cells. Caste, no doubt, is endogamous, but all endogamous groups should not sweepingly be called caste. In my view, each of the three upper varnas consists only of one varna (not caste) with several regional endogamous cells.

Inter-varna and inter-caste marital unions, both hypergamous and hypogamous, at subsequent generations, led to the birth of several castes, such as Puspadh, Avritta, Abhir, Dhigvrana, Pukkas, Kukkutus, Swapak, Vena, Avantya, Jhalla, Malla, Nicchivi, Nat, Khas, Dravid, Karushya, Vijanma, Maitra, Satwat, Sairindhra, Vyadh, Maitreya, Mrgave, Kaivart, Karavar, Charmakar (Chamar) Andhra, Meda, Pandulopak (Dharikar), Ahindak, Sopak and Antyawasayee (Dom).[10]

(b) *Insulation and segregation:* The second factor responsible for the creation of new castes and sub-castes was the practice of insulation and segregation, over the violation of caste rules and conventions. Insulation is a process of withdrawal of contact by the rule and convention-abiding wing of a caste in respect of rule-violative section of the same with a view to protect its purity and rank order. In the course of insulation, all points of contact betwèen the two sections are weaned. Segregation consists in disaffiliating the rule and convention-violative people from the membership of the caste. Both the processes operated simultaneously. Those violating the caste rules and conventions were segregated from the parent body. The parent body weaned all interactions with the segregated people, particularly related to marriage, commensality and co-smoking. Thus, cornered from all sides, segregated people had no option but to form their own endogamous group to sustain themselves. Such a group was joined by the people of similar caste background. In the course of time, such groups evolved all caste traits such as ritual rank, profession and thereby assumed full-fledged caste stature.

A few examples, Sannyasis disaffiliated such members from their midst who fell short of sex norms laid down by the order. So, those segregated, tried to return to their native castes from which they had migrated to the order. But their native castes refused to readmit such tainted persons. Finding all options closed, the segregated lots formed their own group which in due course turned endogamous. This caste came to be known as Gosain. In another case, some famine affected people from high caste, finding no food to eat, joined free food camps (Kshetra). Under the caste rule they were segregated from their caste and branded as Khetarkhai (those who ate in the Kshetra). The segregated people formed their own caste. A third case, where a section of people left the Brahmanic way of life and associated themselves with administration and land ownership. Further, they adopted non-Brahmin titles (Aspad). Being segregated from the parent body, such people formed their own endogamous fold called Bhumihar. Multiplication of caste due to insulation and segregation is also called fission. Differentiation and fission, taken together, account for a large majority of castes.

(c) *Migration:* In ancient times, people migrated from one place to the other, losing touch with their native folk. They formed their own endogamous groups in their new-found land. Such groups ordinarily consisted of people with similar social background from one or several regions. Bengali Brahmins (Chatterji, Banerjee, Mukherjee, also called Chattopadhyaya, Bandyopathyaya, Mukhopadhyaya respectively) are migrated people from Kannauja. They, in their native place, were Kanyakubj Brahmins. But, in Bengal, they evolved an entirely new entity of their own and formed their endogamous groups separate from their original. Kumauni Brahmins consist of Pandeys, Joshis and Pants. They migrated to the hilly areas of Kumaun under the threat of conversion in Mughal period, from three different regions, namely, Karnataka, Nepal and Maharashtra, respectively. All the three have formed a single endogamous group. Kumauni Brahmins have two endogamous sub-groups, namely, Lamdhotia (those with longer Dhoti) and Chhotdhotia (those with small Dhoti). Lamdhotias are deemed superior to Chhotdhotias in rank. The two sub-groups do not intermarry. At the all-India level, Brahmins have 10 major endogamous groups of which five fall in the Gaud bunch (Panch Gaud) at the remaining five in the Dravid bunch (Punch Dravid). The five Gaud Brahmins are Saraswata, Kanyakubja, Gaud, Utkal and Maithil. The five Dravid Brahmins consist of Talang, Karnatak, Dravid, Maharashtric and Gurjar. Saryuparis are a branch of Kanyakubjas, Shakdweepis fall outside the ten-fold category of Brahmins. According to a hearsay tradition, they came to India from Shakdweep as physicians to treat the leprosy of Pradyumna, the son of Lord Krishna. Professionally, Shakdweepi Brahmins are physicians.

(d) *Induction:* Induction is the practice through which a non-caste group is baptised as caste. The moving wheel of Aryan culture intruded into many tribal and non-Aryan groups and varnished (rather casteised) them and thereby raised the number of castes within the varna fold. Many sociologists subscribe to this view, for example, Ghurye believes that caste was originally an exclusive property of the Aryan culture, confined to North India only. Later, it became an all-India phenomenon. In his own words, "I may conclude that caste in India is a Brahmanic child of the Indo-Aryan culture cradled in the land of Ganga and Yamuna and thence transferred to the other parts of the country".[11] B.K. Nair[12] and B.R. Ambedkar[13] talk in the similar tone. Nair alleges that Aryan Brahmins such as Agastya and Pulastya and later several others intruded deep into Tamil society and culture and imposed their own culture and belief through Sanskrit language and varna order. In the process of varnisation, different Tamil groups were accorded ritual rank and status within the varna order on the basis of their own native social position. Thus caste order was thrust on the people who had no caste learning at all. With the passage or time, caste became a legitimate order of the Tamilian society. Essentially egalitarian Tamil social order was hierarchies on the varna pattern.

Ambedkar feels that there is no divinity whatsoever with the varna order. It is just a Brahminic device to divide and rule the society. According to him, Brahmins reserved with them the power to change anybody's caste. They could upgrade or downgrade people in the varna hierarchy at their will. Shivaji, for example, was Kurmi by birth. But a Brahmin from Varanasi, somehow, proved that he was Kshatriya and thus a Kurmi was accorded the status of a Kshatriya. Ambedkar claims that many so-called Shudra castes were originally Kshatriya. Let it incidentally be mentioned here that in Manusmriti, there is a description of varna demotion. Some castes within the Kshatriya fold such as Paundrak, Audra, Dravid, Kamboj, Yawan, Shak, Parad, Pahlawa, Cheen, Kirat, Darad and Khash were downgraded and relegated to the Shudra fold as they had lost their Kshatriya qualities, and had left contact with the Brahmins.[14]

Varna was the hero at the birth phase. Caste occupied the same position at the growth phase. Caste being progeny of varna largely resembles on many points with its parent order. But it has a distinct identity and entity of its own as well. Varna was not so coercive, compressive and regulative as caste came to be. In the birth phase, expulsion-constellation apparatus was initiated to discourage inter-varna marriage, particularly the hypogamous. In the growth and constraint phase, this apparatus was practised more ruthlessly. It virtually became tyrannical. It was the tyranny of this apparatus, which led to the birth of numberless sub-castes and castes within the Hindu fold. In the growth phase, Hindu social order had developed a taste for expulsion, segregation and insulation. It was this taste which led to the multiplication of castes. As I guess, such a taste was the direct outcome of the prescriptive, coercive and compulsive nature of caste.

On the basis of the foregoing accounts, following salient features of caste in the growth phase may be enumerated: (1) Caste emerged as an operative and full-grown institution. It did not however replace the varna order. Rather, varna order functioned as a loose cover of the caste complex. Caste functioned as parallel and co-operative system within the framework of varna. (2) In the second phase, caste came to be thoroughly established and sedimented. Reciprocity marked the entire hierarchy from the top to the bottom. What one unit needed the other provided? Maintenance of social distance, particularly with the Shudra castes, became a taken-for-granted practice. In the extreme cases, the bottom lying castes resented social proximity, even if offered by the higher castes. (3) Segregative, expulsive and insulative practices became highly ferocious and inexorable. Even slightest infringement of the caste rules invited immediate action from the caste guardians whose prying eyes caught every thing that went inside their caste fold. In other words, caste became more punitive and prescriptive in the second phase. (4) All the six attributes of caste, namely, membership by birth, endogamy, rank order, caste-related profession, commensality and untouchability reigned supreme. (5) The number of castes and sub-castes touched all-time high score.

The Current Phase

The supremacy of caste culture came under challenge with the onset of the current phase. Current phase is the story of the decline in the sky-touching glory of caste. In this phase, India came in touch with the western world. Westernisation accelerated the processes of urbanisation and modernisation. Democracy gave of grievous blow to the hierarchical edifice of the Indian social order. The collective forces of all the four factors posed a serious threat to the gigantic strides of the caste culture and arrested its proceeding in some measure. Caste set forth apt responses to the new challenges, adapted itself to new settings. Caste survived though bruised here and there. Caste was partly westernised, modernised, urbanised, even democratised. Caste was westernised in the sense that it got rid of the much tainted attribute of untouchability. Later in 1955 a law was enacted against the practice of untouchability. Westernisation is an extra-mural source of structural change. As against this, modernisation is an intra-mural source. When systems try to attain contemporaneity as prompted by their own internal forces, it is called modernisation. Modernisation in caste was initiated by several Indian reformers such as Ram Mohan Roy and Swami Dayanand Sarswati. Through their organisations called Brahmo Samaj and Arya Samaj respectively, they initiated a cultural renaissance in India. Mahatma Gandhi took this cause and carried it to a higher plane. In his own way, he tried to uplift the downtrodden by calling them Harijan (people of God).

Under the modernisation impact, the system of rank-hierarchy was transformed into the hierarchy of social statuses. Though hierarchy remained but its colour, content and texture changed. Caste in the agro-rural setting was marked by slow movement. Everything moved with easy speed, under the urban setting this movement came to be very fast. The speed difference between the two settings affected the working of caste-related rituals. Such a change was confined to the urban setting only. In the agro-rural settings, things still prevail in the old fashion. Democratisation did cast its impact on caste. Caste under the impact of Indian variant of democracy is used as a tool for grabbing power. Caste at its birth was a religio-social system. Later, it headed towards being purely a social system. In this very process, caste is gathering political dust in and around it. In other words, under Indian model of democracy, caste is being politicised.

Under the general impact of all the four waves, mentioned above, prescriptive, coercive and compulsive traits of caste partly lost their hold. An element of liberalism entered into the caste system. Liberalism partly arrested the operation of the segregative, expulsive and insulative functions of caste which were responsible for caste multiplication and differentiation. It is because of this new trend that in the current phase of caste history, new castes and sub-castes are not coming into being. Not only this, now, a reverse process has set in.

Instead of multiplying, castes are confederating. Caste confederation is taking place on all the three levels – top, mid and bottom. At the bottom level, the so-called depressed (Dalit) castes are congregating on a common platform. Middle castes do not lag behind in uniting themselves. Ajgar (Ahir, Jat, Gujar and Rajput) is an example of mid-caste confederation. At the top level, confederation is in the air, though it has not yet materialised. In the preceding phase castes' emphasis was on hierarchy. Now, it has shifted to horizontality. Castes with common social statuses are in active search for the nexus which may bind them more tightly.

Now, the legitimacy of caste, in the running phase, is being put to scrutiny with double mind. On the one hand, caste is being dragged in all socio-political areas. On the other, it is being cursed full throatily. Reservation is being demanded and granted on the basis of caste. Even converted people claim for reservation on the basis of their erstwhile low castes. Not only this, there is a hot demand for caste-based sub-quota in the reservation for women. Such a double speak on caste shows how undecided people are on whether to go with caste or to bid good-bye to it.

In the social area, people think several times, before overstepping the frontiers of endogamy wherein they are irretrievably enmeshed even today. Caste is said to be possessed of six attributes, namely, endogamy, rank order, membership by birth, caste-related profession, commensality and untouchability. The first three of these attributes are essential and the remaining three are peripheral or subsidiary. Caste is losing only on the subsidiary fronts in its war with the new social forces, but maintaining itself quite boldly on the essential fronts. On the basis of his field study, Yogesh Atal[15] concluded that changes in caste in response to the new social forces are only peripheral. Caste is said to be a highly resilient phenomenon. It is enormously adaptive and keeps itself alive even in the most adverse and unpalatable situations. If caste is so malignantly self-sustaining, how can it be demolished? Until and unless Hindu society evolves a single mind against the caste order, it will continue to prevail in spite of the hue and cry raised against it by the people with vacillating mind.

Caste in the current phase is characterised by a new trend, i.e., craze for enhancement of ritual rank, particularly in the bottom lying caste. Even in the earlier phases of the caste, demand for rank enhancement was there. But, then, such cases were resolved by Brahmin's mediation. Brahmins were empowered to promote, demote or forfeit ranks allotted to different castes and individuals. Now, such cases are resolved by the concerned castes themselves irrespective of Brahmin's mediation by resort to different measures and methods such as raising economic status, sanskritisation and even by conversion. In the Dalit fold, there are three major strata, the inner, the mid and the fringe, marginal or peripheral. All the three strata find themselves ill-adjusted with the ranks and statuses allotted to them under the age-old caste hierarchy. So, they collectively raise the ranks of their respective castes. The inner and mid-strata castes opt for sanskritisation and economic well-being. This leads to the enhancement of their social status. The concept of sanskritisation was evolved by Srinivas[16] on the basis of the study of Coorgs in South India. He, however, modified his original concept in his later book.[17] In sanskritisation lower caste people copy the cultural models of higher caste people. Bailey[18] gives an account of certain castes in Orissa which raised their social status by undertaking new economic enterprises. The stigma of untouchability was erased from the castes related to the inner and mid strata as a sequel to their enhanced rank and social prestige. Such castes though within the Shudra fold came to be known as *Sat-Shudras* (clean Shudras). Their proximity with the castes in the non-Shudra fold rose in course of time. The category of *Sat-Shudra* is very much in vogue in Bengal. The marginal strata castes, such as Chamar, Dom, Mushar and Valmikis, being on the lowest rung of the hierarchy, opt for conversion with no other alternatives left to them for rank enhancement.

In the growth phase, it was caste here, caste there and caste everywhere. Even in the economic area, caste had its way. In the current age, with the recession of caste, class made its presence felt in the economic field. Later class emerged as a 'baby system' in the Indian society only in the mid-course of the current phase. Indian society is primarily caste-bound: class is a subsidiary social phenomenon in the Indian context. One is born in caste and later he moves to class. Both caste and class are similar to each other in the sense that both are hierarchical in structure. But they are dissimilar to each other on two major counts: (1) whereas caste is a sacred institution class is secular, and (2) whereas caste does not allow its members to move out of its fold class lays no such restriction. In class structure, there is free movement from bottom to top and vice versa. Because of the proximity or the two hierarchies, sometimes, they get mixed up and create a situation of *claste*. This is so when caste and class are irretrievably stuck-up with each other. Tripathi[19] gives a detailed description of the caste phenomenon.

Now, the caste as its exists today is different from its counterpart in the growth phase. Following are the points of difference between the two versions of caste:

(1) In the growth phase, caste was uni-centric, now, it has become multi-centric.

(2) In the birth and growth phase, different strata of varna and caste were fully interlaced, which by now have been reduced to loose and semi-discrete units. This is so because different strata have developed their own semi-independent entities and are confined to the narrow interest of their own strata.

(3) In the growth phase status of each caste was determined on the basis of hierarchy principle. Now, it is largely determined by the economic status of the caste concerned.

(4) At the growth phase caste was a fully closed system. Now-a-days, some amount of openness and liberalism are overtaking it.

(5) At the birth phase, the number of castes was very small. In course of time, the number rose due to the practice of expulsion, segregation and insulation. By the close of the growth phase, the number of castes roughly touched the figure of 4,000.

(6) Originally, caste was all occupation and ritual related system. Now, both the original functions of caste have been pushed aside and in their place new functions such as political and social have come it to the fore.

(7) At the birth phase caste was a bifurcated system. The three upper varnas along with their caste complex were on the one side and the castes within the Shudra fold on the other. Now, the system stands trifurcated. The three blocks of the system are the upper, the middle and the Dalit or bottom castes.

(8) By the close of the growth phase, new castes and sub-castes used to come up. Now, the process has reached the point of termination.

(9) Class phenomenon within the fold of caste order has come into being. This was missing in the growth phase of caste. Sometimes caste and class mix up and create a situation of *claste*.

(10) Conversion from the caste-fold is a new trend. It is a new turn in the history of caste.

(11) Caste is changing at the peripheral level but maintaining itself at the essential level.

(12) On the practice plane caste card is played everywhere but at the ideological plane, legitimacy of caste is being questioned.

Notes

1. Rigveda 10–99–12.
2. Yajurveda 31–11.
3. Manusmriti 1–31.
4. Gita 4–13.
5. Gita 9–32
6. Manusmriti 9–23.
7. Manusmriti 10–40.
8. L. Dumont, *Homo Hierarchicus: The Caste System and its Implications* (New Delhi: Vikas) 1970.
9. Manusmriti 10–8–13.
10. Manusmriti 10–21–39.
11. G.S. Ghurye, *Caste, Class and Occupation* (Bombay: Popular) 1961, p. 172.
12. B.K. Nair, *The Dynamic Brahmin* (Bombay: Popular) 1959.
13. B.R. Ambedkar, *Who were Shudras?* (Bombay: Thacker) 1946.
14. Manusmriti 10–43–44.
15. Yogesh Atal, *The Changing Frontiers of Caste* (Delhi: National Publishing House) 1968.
16. M.N. Srinivas, *Religion and Society among the Coorgs of South India* (New York: Asia) 1952.
17. M.N. Srinivas, *Caste in Modern India and Other Essays* (Bombay: Asia) 1962.
18. F.G. Bailey, *Caste and Economic Frontiers: A Village in Highland Orissa* (Manchester: Manchester University Press) 1958.
19. B.D. Tripathi, *Society: Today and Tomorrow* (Bombay: Himalaya) 1990, pp. 58–61.

12

Dimensions of Human Development

Emerging Concerns

S.P. Srivastava

Development has been the continuing pursuit of all nations – rich or poor, western or non-western. The growth of industry, and science and technology, has accelerated the pace of development, creating progress in many walks of life. With the advent of industrialisation and revolutionary methods of production under the powerful and pervasive industrial capitalism, the economic growth-oriented model of development generated enormous amount of wealth, professedly to eliminate scarcity and get rid of the problems arising out of want or dearth of resources. But this econo-centric approach to development has not helped the poor and the marginalised sections of society in enjoying a decent standard of living. This happened because, from the very outset, benefits of development have remained concentrated in the hands of small, elite groups in a few rich countries – mainly the industrialised ones. The classical economists hailed this model of development inasmuch as it increased productivity and profit.

The development debate that began in 1970s and continued till the end of 1990, raised some very fundamental questions, such as whether the growth is the end or means (Srivastava, 1998). The critics of the econo-centric model of development argued that human being should be the end rather than being the mere means. They further asserted that the industrial-cum-technocratic model of development is iniquitous and carries elements of capitalist exploitation. The criticism was based on the ideas of such political economists like Adam Smith, Karl Marx, John Stuart Mill and Alfred Marshall who in their writings had warned about the single-minded pursuit of the wealth-driven model of development. However, such views were largely aside in the pursuit of increased production to satisfy the demands of fast-spreading consumerist culture – a product of capitalism.

The aftermath of the Second World War was a period of taking stock of this model of development. The world community adopted the Universal Declaration of Human Rights, celebrating the victory of human freedom and reasserting strongly and clearly that the principal objective of development was human well-being. In subsequent years there followed a series of UN conventions and conferences establishing the principles of people-centred development. The new debate rejected the idea of development that was determined by the level of productive forces and argued that the people alone are the motive force of development. Political leaders in the newly independent countries of the developing world emphatically argued that the purpose of development is the well-being of people. In 1955, the Nobel Prize laureate West Indian economist Arthur Lewis defined the purpose of development as widening the "range of human choice". But Lewis tended to equate wider choice merely with greater income and had more faith in the old argument of the classical economists that economic growth would inevitably lead to human development.

The contemporary critique of economic development avers that economic growth *per se* does not lead to human development. Economic growth is important but its nature, character and distribution are equally important. A link between economic growth and human well-being has to be created consciously through deliberate public policy measures, such as public spending on social services and fiscal policy to redistribute income and assets. The challenge is to balance the goals economic growth with those of human development.

While exploring the complex relationship between economic growth and human development, the Human Development Report of 1996 emphasised that there is no automatic link between economic growth and human development, but when these links are forged with policy and determination, they can be mutually reinforcing and economic growth will effectively and rapidly enhance human development. The report concluded that the structure and quality of growth demands greater attention than the quantity of growth. Haq (2000: 209) remarked that unless determined policy efforts are made, economic growth can be (a) jobless (expansion of output without expansion of jobs), or (b) ruthless (where the fruits of growth mostly benefit the rich), or (c) voiceless (where the growth in the economy is not accompanied by an expansion of democracy or empowerment), or (d) rootless (which causes people's identity to whither), or even (e) futureless (where the present generation squanders resources, particularly the natural environmental capital, needed by future generations).

Emergence and Growth

The rediscovery of human development is not a new invention. It is a tribute to early philosophers, economists and political leaders who have long emphasised human well-being as the purpose and the end of development. Early quantitative economists – William Petty, Gregory King, Antonie Lavoisier and Joseph Lagrange – followed by political economists – Karl Marx and John Stuart Mills – took a functionalist view of human development and emphasised the paramouncy of social concerns: welfare being the measuring rod of money and human well-being being the core of development. Both of them emphasised the social purpose of national wealth creation, namely, the fulfilment of human choices, which they said, extend beyond economic well-being. The international debate on the changing paradigms of development since the mid-1920s witnessed a significant shift of focus from the economic growth to socio-economic development and later, from socio-economic development to human development. The United Nations Development Programme (UNDP) contributed much to the international economic thinking emphasising that the purpose of development is human well-being, which was rechristened as 'human development' in 1990 with the publication the first Human Development Report by the UNDP.

From a mere idea, human development has now become a vibrant intellectual movement and a practical strategy of development (Haq, 2000: XIX). The trial of human development idea and its strategies have witnessed an unprecedented explosion in the thinking on the subject over the recent years. There is, therefore an extensive amount of writings in the human development field. Commenting on the emergence and growth of human development as a major focus of economic thinking, Mahbub-ul Haq famously wrote: "It appears that human development is an idea whose time has come.

People-centred strategies have increasingly become the focus of all development dialogue" (ibid.). Today, it is widely accepted that the real purpose of development is to enlarge people's choices in all fields – social, economic, political and cultural. Seeking increase in income is one of the many choices people make, but that is not the only one. We have finally begun to accept the axiom that human welfare – not growth – is the true end of development. In a short summation, the human dimension of development is not just another addition to the development dialogue. It is entirely a new perspective, and a revolutionary way to recast the conventional approach to development (ibid.: 11). Human development is a concern not only for the poor countries and the poor people, but everywhere (Streeten, 2000: X, foreword). Human development goes beyond basic needs, in essence it is concerned with all human beings – not only the poor and not only in the poor countries – and not only basic needs. Human development applies to the advanced countries as much as to the middle-income and low-income countries.

Definition and Concept

Since its launch in 1990 the successive Human Development Reports have defined human development as the process of enlarging people's choices by expanding human functioning and capabilities. The most critical ones of these choices are to lead a long and healthy life, to be educated and to enjoy a decent standard of living. Additional choices include political freedom, other guaranteed human rights and several ingredients of self-respect. These are among the essential choices, the absence of which can block many other opportunities. Human development is thus a process of widening people's choices as well as raising the level of human well-being achieved.

The concept of human development embraces a broad range of choices in economic, social and political arenas. It covers more than knowledge, a long and healthy life and standard of living. Issues like freedom, democracy and human security are also important human development indicators. The concept of human development enlarges the notion of human well-being and conceives it more widely to include, not only the consumption of goods and services, but also the accessibility of all sections of population, especially the deprived ones and those who live below the normative minimal poverty line, to the basic necessities of a productive and socially meaningful life. Such a conceptualisation of human well-being encompasses individual attainments in areas of education and knowledge, health and longevity, as well as in the quality of overall social and physical environment of the people.

There is, however, a widespread misperception that human development is only about economic and social outcomes such as reducing income poverty and improving health and education. Though these are important for human development, its aim is much broader – to promote the freedom, well-being and dignity of the people everywhere. Economic growth is a means to these broader ends. Broadly conceived, human development is about people, and about expanding their choices to lead the lives they value. It is about creating an environment for people to develop their full potential and lead productive and creative lives. It is about enlarging human choices for building human capabilities, the most basic being leading a healthy life, being educated, having access to the resources needed for a decent standard of living and able to participate in the life of the community. The concept of human development centres around the development of the people, for the people and by the people. Development of the people means investing in human capabilities, whether in education or health or skills, so that they can work productively and creatively. Development for the people indicates that economic growth that is generated is equitably distributed widely. Development by the people suggests that development must concentrate on giving everyone a chance to participate in development.

Essential Components

There are four essential components in the human development paradigm: equity, sustainability, productivity and empowerment (Haq, 1995). Equity envisages equitable access to opportunities and demands a fundamental restructuring of power in society, namely, the distribution of productive assets, the distribution of income, and access to economic and political opportunities. Thus viewed, equity is a powerful concept that lies at the heart of human development paradigm. Sustainability implies prudent use of all forms of capital – physical, human, financial and environmental – and avers with the view that depletion in any of these forms of capital will mortgage the chances for sustainable development and will rob the future generations of their options. Sustainability in the human development context refers to distributional equity of sharing development opportunities between present and future generations and ensuring intergenerational and intragenerational equity in access to opportunities. Productivity here means investments in people and enabling macro-economic environment for them to attain maximum potential. Economic growth is therefore a subset of human development models – an essential part but not the entire structure. Empowerment here means that people are in a position to exercise choices of their own free will and implies political democracy, economic liberalism, decentralisation of power and involvement of civil society.

Scope and Coverage of Issues

The scope and coverage of issues under the broad umbrella of human development is pretty large to include all such issues, policies and programmers which contribute to strengthening of human capabilities and widening of people's choices. The Human Development Reports, right since their inception in 1990, deal with issues concerned and connected with the promotion of sustainable human development. While the first report (1990) introduced the concept of human development and constructed the Human Development Index (HDI), later reports dealt with (i) financing of human development and the role of the government (1991); (ii) international dimensions of financing human development and the role of global markets (1992); (iii) people's participation in development (1993); (iv) new imperatives of human security in homes, jobs, streets, communities and in their environment (1994); (v) gender and human development and construction of Gender Development Index (GDI) and Gender Empowerment Measure (GEM) (1995); (vi) link between economic growth and human development (1996); (vii) human development and eradication of poverty and the introduction of Human Poverty Index (HPI) (1997); (viii) consumption standards and human development (1998); (ix) globalisation and human development (1999); (x) human rights and human development (2000); (xi) making new technologies work for human development (2001); (xii) deepening democracy in a fragmented world (2002), (xiii) declaration of Millennium Development Goals to end poverty (2003); (xiv) cultural diversities in a globalised world (2004); and (xv) International Cooperation: Aid, Trade and Security (2005); Beyond Scarcity: Power, Poverty and Global Water Crisis (2006); Fighting Climate Change: Human Solidarity in a Divided World (2007–2008); and Human Development on the Move: Migration Both Within and Beyond Borders (2009).

Dealing with the host of issues integrally connected with human development, all these reports have helped in (i) compiling of national human development reports, reflecting the human development scenario with statistics and policy and concerns and commitments; (ii) preparing human development country profiles; (iii) improving human development statistics; (iv) setting up of human development targets; (v) assessing the cost of targets; (vi) clarifying the role of government, civil society, NGOs, private sector and international development agencies; (vii) deciding the financial responsibility of different players/stakeholders; (viii) formulating comprehensive national strategies for human development; (ix) seeking external cooperation through more effective technical assistance and financial; and (x) building political alliances to accelerate the pace and progress of human development.

Measurement and Indicators

To measure human development, the UNDP has devised human development indices such as HDI (Human Development Index), HPI (Human Poverty Index), GDI (Gender-related Development Index), GEM (Gender Empowerment Measurement), HFI (Human Freedom Index) and PFI (Political Freedom Index). HDI is a summary measure of three dimensions of human development concept: living a long and healthy life, being educated and having a decent standard of living (Anand and Sen, 1994). It combines measures of life expectancy, school enrolment, literacy and income to allow a broader view of a country's development than using income alone which is often equated with well-being. The HDI can highlight the successes of some countries and the slower progress of others. Rankings by HDI and by GDP, per capita income can also differ, showing that high levels of human development can be achieved without high incomes – and that high incomes do not guarantee high levels of human development. HPI reflects the distribution of progress and measures the backlog of deprivation that still exists. The HPI measures deprivation in the same dimensions of basic human development as the HDI. It is measured on two indices: HPI-1 and HPI-2. HPI-1 measures poverty in developing countries. It focuses on deprivations in three dimensions: longevity, as measured by the probability at birth of not surviving to age 40; knowledge as measured by adult literacy rate; and overall economic provisioning – public and private – as measured by the percentage of people not using improved water sources and the percentage of those without sustainable access to an improved water source and the percentage of children underweight for age. HPI-2 focuses on deprivation in the same three dimensions as HP-1 and one additional one – social exclusion. The indicators are the probability at birth of not surviving to age 60, the adult functional literacy rate, the percentage of people living below the income poverty line and long-term unemployment rate. GDI measures achievements in the same dimensions and using the same indicators as the HDI, but captures inequalities in achievement between women and men. It is simply the HDI adjusted downward for gender inequality. The greater is the gender disparity in basic human development, the lower is the country's GDI compared with its HDI. GEM reveals whether women take part in economic and political life. It focuses on measuring gender inequality in key areas of economic and political participation and decision-making. It tracks the percentage of women in parliament among legislators, senior officials and managers and among professionals and technical workers – and the gender disparity in earned income, reflecting economic independencies. Differing from the GDI, it exposes inequality in opportunities in selected areas.

Commenting on the value of the human development indices, Paul Streeten in his 'Foreword' to Mahub-ul-Haq's book *Reflections on Human Development* made an important observation worth quoting here. He wrote: "Such indexes are useful in focusing attention and simplifying problems. They are eye catching. They have a considerable political appeal. They have the stronger impact on the mind and draw public attention. The strongest arguments in their favour are that they show up the inadequacies, such as GNP. They reflect our attention from one set of items to others." He, however, added a caveat: "The concept of human development is much wider than what can be caught in any index or set of indicators (Streeten, 1995: XIII).

A Holistic Concept

As human development covers all aspects of development, it is viewed as a 'holistic concept', or a 'holistic development model'. It embraces every development issue, including economic growth, social investment, people's empowerment, provision of basic needs and social safety nets, political and cultural freedoms and all other aspects of people's lives. Most of the recent elaborations of the human development paradigm have been carried out by the annual Human Development Reports, which since 1990 have been commissioned by the UNDP. For over a decade, through its global Human Development Reports, the UNDP has been in the forefront of an effort to generate in the contemporary development discourse a policy focus on the broader attributes of human well-being.

Human development models, as evolved by the UNDP, do not require only the provision of basic service, normally by the state. The models embrace all choices – particularly political, social and cultural – while the basic needs models are generally limited to economic choices. The human development models include all aspects of development. These are: (i) development must put people at the centre of its concern: (ii) the purpose of development is to enlarge all human choices, not just income; (iii) the human development paradigm is concerned both with building up of human capabilities (through investment in people) and with using those human capabilities fully (through an enabling framework for growth and development; (iv) human development has four essential pillars, viz., equity, sustainability, productivity and empowerment; (v) it regards economic growth as essential but emphasises the need to pay attention to its quality, distribution, its link with human life and questions of long-term sustainability; (vi) it defines ends of development and analyses sensible options of achieving them; (vii) it consistently takes the view that growth is not the end of economic development – but that the absence of growth often is. Economic growth is essential for human development but to fully exploit the opportunities for improved well-being that growth offers, it needs to be properly managed; and (viii) there is no automatic link between economic growth and human progress.

The human development paradigm suggests four ways to create desirable link between economic growth and human development: (i) the emphasis on investment in education, health and skills of the peoples to enable them to participate in growth process as well as to share its benefits; (ii) more equitable distribution of income and assets – because it is critical for creating a close link between economic growth and human development; (iii) well-structured social expenditures by the government; and (iv) the empowerment of people, particularly women, is a sure way to link growth and human development. In fact, empowerment should accompany all aspects of life.

In conclusion, it is fair to say that human development paradigm is the most holistic development model that exists. It embraces every development issue. It is neither narrowly technocratic nor overly philosophical. It is a practical reflection of life. Here, it is also pertinent to mention that this holistic model of human development has been pioneered, promoted and intellectually enriched by Mahbub-ul-Haq, the renowned economist of Bangladesh who served the UNDP for more than a decade, and is credited to be the chief architect of the early Human Development Reports launched under the sponsorship of the UNDP. Human Development Reports published annually have made enormous contribution to international development debate. The first Human Development Report (1990) introduced the concept of human development and argued that real purpose of development should be to enlarge people's choices. Subsequent reports have developed the basic concept. Each report has presented the balance sheets for human development for both industrial and developing countries. Since their inception these reports have attracted a great deal of international attention and debate. And, many countries, going beyond discussions and policy statements, are putting human development into practice.

National Human Development Reports

National Human Development Reports are being published since 1992. These reports build on the analytical framework of the global Human Development Reports by examining the countries' most pressing development issues and exploring ways to place human development at the forefront of the national political agenda. These reports are unique country-owned products, drafted by leading national experts and intellectuals and often containing data not published elsewhere. Through a country-led process of consultation, research and report writing, they bring together diverse voices, put difficult issues on the table and help mobilise action for human development policy-making. The reports are also a tool for policy analysis and planning that contribute to progress towards the Millennium Development Goals and provide a unique and valuable resource in analysing global issues.

Since 1992 more than 400 regional and national human development reports have been produced in more than 135 countries. All these reports emphasise key human development concepts. In addition, each national team addresses to specific themes tied to the country's most urgent development issues. The reports have addressed human development approaches to governance, poverty, economic growth, gender, peace and security, survival and health, the environment and information and communication technology. Although 299 national reports have been on general human development, most have addressed other pressing issues facing the nation at the time of publication – including 263 that have analysed governance-related topics such as civil society, youth, human rights, the role of the state, decentralisation, social cohesion and exclusion, participation, inequity and democracy. The reports offer concrete policy recommendations on how to tackle these thematic areas through the human development prism.

Strategies and Policy Perspectives

Human development strategies emphasise the need to allocate adequate public investments in favour of human development priorities such as shelter and quality of housing; sanitation – access to toilet facilities; access to safe drinking water, electricity; road connectivity; and provisions of basic and secondary education and primary health care. However, the human development strategies of the majority of developing countries traditionally and currently emphasise investing in education and health and promoting equitable economic growth. Education and health are indeed the two pillars of human development. Accelerating human development requires universal primary education. This is the foundation on which the secondary and tertiary education and skill training can be built. Central to this is the strategy to provide quality primary education to all school-age children. Public funding of education has to be increased in primary and secondary education. Similarly, health is a sector of human development to provide individuals the choice to live a healthy life – free from illness and ailments – and a reasonable life span – a crucial attribute in the notion of personal well-being. Likewise, a transition from high incidence of morbidity and mortality is considered a desirable and valued social change. Attainments on other dimensions of human developments – water, sanitation and shelter – can reinforce the transition towards better health and longevity of the population. However, systems of health and education are severally underfunded in most of the low-income countries. With small and inadequate budgets, and poor people lose out.

Countries with low human development – particularly those stuck in poverty – have the most pressing needs in terms of food, clothes, shelter, health, education, water and sanitation – the essential ingredients of human development. All developing countries must construct coherent strategies for achieving Millennium Development Goals and to increase investment on human development measures. Each of these countries must, therefore, pursue a human development strategy that meets its specific needs. National strategy should be based on solid evidence, good science and proper evaluation and monitoring.

With regard to policy perspectives the top priority has to be accorded not only to sustained economic growth but also to equity, good governance and an effective human rights regime to remove discrimination, secure social justice, and promote the well-being of all people (HDR, 2003: 4). Equally important is to strengthen welfare, development and empowerment policies and institutions for the upliftment of the weaker and vulnerable sections of society. Public policy needs to respond to the issues of resource levels, performance standards and efficiency and effectivity of such social development policies and programmes that directly focus on rural areas, poor communities and women, children and the aged. What is needed is that the efforts be properly made, and services to be distributed more fairly and efficiently.

The Indian Scenario

While the country has made tremendous progress in economic development, infrastructural resources and technological advancement, all these have, however, not resulted in the materialisation of universal human well-being as a product of development efforts. Concededly, the impressive economic growth has not been accompanied by sustainable improvements in social well-being. The new thinking, therefore, is that the prosperity of the few and the penury of many would create such imbalances that would generate tensions and conflicts resulting in the tearing apart of the social fabric of society. Accordingly, human development has been accorded priority in the planned programmes of development since the inception of the planning progress and constitutes the first and an important area of concern for India Vision 2020 (Ray, 2004: 19). Despite budgetary limitations the central and state governments continue to invest more in social development sectors – demography, food security and nutrition, employment, education, health and vulnerabilities. However, despite impressive achievements, the country's record of human development is far from satisfactory. The country is being ranked low in the successive Human Development Reports of the UNDP. The poor ranking of the country is a reminder of the daunting human development challenges in the face of the unacceptable and yet persisting levels of deprivations in many aspects of people's lives.

Following the UNDP's human development framework, the National Human Development Report (2001) of the Planning Commission, Government of India has broken fresh ground in quite a few ideas in presenting the status of the human development at state level in India. It has, for the first time, put together an extensive data base for social indicators – on various aspects of the quality of life on three critical dimensions of well-being, namely, longevity (the ability to live long and healthy life); education (the ability to read, write and acquire knowledge); and command over resources (the ability to enjoy a decent standard of living). The report presents a comprehensive profile of the state of human development in India. It notes with some satisfaction that the overall human development as reflected in the HDI has improved significantly between 1980 and 2001. At the national level, during the eighties, the index has improved by nearly 26 per cent and by another 24 per cent during the nineties. There have been improvements both in rural as well as in urban areas. Though the rural-urban gap in the level of human development continues to be significant, it has declined during the period. Inequalities across states on the HDI are less than the income inequality as reflected in the per capita State Domestic Product. At the state level, there are wide disparities in the level of human development. The economically less developed states are also the states with low HDI. Similarly, the economically better off states are also the ones with relatively better performance on HDI. However, the relation between the HDI and levels of development does not show any correspondence among the middle-income states in the country (NHDR, 2002: 34).

In respect of two very critical components of HDI, i.e., literacy and longevity, the scenario seems to be stupefying. At present, India has achieved a literacy rate of 64 per cent but still has the gross number of illiterates (approximately 300 million adults, 30 per cent of the entire population is the largest in the world). The current enrolment rate for primary education is around 77 per cent and for secondary education it is about 60 per cent. The education sector has a high dropout rate – only two out of 10 students reach the 9th standard.

Measured in terms of infant mortality, maternal mortality, life expectation and nutrition, the health of the Indian population has improved dramatically in the past 50 years. Life expectancy has risen from 33 years to 64 years. The infant mortality rate (IMR) has fallen from 148 to 71 per 1,000. The crude birth rate (CBR) has fallen from 25 to under 9. The couple protection rate (CPR) and total fertility rate (TFR) have also improved substantially. Yet, despite these achievements, wide disparities still exist between different income groups, rural and urban communities, states and even districts within states. Communicable diseases remain the major cause of illness. The IMR among the poorest sections of the population is 2.5 times higher than among the richest. Maternal mortality also remains very high. More than one lakh women die each year due to the pregnancy-related complications.

Human Development Parameters at a Glance

Parameter	*Present percentage*
Poverty as per cent of population below poverty line	26.0
Male adult literacy rate	68.3
Female adult literacy rate	44.0
Net primary school enrolment ratio	77.2
Life expectancy at birth in year	64.0
Infant mortality rate per 1,000 live births	71.0
Child malnutrition as of children under 5 years based on weight for age	45.0

Having assessed the country's human development scenario in terms of specific human development indices, the National Human Development Report (2001) makes certain candid admissions showing: (a) slow improvements in gender equality; (b) considerable decline in human poverty along with persistence of striking inter-state differences; (c) low attainments for women and for people residing in rural areas; (d) women, children and other poor/socio-economically backward and vulnerable people in both rural and urban areas are typically progressing slower than the national average; and (e) the urban-rural gap appears to be persisting or worsening in all sectors of human development.

Notwithstanding the inadequacies of human development infrastructure and the financial constraints and budgetary limitations of the central and state governments, the National Human Development Report highlights the centrality of human development paradigm, and suggests, amongst several measures, the need to formulate and prescribe appropriate public policy measures, institutional structures, and approaches and perspectives to accelerate the pace and progress of human development. In his 'Foreword' to the Report, K.C. Pant, the then Deputy Chairman of the Planning Commission, emphasised the necessity of having a framework of such development strategies that forge and strengthen the link between economic growth and human development, for furthering the well-being of the people. For any public policies and programmes, it has to be anchored in a social context. It is therefore necessary for countries like India to develop a contextually relevant approach to human development, and identify and devise appropriate indicators to help formulate and monitor public policy. The imperatives of human development require more government interventions, greater presence and better allocations. The publication of National Human Development Reports has now been suspended/stopped and several state governments are publishing their annual reports.

References

Anand, Sudhir and Amartya Sen (1994) *Human Development Index: Methodology and Measurement*, Human Development Report Office Occasional Paper 12, UNDP, New York.

Haq, Mahbub-ul- (2000) *Reflections on Human Development*, Oxford India Paperbacks, New Delhi.

Planning Commission (Government of India) (2004) *National Human Development Report (2001)*, Oxford University Press, New Delhi.

Planning Commission (Government of India) Amit S. Ray (2004) *India Vision 2020 (The Report of the Committee on India Vision 2020)*, Academic Foundation, New Delhi.

Srivastava, S.P. (1998) *The Development Debate: Critical Perspectives*, Rawat Publications, Jaipur and New Delhi.

Streeten, Paul (2000) "Foreword", in Mahbub-ul-Haq, op. cit.

United Nations Development Programme (UNDP) *Reports (1990–2004)*.

13

Globalisation and Gandhian Economic Thought

Bindeshwar Pathak

Of a large number of old as well as recent writings on Gandhiji and Gandhian thought (Gandhism) only few of them directly refer to the core themes of Gandhian economics vis-à-vis the beneficial and the baneful effects of globalisation on Indian society, culture, economy and polity. The scarcity of literature on this important subject has rendered the present-day critiques of globalisation devoid of several critical ideas which surely and certainly offer new insights and understandings to shape up India's response to the sweeping tide of globalisation. Many Gandhian scholars are now realising the need to discover the relevance of Gandhian economics against the social and economic aftermaths of globalisation in the developing countries, including India. Here, for obvious reasons, the Gandhian scholars are turning their attention Gandhiji's *Hind Swaraj* – a small but enormously powerful publication of 1938. Not that Hindi Swaraj had not been extensively quoted in the writings of Gandhian economists (alas! Few in number are alive today), but the fact had been that the views of these economists had been contemptuously termed as 'archaic', 'unproductive' (even 'counterproductive') and 'too old-fashioned' as to be given little or no credence – by pro-growth development economists dazzled with the glitter of globalisation in many parts of the world. As a consequence, the feeble voice of the

Gandhian economists had been drowned in the cacophony of loud noises raised in favour of globalisation by a bunch of IMF/World Bank-inspired economists. Now, when the things have gone awry, and the sweet songs of globalisation are turning sour, many people in the country, including several economists, are remembering Gandhiji, as if he was the prophet to forewarn us against the evil impacts of globalisation, as we see in the country today. I am not surprised at this turn around, and am inclined to believe that we Indians have the habit of being charmed by many western ideas and thought processes (ideologies to be precise) which promise to take us to a make-believe world of progress and prosperity promised by economically and technologically advanced western nations. When things do not happen the way we want them to be, we get disappointed and start looking for subterfuges. Realising our mistakes, we turn to rediscovering the relevance of the ideas, views and opinions of the founding fathers of the country, who had envisioned India of a different sort. It is, therefore, no wonder that we are now remembering Gandhiji when confronted with the baneful effects of globalisation.

Given this situation, I wish to examine the relevance of what Gandhiji had said long ago about the kind of economy which would suit most to the country like India. This I am doing with the sole intent of contemplating whether or not the spirited implementation of Gandhian economic thought would have helped us laying the foundation of an economy of equity with its eyes fixed on the welfare and the well-being of the poor. Since globalisation (of the kind we see today) was not there when Gandhiji was alive, the term 'globalisation' does not figure in any of his writings and speeches. This renders the exercise of situating Gandhiji's gospel of economic growth little problematic in the context of globalisation and its menacing manifestations in India today. Having this problematic in mind, I now wish to refer to the echoing critiques of globalisation to make clear how Gandhiji had forewarned us not to drift from what he thought was best for India. Having done that I would, in the latter part of this paper, reiterate the relevance of Gandhiji, as a Man of the Millennium, who had a vision of a different social and economic order best suited to the existing conditions. And, that I think is the objective of this paper. But, let us first understand the dynamics of globalisation to see how good or bad it is for Gandhiji's conception of Indian society.

Understanding the Dynamics of Globalisation

Globalisation, its different articulations notwithstanding, generally speaking, refers to a process through which national economies are becoming more open and thus more subject to supranational economic influences and less amenable to national control (Mishra, 2000: 4). Globalisation proper (as distinct from internationalisation of economies) refers to a situation where distinct national economies cease to exist in that they are subsumed and rearticulated into the system by international processes and transactions (Hirst and Thompson, 1996: 10). Globalisation, in its fundamental features, is the closer integration of the countries and the peoples of the world which has been brought about by the enormous reduction of costs of transportation and communication, and the breaking down of artificial barriers to the flows of goods, services, capital, knowledge and people across borders (Stiglitz, 2000: 9).

Globalisation, in operational terms, means: (a) globalised production and marketing networks; (b) economic interdependence between countries in the economic field – trade, technology, labour and internal capital flows: and (c) international integration of culture, technology, labour standards, governance and media management. In simpler terms, globalisation means free movement of goods, services, people and information across national boundaries. In essence, it is the global integration of national economies and societies – meaning internationalisation as well as transnationalisation of economies – the world becoming a global market.

Globalisation has become an increasingly, dominant feature over the past decades as more and more countries are getting integrated into the global economy through trade and capital flows, and also transfer of information and communication technologies. The nature and speed of the processes of globalisation have been facilitated and accelerated by new developments in information and communication technology. The era of globalisation, as its protagonists claim, is opening many opportunities for millions of people around the world. The protagonists of globalisation, who, indeed, are singing the sweet songs of globalisation, maintain that it: (i) promotes production and enhances productivity; (ii) opens up markets and allows free movement of goods which generate competition and augment the quality of goods and services offered; (iii) increases the rate of economic growth through liberalisation; (iv) makes the economies of the developing countries more robust due to flow of foreign investments; (v) benefits the consumers by offering them vast choices of goods and services that they can avail of in the domestic market; (vi) develops local economies owing to increase in international economic cooperation; (vii) boosts production due to structural adjustment processes favouring liberal and forward-looking economies (viii) promises better prospects for increased employment, enhanced growth rate and sustained development, which lead to better quality of life; and (ix) leads to the availability of more comforts, more leisure and more affluence in society.

On the contrary, the antagonists of globalisation maintain that (i) it is ruthless in its functioning as it obeys the command of money powers; (ii) it tries to perpetuate a system where the poor are always kept deprived and craving for more; (iii) it has urban bias which will certainly lead to lopsided growth in the developing countries and would increase the rich-poor and rural-urban divide and disparities; (iv) it helps MNCs prey on the erosion of traditional values and knowledge systems through their propaganda, advertisement and brand creation; (v) it aggressively promotes privatisation and liberalisation resulting in the weakened hold of governments over their economy and polity; and (vi) it is driven by the advanced industrialised countries of the West to exploit the markets of the developing countries through the penetration of MNCs and an uncontrolled access of international monetary institutions like the IMF and World Bank.

Notwithstanding the powerfully persuasive stands of both the protagonists and antagonists of globalisation, the fact, however, is that globalisation is all set for its long march and triumphant journey in most parts of the world. Given the nature of global politics and the instrumentalities of international economic governance, globalisation is an irreversible process that cannot easily wished away. All countries have to learn to live with it. Even the World Bank admitted that globalisation creates opportunities but also produces risks. Unfortunately, for the majority of developing countries, the risks outnumber the opportunities. Let me briefly explain why is that true in a country like India.

Globalisation is making its impact felt in India in a variety of ways. It has already made new inroads in the economy of the country with its positive, innovative and dynamic aspects, which at the same time entailing negative, disruptive and marginalising aspects. The balance sheet of its benefits compares poorly with its baneful results.

This is why it has become a matter of intense controversy. Let us understand why this is so?

India's tryst with globalisation tallies with that of the experiences that several developing countries in Asia, Africa and Latin America have had in the recent years. Globalisation has created a growing divide between the haves and have-nots and has pushed a large population into situations of deprivation and destitution. The lesson learnt is that its golden promise of reducing poverty has remained largely unfulfilled. The introduction of market economy, for many such countries, has proved to be an unmitigated disaster. A distinguished American economist, Joseph E. Stiglitz (2002: 6) has asserted that when the critics of globalisation accuse western countries of their planned conspiracy, full of hypocracy, deception and deceit, they are right. The powerful western nations have driven the globalisation agenda in a manner as to ensure garnering of disproportionate share of benefits at the expense of the developing countries. The hard reality is that the developing countries, including India, cannot compete with the advanced industrialised countries of the developed world. In all respects the developing countries have remained at a disadvantageous position. In too many spheres the benefits of globalisation have been much less than what its advocates claim. Contrary to expectations, the two prominent accompaniments of globalisation – 'liberalisation' and 'privatisation' – have not resulted in the promised economic growth. As a result, it has become abundantly clear, not just to ordinary citizens, but also to policy makers that globalisation, as it has been practised, has not lived up to what its protagonists have promised. In some cases, it has not even resulted in growth, but when it has, it has not brought benefits to all – the net effect has all too often been to benefit the few at the expense of many. In many cases, says Stiglitz (ibid.: 20), commercial interests and values have superseded the people's concern for environment, democracy, human rights and social justice. Globalisation, observed the former President of France, Jacques Chirac (1996), "is not making life better for those who are most in need of its promised benefits".

The problematic of globalisation today is that it has provoked such controversies which suggest that it: (i) assaults national sovereignty, erodes local culture and traditions and threatens economic and social stability; (ii) brings instability and unwelcome changes in society, culture and tradition; (iii) exposes workers to competition from imports; (iv) undermines governments and nation-states; (v) diminishes employment, hurts people without assets, without education and without high skills; and (vi) unsuits small firms, weak investors and business houses without market access and branded items. Given these threats, the hard critics of globalisation repeatedly cry aloud, through their writings and speeches at the global economic fora, that it is not working for many of the world's poor.

Globalisation and Gandhian Economic Thought

Against the backdrop of current critique of globalisation, let us surmise for a moment. How Gandhiji would have responded to factors and forces fuelling LPG (liberalisation, privatisation and globalisation) in the contemporary Indian society, had he been alive today. My guess that being a visionary and a realist, combining in himself the qualities of an idealist as well as pragmatist, Gandhiji may not have opposed globalisation *per se*, but may have argued against it inasmuch as it affects the common man; the village-based cottage industries; usurpation of the benefits of globalisation by the minority of people already in positions of social and economic advantages cornering of wealth by a select few business and industrial families; and drastic reductions in the financial allocations for the 'welfare state' spending. But, in so doing too, Gandhiji may have taken pragmatist position on the powerful paradigm shifts in the fast changing global economic scenario where under only the industrially, techno-scientifically and economically advanced country can dominate the policies, programmes and operations of the World Bank, IMF and WTO – the three major institutions of global economic governance – which provide support and sustenance to the forces of globalisation sweeping over the globe. But, Gandhiji, under no circumstance, may have compromised with the sovereignty of the nation-state to decide what economic path is best suited for the country. Had he been alive today he would have relentlessly campaigned against the adverse impacts of globalisation by sticking to his seminal economic thoughts which envisioned of an economy of a different sort.

Without being a distinguished economist, Gandhiji stuck steadfastly to a simple route of economic well-being of village economy to usher in an era of economic growth best suited to the augmentation of village industries and generation of rural employment – both of which are today hit by the processes of globalisation. He would have pointed out the ill-effects of the Indian society being subordinated to the modern scientific and technological consequences of globalisation under which poverty has been accentuated, unnecessary wants have been created, large-scale unemployment is in place, ruination of the countryside is evident and the village industries and handicrafts are on the brink of extinction. He would have resented the paradoxes of the present-day world where there is poverty amidst plenty overproduction in face of undernourishment; resurgence of affluence and wasteful life in contrast to bare survival; overdevelopment versus underdevelopment; economic growth versus ecological crisis; consumerism for few as against denial of basic needs of the millions; explosion of knowledge as against vast masses of illiterates; and globalisation versus intense parochialism and ethnicity.

Given this scenario, Gandhiji would have more forcefully propagated his old economic thoughts on the removal of poverty, elimination of inequality and adoption of an economics of social welfare based on ethics. Interestingly, Amartya Sen's economic thought seem to be inspired by the economic philosophy of Gandhiji. N. Mahalingam, in his article on Amartya Sen's economics and Gandhian idealism, finds too much in common in the economic thoughts of both Gandhiji and Amartya Sen. He wrote: "Both did now want to divorce social welfare as the goal of economic activity; both looked upon the removal of poverty and social equality as the goal of economic policies. While Gandhiji said 'economics without ethics is rootless', Professor Amartya Sen stated that 'economics without human welfare is fruitless'" (Mahalingam, 2001: 223).

Gandhiji's economic thought stressed the following:

- Removal of poverty and inequality.
- Curtailment of wasteful expenditure by the prosperous section of society so that all could be free from penury.
- Villages to function as self-sufficient economic units.
- Villages to serve as production centres rather than as markets.
- The emphasis on heavy industries and power-based industries should be reduced.
- The purpose of any economic plan should be to promote greatest happiness for the greatest number.
- The basic needs of all should be satisfied.

The essence and the foundation stone of Gandhian economic thought, which several critics of globalisation now endorse, is the removal of economic inequality through the mechanism of equal opportunity. Let us remember here that Gandhiji did not say that all are equal; he only said that all should be treated equally without discrimination. "Economic equality of my conception," said Gandhiji, "does not mean that everyone literally has the same amount. The real meaning of economic equality is to earn according to his/her need." Gandhiji's idea of society is one where all have right to equal opportunity. In the words of Gandhiji, "The real implication of equal distribution is that each man shall have the wherewithal to supply all his natural needs and no more." Gandhiji further said, "Cut down you wants, all your economic problems will be solved". By this statement Gandhiji meant a simple living bereft of superficial wants which globalisation has created. Gandhiji emphasised village development (as opposed to city development in the era of globalisation) for very pragmatic reasons, for he thought that without developing its villages, India cannot become a developed country. He wanted villages to be self-sufficient economic units with local production centres, only because that alone will create massive rural employment opportunities to enable reduction of poverty. "More employment", said Gandhiji, "will make our villages become self-sufficient economic units." Heavy industries, he argued, cause unemployment, the like of which we are seeing today in our midst. He was of the view that labour can be enthused to improve productivity only if it is assured that improved productivity (which globalisation seeks to encourage) will not lend them in loss of jobs. The repeated argument that improved productivity would bring higher wages, which in turn would unleash demand for consumer goads – and durables and thus create more jobs, at the micro level, can hardly bring any solace to the worker who faces redundancy as a result of higher productivity. The former President of India, R. Venkataraman writes: "This theory has relevance to countries with shortage of manpower and single-digit unemployment. In countries with astronomical figures of unemployment, it is difficult to enthuse workers in productivity schemes unless they are assured of job security" (2001: 16). Here, we must bear in mind that globalisation is no guarantor of job security to anyone, whether skilled or unskilled, knowledgeable or illiterate. Everyone can be thrown out if company does not earn profit.

In a very perceptive article on "Globalisation and Gandhi," Professor Lallan Prasad, Head, Department of Business Economics, University of Delhi regrettably writes that "in an era of globalisation we are paying for our sins by not following him (Gandhiji). We have done practically nothing which he wanted; and which would have made us strong to face the competition which is on our doors, destroying our economy and culture" (2001: 40–43). Globalisation, by all reckonings, is the antithesis of Gandhian economic thought which aimed at self-reliant model of economic growth, development with a human face, and prosperity without widespread penury. Thanks to the cozening stranglehold of forces unleashed by globalisation, we have plethora of problems facing the country. Whilst the urban India may be shining, the rural India is whining. While there is glitter in certain parts of our cities, there is enough gloom in our urban slums, where nearly 40 per cent of our urban population lives. While the percentage of poor has declined, there is not much reduction in the absolute number of the poor in the country. Almost a third of population is below poverty line. Literacy in villages is one of the lowest and even the basic amenities like drinking water and sanitation are scarce. The trickle-down theory of our planners has failed. The city-based rich have been accumulating wealth, whilst the people in villages are facing poverty of means and resources. The planning had been urban and industrial development oriented, with the result, adequate employment opportunities could not be created in rural areas. Whatever production was available to small-scale sector has been gradually withdrawn, leaving the village artisans and craftsmen on the mercy of traders and moneylenders. Multinationals are economic powerhouses of the new global economic order. They have their eyes on India only as a vast market far their goods and services at the detriment of local producers of consumer goods. A country which lacks in roads and energy having a marked penchant for more and more luxury cars manufactured by multinational automobile giants. In the garb of level playing fields, the planners and policy makers are persuaded or allured to make concessions to MNCs which are not always in the interest of the country's economy.

Today, in the name of globalisation of trade, i.e., buying the best and the cheapest from anywhere in the world, we are abandoning national industries to the mercy of multinationals. In the first place, multinational corporations have the advantage of huge capital resources, advanced technologies, procurement of inputs from their own concerns scattered all over the globe and manipulating price so as to stifle local competition. With all these advantages, the multinationals want level playing ground with indigenous industries. One would like to ask whether indigenous industries in developing countries are on level playing ground with the multinationals.

The crucial questions that the advocates of globalisation in India have to answer are: Who are those who have been benefited from the process of globalisation? To what extent has globalisation aided peasants, disadvantaged sections, women and ordinary working people? Has it decreased disparities in wealth and income? How has globalisation strengthened the capacities of the states particularly with low levels of human development and lacking in economic resources to meet their basic human rights obligations to their citizen? In responding to these questions the protagonists of globalisation may advance ingenious arguments in support of their viewpoints, the fact, however, is that only a small section of humanity is basking in the glow of globalisation, whilst the larger segment wallows in increasing despondency and despair – a phenomenon which Soli Sorabjee, the former Attorney General of India, described as "the concurrence of globalisation and marginalisation". The anti-globalisation demonstrations in cities across the world, he says, should not be dismissed as extravagant protests of misguided persons. They symbolise the voice of millions who lose out in the trading game. The urgent need, he opines, is to ensure that the processes of globalisation are sensitive to the goals of sustainable human development of which the promotion and protection of human rights is paramount.

Too many critics of globalisation now argue that the policies of privatisation and liberalisation in business, commerce and industry; heavy dependence on market forces, retreat of the state from its welfare commitment; and substantial resort to the policy directions and dictates of the World Bank, IMF and WTO do not necessarily work to the benefit of the poor and deprived people of the world, more so in India. Pressures of global integration have led to the curtailment of social welfare. Conditionalities imposed by the World Bank, IMF and WTO compel such structural adjustments that work to the detriment of the needy. The development paradigm that depends mainly on economic growth seems to ignore the demands of equity. New agenda under the external pressure of globalisation has distorted development process, making the state lose its credibility and capacity to serve its own people adequately. The inescapable conclusion of all this is that neither the state nor the market can meet the emergent needs of people. Market is a very double-edged weapon. It is ruthless, insensitive and does not care for the losers. It is also a war where those unable to compete have no place. They have to suffer, get subjugated and follow the dictates of the mighty, i.e., the MNCs.

Relevance of Gandhian Economic Thought

In this part of the paper, I would like to take a position in line with many of the Gandhian scholars who have written extensively on the relevance of Gandhian economic thought. I would reiterate and reaffirm that what Gandhiji had said about the righteous path to economic growth in the country is still relevant in the era of globalisation. To appreciate the continued relevance of Gandhian economic thought, we must read his writings and speeches very carefully and stop being swayed by the propaganda that he was against science, technology, industrialisation (heavy industries) and modernisation of Indian society and culture. Such a misconception of Gandhiji's opinions and views is completely bereft of his correct understanding and is both mischievous and misconstrued. For example, when Aldous Huxley wrote in an article that "Mr Gandhi wants to take humanity back to the primitive age", Pandit Jawahar Lal Nehru gave a spirited reply, saying, "You have not understood Gandhi and that is why you say he is anti-science. I know Gandhi much better than anybody else, and he has said that he was not anti-science. On the other hand, he had cautioned humanity against the consequences of using science and technology in an indiscriminate manner." Actually, he not against science and technology, but against science and technology being used for the exploitation of man by man. Today, if we look at the global development that has taken place on the basis of science and technology, we find that the advances in science and technology have created an unstable equilibrium in human family. Several assessments made with regard to the main beneficiaries of global economic developments tellingly reveal that at a global level 20 per cent of humanity has access to more than 80 per cent of global production and the bottom 20 per cent had access to only 1.4 per cent of global production. This is the state of disequilibrium that has come about. There is affluence at the greatest level on one side and abject poverty at the other. Gandhiji had pointed out that if science and technology are used for the exploitation of man by man, this equilibrium is bound to come into existence. At that time he opined that there is enough to meet the needs of all persons but there is not enough to meet the greed of even a small percentage of people. Therefore, he said, everyone should be satisfied with what one has and not go on increasing one's wants. This is even more relevant today than at the time he said it.

Today, we find that with the development of high technology, there is more and more unemployment not only in the developing countries but even in the developed countries. In modern scientific and technological society man is subordinated to machine and he is measured in terms of money. The modern science and technology promise plenty but result in poverty, creation of unnecessary wants, large-scale unemployment, the ruination of the countryside, the growth of cities and slums, the extinction of village handicrafts, and the general erosion of moral values. All this has happened because we have not given a fair trial to his economic programmes and philosophy, and the result is there for all of us to see. After over four decades of socialist experiments and over two decades of globalisation, today the people living below poverty line are almost equal to the population of our country at the dawn of independence.

Gandhiji's critique of modern civilisation was influenced by the writings of some western thinkers. Edward Carpenter's *Civilization: Its Cause and Cure* greatly influenced Gandhiji for critical attitude towards modern science and technology. He decried modern civilisation because it is materialistic and exploitative. Speaking at the Meccano Club, Calcutta, in August 1925, he said: "Do not for one moment consider that I condemn all that is western. For the time being I am dealing with the predominant character of modern civilisation, do not call it western civilisation. The predominant character of modern civilisation is exploitation of the weaker races of the earth. The predominant character or modern civilisation is to dethrone God and enthrone materialism." Modern civilisation, according to Gandhiji, is based on a faulty concept or model of man as materialistic or body-centred and limitless consumer of utilities. Such a view of man places sensual or materialistic wants over and above the spiritual or moral values. It regards the individual as wholly independent and self-centred atom with no moral or spiritual bonds or obligation.

Gandhiji maintained that modern civilisation seeks to increase our 'bodily comforts' through better houses, better clothes, and faster modes of travel and transport, and mechanised production. These, however, have failed to bring real happiness to the people. On the contrary, they have brought about newer diseases, dehumanisation of workers, and more efficient and large-scale means of the destruction of life. "Formerly", writes Gandhi, "men were made slaves under physical compulsion. Now, they are enslaved by temptation of money and of the luxuries that money can buy. There are now diseases of which people never dreamt before." Divorced from ethics or morality, the modern self or the individual is left to the play of self-entreasured, competition, exploitation, brute force violence, etc. Modern man feels no moral or spiritual restraints in conquering or colonising other people. Gandhiji said, "I do not want my house to be walled in on all sides and my windows to be stuffed. I want the cultures of all lands to be blown about my house as freely as possible. But I refuse to be blown off my feet by any."

Gandhiji supported 'Swadeshi' for the development of the country and keeping its identity intact. He said, "Much of the deep poverty of the masses is due to the ruinous departure from Swadeshi in the economic and industrial life." He continued, "We have labored under a terrible handicap owing to an almost fatal departure from the Swadeshi spirit." Gandhiji further said, "It has often been argued that India cannot adopt economic life at any rate. Those who advance this objection do not look upon Swadeshi as a rule of life." In favour of promoting small-scale industry, he wrote, "I have no doubt in my mind that we add to the national wealth if we help the small-scale industries. I have no doubt also that true Swadeshi consists in encouraging and reviving these home industries. That alone can help the dumb millions." According to Gandhiji, any country that exposes itself to unlimited foreign competition can be reduced to starvation and, therefore, subjugation if the foreigners desire it. This is known as 'peaceful penetration'. Mechanisation is good when the hands are too few for the work intended to be accomplished. It is an evil when there are more hands than required for the work, as is the case in India.

Gandhiji was not against machinery as such but he was against centralised mass production and profit motive. He welcomed simple tools and instruments and all such machinery that saves individual labour and lightens the burden of millions of workers. "Machinery," he said, "must not be allowed to displace necessary human labour." Replying to a question whether he was against all machinery, Gandhiji said, "How can I be when I know that even this body is most delicate machinery? The spinning wheel is a machine; a little toothpick is a machine. What I object to is the craze for machinery, not machinery as such. The craze is for what they call labour-saving machinery. Men go on saving labour till thousands are without work and thrown on the open street to die of starvation." "Industrialisation on mass scale", Gandhiji said, "will necessarily lead to passive or active exploitation of the villagers as the problems of competition and marketing come in." He wrote, "Europeans pounce upon new territories like crows upon a piece of meat. I am inclined to think that this is due to their mass-production factories."

A very significant concept with a potential to change the economic and social order is Gandhiji's philosophy of trusteeship. An original thinker, as he was, Gandhiji was probably the first to see the inherent contradiction of both capitalism and communism, and, a practical idealist that he was, he propounded the theory of trusteeship which could be an alternative way of life, an economic system in place of capitalism and communism. Trusteeship provides a means of transforming the present capitalist order of society into an egalitarian one. It gives no quarter to capitalism, but gives the present owning class a chance of reforming itself. Trusteeship is the concept of universal consequence, a new alternative to correct the ills of social accumulation, and at the same time gives inspires those with managerial and entrepreneurial expertise to use the same for the good of the society.

Conclusion: Need for a Reasoned Response

In this final part of the paper, I rush to state my position vis-à-vis globalisation, lest my above articulation on Gandhian economic thought creates an impression that the adherence to the guiding principles of Gandhian economics alone is the best safeguard to ward off the deleterious impacts on globalisation on Indian society, culture and polity. My position simply is that whilst Gandhiji's opinions and views on the best ways to handle the problems of economic growth scenario are relevant, but they have to be recast, reformulated and restructured in coping with the factors and forces that make globalisation a reality not to be easily wished away and confronted with. Globalisation is inevitable, in view of the efforts of all nations to accelerate their economic growth and modernise their societies. Given the nature of global politics and the instrumentalities of international economic governance globalisation is an irreversible process which cannot be stopped. All countries have to learn to live with it and adjust to. Given also the inevitability of globalisation processes, it is imperative for all nations to participate in this process in order to draw its potential benefits. It requires many enlightened social, economic, scientific and technological policies on the part of national governments, international organisations, private sector and civil society organisations to translate the benefits of economic growth that result from globalisation into enriching the lives of ordinary people.

The problem, however, is not with globalisation, but with how it has been managed in different countries. Part of the problem lies with the international economic institutions, i.e., IMF, World Bank and WTO, which help set the rules of the game. They have done so in ways that all too often have served the interests of the more advanced industrialised countries, and of particular interest groups within those countries, rather than those of the developing countries and their poor and deprived masses. They have approached globalisation from a particular mindset shaped by a particular vision of the economy and society. There is, therefore, need to assess globalisation from the point of view of human development and poverty reduction. And that economic growth and human development must move together. This is what Gandhiji wanted and worked for. Gandhiji wanted economic growth model which is job-led, labour-intensive, pro-village and pro-poor. Gandhiji, I suppose, would not have opposed globalisation which does not (i) decrease employment opportunities for semi-skilled and unskilled labour; (ii) displace labour-intensive low-cost technology industries; (iii) increase disparities in income and accentuation of income and resource poverty of the marginalised sections of society; (iv) result in the rising social unrest; (v) decrease the public provisioning of social welfare services; (vi) downsize the government and scale down their social protection policies and programmes; (vii) erode the sovereignty of nation-states, particularly their role in economic decision-making; and (viii) rob of the autonomy of national governments to manage their economies in a manner which may ensure full employment and equitous economic growth. If Gandhian economic thought is correctly understood, the challenge is not to oppose globalisation *per se*, but to ensure that it works for people, not just for profits. The challenge further is economic growth sensitive to ethics, equity inclusion, human security and sustainability. What is of paramount importance in meeting the challenges thrown by the processes of globalisation is to adopt such alternative courses of action which suit to the Indian society, culture, economy and polity. This necessity requires alternative modes, not just those recommended, promoted or pressured by IMF, World Bank and WTO. Many governments have done that to their best advantage – Malaysia, South Korea, Taiwan and China. The evidence suggests that governments can, and have, crafted their reasoned responses to mitigating the adverse impacts of globalisation. The point, I am labouring to emphasise simply is that globalisation can be managed if it accompanied care, caution, regulation and reasonableness. If Gandhian economic thought is relevant in any way in our efforts to globalise our society, we should give credence to it. That would be the best way to remember Gandhiji in these troubled times when things look so uncertain under the market fundamentalism and forces of neo-imperialism.

References

Chirac, Jacques (1996) The Economy Must be Made to Serve People, Address at the International Labour Conference, Geneva.

Cornia, G.A. et al. (1987) *Adjustment with a Human Face*, Oxford: Clarendon Press.

Gandhi, M.K. (1938) *Hind Swaraj*, Ahmedabad: Navjeevan Publishing House.

——. (1947) *India of My Dreams*, Ahmedabad: Navjeevan Publishing House.

Garret, V. (1998) *Partisan Politics in the Global Economy*, Cambridge: Cambridge University Press.

Hirst, P. and G. Thompson (1996) *Globalization in Question*, Cambridge: Polity.

Mahalingam, N. (2001) "Amartya Sen's Economics and Gandhian Ideals", in Suresh Rao Chavan (ed.), *Mahatma Gandhi: Man of the Millennium*, Bombay: Bhartiya Vidya Bhawan.

Mishra, R. (2000) *Globalisation and the Welfare State*, Northampton, USA: Edward Elgar.

Prasad, Lallan (2001) "Globalisation and Gandhi", in *Concept Papers of the National Convention on Gandhian Agenda for the 21st Century*, New Delhi: Gandhi Smriti and Darshan Samiti.

Schaefer, R.K. (1997) *Understanding Globalisation*, Lahman: Rowman and Littlefield Publishers.

Sorabjee, Soli (2001) "Globalisation", *Sunday Times of India*, New Delhi, August 19.

Stiglitz, J.E. (2000) *Globalisation and its Discontents*, London: Allen Lane.

Venkataraman, R. (2001) "Gandhi: The Architect and Author of Spiritual Regeneration of India", in Suresh Rao Chavan (ed.), op. cit.

14

Experiments in Workers' Participation for Effective Industrial Democracy

An Analysis

R.C. Sarikwal

This article is a humble tribute to Professor S.P. Nagendra, an eminent professor and scholar of sociology. While inaugurating the Indian Chapter of RC-10 of International Sociology Association during the course of XI World Congress held at New Delhi, India in 1986, Professor Nagendra posed a genius query about the workers' participation in management saying whether this concept is a 'fact' or 'value'. Obviously this enquiry became mind-boggling for many and I was am not an exception to it.

The concept of workers' participation appears to be as much shrouded in vagueness as is the concept of industrial democracy. Various authors have provided tentative or context-specific definitions which appear inadequate when viewed in a global perspective. The diversity of definitions notwithstanding, workers' participation in the industrial relations context means workers' partnership in management. It denotes workers' involvement in the conduct of enterprise affairs. It means participation of employees in the managerial functions of the enterprise or, in other words, involvement of those at the bottom of the enterprise hierarchy in areas which had previously been reserved exclusively for the management as their prerogatives. In more specific terms, workers' participation is an act of taking part in managerial functions like planning, organising, directing and controlling, either directly by workers or indirectly by their representatives. By implication, therefore, workers' participation means taking part in the managerial functions by the workers or by the representatives of the workers (trade unions). The concept of workers' participation has different assumed names in different industrial economies and is being used interchangeably with labour management cooperation, joint regulation, joint management, co-determination, etc.

According to Walker (1974), workers' participation in management occurs when those at the bottom of an enterprise hierarchy take part in the authority and managerial functions of the enterprise, that is, employees become involved in extended areas of decision-making and control which had previously been reserved exclusively as management's prerogatives. Thus institutionalised workers' participation emphasises changing the balance of decision-making within an enterprise. But, the writers use different words, such as 'influence', 'decision-making', 'control' in defining participation. This, in our view, would narrow down the actual meaning, scope and coverage of workers' participation.

On the basis of above definition, therefore, participation can be classified into two categories: (1) taking part (involvement) in the managerial functions by the workers (who do only directed functions within the enterprise); and (2) taking part in the managerial functions by the representatives of the workers (trade union). The first type involves direct participation in day-to-day activities related to task (work-related matters) whereas the second type involves indirect participation. In direct participation, the workers take part in managerial functions from their own level (for example, self-planning, self-direction and self-control in task performance). It means delegation of managerial responsibility and authority to the workers' level. The degree of delegation would certainly depend upon the task need, capability of the individuals and the situation. In indirect participation, the representatives of the workers (trade union) take part in managerial functions at levels above their own (for example, wage determination, bonus settlement, etc. The first type is visible under different sponsored (by the government/management) workers' participation schemes in most of the industrialised countries like, works committee, workers' council, joint management council, shop council, joint council, unit council, etc. The second type is visible under collective bargaining – and process of joint regulation, which can be said to remain the major form of workers' participation in the USA, Britain and to the significant extent in Japan, as well as in most of the countries in English-speaking Africa. In this context, however, it may be mentioned that many writers in this field do not want to consider collective bargaining as a major form of workers' participation. This may be because of the lack of comprehension about an appropriate definition of workers' participation. The above deliberation on the definition might be able to give a perspective in that direction. Earlier, H.A. Cleggec, C.J. Lammers, K. Odaka, J. Schregle, A. Gladstone and R.M. Greve and some others also made their propositions in this regard. A common agreed definition may, therefore, be needed for proper understanding of the situation in the industrial enterprises and the process of functioning thereof, instead of a hypothetical one.

Existing Framework for Workers' Participation

Ever since the inception of the idea of industrial democracy and its unquestioned need and importance, there is an ongoing international search for effective models. The search has been both rewarding and frustrating: rewarding in the sense that many models of industrial democracy have emerged that are tampering enough to be replicated in different socio-cultural and politico-economic situations, and frustrating in as much as the replicability of imported models have been seriously questioned in terms of their feasibility and effectiveness. The real trouble with the models is that all of them are culture-specific and therefore difficult to be transplanted in alien environments. The great disparities in the countries in terms of the level of economic development and industrialisation, the political and economic structures of their systems of government, and the complexion of the state and industrial relations, present insurmountable hurdles in launching successful models of industrial democracy for the benefit of developing societies. Owing to these difficulties, presumably, there is no single model to be followed. The model, as experts aver, has to be created on specific grounds of each society. If at all non-indigenous models are to be adopted, they have to be appropriately modified to suit to the genius and cultural ethos of the country concerned. The simple reason is that in an international perspective owe do not have one way, not to speak of the best way.

The way out in this complex and confused scenario lies perhaps in examining the experiences of other people, of other systems and of other nations. The exercise necessarily calls for accumulation of case studies of participative structures and practices and subjecting them to critical appraisal against the background of specific countries where the new innovative systems have to be introduced. Examination of international perspectives on industrial democracy is considered necessary for model building. The comparative study of different models would help deepen our understanding of specific features of a given country. With this preliminary observation, we would like to describe briefly certain models of industrial democracy in a global perspective.

The Japanese Model

The Japanese model of industrial democracy envisages the adoption of a system of workers' self-management through voluntary and autonomous groups, popularly known as 'quality circles'. These groups ere spontaneously formed amongst the volunteer workers and are independently organised for the purpose of studying problems chosen by the participant themselves. There are today three types of groups that carry out autonomous work activities in Japanese industry: (a) voluntary type – small study groups of volunteers allowed to engage in spontaneous study and training activities outside regular work hours; (b) transitional type – intermediate or mixed groups falling between or consisting of older and new type features; and (c) autonomous type – small groups which engage in regular productive work and which are organisationally allowed autonomously to determine their operational procedures and to be responsible for results. In the public sector undertakings, the joint consultation system operates. The public sector corporations have their respective joint consultation systems to smoothen communication between the management and the unions to prevent the outbreak of industrial disputes concerning technological innovations. The Japanese joint consultation system is very much akin to collective bargaining in terms of its functions. In fact, joint consultation and collective bargaining systems in many large companies cannot be separated in their substantial functions. Although the Japanese system has not solved all problems, yet it has contributed to improvements in communication between management and the trade unions in public corporations. The system, however, does not suggest built-up participatory industrial relations. The system has only enabled the trade unions to have an enlarged opportunity for negotiation with management and have, to some extent, succeeded in influencing the management policies. It does not intend the sharing of power of decision-making between the trade unions and management. The processes and conditions of workers' participation in management are more closely related to morale-building and improvement in productivity than to the problems of wage and employment.

In Japan, workers' participation has been promoted not mainly by trade unions' demand for industrial democracy, but in most cases by the employers' intention to stabilise labour-management relations with a view to increasing productivity. In other words, the workers' participation is effected without trade unions. Unlike other countries, various procedures of workers' participation – joint consultation system, the autonomous groups, the ringi system and the employees' shareholding system – have not been realised by legislation or by national agreement between workers and managements. In most cases they have been introduced on the employees' initiative, or by agreement between the employer and the trade union of each company. The smooth functioning of internally induced industrial democracy in Japan is largely because of certain unique features of labour-management relations and workers' participation in management. The chief ones are: lifetime employment, trade union organisation within the company, the seniority wage system and a well-developed system of workers' welfare. In addition, Japanese labour-management relations are characterised by family and community consciousness (integration) within companies, differential treatment of outsiders, diligence or priority on work, informal decision-making, i.e., implicit consensus before formal decision, continuity between company life and private life, harmony within groups, informal and daily communication between employers and labour union leaders, employees' pride in their company, strong desire for promotion and national character placing premium on collectivism in all walks of life.

The German Model

The German model of industrial democracy is known for its co-determination system. The co-determination model envisages employees' participation in decision-making with extensive repertoire of instruments for workers' control. In Germany there are works councils and co-determination committees with wider jurisdictions and extensive powers. Elaborate mechanisms have been devised to settle all relevant economic, social and personnel related issues. Cooperation, collaboration and consultation are the key methods to determine priorities in the business and industry. The encouraging results of co-determination model in Germany have prompted Sweden to shape up its industrial relations system.

The Swedish Model

The Swedish model of industrial democracy emulates the German model of co-determination. The Swedish Co-determination Act (1976) applies to both private and public employees. It entitles union representatives to special safeguards with respect to the right of association and carry on union business during paid working hours. It vests considerable decision-making powers in the workers' representatives. It aims to provide joint decision-making in all matters of concern to the employees. The Act also provides a number of general instruments whereby trade unions can exert considerable powers to demand negotiation on all matters pertaining to employer-employee relations, and those connected with day-to-day supervision of work and with top-level decision-making within the company or public authority concerned. The Act awards the trade unions what is termed as the reinforced right of negotiation on questions of particular importance. If any issue is not covered by the primary duty of negotiation, the employer is still obliged to enter into negotiation before reaching a decision, if the employees' organisation so requests.

In Sweden co-determination is progressing most satisfactorily at big workplaces with strong local trade unions. At small places cooperation and participation often proceed spontaneously without any contractual formalities. The Swedish trade union movement is probably one of the strongest in world. Social democracy through its prolonged tenure of power has contributed a great deal towards the importance of trade union organisations. Unions are officially consulted in drafting of proposed legislations, join government commissions, and are represented in central agencies. Several trade union leaders are also nominated to the Swedish Parliament.

The Yugoslav Model

The socialist bloc practices the Yugoslavian model of 'self-management'. It implies complete control of management by worker, through an elected board and workers' councils. Decentralisation and democratisation are the central elements of self-management. Decision-making is decentralised and is practised both at the level of enterprises and also at the level of various units of the enterprise. The system of self-management can exist only in socialist societies where all power belongs to the workers. It can work in such socio-political systems where means of production are socially owned. The main and the long-term aim of the system of self-management is to assure the realisation of direct political and economic authority of the working class and of all working people. Self-management was introduced in Yugoslavia in 1950. During these four decades, self-management has become an integral part of the Yugoslav social, economic and political system. The main characteristics of the system are: (a) means of production are socially owned and workers themselves directly manage the enterprise in the interest of the society, as also in their own, but do not own the enterprise; (b) workers themselves decide about the whole result of their labour; they all have the same rights in decision-making; and all basic decisions are made through direct participation of all workers in their basic self-management organisations; and (c) decision-making bodies on higher levels of organisations are composed of workers' delegates from basic self-management organisations.

Conclusion

In view of taking into consideration the long and detailed discussion held in the preceding pages, there is no disagreement about the merit and quality of the models implemented different countries. But when it comes to gauge the success, it varies from 70 to 90 per cent. The situation in our country is much more adverse. The reason being that India has a divergent culture full of countless varieties. Besides this, the existing factors immediately after independence were acutely adverse for taking up welfare provisions, viz., 85 per cent illiteracy, merger of approximately 500 big and small states, unemployment, settlement of lakhs of refugees and on the top of it explosion of population. Nevertheless, we tried our best to try one or other model envisaged by our planners.

Despite this, to my mind, four factors, viz., (i) the half-hearted nature of state intervention; (ii) employers' reluctance to accept innovative changes; (iii) absence of unified, strong and responsible trade union movement; and (iv) workers' participational incompetence and their single-minded concern, with only interest-related issues, were responsible for the slow progress of workers' participation in management.

However, in the given state of affairs, both the workers and employers look at the experiments of industrial democracy with half-hearted smiles, almost bordering on cynicism (Das, 1964: 154), though it can be said that the 'fact' remains that industrial democracy in India has not yet taken firm roots, it is still in its nascent stage of growth but with the kind of continuous and whole-hearted efforts I am quite optimistic that the future of industrial democracy in the country is bright and the signals are such that the whole concept may turn into 'value'.

References

Alexander, K.C. (1972) *Participative Management: The Indian Experience*, Shri Ram Centre of Relations, New Delhi.

Arya, P.P. (1980) "Nature and Extent of Workers' Participation in Decision-Making", *Indian Journal of Industrial Relations*, Vol. 16, No. 1, July.

Aziz, Abdul (1980) *Human Relations in Industry* (New Delhi: S. Chand and Co.).

——. (1980) *Workers' Participation in Management* (New Delhi: Ashish Publishing House).

Bhatnagar, Deepti (1977) "Workers' Desire for Participation: An Empirical Study", *Productivity Journal*, Vol. 17, No. 4.

Birmani, B.R. (1978) *Workers' Participative Management: Some Experiences and Lessons* (New Delhi: Macmillan).

Chandra, Sushil (1976) "Participative Management: Strategies for Success", *Financial Express*, New Delhi, Part I, 6th Nov. p. 4, Part II, 7th Dec. p. 4.

Clegg, H.A. (1960) *A New Approach to Industrial Democracy* (Oxford: Blackwell).

Das, Nabgopal (1964) *Experiments in Industrial Democracy* (Bombay: Asia Publishing House).

Dasgupta, A. (1974) *Business and Management in India* (Delhi: Vikas Publishing House).

Dhingra, O.P. (1972) "Participation Pre-Disposition of Public Sector Manager", *Lok Udyog*, Vol. 5, No. 12.

Dholakia, Jitendra (1981) "Industrial Democracy: Is it a Myth or Reality?" in S.K. Deshmukh (ed.), *Worker's Participation in Industrial Management* (Pune: Link Publications).

Fonseca, A.J. (1978) "Workers' Participation in Industry: A Study of European and Indian Experience", *Social Action*, Vol. 28, No. 2.

Gladstone, A. and W.H. Schmiat (1984) "Workers' Participation in Management: A Framework for Discussion", *Labour and Society*, Vol. 9, No. 3.

Gopal, L. (1977) "Industrial Democracy: The Indian Experiments", *Indian Journal of Commerce*, Patna, Vol. 30, No. 110.

Gopal, V. (1984) *Industrial Democracy in India* (Allahabad: Chugh Publications).

Government of India (1969) *Report of the National Commission on Labour*.

——. (1985–86) *Annual Report of the Ministry of Labour*, Vol. 1.

——. (1990) Status Paper of the Seminar on Labour Participation in Management, New Delhi.

Guest, D. and D. Fatchett (1977) *Worker Participation: Individual Control and Performance* (London: IPM).

Hallen, G.C. (1964) Labour Participation in Management in India, Doctoral Dissertation, Agra University.

Hersey, Paul and K.H. Blanchard (1972) *Management of Organizational Behavior: Utilizing Human Resources* (Englewood Cliffs, NJ: Prentice Hall).

Institute of Economic Growth (1962) *Participation in Management: The Indian Experience*, Delhi.

Kennedy, Van D. (1986) *Unions, Employers and Government: Essay on Indian Labour Questions* (Bombay: Manaktalas).

Khanolkar, S.G. (1981) "Labour Participation in Management", in S.K. Deshmukh (ed.), *Industrial Management* (Pune: Link Publications).

Lammers, C.J. (1967) "Power and Participation in Decision-Making in Formal Organizations", *American Journal of Sociology*, Vol. 73, No. 2.

Liberman, S.M. and R.L. Liberman (1978) "Two Case Studies in Worker's Participation in Management", *Indian Journal of Industrial Relations*, Vol. 13, No. 4.

Likert, R. (1967) *The Human Organization: Its Management and Value* (New York: McGraw Hill).

Mathew, M.A. (1976) "Worker's Participation in Management: A New Prospective", *Indian Manager*, Vol. VII, No. 2.

Mhetras, V.G. (1966) *Labour Participation in Management: An Experiment in Industrial Democracy in India* (Bombay: Manaktalas).

Myres, C.A. and S. Kanappan (1970) *Industrial Relation in India* (Bombay: Asia Publishing House).

Odaka, K. (1975) *Toward Industrial Democracy: Management and Workers in Modern Japan* (Cambridge, MA: Harvard University Press).

Pandit, D.P. (1962) *Workers' Participation in Management: The Indian Experiment (Report)*, Delhi: Institute of Economic Growth.

Poole, M. (1980) "Managers, Industrial Democracy and Control", in M. Poole and R. Mansfield (eds.), *Managerial Roles in Industrial Relations* (Aldershot: Gower).

Punekar, S.D. (1967) *Trade Union Leadership in India: A Survey* (Bombay: Lalvani Publishing House).

Pylee, M.V. (1975) *Workers' Participation in Management: Myth and Reality* (New Delhi: N.V. Publishers).

Schregle, J. (1981) "Comparative Industrial Relations: Pitfalls and Potential", *International Labour Review*, Vol. 120, No. 1.

Sharma, B.R. (1987) "Indian Democracy: The Indian Experience", *Indian Journal of Industrial Relations*, Vol. 22, No. 3.

Sharma, J.N. (1976) "Experiments in Industrial Democracy", *Yojna*, Vol. 20, No. 20.

Sharma, N.K. (1976) "Workers' Participation in Management", *Indian Labour Journal*, Vol. XVII, No. 9.

Sheth, N.R. (1972) *The Joint Management Council: Problems and Prospects* (New Delhi: Shri Ram Centre for Industrial Relations).

Shri, G.K. (1973) "Participation and Productivity with Special Reference to Scanlon Plan", in C.P. Thakur and K.C. Sethi (eds.), *Industrial Democracy: Some Issues and Experiences* (New Delhi: Shri Ram Centre for Human Resources).

Singh, J. et al. (1976) *Effectiveness of Constructive/Participative Bodies in Industry (Report)*.

——. (1976) "Workers' Participation in Management", *Mainstream*.

Srivastava, K.N. (1954) *Industrial Peace and Labour in India* (Allahabad: Kitab Mahal).

Subramanian, K.N. (1967) *Labour Management Relation in India* (Bombay: Asia Publishing House).

Tanic, Z. (1969) *Workers' Participation in Management: Ideal and Realty in India* (New Delhi: Shri Ram Centre for Industrial Relations).

Tannbaum, R. and W.H. Schmidt (1958) "How to Choose a Leadership Pattern?" *Harvard Business Review*, Vol. 36, No. 2.

Thakur, C.P. and K.C. Sethi (1973) *Introduction to Industrial Democracy* (New Delhi: Shri Ram Centre for Industrial Relations and Human Resources).

Upadhyay, L.P. (1979) "Workers' Participation in Industry: Expectations and Experience", *Integrated Management*, Vol. 14, No. 5.

Verma, Pramod (1987) *Labour Economics and Industrial Relations* (New Delhi: Tata McGraw Hill Publishing Co. Ltd.)

Walker, K.F. (1974) "Workers' Participation in Management: Problems, Practice and Prospect", *Bulletin of the International Institute for Labour Studies*, Vol. 12.

Zivan, Tanic (1969) *Workers' Participation: Ideal and Reality in India* (New Delhi: Shri Ram Centre for Industrial Relations).

15

Globalisation, Cultural Change and the Issue of Global Uniformity

P.N. Pandey

Globalisation is a multidimensional concept that refers to the transformation of trade, technology, industry and economy in a universalising direction. It is a cultural process as well but more specifically, it is projected by the western industrially developed countries, i.e., the US, France, Germany, Italy and the UK, as a worldwide trade mechanism. In cultural terms, it refers to both as compression of the world and intensification of the consciousness of the world as a whole (Robertson, 1992). It is a process that transforms institutions of modernity in universalising directions (Giddens, 1991). Capitalism, industrialism, surveillance and monopolisation of means of violence are its major institutions.

Globalisation, as a worldwide trade mechanism, is a new approach but its roots lie in the last five decades of post-World War II period. The dictates of 1960, 1970, 1980, 1990 started with the agenda of growth, modernisation, social transformation, development and sustainable development and finally at the end of the 20th century it led to globalisation with emphasis on liberalisation and privatisation (Pandey, 1997). The chief motivators for globalisation are: (i) search for market place, (ii) multinational investments, and (iii) new tools of technology and electronics with computer network. The most paradoxical aspects of globalisation are disparity, inequality, injustice and insecurity prevailing in the economic, political and social structures of different societies of the world. The industrially developed countries of the world represent 20 per cent of the world population which holds control over 80 per cent of world resources while the developing world that represents 80 per cent of the world population holds just 20 per cent of the resources of the world. Countries like the US, the UK, France, Germany and Italy are moving from manufacturing to service economy. They are, therefore, in urgent need of market place for their products. It is developing countries of Latin America, Africa and Asia which appear as prospective markets for their products. These countries are apprehensive of identity loss. They do not want techno-electronic imperialism.

Sad Impressions of Modernisation, Development and Sustainable Development

The so-called phenomena of modernisation, development and sustainable development have created more disparities, discrepancies and discriminations, though the slogans of globalisation sound more attractive.

The outcomes of the western developmental programmes have disheartened the developing nations. The ever-increasing social and economic disparities, discrepancies, differentiations and the gap between the rich and the poor indicate that the very ideology of development based on egalitarianism and equity has proved to be elusive and dilemmatic to the societies of Asia and Africa (Hudson, 1971; Bauer, 1972; Mende, 1973; Hayter, 1972; Beteille, 1993; Wallerstien, 2000).

The borrowed patterns and paradigms of development not only create value conflict but also lead to the conflicting lifestyles in the developing societies. The Marshal Plan, under which the societies of western Europe were restructured after the World War II, was drawn into these countries and failed miserably. For example, heavy industries and factories, dams and projects, with borrowed technology and capital from the western countries, have tried to restructure the developing societies with a view to push them forward to join the developed nations but at the same time the perpetuation of poverty, unemployment, growing distance between the rich and the poor, ecological imbalances, environmental degradation with excessive deforestation, loss of ethnic identities, cultural specificity and displacement of primitive people have caused baffling problems of socio-cultural differentiation in the name of structural transformation and changes.

For more than five decades the idea of development has affected the policy and programmes of structural transformation of the vast majority of the countries of the world. As a major ideology of our times, development has shaped the purposes and efforts of states and that of public as well as private organisations (Sutton, 1989: 137). It has been characterised by some scholars as a secular theory of salvation (Nandy, 1987, 1989). Then, there are others who viewed it as a modernising myth (Furtando, quoted in Wolfe, 1981).

The origins of the concept can be traced to the nineteenth century idea of progress. These, in turn, draw on the work of the philosophers of the eighteenth century. The orthodox theory of development has the following premises (Baruni, 1989; Sutton, 1989):

(i) The industrially developed countries of the West are advanced and developed whereas others, primarily non-industrial countries, are underdeveloped.

(ii) People everywhere have equal capacities and rights, i.e., inequalities between societies and within societies are not natural or preordained. They can be removed or minimised by concerted action. In this sense, the so-called underdeveloped countries are also developing.

(iii) Development is possible through rationality, organised planned efforts and the application of science and technology. It is the key to experience the increases in economic productivity.

(iv) The national governments, as the representative bodies of the aspirations and hopes of citizens, have a pivotal role to play in initiating and carrying out development programmes.

(v) The pace and degree of development in economic terms is judged by economic indicators, i.e., Gross National Product (GNP) and per capita income. The less developed countries are dominated by large agricultural sector, whereas the highly developed countries have greater share of industry and services.

(vi) The prima facie goal of development is to improve standard of living apart from increases in productivity and income.

In the light of the above theory of development, when examined intensively, it is held that the concept of development is based on the philosophy of equity or egalitarian ideology, that is to say, the distance between the rich and the poor, developed and underdeveloped may be minimised (Sachs, 1990). But, the entire Third World countries in general and India in particular are seriously facing with various dilemmas, which can be traced in the following context of structural transformation and changes:

(i) *Development versus social equity:* The global experiences of development indicate that social distance among the different nations, and between the nations, in terms of affluence and scarcity, well-off and deprived, rich and poor, and powerful and powerless has increased (Beteille, 1983, 1993).

(ii) *Development versus cultural diversities:* The race of globalisation is faced with a baffling issue of continuity and survival of cultural diversities, heterogeneity and distinctiveness. The challenges emerging on the regional and ethnic levels in India are alarming signals – be it Sardar Sarovar Project Movement by Medha Patkar or Tehri Dam Movement by S.L. Bahuguna or several others like Bodo and ULFA movements in Assam and also in different regions. This shows that the mood of the nation is reversed to accept the benefits of globalisation at the cost of identity loss. Such symptoms are also perceptible in the other countries of the Third World.

(iii) *Development versus ecological and environmental protection:* Development has posed a serious challenge at the global level not to say about India alone. On the one hand, there are lures for development but, on the other hand, its alarming consequences and probability of horrible images of future have drawn the attention of the scientists, ecologists, environmentalists, technologists, sociologists and economists towards establishment of the mega projects and heavy industries causing deforestation, ecological imbalances, loss and erosion of soil fertility, desertification, devastation of hilly regions, increasing pollution as a result of industrial refuges and garbage, air and sound pollution, loss of flora and fauna, ever-increasing ambivalence in the eco-system (Reddy, 1986; Guha, 1988) and – depopulation and displacement of tribal population resulting in the elimination of tribal identity and its cultural diversities. Such an outcome of development is undoubtedly leading to a situation of anarchy and structural and ecological strains (CSE, 1982, 1985).

The studies and investigations made by the western social scientists in recent years about the socio-economic development of the Third World countries show a major contradiction. For example, Michael Hudson (1971: 13–14) concludes in his survey that the foreign aids have created adverse consequences in these countries. Similarly, Tiber Mende (1973: 36) has traced out that a tendency of strong resentment and protest has been evoked among the developing nations against the developed western countries. The developing nations are realising that foreign aids are instrumental in perpetuating long term dependency and as such it is a strategy to place the developing societies in the grip of foreign trade and technology. The profiteering motives and interference in the economy and polity of the developing countries by the western nations will always put them in the subservient position. Hence, they are scared about their identity loss. In this state of affairs the developing countries must evolve their own indigenous models and parameters to their social and economic development. This will help them restore their identity. Teresa Hayter (1971: 151–52) goes a step forward and emphatically argues that the policies and programmes initiated by various development agencies such as International Monetary Fund, World Bank, United States Agency for International Development and Inter-American Development Bank accord and approve both the international and national character of western capitalist countries and their supremacy over developing countries. These agencies motivate for creating free market, trade and technology and encourage to rely on them with a sense of attachment and commitment. P.T. Bauer (1972: 49–68) is another social scientist who, while presenting a critical assessment of the nature and form of western aid, has concluded that the western developed countries have attempted more to create a vicious poverty cycle in the Third World countries rather than improving their economy and social standards of life. Immanuel Wallerstein (2000), in one of his latest works entitled *After Liberalism,* has expressed his apprehensions about the immanent crisis sprouting out of the late capitalism. A contemporary economist of the US, George Soros (2000) in one of his latest works entitled *The Crisis of Global Capitalism: Open Society Endangered,* is very vocal and clearly highlights that globalisation is an inevitable outcome of the crisis of post-industrialisation in the western world, specially the US, France, Germany, Italy and the UK. A well-famed Canadian economist Sislia Ostry (1999) observes that the western industrially developed countries are facing crucial problems in the sale and consumption of their products and are setting their eyes on the countries of Asia and Africa. Thus, the proper coordination between man, machine and social values in the western world is disturbed and is coming to an end. The western social system is silent on the issue of cultural destination of man through the process of globalisation. The excessive production in the West requires a large and wide market place for its sale and consumption. The increasing demand of consumption is a decisive factor in this regard and this is feasible only when there is extensive market place. In this context, the Third World countries appear as the only alternative for the West.

The principle of justice, associated with socialist welfare states, is ridiculed in the agenda of globalisation. The nature and quantum of electronic appliances, computers, email, internet, etc., is not equally available to all the countries of the world. Research and development (R&D) is the lifeblood of any economy. The initiatives are taken by multinationals more frequently for infringement of powers and capacity of the developing countries in policy making which means multinational corporations will have upper hand in the developing nations. Globalisation proceeds with consumerism while 80 per cent of the world is in need of productive economy. It is elusive to the needs and expectations of the poor and the weaker sections. This widens the gap between the rich and the poor. Accepting globalisation means accepting the primacy and rule of the integrated minority over a huge majority of the world. At the structural transformation level, the programme of globalisation is against participatory democracy as 80 per cent of world population has little representation and interference in its policies and decision-making. Apparently, the developing nations at Seattle in the US, and also in Geneva at the WTO summits, denoted that they are not ready to accept the terms and conditions of WTO as binding on their social and economic liberty. The theft of intellectual property by multinationals and putting on their patent is nothing less than imperial exploitation. It has shattered the nerves of the egalitarian ideology and obsesses the poor countries with ruthless domination and super bossism of the West. The western industrially-developed countries show a deceptive crocodile sympathy to developing countries, which have different culture, history, tradition, national ethos and ideology. In fact, the programme of globalisation is the outcome of western crisis of post-industrialisation and is devoid of human concern and issue of uniformity. The Third World countries must come out in a consensual way to make a forte of their own to face the challenges in the new millennium. Raising such awareness by SAARC and ASEAN in Asia is a commendable step.

Cultural Change and Euphoria of Post-modernism

The post-industrial developments emerging from the land of the industrially-developed capitalist countries of the West, specially the US, France, Germany, Italy and the UK, have posed a number of challenges and crises before the developing countries of Asia and Africa, after World War II. The western countries have attempted to restructure their economy, polity and social structure. In doing so they started with the agenda from modernisation, development, sustainable development to overall globalisation of economy and social structure. But all these have ironically aggravated a number of crises for peace, prosperity and social solidarity in the developing countries. These crises are ranging from poverty, unemployment, health hazards, religious fanaticism, communal riots, environmental degradation, international and cross-border terrorism to internal insecurity and political destabilisation. These are not challenges to the developing world only but have also created unprecedented chaotic situations for the developed countries of the western world as well. A crisis virtually denotes a major dislocation, an interruption in the fundamental institutions and agencies of a social system. It requires collective and organised national efforts to be absolved.

The unprecedented changes have occurred during the last two decades because of the excessive developments in the industrially developed capitalist societies of the West. These societies, having been equipped with technical manpower and production, have entered into a stage of post-industrialism and post-modernism. They have shifted their focus from modernity to post-modernity and overall globalisation of economy and polity on their agenda for the 21st century. The success and relevance of modern technologised production depends on the success of excessive consumption. All this has led to commercialisation, computerisation and commmodification of knowledge. The capacity to deliver outputs at the lowest cost replaces truth as yardstick of knowledge. The character of this so-called post-modern culture, can be termed as depthless, ahistorical, timeless, conceiving the world as a technological entity rather than an ecological balance. Most of the western social scientists now perceive that the proper coordination between man, machine and values is disturbed.

The experiences of the last fifty five years since World War II, reveal that all the major agendas of the western world right from modernisation, development and sustainable development to globalisation, preceding with liberalisation and privatisation, have miserably failed as they have not bridged the gap and brought homogeneity between the developed and the developing world.

The supreme paradox of the existing world order is that 20 per cent of the world population is enjoying 80 per cent of the world resources while 80 per cent of the population of the globe is surviving on mere 20 per cent of the resources. In such a situation, a major crisis is alarming the world about its disastrous consequences. Further, the emerging crisis of western capitalism in search of alternative market place in the countries of Latin America, Africa and Asia is another major concern for the developing world. Modern technology, electronics, information technology and cybernetics are no doubt additions to human civilisation and but their hegemonic control by few capitalist countries of the West has presented a number of challenges before the developing world by threatening the peace and co-existence and creating more of economic and political instability. The exercise of power game by having arsenals, deadly biological, chemical and nuclear weapons, hiring mercenaries for massacres, bloodshed, and international and cross-border terrorism have shattered human conscience. The other most horrendous challenges are ecological and environmental crises, women atrocities, health hazards and creation of vicious poverty cycle, etc., which are to be faced by the developing nations of Asia and Africa.

In this overall changing scenario, the social scientists in general and sociologists in particular have to review the global social order with a view to resolve these issues and present the responses and reactions to procure peace and stability for humanity at large.

The most recent theoretical debates about culture centre on the issue whether it has taken a new turn, and entered a new phase, at the end of the 20th century. The cultural registers analysed by the neo-Marxist and neo-Weberian scholars are essentially modern in character. If society prefers to be dominated by a single set of ideas, then Gramsci of Frankfurt School can investigate how these ideas are manufactured; if society is divided by men into a small and fixed number of classes, then Bourdieu or Abercrombie, Hill and Turner can investigate if culture exhibits similar internal differentiations. The post-modern culture is a chaotic mass mediated, individual preference based phenomenon.

The recent Marxist version comes from Jameson (1984) who interprets cultural change as the 'cultural logic of late capitalism'. He proposes a three-fold perception of capitalism, which comes originally from Mandel, as under:

1. Market capitalism, which involves markets within nation-states.
2. Imperial or monopoly capitalism, in which the capitalist states establish colonies so that they could catch both suppliers of raw materials and international markets.
3. Multinational consumerist capitalism, which establishes a new integrated global place for capitalist expansion and within that expands markets by expanding individual acquisitiveness.

This expansion of capitalism into global arena is percolated by a global expansion of culture which liberates it from particular social context. There is a prodigious expansion of culture throughout the social realism. This is so-called post-modern culture. The post-modern culture, which focuses on the centrality of the global space and dislocates individuals from the realities of their own situation, has four characteristics as under:

1. It is depthless (i.e., what you see is what you get) which has risen on the collapse of grand-narratives and meta-theories.
2. It is ahistorical and immediate: it provides no reference back to human suffering and struggle. Traditions can be mixed and matched in pastiche rather than drown upon or resisted.
3. It is timeless. It focuses on organisation of fragments of culture meanings in space. The time relations of these fragmentations are not signified.
4. It conceives of the world as a technological entity rather than as a natural one, as computer network, rather than an ecological balance.

If we count Jameson (1984) and Harvey (1989) along with Bell (1993) and Habermas (1981) as critics of post-modernism, then among its best friends must be Lyotard (1984) and Baudrillard (1988). The move from modern to post-modern knowledge parallels social development. The status of knowledge is altered as societies enter what is called as the post-industrial age and culture enters as what is known as post-modern age. The post-industrial developments include the computerisation and commmodification of knowledge. Increasingly, the capacity to deliver outputs at the lowest cost replaces truth as yardstick of knowledge.

- Modern culture is highly differentiated but post-culture moves towards hyper-differentiation. Post-modern culture can be seen as a dazzling variety of styles which can be mixed and matched with various packages.
- Modern culture is highly rationalised pattern of technical cultural expertise located either in tradition or its transcendence. Post-culture is so hyper-intensified that there can no longer be any claim to expertise or any development of tradition.
- Modern culture is highly commodified whereas post-culture is so hyper-commodified that material commodities are subsumed by signs which represent them.

Information Technology and Global Change

The medium of mass communication revolutionises culture and the knowledge of science, technology and electronics enhances it to give wider coverage to the global space. The society is transformed into a 'technetronic' culture with computer networking. The 'culture specifics' are attempted to be subsumed into multi-ethnicity and multi-culturalism as smaller clenches with secondary importance. The printing press, radio, film, television, the cybernetics and informatics are controlling the global network. The information technology and tele-communication systems with digital codifications are reducing the vast pool of human knowledge to a codified structure embedded into the floppy of computer websites.

In the words of Habermas, this process of globalisation is going to decouple the integration of life world and the system and is tended to proceed towards internal colonisation. In the modern techno-electronic set-up individuals are forced to go through purposive rationalisation (in Weber's term Zweck rationalitat). The purposive rationality is marked with contractual morality, i.e., non-critical, object-oriented, and not by communicative rationalisation, i.e., critical reasoning (in Weber's term Wert rationalist). Excessive bureaucratisation and commmodification of knowledge are the outcomes of post-industrial development. The character of this so-called post-modern culture can be termed as disethisised, shameless. The individual is emerging as a client leaving aside his/her real identity and the whole world system is being regulated by purposive rationality. The whole world is going to emerge as a computerised networking rather than a natural entity, a technological entity rather that an ecological balance. The developing countries in general and India in particular have a long history of grand narratives, meta theories, legends and myths. Globalisation cannot assimilate all of them. In my assessment India and other developing countries of Asia and Africa will ever manifest a peculiar blend of their historical identity even in the global modernising attempts.

References

Baruni, Tariq (1989) *Modernization and Its Discontents: A Perspective for Sociology of Knowledge*, Helswki: W.I.D.E.R.

Bauer, P.T. (1972) *Dissent on Development*, Cambridge, Mass: Harvard University Press, pp. 49–67.

Bell, Daniel (1973) *The Coming of Post-Industrial Society*, New York: Basic Books.

——. (1979) *The Cultural Contradictions of Capitalism*, London: Heinemann.

Beteille, Andre (1993) *Equality and Inequality*, New Delhi: Oxford University Press.

CSE (1982 and 1985) *The State of India's Environment: A Citizen's Report*, New Delhi: Centre for Science and Environment.

Giddens, Anthony (1990) *Consequences of Modernity*, Cambridge: Polity.

——. (1991) *Modernity and Self-Identity*, Cambridge: Polity.

Habermas, J. (1981) "Modernity versus Postmodernity", *New German Critique*, No. 22 (Winter), pp. 3–14.

——. (1984) *The Theory of Communicative Action, Vol. I, Reason and Rationalization of Society*, Boston: Beacon.

Harvey, D. (1989) *The Condition of Postmodernity*, Oxford: Blackwell.

Hayter, Teresa (1971) *Aid as Imperialism*, Harmondsworth: Penguin, pp. 151–52.

Hudson, Michael (1941) *Myth of Aid*, New York, pp. 13–64.

Jameson, F. (1984) "Postmodernism or the Cultural Logic of Late Capitalism", *New Left Review*, No. 146, pp. 146–53.

Lyotard, J.F. (1984) *The Postmodern Condition*, Manchester: Manchester University Press.

Mende, Tiber (1973) *From Aid to Re-colonization: Lessons of a Failure*, New York: Pantheon Books, p. 36.

Nandy, Ashish (1987) *Traditions, Tyrannies and Utopias*, New Delhi: Oxford University Press.

——. (1989) *Science, Hegemony and Violence: A Requiem for Modernity*, New Delhi: Oxford University Press.

Ostry, Sislia (1999) *The Crisis of Global Trade*, New York.

Pandey, P.N. (1997) "Dilemmas of Development: A Case of the Third World", *Samajiki, Journal of U.P. Sociological Society*, Varanasi, Vol. 10, Joint Issues 1–2.

Robertson, R. (1992) *Globalization*, London: Sage.

Sachs, Welfgand (1990) "On the Archaeology of Development Idea", *Lokayan Bulletin*, Vol. 8, No. 1, pp. 7–37.

Soros, George (2000) *The Crisis of Global Capitalism: Open Society Endangered*, New York: Public Affairs.

Sutton, F.X. (1989) "Development Ideology: Its Emergence and Decline", *Daedalus*, Winter, Vol. 118, No. 1.

Wallerstein, I. (2000) *After Liberalism*, New York: The New Press.

Wolfe, Marshal (1981) *Elusive Development*, Geneva: United Nations Research Institute for Social Development.

16

Culture of Hierarchy and Power

Local Socio-Historical Perspectives Indian Case Study

D. Sundaram

In all discourses on inequality, there is an uncritical assumption on (a) dynamic nature of hierarchy, power and thereby (b) on the socio-economic and cultural co-ordinates of hierarchy in local historical situations. With this background, an analytical study of Indian social structure and institutions within a specific time and space has considered the significance of the cultural tradition on which Indian society was based. The methodological understanding of this process was through description of the issues. The traditional methodological approaches appear to be an excessively reductionist one in terms of style and process rather than that of the context and content of the process. This descriptive focus is a modest one to study the culture and society in India marked by a form of social structure, which has a selective incorporation of cultural elements constructing a general civilisation process within a specific historical event. Indian society through the historical dynasties is an abundant source to state that hierarchy is not a static concept. It is as dynamic as the culture of tradition in Indian society. The social structure and institutions were

---

This paper is revised version of the report on the project on Life Thought and Culture for the Indian Philosophical Sciences Research Council March 1994 and was presented at the second international conference on Hierarchy, Power and Civilisation, Institute of Oriental Studies, St. Petersburg, Russia, on 4 July 2002.

in fact subordinating the cultural tradition of hierarchy in Indian system to such an extent that subsumption of power into status took place more by an act of individuals conditioned by society, and not through the textual prescription of the social order. Thereby, the form and shape of hierarchy got transformed over the cultural bases. Thus, the understanding of the issue of inequality through the culture of hierarchy is of how the hierarchy as a component of inequality is a locally variant one with the potentials of continuity and change. The knowledge and scholarship on such local variant of the hierarchy within a historical and cultural context will be an added input into the inequality dimensions of the development paradigm.

The need for giving pre-eminence for such approach to inequality/equality could not have been clarified much better than Alexis de Tocqueville, who compared the two historical situations, namely, France and America, in 18th and 19th century along with the respective socio-cultural co-ordinates. Though, he has not deliberately intended with the perspectives as we seek, the case is an illustrative significance of the dynamic nature of equality/inequality under the given local socio-cultural conditions characterised with ranking, hierarchy and difference (Tocqueville, 1946). The issue of social equality versus social inequality by Tocqueville under the two distinctively different structured conditions of society, namely, France – the aristocratic and the US – democratic, is a point of reference here. The conditions where equality was minimised or maximised are socio-culturally different and separate. Tocqueville exposition of how the aristocratic society in France in a given historical situation has eroded the principles of equality while in contrast how democracy in the US in a given historical time influenced the principle of equality is significant. The social and cultural conditions that have generated ideas and social outlook on equality in these two historically different situations constitute his basic approach (Tocqueville, 1945).

Similarly, the inequality eradication programme in India through affirmative action, i.e., the backward classes' development, is another case in point. The criteria of identifying individuals for social, educational and economic backwardness through the social group to which he/she belongs to as individuals was more on cultural factors rather than on economic dimension. And, it is nothing but dismantling the hierarchical ranking and status due to social backwardness of the social group to which he/she belongs as individuals. This version of social backwardness is explicitly stated more as a historical disadvantage and, thereby, the caste/class as socially backward has been seen in a historically conditioned socio-cultural context and background where the issue of hierarchy was more pronounced. Andre Beteille (1981) has stated that the problem of the backward classes in achieving equality in a world permeated by inequality, i.e., the significance of the backward class lies not only in its size and content but also in the uniquely Indian way of defining the boundaries, i.e., the hierarchical boundaries. This uniqueness is a reflection of specific social and historical conditions, which may be formulated as "culture of hierarchy".

Dipankar Gupta (1991), in his work on stratification, has elucidated the extent to which the hierarchies have inherent characteristics of inequalities by virtue of social enforcement at a particular point of time and by the contingencies, which strive for imposed order to ranking the human differences as a dynamic structure. His vision of bracketing the hierarchy of Brahminical version as capricious, as non-Brahminical version and also the need to give cognisance to the fact that they should also hierarchise differently and separately in as much as castes are different and separate is the point to be pondered over. I.P. Desai (1988) joined the Dumont version of hierarchy in the context of the real and apparent differences in the caste system in India, which have internally multiple identities and tensions. Also, in this context, the precedence of the difference over hierarchy or hierarchy preceding differences – the concern of I.P. Desai – are the other points of view on hierarchy.

Gupta, while acknowledging further on the variety of the form and shape of hierarchies – an inevitable component in the study of inequality and stratification – has noted that the different hierarchies are contextualised through different socio-economic and cultural co-ordinates. As already stated, Indian society through the historical dynasties is an abundant source to state that hierarchy is not a static concept. It is as dynamic as the culture of tradition in Indian society. The social structure and institutions were in fact subordinating the cultural tradition of hierarchy in Indian system to such an extent that subsumption of power into status took place more by an act of individuals, and not through the textual prescription of the social order. Thereby, the form and shape of hierarchy got transformed over the cultural bases. Thus, the understanding of the issue of inequality through the culture of hierarchy is of how the hierarchy as a component of inequality is a locally variant one with the potentials of continuity and change. The knowledge and scholarship on such local variant of the hierarchy within a historical and cultural context will be an added input into the inequality dimensions of the development paradigm. The current inequality eradication programmes of development paradigm are not only of income generation but also of delinking the occupation from the traditional characteristics with symbolisation towards material advancement. The cultural connections of hierarchy, particularly of the culture at the local dimensions of inequality, is given due significance as is in the case of development and welfare of backward classes and weaker sections in Indian society. The issue of culture over the issue of inequality has to be analytically taken up not necessarily within the model of culture and modernisation theory, nor even within the pronounced economic determinist model of Marxism, followed by an engagement of this by a host of scholars like Sahlins, Frank, Wolf, Laclaw and Wallerstein, Banaji and Hindess. Rather, it is on the other side, i.e., beyond the determination model. The issue is not in contesting, rebutting, challenging or social action groups practice negotiating the issue of culture as it is within the framework of continuity and change of the form and shape of culture connections over several social dimensions of society, which include inequality, hierarchy and social stratification.

While studying the culture and society in India marked by a form of social structure that has a selective incorporation of cultural elements, constructing a general civilisation process within a specific historical event, the emphasis has been on the context and content of the process through the description of the issues in the given consciousness of the historical period.

The knowledge, in this context, to be derived is supposed to be the one on the 'historical consciousness' of social institutions rather than on the dynastic chronicle alone. In this context, social significance is on the consciousness of the event, process or act. No specific methodology of the traditional scientific outlook could be effective because the social framework of Indian society through time and space cannot be looked through the holistic tradition without its variants, namely, religion, culture, values and political contextualities. Also, to see them through text and theory without reference to context and practice will be an academic fiasco. An attempt is made to look into the state and society in a specific historical space and time to analyse how the ideological interests of hierarchical socio-cultural order of the period are fostered by social structural conditioning. In this process, the social reality of Indian society has been discussed in a sociological ethnography of persons as individuals, in a group, community and society through the social structure of the state. Thus, the dynastic chronicle of the state is analysed along with the social chronicle of society. The dominant trend of caste analysis is reversed with a specific period, i.e., 300–1000 A.D., through the history and person-oriented approach.

The kings and dynasties during this classical age were not bound by the rigid legitimisation of caste right even when society was ridden with caste-based social relationship. For example, Chandragupta married a princess from the great aboriginal tribe of the Lichchhavis; the Parthiharas were said to be descendants of a Gujara tribe from Central Asia; Pallavas were said to be aboriginals, while the Chola, Chera and Pandya rulers were of Kshatriya origin. From this, it is clearly evident that in the quest for political power and also to sustain themselves in it, by certain individuals, there was an element of desire for 'mobility and social change' to seek socio-economic opportunities. Although the normative prescription of scared scripts disallowed the Brahmins to become a king, the Brahmins with their superiority in Sanskrit language and literature remained on top by holding themselves strongly in the higher ranking in ritual hierarchy. They ignored ethnic fission and fusion in the social order and continued to patronise the exclusive social authority of power. As far as south is concerned, the dynastic history of the classical age during this period reveals a long march of Samudragupta to the south reaching as far as Kancheepuram. To sustain his rule in the distant south, he devised a method by arranging the marriage of a Gupta princess to Vakataha prince of the Deccan dynasty. During the same time, the Pallava dynasty was extending its boundaries in Tamil Nadu in south. Of the greatest kings of Pallava was Mahendra Vikrama Varman I and Narashimha Varman III who ruled Pallava kingdom. Southernmost India had a division of Pandya, Chola and Chera kingdoms, which bore the history of small kingdoms and principalities. Imperial Cholas were the exception for a short period. They had a great empire with suzerain authority over the largest geographical area crossing nautical boundaries.

During this period, the tradition of Indian social organisation had a unity of purpose among the different social groups. There were differences in tradition without assimilating with the other, although they co-existed together. This non-assimilative nature is described as an inter-cultural autonomy, which flourished through the ages. In a way, work of every nature was occupationalised with hierarchical authority, as described in Hindu jajmani system. Although this system is described as a reciprocity, it depicted exploitative reciprocity. With such cultural and structural characteristics of the groups, people were working in the different occupations. The fundamental relationship between culture and social structure in Indian society is manifested abundantly in the form of the caste system. There were number of tiny social groups with distinct culture, occupation and systems of belief with which these groups lived side by side. The autonomy of each tiny group has been respected while, at the same time, cooperation has been ensured between them. This kind of theoretical standpoint of the Indian tradition about man and society, within a matrix of the relationship between culture and structure and within the conceptuality of king, state and social order in organising the society, have several issues like 'individuality' to name one among few.

Accordingly, the individual's consciousness within the then existing framework of political power, economy and society/social group was one of the frameworks, which was purely a functional element. Here, the quest of individuals and groups as intermediaries between kings and subjects appeared to be a functional one cutting across caste. The social structures and institutions played a significant role in absorbing the tradition of cultural features of caste in an adaptive sense.

The system of a leader or feudal lord or intermediary or local chieftain and so on mostly characterised the angle of individuality without individualism – being Indian values. They were fostered mostly by the power of the state and not by the sacred perceptions of theoretical social order. This was one of the hallmarks of the institutionalised social power away from the power of the king and his authority. It was the social power circle vested by the king to wield his authority from a distance. In this context, the principle of hierarchy within and between castes did not shape the form of individuality. It emerged from the Indian values of individuality without individualism, i.e., from the culturally stipulated attributes of an individual for being the leader either in the group or village or region. These were the principles that highlighted the "co-existence of group mind and individuality without individualism". All these denote the meaning of the social bases of power to regulate the mechanism of people's interest. They were fostered from the point of view of land, social control and the maintenance of the economic organisation of society. The social division was not purely a caste-based one, i.e., it was based on the practice of social power vested among the individuals. But, the social relationships were on caste lines. It was mainly because of the possible economic interests that certain individuals in the society and village were forced to be the holders of socio-political power positions. Thereby, the groups and the castes in the villages had to accept these individuals as distinct persons and, thus, these distinct persons acted as intermediaries between the king and his subjects.

The individuality in Indian context, unlike in West, where it depicts personal liberty and freedom was in essence a 'group mind', Rather, the individuality in Indian social organisation was characterised with the values of dependency of the group or the compulsions for the group to look towards some one who was socially powerful/tall and locally influential with willingness to meet the group demands and also to fulfil the needs and aspirations of the people in the social group irrespective of caste, kind or class in a given region. So, the group's quest or someone among them as individual to lead and to give direction was the hallmark of the Indian social organisation. Accordingly, social institutions of Indian social organisations were not as depersonalised as that of the West either by way of power having a meaning of coercion over others or remaining apart from the group from which the individual transforms into a leader. The group functioned at the level of personalised social interaction by reposing faith and confidence among those 'individuals' who were believed to be above everyone else in the social group. Accordingly, Dumont's paradigm of 'individuality' in Indian social organisation may be reformulated on the fact that he superimposed the western values of individualism and tried to evaluate it in the Indian context.

In this context, the existence of a 'significant man', which reflected the central importance of 'individuality' among the groups/castes in the organisation of society in India as a social reality, has to be searched for its historical consciousness. There is no dearth of academic exercise on 'individual and group' among the Indian academia who used the framework of 'caste and hierarchy'. They have, at the same time, tried to see the need for co-existence of 'individuality with the groups' in caste, clan, kinship and village. In reality, the emphasis of caste hierarchy used to be only partial even though the scholars of Indian civilisation have enunciated the issue of 'cultural holism'. To put it differently by borrowing the existing academic versions on the subject, the version of individual and his relationship within the caste, as that of the one occurring in social space, seems to be only a cognitive reality, very much different from the existential reality. It may appear that the caste as an insular social space of an individual reflected in the restriction of the hierarchical relationship to certain specified areas of social needs. The transition from the *varna* to *jati* framework was essentially a transition from the form and shape of existential reality conditioned by the necessities of certain social situations. There, the divisions of interest of certain social elements of groups within the larger groups had a quest for a separate social identity. The dissonance of cognitive reality from that of the existential reality is not only a transition, as is in the case of *varna* to *jati*, but also an inevitable existence of individuality with group mind in Indian social organisation.

Certain individuals in society emerged into a socially nodal point of the group/caste (to which the individual belongs) based on "the supremacy of the accumulative and distributive potential of individuals". It was considered as a significant socio-genesis of power relationship in Indian society. In terms of social history of a person and group, the Indian civilisation is replete with the occurrences of such 'accumulative and distributive' relationships between the king and his subjects. The social salience of dominance of individuals either single or as group apart from the hierarchical features of the caste was visible among the analytical contributions of Indian society by Gloria Raheja (1988a), Carol A. Breckenridge (1977), Nicholas Dirks (1987) and Arjun Appadurai (1986). The issue of dominance and authority of individuals in the several social contexts of Indian social organisation is of great significance. These scholars have observed that there were several community level agents and agencies that had "distributional social power and status among them cutting across social relationships at the caste level". Therefore, the emergence of individuality without individualism in Indian social organisation was legitimised by the forces of social obligation of individuals for the social group comprising of several castes and not of one caste in which he was socially located although, he belonged to a particular caste. This social obligation was, besides his self-interest, with no quest for personal freedom and equality.

In reinventing such social salience of 'individuality' in the classical age of our Indian history, without in any way discarding the existence of caste hierarchy, an analysis of the prevalent social economy and the socio-political order may be relevant. Thus, the evolutionary form and type of state control over its subjects in terms of the right over the landforms is a piece of social history. The form and shape of the state control over land right from the Gupta period to the emergence and consolidation of empires not a simple 'land and state' relationship. They were the mechanisms of enforcing economic relationship through a kind of social formation of peasantry. For example, land was the primeval source of socio-economy of the society to maintain socio-political authority. Such land, with all its wealth potential to maintain the army and the subject for the kings of a given region in India, had the features of the system of land tenure and also associated features like land grant and revenue system. Unlike Europe, where land feudalism prevailed with all its private potential, i.e., private landlordship, the kings in India merely provided rights of power over the land to some selected subjects in various regions to collect the revenue purely within the framework of land as a property of the state. The king and the state had discretion to remove this right and power over the lands among the subjects and, thus, the private ownership of land was absent. To cite an example, the Gupta empire under the classical age of India, like other empires in India, was primarily relying on revenue share from the lands that Indian peasants had to part, a specified amount out of every harvest to the kingdom. It was often said that there has been a crystallisation of feudalism, i.e., over the land and its products during this historical period. A survey of land control and king's relationship with the subjects revealed that there was a system under which lands were transferred to local feudal lords. There were two different ways of controlling the land tenure. One way levying tributes in kind from local leaders and tribal chiefs without an intermediary class and the other was to locate intermediaries and give them the responsibility to collect tax and remit it to the feudal hierarchy.

It is said that "in the course of time, it was the intermediary structure between king and society which emerged into a ruling class whose function was to appropriate the surplus of the peasantry". An incisive analysis of land tenurial relationship under this semi-feudal system demonstrated the development of 'accumulative and distributional' power having been vested among the intermediaries between the king and his subjects. This kind of dependency-dominance syndrome is assumed as a 'significant man-centred individuality' as is conceptualised by Mattison Mines in a different context. This explains that this 'power of wealth and resource' did not have economic significance alone without having the features of the 'power of ruling' vested in the leaders by the kings during their conquest of a region. The real issue was the social dependency of the 'subjects' on these 'feudal lords'. This ultimately results in the debate whether there was feudalism. Much more than the argument on the existence of feudalism, the issue is beyond the social formation of peasantry and is in the cultural forms of peasantry. The cultural forms, in this context, were in the co-existence of political, economic and social power at the level of peasant society. The social power in the form of caste hierarchy remained so constant that it continued as a structural tradition for a greater social mobilisation and identity. But, the equilibrium between the political and economic power at the peasantry level was in the form and shape of culture individuality, which should be a subject of debate in the context of the question of hierarchy.

To contextualise this issue, the position of 'land' may be taken up for an analysis. The account of pilgrims during the 5th and 6th centuries A.D. provided an indication that there was no land registers in terms of household allotments at the hands of king's authority. It only showed that the state was not directly operating the land tenurial system, although the lands with mineral value were at the command of the state. Also, there were records of land grants to guilds and Brahmins. Essentially, the intermediaries between the king and subjects directly operated lands. The statements of Fa-hsien during the Gupta period show that their officials and the conquered princes were granted lands. These princes and petty officials were more visible with their economic power over the merchant and professional guilds. During the Gupta period, these princes who commanded the various groups, including merchants and professional guilds, also demonstrated their political power vested in them as individuals. The political power of these individuals was restricted within the vicinity of space and regions to which the kings have given them authority. These individuals through their 'individuality', i.e., social individuality, played a significant role in shaping cultural and social relationship at the local level. The subjects under the different dynasties including Pallava and Chola were both inside and outside the caste groups. This is a complex tradition with a 'culture of hierarchy' in Indian society.

To sum up, the social order during the classical age was of continuity and change in the cultural features of hierarchy. The framework of 'individuality' without individualism represented how the hierarchical concept could undergo change or transformation in a given context. By narrowing this discussion to the nature and characteristics of hierarchy, an endeavour is made to capture the cultural forces of hierarchy in the Indian social order.

The Indian social system and institutions in the classical ages did represent a situation where the features of hierarchy were located within the dynamics of change in the structural features. The knowledge and scholarship on hierarchy in the Indian context, by their explanatory endeavour, invoke the concepts of tradition, changing dimensions of power, economic arrangements, and social reward and also of moral values and ideas. In the textual clarification of the Indian social system, there was a description of moral obligations on the part of the individuals and groups to stay within the hierarchy of the social order. The significance of such moral obligations was in the inflexible attitude among the mobility of individuals from one status to another in the social order. These features were effectively institutionalised also in various forms of social categories. The issue is whether or not these textual prescriptions were practised in the social contexts.

Here, a brief survey of commentaries of the hierarchy in Indian society may be relevant. Attempts were not made to look into the conditions of hierarchy in an exclusive manner. Instead, there were attempts to know as to who were actually advocating and practising the principles of hierarchy as per the texts and also in which contexts. It is concluded that all the people entered into the hierarchical relationships, i.e., obligations emanating from the cultural structure of hierarchy from the point of view of the four-fold stages of Hindu way of life, a system of hierarchical ways of life was enunciated in the forms of stages of Brahmacharya, Grahastha, Vanaprastha and Sanyasa. In reality, the absoluteness in the practice of passing through all these four stages for every individual or group in the society was not there. There were clear-cut deviations that a majority of the masses did not adhere to this in the strict tradition. Many of them remained purely ideological with certain elements of motivational force. Such motivational force was impelling some individuals in society to translate the precepts into practice. In this context, the institutionalisation of the ideology was not completely resulting in the nature of culture that mediates the structure of the social relationships for various individuals in different ways.

In terms of conformity to the ideological aspects of Hindu divisions of life featuring a form of hierarchical orientation, there was the least rigidity and, thus, they remained purely a hierarchical culture without rigid institutional roles. In this context, if one goes to the extent of saying that the Indian caste society is holistic and hierarchical and the expression of individualism is subordinated to collectivism, it may not match perfectly as there was no proper *FIT* between ideology and fact, or precept and practice. The absence of such a *FIT* between ideology and fact or percept and practice of hierarchical features either in the ways of Hindu division of life or in the *jati* system could not be explained by the lack of institutional complexes alone. The basic features of hierarchy in the Indian social order are in the co-existence of separation and interdependence as far as the formulation of social relationships is concerned. The *jati* model of caste and its transition from *varna* (although it is yet another cultural subordination of the structure) has been seen in practice during the Gupta dynasty and their counterparts in South at that time. There was flexibility in the practice of the behavioural norms, which differed from the text. It was evident in the pursuit of power by some people or clans. They located themselves in institutionalised forms like monarchy as in the case of kings and princes who have their marriage alliances from the caste other than their own as stated elsewhere in this paper. This is a situation where there was a chance for a clan or a group to move away from the hierarchical restrictions provided by the caste-based social relationships.

Similarly, the features of individuality as located among the chieftains or local persons in the name of intermediaries through the system of land grants and power to collect the revenue were yet other forms of lack of *FIT* between the hierarchical ideology and fact, although it may look like performing the royal function by the local chieftains. These persons sustained themselves in a social power that raised them to a status of position; the groups and castes in the region and locality looked towards them. Then, these persons became dominant individuals cutting across the caste-based hierarchical relationships. Dumont and others discuss this issue of dominant individuals at the local level within the framework of power and status. Differentiating the levels of power and status into primary or non-segmented level, Dumont discovered that the power is subordinated to status at the former level and the same becomes equal to the status at the latter level. M.N. Srinivas in his commentary on the position of Dumont about the relationship between power and status at these different levels has stated that there is a different legitimatised exercise of power. The differentiated levels like kings getting coronated and the local chiefs not getting coronated and the usage of Brahmin priests in the process are the classic situations of relationship between 'individuality' and 'hierarchy' within the cultural features in defining the individual and his status.

The separateness and interdependence of caste-based hierarchical relationship at the social level was also replicated at the level of individuality and hierarchy. The local chieftains get grouped into individuality not by subordinating the power, both social and political, to the status determined through hierarchy. Thus, the question of uncritical assumption of traditional hierarchy is significant. The 'individuality' obtained by the local chieftain during the periods was not within the textually prescribed hierarchy. This kind of transformation in hierarchy in Indian social order may be yet another focus and thereby a knowledge and scholarship on culture of hierarchy can be constructed. Already, there is enough evidence generated by the sociologists of Indian society on this question of culture of hierarchy. The relevant issue in their analysis is the culture of hierarchy, its transformative nature and the need for understanding the social service to the needy.

References

Appadurai, Arjun (1981) *Worship and Conflict under Colonial Rule: A South Indian Caste*, Cambridge University Press, New York.

Appadurai, Arjun and Carol A. Breckenridge (1976) "The South Indian Temple: Authority, Honor and Redistribution", *Contributions to Indian Sociology (N.S.)*, Vol. 10, No. 2, pp. 187–211.

Basham, A.L. (1975) *A Cultural History of India*, Clarendon Press, Oxford.

Beteille, Andre (1981) *The Backward Classes and the New Social Order*, Oxford University Press, Delhi.

——, (1986) "Individualism and Equality", *Current Anthropology*, Vol. 27, No. 2, pp. 121–34.

Desai, I.P. (1998), *Division and Hierarchy: An Overview of Caste in Gujarat*, Indian Council of Social Science Research, New Delhi.

Dirks, Nicholas B. (1987) *The Hallow Crown: Ethno History of an Indian Kingdom*, Cambridge University Press, New York.

Drekmeier, Charles (1962) *The Kingship and Community in Early India*, Stanford University Press, California.

Dumont, Louis (1970) *Homo Hierarchicus: The Caste System and its Implications*, University of Chicago Press, Chicago.

Gupta, Dipankar (ed.) (1991) *Social Stratification*, Oxford University Press, Delhi.

Sundaram, D. (1994) Indian Social Structure and Institutions: A Social History in Retrospect, AD 300–1000: Culture of Hierarchy, a paper presented at the seminar on Society and Culture for Indian Philosophical Research Council, March.

Tocqueville, Alexis de, 1945, Democracy in America and Old Regime and French Revolution, Winkle Book edition, pp. 14, 338–339 and p. XII).

——, (1946) *Democracy in America (1835) and old regime and the French Revolution* (1856).

17

American Social Theory and Indian Social Reality

The Case of Reference Group Theory

Jagdish Kumar Pundir

The present paper attempts to explore first the basic premises of a social theory and its usefulness which had its origin solely in the United States of America, as it was introduced at first and developed systematically by American social scientists. The social theory, a unique theory in understanding the gradual changes in the behaviour of individuals and groups, is that of reference group behaviour. It was at first introduced by H.H. Hyman in 1942 but systematically developed and presented by R.K. Merton in 1950. It is only after Merton's writings, the theory has become widely known in social and behavioural sciences. It has been widely applied in different social contexts across the length and breadth of the globe. India provides a case of a unique culture-specific historicity of human civilisation and thus a unique society. If a social theory becomes applicable and found useful in various situations, its universality of scope is likely to get established. That is the demand on a theory to become a theory in real sense. The present effort is in this direction to look into the applicability of the theory of reference group behaviour to the Indian social reality. The paper at first attempts to clarify the basic assumptions of

Provisional draft of this paper was presented at the First Inter-Cultural Dialogue Colloquium held at Udaipur, 2–3 March 1997.

theory and its level in comparison to theories in natural science. Secondly, the premises and characteristics of reference group theory are briefly described from its initiator and systematic formulation by R.K. Merton and others. In the third part an attempt has been made to survey a few studies, where and how this theory has been used to understand Indian social reality. Its strengths and weaknesses are analysed towards the end of the paper.

Social Theory: An Elementary Formulation

Whether there are social theories? R.K. Merton, the most quoted scholar of USA at one time, arrives at a conclusion that social theories may be applicable to a limited universe. He calls these theories as 'the theories of middle range' (Merton, 1968). These are not universal theories as such, as the case in natural sciences. In social sciences, the theories have attained the level of generalisation and concept formation. These theories can further be applied and verified in various empirical situations. Even empirical situations may give rise to such modification and initiation of new theories. The theory of reference group behaviour emerged from the empirical material of the *The American Soldier*. This is one of the well-known theories that have emerged during later half of twentieth century in the social sciences in the USA. A perfect theory in its true sense of the term is defined as a set of interrelated propositions (propositions containing the relationship of several social phenomena) in which (a set) a conclusion, even of the relationship of social phenomenon not empirically verified, follows from the premises. Even though such a set may constitute an argument in logic in which relationship of imaginary, unrealistic, non-empirical phenomena may follow. But in theory such a conclusion that follows in the form of a relationships of social phenomena is indicative of the relationship of those social phenomena which are empirically verifiable. It is in this background that Merton arrives at the above affirmed conception of theory in social sciences that there are 'theories of middle range', applicable to a limited universe, attained the level of generalisations and concept formation. The reference group theory has thus emerged as a theory of the middle range, which may further be applied and verified in various empirical situations. This application and verification in the context of unique social reality like Indian society may widen its scope of universal applicability. But before examining this applicability, we look at the basic clarification and formulation of this theory.

Reference Group Theory: Premises and Characteristics

The term 'reference group' was introduced by an American social psychologist, Herbert H. Hyman, in 1942 in an inquiry into the psychology of status. He was seeking to understand the way the individuals ranked themselves in their choice of a social framework for comparison. He explored the reference groups employed by the subject and the dynamics underlying such selection as well as the effects of such particular groups on self-appraisal. At the same time, Newcomb (1943/1965) explored the various ways in which individuals related themselves to the community or choose it. These initial studies stimulated no more but few notably Hartleys and Sherif. Sherif (1948) in *Outline of Social Psychology* included a summary by Newcomb's study, rephrased in terms of the explicit concept, 'reference group'. This had clarified paradoxical findings for Newcomb. On the other hand, Stouffer and his associates were led, in their studies of the *The American Soldier* (1949), to the concept of 'relative deprivation'. They confronted the apparent contradiction between feelings of satisfaction, or deprivation and the objective conditions/situations among the groups of soldiers. A soldier's sense of deprivation was not dependent on an absolute level, but was relative to the perceived level among the groups with which he compared himself. These ideas and concepts, however, had little prominence until 1950 when R.K. Merton (with Alice Kitt Rossi) synthesised and systematically presented in the classical essay, *Contributions to the Theory of Reference Group Behaviour.* Since 1950 the concept has achieved meteoric prominence and has figured in so many writings that the more recent history defies brief review (Hyman, 1968).

Merton's comprehensive outline stresses, "Reference group theory aims to systematise the determinants and consequences of those processes of self evaluation and self appraisal in which the individual takes the values and standards of other individuals and groups as a frame of reference" (1950: 35). This statement indicates the comprehensiveness of the classical writing. In arriving at this comprehensive statement, he uses empirical data, especially the nine excerpts from the study of *The American Soldier,* as illustrative evidence for further analysis. This was a stage of the development of social science when the studies were also governed by military and economic considerations. It was this further interpretation of the ocean of empirical material that Merton and others set for *The Continuities in Social Research* (1950) and the classical essay came into being for wider circulation among the social science scholars.

The theory of reference group behaviour got initiated from the further interpretations of empirical material and the concept of relative deprivation, though the two words existed much earlier. 'Relative deprivation' was a major concept employed to interpret the findings of *The American Soldier*. Merton concentrated on the following excerpts in the formulation of reference group theory (only few related words are reproduced here), analysis of these gave rise to the theoretical problems:

1. Drafted married man "comparing himself with his unmarried associates and comparing him with his married civilian friends";
2. "... High school graduates or college men ... compared themselves with their civilian friends ..." (who have been deferred from induction in army);
3. "... The better educated man had more to loose ... in the eyes of his friends ... by failure to achieve status in army";
4. "... Overseas soldiers, relative to soldiers at home and the combat soldier ... relative to the soldier not incombat";
5. "... differentials between officers and men in the enjoyment of scarce privileges";
6. "... Those advance slowly relative to others ... . With equal longevity ... are critical ... (expected) ... Better educated will complain of the slowness of promotion";
7. Officers' ... Level of expectation and level of achievement ... relative to that of one's acquaintances ...";
8. "Northern-Southern Negroes ... Negro soldier has a position of wealth and dignity ... (compared to Negroes in Southern)"; and
9. "... Negro soldier in the south relative to Southern Negro Civilian ... exceeded that values of army life ... to the Negro Soldier in the North relative to the Northern Negro civilian" (Merton, 1968: 282–92).

Thus, the concept of 'relative deprivation' grows out of the 'surrenderipty pattern' of the empirical research and gave rise to new theory, i.e., "the theory of reference group behaviour". For the authors of *The American Soldier*, relative deprivation was problematic with emphasis on deprivation. The attitudes of soldiers were taken as the dependent variables which depended on various attributes of their status (e.g., married, graduate, officer, Negro, Southerner). Comparisons were made with the persons of same status and also with those in a different category. This gave rise to the 'two' contexts – membership groups (in groups) and non-membership groups (out of groups). This difference formulates the general question of central importance for Merton ... Under which conditions are associates within one's groups taken as frame of fence for self evaluation and attitude formation and under which conditions do the outer groups provide significant frame of reference (ibid.: 292–97).

This seems to be a central sociological concern of the reference group theory. There are innumerable reference groups in principle, e.g., multiple reference groups. The important fact is not one's own group, more such groups other than one's own ... search out the processes through which individuals relate themselves to groups to which they do not belong. In this context, Merton (ibid.: 290–316) outline the theoretical scheme or range of specific problems along the following points:

1. Membership groups operating as reference groups;
2. Conflicting reference groups and mutually sustaining reference groups;
3. Uniformities of behaviour derived from reference group theory;
4. Reference group theory and social mobility;
5. Functions of positive orientation to non-membership groups;
6. Social processes sustaining or curbing these orientations; and
7. Psychological and social functions of institutions regulating passage from one membership group to another.

For Merton these are the guiding points for elaboration of the theory of reference group behaviour. These also indicate the possibilities for observation in a given social context. These may have further theoretical implications. The consequences and determinants of reference groups behaviour may be judged (i) for individuals engaging in them, and (ii) for groups in which they are a part and the larger social system. To the extent to which legitimacy is accorded to the structure of these groups and the status of their members may effect the range of groups or strata taken as frame of reference. It may call for the linkages between the reference group theory and the theory of organisation. It can be examined from both psychological and socio-logical frameworks, e.g., 'temporary grouplessness" ... degroupping may take place, and it may be dysfunctional for the individual, may have functional consequences for the organisational units.

Later, Merton (1957/1998), in another essay "Continuities in the Theory of Reference Groups and Social Structure", as distinct from socio-psychological implications of the current enquiries into reference group behaviour, examines some theoretical problems of social structure. He clarifies the reference group and its functional types, groups of various types, and the process of selection. Men frequently orient themselves to groups rather than on their own, in shaping their behaviour and evaluations and this is the problem centred around this fact of orientation to non-membership groups that constitute the distinctive concern of reference group theory. Two types of groups are identified: (1) *normative type*, which sets and maintains standards for the individuals, these are source of values assimilated by designated individuals; and (2) *comparison type*, which provides frame for comparison relative to which individual evaluates himself/herself and others, provides a context for evaluating the relative position of oneself and others. This distinction is analytical since the same reference group can serve both the functions. It opens up various other theoretical problems like that of groups collectivities, and social categories; positive and negative reference groups; reference groups versus reference individuals; the selection of potential reference groups; and also to the processes like anticipatory socialisation. These are analytical dimensions/deriva-tives from the basic concept of the reference group.

Thus, the theory of reference group behaviour, systematically advanced by Merton, in his two classical essays, provide a broad framework for applying the theory in a wide variety of situations in various social contexts. Limiting ourselves to the Indian social reality, we examine some of the studies here. How far the American social theory, i.e., the theory of reference group behaviour, as advanced systematically in detail by Merton, finds wider applicability in under-standing Indian social reality, which has a complex unique cultural context. Such a step is in the direction of broadening the scope and generalisability of social theory and indicates a reflection on the very nature of sociological theory.

The Theory of Reference Group Behaviour and Indian Social Reality

Merton observes the functions of positive orientation of non-membership groups and this gives rise to the process of anticipatory socialisation, states: "It appears further that anticipatory socialisation is functional for the individual within a relatively open social structure providing for social mobility … . By the same token, the pattern of anticipatory socialisation would be dysfunctional for the individual in a relatively closed social structure" (1950, 1968: 58–59). Looking at social structure of a society, especially like the one in India, the members of the lower stratum are not likely to adopt higher stratum as a reference group and it could not be a source of mobility in such societies (Fishbein, 1963: 271–86). Thus, logically, it follows that in Indian society, being a closed society, lower castes cannot consider higher castes as their reference groups because such mobility is not possible in a rigid social structure. In caste-based Indian society change in one's stratum would amount to change in caste but this change in caste is not permitted thereby social mobility in ideal condition is not possible. Thus, from the basic premises of reference group theory, as formulated by Merton, it becomes clear at the outset that it may not be applicable in the understanding of Indian social reality.

But, there is a basic question about the very unique characteristic (i.e., caste) of Indian society: Has the caste system been an idealistic rigid system? Was any mobility in the position of castes never permitted? One view, an important one, considers and traces it from social history, that some mobility was always allowed, change in the status of a caste has always been possible (Srinivas, 1962). But caste as such allows a small rate of mobility (Damle, 1968: 96–102). If we look at status in secular, rather than sacred sphere, like position in power structure, economic categories, and alike, then greater individual mobility is permitted and such mobility has always taken place.

In this context, and to understand such processes, a few authors, writing on social mobility, have noted and applied apparently or inherently some dimensions of the theory of reference group behaviour in the understanding of Indian social reality. B.N. Verma (1965), for example, observes that mobility in the status of a caste has been possible whenever a lower caste followed behaviour patterns, rituals and other observances of a comparatively higher caste over a time span, and in due course of time, it achieved higher status. A lower status liquor selling caste in Orissa enhanced its social status in the social hierarchy or rural social structure by improving its economic position and thereby becoming land owners like the upper castes (Bailey, 1961).

The well-acknowledged process of sanskritisation, in which a lower or untouchable caste, considering Brahmins as a model, follows their patters of behaviour and consequently at least a positional change takes place, not a structural change as such (Srinivas, 1962). Thus, in a sense, this process of sanskritisation becomes a species of the general theory of reference group behaviour. Of course, this became a debatable concern since 1950s and still not resolved. At least sanskritisation has been acceptable as a culture-specific process of social mobility in India. But this is obvious that mobility in one caste has been possible by considering another caste as a 'positive model' thus, 'reference group' in other words. In other parts of south India, lower castes observed the patterns of behaviour of higher castes in secular and sacred spheres of social life and achieved higher status than where they were placed earlier (Alaxender, 1968).

These illustrations provide the context of operation of castes as positive non-membership reference groups. The instances of not considering higher castes like Brahmins as models of positive orientation, but rather rejecting their patterns, are also observed. The other middle and upper middle groups become reference models for the lower stratum. This provides a clear case of the operation of the theory of reference group behaviour, where simultaneously negative reference orientation works for one stratum and positive for another but for both being non-membership groups (Deiva Sigamani, 1981). In south India in revival of their own traditional cultural patterns and feeling in them, the lower social groups have asserted themselves and rejected the values of Brahmins. This case of negative reference orientation towards non-membership groups and one's own group as a positive reference orientation has been observed (ibid.).

Among the lower caste elites, it has been found in north India that the leading persons of the community and also acquaintance from among the higher castes, are very much considered as positive reference individuals and groups by lower caste upcoming individuals (Pundir and Kahlon, 1986). Even among some of the tribal groups in India, it has been possible to consider other groups as their models of behaviour and change accordingly, though it entailed certain negative consequences. The process of tribal integration in the context of planned development and cultural context has been understood in this framework of reference group theory. Four models, viz., (1) the caste Hindu, the agents of change who are engaged in tribal development, (2) missionaries, (3) social workers, and (4) the non-tribals, inducted in the settlements provided four non-membership groups as reference groups for the tribal (Mann, 1988).

The process of imitation (crucial in reference group theory) on the part of the lower social groups has become more complex in contemporary India. There are multiple reference groups and further compartmentalisation takes place in those reference groups. A person appears to have one reference group in one respect, say in political matters, another in religious matters and a third in economic sphere (Alaxender, 1968). A symposium in the late 1960s (Silverberg, 1968) discussed the issue of social mobility in the caste system in India. Reference group as 'frame of reference' was emphasised and indicated at least as a provisional conceptual tool for understanding social mobility in India. Applying reference group theory to a society which is structured by rigid caste divisions, one view emphasised that caste system allows a small rate of social mobility (Damle, 1968). Positive orientation for reference and imitation is permitted and even encouraged. Anticipatory socialisation can thus take place and it has effect of inducing distance and repulsion between castes even if it does ensure ultimate absorption or inclusion (ibid.).

Although lower caste people cannot expect to be included in higher castes but positive orientation for reference and imitation is permitted and even encouraged. Individuals may gain identification other than those ascribed by birth (Lynch, 1974). There have been many cases of upward mobility of lower caste individuals by suitable role adaptation of higher caste non-membership group. Prestige determinants of individuals may go beyond caste in ranking of individuals much higher or much lower than their caste standards. The selection of reference individuals however depends upon established social relations and cultural definitions. Thus, reference individuals may be 'local' or 'cosmopolitian' (Chauhan et al., 1975).

At individual level, reference groups may undergo changes over a period of time. This has been observed in case of lower caste individuals accepting the facilities provided by the state under special provisions. At the first instance, these recipients were rejected by their own caste persons thus presented as a negative reference group but later these initial recipients were considered as positive reference group by the same persons who rejected them earlier. Thus, the membership group was considered as a negative reference model and with change in time the same considered as a positive reference model. The competing individuals among various higher castes, in supporting and guaranteeing for lower caste individuals, became reference models for others who aspire for positions at local level (Pundir, 1998).

The above studies are some of the illustrations of applying and examining various dimensions of the American social theory, namely, the reference group theory, which was systematically advanced by Merton, in the context of culture-specific Indian social reality. The above brief survey of select literature is only illustrative and not exhaustive but it is suffice to point out the main issue raised initially in the present paper. Now, we can comment on the strength of the theory and its applicability in Indian situation and its generalisability.

Concluding Remarks

If we look at how the American theory of reference group behaviour has been applied, extended and examined in the Indian social context, we find a vivid picture. The illustrative studies mentioned in the earlier part are indicative of this picture. At the outset it can be stated that sociologists, political scientists and anthropologists have made use of various dimensions of the reference group theory. Most common application appears to be in the understanding of social mobility, particularly in the lower social groups, which are striving for upward mobility. It covers both the secular field of life as well as the religious sphere. But as it appears the later lesser highlighted in these studies.

In caste-based Indian society the status of an individual is determined by birth, and rights, pre-requisites and obligations of each stratum are generally held morally right and considered a religious duty. Thus, in Merton's systematic analysis of reference group theory, the scope of application to such a rigid society was obsolete. But, the illustrative evidence suggests that reference group theory can be useful and applied to certain situations even in such a rigid society.

This appears to be on two scores. First, that the very caste system is absolutely rigid and is not a true fact as has been highlighted above. Secondly, the processes of social mobility are taking place in Indian society if less in religious sphere but more in several other aspects of life of the people. Though degree and rate of mobility varies but it is a fact that social mobility is taking place. This has happened in the case of lower social groups in particular and more at individual level rather than at group level. In some cases it has been found that certain mobility takes place in the position of a social group (caste) as a whole by imitating the patterns of behaviour of higher castes though structural change does not take place.

In sacred sphere also, the lower castes, following the Brahminical model as a positive reference, have been observed and the culture-specific process of imitation has come to be known as a processor theory of sanskritisation (Srinivas, 1962). But there has been used, though a lesser known, concept, of 'enhanced ritualisation' (Chauhan, 1967) that seems to have helped lower castes to attain better position and lessening of social distance between the castes, though the structural whole remains intact.

There appear to be various reference models in Indian society for individuals and groups – some are membership groups and others non-membership groups. Both types of groups operate as positive reference groups whereas in a few other cases such groups also act as negative reference models. Even caste, as the core and unique social reality of Indian society, has been considered as a reference group by others and also by its own members. In other situations, such possibility has been noted just opposite. Beyond castes as groups some other groups in secular spheres of life have also been studied by making use of the theory of reference groups in Indian context. These models of comparison and imitation have been noted not only by sociologists but by anthropologists in tribal situations and by political scientists in the context of political mobilisation and uprisings.

Thus, when it is concluded, though tentatively, that the theory of reference group behaviour as an interpretative tool for understanding the social processes in Indian society seems to be an efficient theory even when India is considered as a rigid society. Particularly this has been used in understanding social mobility processes. The Indian society, with these ongoing processes, appears to be somewhat changing, loosing though very little, the rigidity labelled on it. The various dimensions of the reference group theory have been found useful in understanding these processes of mobility or change. Whether the reference group theory or the culture-specific theory of sanskritisation is exhaustive in understanding Indian social reality, remains open and more confirmation is needed before either is to be confirmed as the social theory is enlarged when comes to Indian social reality and its generalisability broadened. In the emerging era of (international) globalisation the models in economic – secular spheres may get multiplied further beyond the boundaries. This may further, expected if not sure, extend scope of the application of the reference group theory in the context of Indian society. The present context appears to be different than what it was when Merton indicated the rigidity and non-applicability of the theory of reference group. Now, the context gets extended beyond the geographical boundaries many times more than that could be expected around the middle of the twentieth century.

References

Alexander, K.C. (1968) *Social Mobility in Kerala*, Pune: Deccan College.

Bailey, F.G. (1958) *Caste and Economic Frontier*, London: Oxford University Press.

Chauhan, B.R. (1967) *A Rajasthan Village*, New Delhi: Veer Publishing House.

Chauhan, B.R., T.R. Singh and G. Narayana (1968) "Reference Group Theory with Regard to Mobility in Castes", in James Silverberg (ed.), *Social Mobility in Caste System in India*, The Hague: Mouton, pp. 95–108.

Damle, Y.B. (1975) *Scheduled Castes and Education*, Meerut: Anu.

Deiva Sigamani, K. (1982) Social Movements and Identity, paper presented in the XVI All India Sociological Conference, Annamalai, Dec. 29–31.

Fishbein, Martin (1963) "The Perception of Non-Members: A Test of Merton's Reference Group Theory", *Sociometry*, Vol. 26, No. 3, pp. 43–52.

Hyman, H.H. (1942) "The Psychology of Status", *Achieves of Psychology*, No. 269, pp. 3–38.

——. (1968) "Reference Groups", in *Encyclopedia of Social Sciences*, Vol. 13, New York: Macmillan, pp. 353–69.

——. (1968) "The Psychology of Status", in H.H. Hyman and Eleanor Singer (eds.), *Readings in Reference Group Theory and Research*, New York: The Free Press, pp.147–65.

Lynch, O.M. (1974) *Politics of Unsociability: Social Mobility and Change in a City of India*, New Delhi: National Publishing House.

Mann, R.S. (1988) "Reference Group Dilemma in Tribal Development", *The Eastern Anthropologist*, Vol. 41, No. 3, pp. 251–58.

Merton, R.K. (1950) "Introduction", in R.K. Merton and P.F. Lazarsfeld (eds.), *Continuities in Social Research*, New York: The Free Press, pp. 9–15.

——. (1968) *Social Theory and Social Structure*, New Delhi: Amerind, pp. 107–13.

Merton, R.K. and Alice Kitt Rossi (1950) "Contributions to the Theory of Reference Group Behaviour", reproduced in R.K. Merton (1968), op. cit.

Newcomb, Theodore (1943) (1965) *Social Psychology*, New York: Holt, Rinehart and Winston.

Pundir, J.K. and N.R. Kahlon (1986) Reference Groups of Scheduled Caste Elites in Urban Punjab, paper presented in IX U.P. Sociological Conference, Meerut, July 2–4.

Sherif, M. and C.W. Sherif (1964) *Reference Groups*, New York: Harper & Row.

Silverberg, James (ed.) (1968) *Social Mobility in the Caste System in India*, The Hague (Paris): Mouton.

Srinivas, M.N. (1962) *Social Change in Modern India*, Bombay: Asia Publishing House.

Verma, B.N. (1965) "Community Studies and the Concept of Caste", *Indian Journal of Social Research*, Vol. 6, No. 3, pp. 251–62.

18

Secularism in Theory and Practice

A Derivative Discourse in Indian Context

Ashok Kaul and Anita Mattoo

The concept of secularism as "a mode of orientation to the phenomenal world, which is indifferent to or actively rejects the traditional orientation in preference for exclusively humanistic this worldly orientation" (Flint, 1968: 193), has passed through many phases. Emerged as a European doctrine with the rise of capitalism, it became an established political ideology that was propagated through the Enlightenment Project. The United States constitutionally accepted it in 1791. India inherited it from Britain to go well with its immense diversities and pluralities in its nation-building process. Though it has stayed with other ideals like representative democracy, yet its journey has been thorny, struggling to strike its roots.

I

The rise of Christianity was a rejection of the ideological system of the 'Greek polis' and the 'Roman civitas'. Its evolution in subsequent centuries, through Reformation Movement, initiated a process that separated the church from the state. The emphasis was on the doctrine of two ends – the temporal that alone belongs to the state and the spiritual, which is purgative of the church. The success of the Reformation Movement and the Renaissance consolidated the foundations of secular values. In the construction of a new social organisation, the modern philosophy proliferated a rational picture of universe on the basis of empirical knowledge, wherein the world of human affairs was seen as "self-contained realm as against the earlier notion of supernatural criterion". The contributions of both Rationalists and Empiricists brought out the essences of secularism in metaphysical terms while in the modern project, it was shifted to a more empirical and intensive quest for knowledge in its pragmatic world view. In the comprehensive works of Descartes, Hobbes, Spinoza and Leibniz, the rationalism presented a rational picture of the universe. In perpetuating this scientific basis of knowledge, the eighteenth century gradually shifted the emphasis of secularism from explanation in "metaphysical terms of universal ultimate to a more empiric and intensive quest of knowledge in its concrete practical manifestations" (Groethuysen, 1937: 631). It was an attempt to create a subjectivity that would overcome the traditional mindset of different and diverse social, economic and political rungs of society to work together. These eighteenth century philosophers like Locke, Montesquieu, Hegel and Mills strongly argued against the enforcement of any religion by the state. This utilitarianism argument had the tacit implicit of European expansion and the subjugation of colonies across the world. Locke fused the various elements of religion into an Integra – integrated system, which was to provide a working agreement and readily seized upon by his successors (ibid.: 633). The Enlightenment thinkers perceived social change holistic that would give birth to a new society, which would stand in contrast to the previous one. Therefore, this new society would perceive secularism as its ideology in public dominion. The Enlightenment Project made it a must instrument in the formation of nation-states. No doubt, by the nineteenth century, the philosophical debate on secularism in its ideological essence was resolved to a major extent, however even in Europe, its manifestations appeared in various forms. The reformative church, to go well with the nation-state, was recast. In addicting changes, England and France became the pacesetters. This was because of the prerequisite middle class and the internal unity and achievements in trade and exchange. England with its new geographical position as the enter pot between Europe and America, its achievements of internal economic unity about two centuries before Germany, its constitutional revolution, and its powerful bourgeoisie of bankers, ship owners and merchants, the transformation of the structure of the society is earliest, in its essence is the secularisation of social and economic philosophy (Tawney,

1970: 11). With the opening up of its barriers, a sizeable migration and a religious minority also lived in. These new changes were not in uniformity. In the Protestant-dominated countries, the human conduct appeared more individualistic and private, whereas, in the Catholic society, it was much diffused. With the passage of time, the state no longer could remain Catholic or Protestant, as in some cases the dominance had become quite balanced. To quote Sabine, "only slowly and under the compulsion of circumstances that permitted no other solution, did a policy of religious toleration emerge, as it was discovered that a common loyalty was possible to people of different religions" (1952: 166). Thus, with the conception of an independent sovereign state, the national objectives became the crucial determinants in the interpretation of secularism. The early twentieth century witnessed an altogether different brand of secularism propagated by the former Soviet Union. It was an attempt of the proletariat to build up a system perpetuated in socialist theories. Now, it has become a part of the history. Though with varied political ramifications, the secularism soon found acceptance as a guiding political philosophy all over the world. The United States became constitutionally a secular state in 1971, through the first amendment to the US Constitution that Congress shall make no law respecting an establishment, or religion or prohibiting the free exercise thereof. Being the country of immigrants, USA could become a secular state without much difficulty. And to a major intent, secularism has struck its roots, yet at times, its completeness is put to a question. To a large extent, the church and state are separated in America. The church is not interfering in the affairs of the state but in some exceptional cases, it is in a position to influence the affairs of the state. This has led critics to proclaim that the separation of the state and the church does not exist in the truest sense. To quote, "So called great American principle of complete separation of church and state as spurious ... there is no such great American principle and there has never been" (Pfeiffer, 1953: 118). From time to time, such criticisms have frequently appeared in the popular press, the church in America is very much in politics and will continue to be there for a long time to come. Regardless of its variations and criticisms, the secularism has come to live in plural societies without any alternative. To see it in retrospect, it can be stated that secularism is an ever-evolving ideology. Its intellectual origins can be traced from the beginning of Christianity; it found its logical climax in the seventeenth century, when the age of religious struggles came to end with the Treaty of Westphalia in 1648. The state, first in England, then in France, Germany and America, found its sanctions, "not in religion but in nature, in a presumed contract to establish it ... It appeals to no supernatural commission, but exists to protect individuals in the enjoyment of those absolute rights which were vested in them by the immutable laws of the nature" (Tawney, 1970: 10). As mentioned elsewhere also, from this ideological position, secularism in practice has assumed varied forms. It is evident today that the line of division between the religion and state is fast shifting due to new formations appearing at global level. With the end of the Cold War, there are no ideological dreams and the capitalism seems to have no alternatives. As such, the new religious identities, complementary with the capitalism, are gaining ground. This has placed the ideology of secularism at varying points on a continuum, both in the developing and the developed countries.

II

India has evolved to a multicultural society with layers over layers through the dialects of thousand years of continuous history. Predominantly a Hindu society, it has no organised church, no clergy, no religious codifications and not even commonly accepted scriptures. It can accept any variety of beliefs, and mode of worship, any cult of reference as long as its holistic social structure remains intact.

In the ancient India, there was no institutionalised boundary between religion and the kingdom. But, the king had no powers to change the rules and regulations of the Hindu social system. The spiritual powers were not institutionalised. Caste was a predominant in the division of labour. The basis of justice was hierarchical. The system continued to work even after the advent of Islam in the medieval period. From Nehru's recounting of Indian past, Chatterjee writes, "it would appear that there are two great movements in the Nation's history, consisting of a long cycle and a short cycle. The long cycle begins with the earliest known historical period, that of the Indus valley civilisation, and ends with the first Turko-Afghan invasions of the eleventh century" (1986: 134).

In the absence of any organised form of religion, the Hindu social system had formed an elite social formation, which had a capacity for adaptation and transformation. Despite the long Muslim rule in India, the process of Islamisation did not make any structural changes. The effects were "more or less superficial and social culture remained much the same as it used to be. In some respects, indeed, it became more rigid" (Nehru, 1946: 261). The Islam proved only to be a veneer, its religious tenets of monotheism accommodated Hindu form of practice in its all form or another. Similarly, it did not remain a homogeneous and monolithic Muslim entity, but gave way to different patterns of social stratification, which were observed before the advent of Islam. Therefore, a short synthesis occurred, which perpetuated the sense of co-existence. During Akbar's regime, the spirit of national unity received some considerations, but this direct approach did not succeed, as it has seldom succeeded elsewhere. The same historical period had undergone far-reaching transformational changes in Europe, however "Asia static and dormant still carried on in the old traditional way relying on man's toil and labour" (ibid.). With the colonial subjugation, there was a qualitative structural transformation of Indian society. The colonial social engineering with its degenerative and regenerative roles produced enough material bases that laid the foundations of various reformative movements in the eighteenth century. The new western education, means of transport, communication and judiciary produced a new educated middle class, which became the agent of development, reform and modernisation of the entire Indian society. Since the traditional Hindu elites were quick to respond to the new avenues and opportunities offered by the British rule, its adaptation and modernisation was quicker than the Muslims. In fact, during the colonial rule, Muslims lost their hold more than proportionality, partly due to the erosion in the Muslim rule and more significantly due to their apathy towards westernisation. The 'lag' between the two communities in the development of educated middle class was the main factor in the rise of Muslim communalism. Nehru conceptualises it as 'the narrow middle class mentality' due to the cultural gap. During the freedom struggle, the communal issue appeared on the surface and resulted in the fragmentation of the national movement.

Thus, secularism in the Indian context provided the basis for the inner group accommodation to highly communalised communities on the eve of independence. During the national movement, the secular polity remained abortive, "it is not sufficiently well known, and excepting to a few specialists that Indian nationalism has been frequently forced to compromise with its secular ideals throughout its long and torturous history" (Rao, 1989: 34). Therefore, it is hard to agree that the Indian awakening with the reform movements of the eighteenth century should really be called a Renaissance. Neither the Indian society experienced a long gradual transformation in an indigenous social context, like the Europe, nor there was any end to the communalism with formation of Pakistan on the basis of 'two-nation theory'. The new social transformation did not result in such a social formation, which could be cordial to the ideology of secularism. The political unification preceded the cultural integration and with tragedy of communal award, "a tradition bound, caste ridden and authoritarian society, unwilling to make breach with the past, does not provide a nourishing soil for secularism to strike roots" (Sinha, 1968: 20). Nehru had to reckon with the historical truth that the new nationalism in India as elsewhere in the East was a religious nationalism, the modernist's vision no doubt had a secular outlook, but they lacked a mass base, the masses were with Gandhi, who was not sectarian but his world view was deeply influenced by religion (Mishra, 1992: 161–62). Therefore questions of inter-faith existence and in-group accommodation remained persistently hobbling the minds of the nationalist leaders. Since the content of the national movement was based on the liberal rational core, though culturally fragmented with the partition, Nehru tried to articulate the ideological fervour of the state on secular lines. His emphasis was that the post-independent state must involve all the rungs of the society, give every one an equal right of citizenship, irrespective of sex, language, religion, wealth and education, in particular it must be based on a consciousness of national solidarity which includes an active political process (Chatterjee, 1986: 146). This ideological construction was the interpreting view of the Indian secularism at the arrival of the freedom from colonial subjugation.

III

Unlike the West, India achieved independence and political unification without the integration of its sub-cultures. Its complex diversities did not disappear with the partition of the country. Rather, the creation of Pakistan on the basis of religion was causality for the composite national culture. Thus, in the making of modern India, a secular state was deemed necessary in view of the complex situational realities. This was provided through the constitution that came into force on 26th of January 1950. It proclaims through the Article 15 (1) that the state shall not discriminate against any citizen on grounds only of religion, race, caste, sex, place of birth or any of them. Similarly, the Article 16 (1) states that "there shall be equality of opportunity for all citizens in matters relating to employment or appointment to any office under the state". Again, the Article 16 (1) is clear that "no citizen shall on grounds only of religion, race, caste sex, descent, place of birth, residence or any of them be ineligible for, or discriminated against in respect of, any employment of office under the state".

The early leadership under the guidance of Nehru visualised a new nation-state on the principles of democracy, secularism and socialism. For Nehru, the secularism was a scientific temper, a rational outlook and a necessary instrument for the modernisation and overall progress of the country. He was convinced that "the organised religion invariably becomes a vested interest and thus inevitably a reactionary force that opposes change" (Shah, 1968: 140). Through an interventionist state, the democratic institutions were established to build up a federal plural society. Therefore, a liberal centrist state promoting a secular society was envisaged as an effective functional instrument to achieve these nationalist objectives. With secular elite in command, the earlier decades did not witness any sporadic growth in the rise of conventional parties, nor were the caste conflicts, as prevalent in the present degenerative form, observed. India was recognised as a potential democratic plural society with a promise, while representative democracy and secularism in its neighbourhood were distant dreams. With a little wonderment, the western authors started commending the Indian state and its governing principles, "despite various undemocratic features of Indian politics and government, parliamentary democracy is functioning, and with considerable vigour. Similarly, the secular state, the ideal is clearly embodied in the constitution, and is being implemented in the substantial measure" (Smith, 1963: 499–500). Secularism proved to be a needed ideology to manage the highly volatile Indian society after the partition. It was not meant a clear-cut separation between religion and politics, but some arrangement that would guarantee the inter-faith relationship and freedom to observe religion of choice. No doubt, during the national movement, since Nehru perceived communalism as a lag in the development of the communities that would disappear with the process of development, therefore he wanted to retain the original notion of secularism, as supposed to be in the West. History and the culture being different,

Nehru had to modify his position of early radical stance to a new workable concept of secularism, as a positive mental attitude with an equal respect for all religions. Not a compromise, but a strategy proclamation in order to march on from the transitional phase of development. To a question what his hardest task was after independence, Nehru's reply was "to build a just society by just means ... perhaps too creating a secular state in a religious society" (Madan, 1995–96). His secularism envisaged in the constitution was his personal triumph. The post-Nehru era marked a gradual shift in the discourse of secularism. The world was witnessing sharp Cold War rivalries. The Marxian ideology was gaining acceptance in the developing countries. The religious discourses at the national as well as the international level had become insignificant before the debate of socialism and the capitalism.

The creation of Bangladesh was a psychological victory for the practice of Indian secularism. Indian state had become quite strong with the triumph in the decisive war against Pakistan in 1971. The developmental structures established in the 1950s had started giving dividends, especially in the field of agriculture and the industrial production. The secularism was thought to be getting acceptance at the societal level. In the progression of the Cold War rivalries in mid-1970s, Pakistan was thought to be a strategic asset by the United States, and in return Pakistan used this relationship to weaken the secular federal India. By 1970s a new rich class had emerged out of the developmental and democratic processes of decades that searched its identity in primordial loyalties to claim its share in political power. This new rich class took refuge in narrow loyalties, promoted its cause by breaking the traditional order with its value system. Its acquiring of political power was a natural outcome of the process of democratisation. But without the spread of civic culture and education, the excess of democratisation produced a collapse in the political culture of the country. With the declaration of a state of emergency in 1975, the parliamentary democracy received a severe setback. Consequently, Congress, in the eventful national election of 1977, lost its power first time since the independence of nation to a unified opposition. This was a fundamental change in the socio-political journey of Indian nationhood. It was not only a replacement of traditional secular elite at the centre but also unfolding the regional and local aspirations and its assertion in the power politics of the country. The state became tilted and weak with a soft centre. Also, in the absence of any national culture, the primordial loyalties and religious issues found articulations in the ethno-national movements through the regional parties. The rapid and the unpredictable global changes in the post-1980s have compounded the problems. The demise of the Marxian ideology and the collapse of socialism, first in the Eastern Europe and then the disintegration of former Soviet Union, brought an abrupt end to the Cold War. The world has now become unipolar. The established paradigms of knowledge have collapsed. It has created a vacuum in the thought process of human history. The most cherished ideals of nationalism, pluralism and secularism have been put to doubt. As an alternative to the capitalism, the religious revivalism is gaining ground. More specifically, the religious war in the former Yugoslavia and the political religion as championed by Iran for the Muslim universalism, the armed insurgency in Indian Kashmir by a dozen of Muslim extreme outfits is the crude forms of Islamic revivalism. It seems, "Islam has closed itself on itself .... Fundamentalism may still be contained with the help of state machinery where there is a long tradition of strong state, but on the ideological plane, it has no rival in the Muslim world" (Jain, 1992: 6). The rise of Muslim extremism in the various parts of India, on the lines of West Asian fundamentalism, is proving counter-productive for the growth of Hindu confessional parties. The exodus of non-Muslims from Kashmir, mushrooming of *madrassas,* activities of Students Islamic Movement and the conduct of Islamic Sevak Sangh in the south have provided enough planks for the Hindu confessional parties to seek the roots of Indian nationalism in 'Hindutva'. This is a new subjectivity feeding on acuity that the Muslims are the cause of national weaknesses, a negation to the synthetic composite culture. It is a nemesis of partition that has eaten away the potency of cultural strength of the Indian society and made it vulnerable to the disintegrating forces for further divisions. The fragile nature of Pakistani state uncomfortable with the pre-partition history and culture is struggling for its nation-building process. It is a failed state. Its military leadership awfully convinced that its domination and retention of power and cementing of its federal structure would come from anti-India tirade. A secular composite India vibrant with parliamentary democracy is treated threat to its existence. Therefore, it found Talibanisation of Afghanistan, as its strategic depth and *jihad* in Kashmir its strategic asset to weaken the secular fabric of Indian society. The decade of 1990s witnessed the resurgence of political Islam on the West Asian lines. It suited to jingoists, militarists, ideologues, spin doctors, bureaucrats and respective Hindu and Muslim baiters to serve their interests. The emergence of radical confessional movements working on religious nationalism did bring out chain of consequential events across the boundaries of nation-states. It was with the concurrence of the oil-rich elite, which was instrumental in reshaping the political economy with the religion. This was perceived as threat to the domination of resources as well as to the survival of civil society, as envisaged in the modern project, particularly in a world that is devoid of any ideology. The world community is divided and fragmented at a point of history when the culture and capitalism is in a confronting disposition to form any viable alternative tradition.

IV

To sum up, this narrative discourse might appear as requiem for the ideology, but undoubtedly in the changed world order, where information technology and electronic media have made public and private gawked in surveillance. The fast-emerged cultural attributes are again finding assemblage in power and domination. The identity questions are clubbed with passports, even though the borders seem to be open and diminishing. Therefore, the difference and diversity within a nation-state need a new articulation. The earlier models have come to abyss. The Nehruvian liberal model taken from the West that shows a complete separation of the religion and state does not hold ground with the sustainable elements of the old society. The dialectic model that political becoming transformed into sacred has collapsed. The possible way out seems to come from the Gandhian perspective that stresses "a transformed religious consciousness among the Hindus, no less than among the Muslims and the followers of the other religions, could offer the basis for creating a national unity". Since the society is passing through a transition, the constitutional provisions have proved inadequate instruments of social transformation due to the failure of the modernisation process in creating a melting pot amalgamation of the society. The processes of democratisation and development have set in motion a non-violent revolution of transfer of power to those rungs of society that have remained neglected or ignored in history. The historical unevenness contradicts the rationale of the established value system of the civil society, when it comes to power matrix. The problematic of power politics has brought out two extreme types of social forces, one apt to set for an alternate tradition, but unable to articulate an over agenda for social transformation and the second purveyors of Hindutva set out for mythologising the past to bridge the lag. The demise of the Cold War had created a vacuum that confessional religion attempted to fill it up by transcending boundaries with an agenda to undermine the functionality of the state. Before it would achieve a legitimisation, a governing role to dismantle the fragile secular civil societies, its menace was acknowledged by accrediting it with a sort of terrorism. The fall down of twin towers in New York has set in motion a new configuration that apparently would give credence to the secular politics and inter-faith accommodation, at least in public realm. The visible dividing lines of secular versus confessional are not the exclusive demarcations. Deep down in the society across the nation-states, it is packed with contradictions shaped and reshaped by the culture confronting capitalism. The fusion of radical technology and religious extremism on the one hand, and its subtle and tacit endeavour to retain the resource base, on the other, has led to the break down in the process of a civil society formation. The inconsiderate market fundamentalisms feeding on the belligerent consumerism on diminishing resource base have created an epoch of uncertainty. In this era of 'manufactured uncertainties', the Indian secularism reaffirms its expression for a new articulation, possibly its evolution will be determined by 'history itself'.

References

Atkinson, J. (ed.), *Alexander to Constantine* (Oxford: Clarendon Press, 1966).

Barker, E., *Principles of Social and Political Theory* (London: Oxford University Press, 1961).

Chatterjee, P., *Nationalist Thought and the Colonial World* (Delhi: Oxford University Press, 1986).

Flint, John, "India as a Secularising State", in *Secularism in India*, edited by V.K. Sinha (Bombay: Inland Printers, 1968).

Groethuysen, B. "Secularism", in *Encyclopedia of Social Sciences*, (New York: The Macmillan Company, 1949).

Jain, Giri Lal, "Closed World of Islam", *The Times of India*, August 27, 1992.

Mishra, R.K., Nehru and Secularism, presented in the seminar on Nehru and the Constitution, Dec. 31, 1988, Banaras Hindu University (unpublished).

Nehru, J., *Discovery of India* (New York: John Day, 1946).

Pfeiffer, L., *Church, State and Freedom* (Boston: The Beacon Press, 1953).

Rao, R., "Religion and Secularism", in *Religion, State and Politics in India*, edited by Moin Shakir (New Delhi: Janta Publications, 1989).

Sabine, G.H., *A History of Political Theory* (London: George G. Harrap, 1952).

Shah, A.B., "Secularism in India", in *India as a Secular State*, edited by D. Smith (New Jersey: Princeton Press, 1963).

Sinha, V.K., "Secularism and Indian Democracy", in *Secularism in India*, edited by V.K. Sinha (Bombay: Inland Printers, 1968).

Tawney, R.H., "The Medieval Background of Modern Social Thought", in *The Impact of Sociology*, edited by Jack D. Duglas (USA: Meredith, 1970).

Index